HERE BE SEXIST VAMPIRES
The Deep In Your Veins Series

Suzanne Wright

The characters and events portrayed in this book are fictitious. Any similarity to real persons, living or dead, is coincidental and not intended by the author.

Copyright © 2012 Suzanne Wright

All rights reserved. This book or any portion thereof may not be reproduced or used in any manner whatsoever without the express written permission of the publisher except for the use of brief quotations in a book review.

ISBN-13: 978-1481978064
ISBN-10: 148-1978063

For Bev and Melissa – my gorgeous girls

CHAPTER ONE

(Sam)

I knew before I even reached the doorstep of the building that someone was in my flat. I knew that they were unfamiliar. I knew that their mood was calm, cool. And I knew that they were a vampire. Like me.

When I reached the top level of the building I found my Sire's two dull looking vampire guards stood outside my door as usual, seemingly unaware of the vampire inside. I thought about alerting them, but then curiosity came to call. The strange vampire had to be powerful in order to remain off the radar of the guards and yet he, or she, apparently had no interest in concealing their presence from me. Okay, they had me intrigued.

Just as calm and collected as the intruder, I unlocked the door and headed straight for the tiny, outdated kitchen. While rooting through my plastic shopping bag for the carton of milk, I called out, "I don't have all night so I'd appreciate it if you told me what you want."

At this point I had established by their scent that they were male, seeing as females tended to smell sweeter. I was also able to tell, going by the fizzing feeling in the flat, that this particular vampire was extremely powerful: a master vampire for sure.

The footsteps behind me were soft, slow, non-threatening. Whatever this vampire wanted, it wasn't a brawl. "Evening Miss Parker," he said politely, "I've been waiting for you." It was rare that

I heard such a well-spoken voice around this area of London. My neighbours – most of whom were drug addicts, poverty stricken, or criminals – would be more than tempted to try to mug the bloke. Well they would be in for one hell of a surprise if they did.

Milk carton in hand, I finally turned to look him. "So I see."

As with all vampires, he had incredible sexual appeal, but his allure was even more intense because he was a Keja vampire – something I knew just by the slight tint of amber in his irises. That amber would glow whenever he was angry, thirsty or horny. Luckily enough, they weren't glowing now. All Keja vampires had hypnotic beauty and females were often called Enchantresses. Why couldn't I have been a Keja? Instead, I was a Sventé vampire; the dullest of all three breeds.

Three breeds? Well you see, basically, you know how there are varying accounts of vampires? Some humans report us to be terribly aggressive with hulk-like strength, some report us to be entrancingly beautiful and charming, and others believe that we are actually more human-like than the stories say. Well the reason for all the confusion is that there are actually different breeds. Sventés, like me, don't have hypnotic beauty like Kejas or have super-super-super strength and speed like Pagori vampires, though we are stronger and faster than any human. But our bloodlust isn't overpowering, which means that we can walk amongst humans without becoming overwhelmed and tempted to cling to someone's artery.

This particular Keja had the most penetrating set of eyes, his lips were full, and his peppery black hair perfectly framed the upper part of his face, tickling his high cheekbones. His black shirt and black trousers had to be made to fit; they were snug enough to hint at his athletic build. Armani, I'd bet. He obviously wasn't some rogue vampire.

So what was a posh, rich, master vamp doing here? I folded my arms across my chest. "Make it quick."

"My name is Sebastian. I've been following you around for the past week."

I hadn't expected that. I'd thought he was here for Victor, my Sire – or as I liked to think of him, the spawn of the Devil. Studying the Keja's expression, I knew that he wasn't lying, but how could I not have noticed him? I considered myself a pretty alert, aware person. Either I was losing my touch or he was really good. "Who exactly are you?"

He mirrored my posture. "I work directly for the Grand High Master."

The Grand High Master? Ooh, this couldn't be good. He was the vampire of all vampires. I'd never met him as it was a matter of invitation only. All I knew was that he lived somewhere in the Caribbean on an off-the-map private island which he very rarely left. "What is it I'm supposed to have done?"

Sebastian smiled. "As a Tracker, it is my job to hunt and seize felons as directed by our Grand High Master. However, my main role for the past two weeks has been to seek out suitable candidates."

"Suitable for what?"

"To keep it brief, His Grandness wishes to replace an exterminated squad in his private army – his legion. I spotted you when I attended your Sire's gathering last week. He had you duel with a vampire of another bloodline and I have to say you are, indeed, a tremendous fighter: very strong for a Svente, but also very controlled. And your gift is substantial. I was most entertained. I believe you would make an excellent addition to the legion."

"Hang on a minute…you want me to fight for the Grand High Master?" He had to be blowing smoke up my arse. In terms of hierarchy, my Sire was low, low, low, low down which was why he persistently duelled for more territory and had used me for the past three years to help with his pursuit of it. Add to that the fact that Sventés were considered lower class by the other breeds because we were thought of as 'too tame' and this whole thing felt surreal. My being noticed by Sebastian was the equivalent of a homeless person being singled out by the Royal Family. "You want to recruit me?"

He nodded. "I will take you to the location where our Grand High Master resides and you will partake in a test, along with the other potential candidates that have been selected by other scouts. If you are chosen, you will then join the legion."

A short laugh of incredulity popped out. "Thanks for the offer, but I must respectfully decline. You can let yourself out, seeing as you let yourself in." I filled the kettle with water and switched it on to boil.

"You wish to decline?" he said disbelievingly, slowly walking toward the kitchenette.

"If the guards overhear this conversation—"

"They will not hear a thing, just as they cannot sense me: I placed a mental shield over the flat."

Oh. Handy gift. That explained why I hadn't sensed him following me around. "My Sire could walk in any second—"

"And we would sense him well in advance." Sebastian clasped his hands together. "Now, tell me why you are rejecting my offer."

"I don't have the luxury of a choice," I said sulkily as I prepared my cup of coffee. "Victor would never let me go." The prick.

"Yes, I find Victor particularly territorial, even for a vampire. When did he Turn you?"

"Three years ago. He found me when I was dying and told me that he could heal me, but that I would have to agree to serve him until he freed me from his hold. I hadn't known what the bloody hell any of that meant, I just hadn't wanted to die so I'd said 'yes'. If I *had* known, I wouldn't be standing here now."

Sebastian narrowed his eyes. "Miss Parker—"

"Sam," I offered.

"Sam, do you realise that by joining the Grand High Master's legion, your freedom from Victor would instantly come into effect?"

That made my head snap up.

"I've got your attention now, haven't I," he said, smirking. "He would not be able to override the decision of the Grand High Master."

I leaned against the counter as I sipped my coffee. "Yeah, well, I don't see the point. I loathe Victor, but from what I've heard once you sign up to run around after the Big Man, it's a lifelong position. If I took you up on your offer and was chosen to join the legion, I'd still be serving someone. What's the difference?"

Sebastian seized my gaze, his tone all seriousness and assurance. "That is true, any immediate employees of his are required to serve him for the entirety of their immortal lives. But I can assure you now that being in the service of his Grandness would be very different from your current circumstances. He is very fair, very principled, and would value your service and reward you, rather than exploit you and your gift the way your Sire does."

"My gift," I echoed. "That's what got your attention, isn't it?" It got everyone's attention. Typically Sventé gifts were only ever defensive as opposed to offensive. Or 'boring', as many complained. My individual gift, however, was far from it. Sebastian wasn't the first vampire to try to coax me to leave Victor, but he was the first vampire to ever offer me a position that seemed worth risking Victor's wrath for.

"As it happens, you had my attention well before you used it in the duel. But yes, I do believe that your gift would make you an excellent addition to the legion. Wouldn't you consider serving your Grand High Master as an honour?"

"Yeah, but—"

"By joining the legion, you can be part of something momentous. Your name would go down in vampire history. You would be respected, admired, and prized by all of vampirekind. You cannot tell me that this is not something that appeals to you."

If I was being totally honest, I'd admit that being part of something so grand was tempting, especially when I hadn't really done anything that I could be proud of in my twenty years of human life before then being Turned into a vampire. Even before I was Turned, and had to disappear from my family's radar, I'd never had much to boast of. I'd always wanted to be something more and had wanted to attend university so that I could do a degree in Law. Of course the vampirism put a stop to that.

Sebastian sighed as he leaned against the refrigerator. Then he cast a look at the faded, slightly rusty thing and moved away from it as though it might stain his suit. I stifled a smile. "Since observing you duel last week, I have followed you and observed you further. "I have seen that, even in spite of your strong dislike of Victor, you are loyal and trustworthy. I have noticed that you are also headstrong and ambitious. Good qualities, both of which Victor seems determined to crush."

I shrugged. "What can I say? That's Victor."

"He already controls your actions. Do you want him to have control over your emotions and strengths as well? Of course you don't. His Grandness would respect these qualities, respect you, and give you room to be your own person. He certainly wouldn't force you to be his lover."

This bloke really knew how to play someone. "Haven't you heard that being a vampire's consort is an honour?" I said bitterly.

"That all depends on the vampire."

"Look, you can't be sure that *His Grandness* would be interested in having me in the legion. I'd only be a possible candidate. I can't just flit off to attend some try-out. Victor would lose the plot. Would you like to know what he does whenever he's stressed out or I rebel? Drags an innocent human – usually a kid – off the street and kills them slowly and painfully. He gets off on fear and pain."

Sebastian's face and voice softened. "Is that not all the more reason to escape his hold? Sam, I know his Grandness extremely well. And I know that he will have the same opinion about you and your potential that I do. I am more than confident that you will impress him as you have impressed me."

I rubbed my temples, totally undecided. It wasn't just Victor's response I was wary of. It was all very well Sebastian saying the Big Man was super, but of course he'd say that. The last thing I wanted was to be serving an even more powerful arsehole. But then he couldn't be the Grand High Master if he was all that bad, could he? Then again, neither option was particularly fantastic to someone who hadn't wanted all this. It wasn't exactly a childhood dream to become a vamp and join a vamp-type army for the whole of eternity.

Sebastian clearly picked up on my inner conflict and pounced on it. "You may not particularly like the fact that you are a vampire, but you have the opportunity now to take your situation and make something good of it. To rise above the suppression that it has so far had on you. To illustrate to vampirekind and to Victor that you are much more than his pet; that he cannot control you any longer. And if you decline, you will have the remainder of your immortal life to question that decision, and wonder what would have or could have been. So, which will it be?"

A queasy feeling overcame my stomach as I was teleported by the vampire that Sebastian summoned to bring us to the Grand High bloke's mansion. It was more like a museum with its ornate columns, rare artefacts, and statues of unnecessarily naked people. The walls were a brilliant white with massive pieces of art scattered here and there. The floor was a beige marble that was so well polished I could see my reflection in it.

The bright walls and marble flooring continued throughout the house as I followed Sebastian along a corridor that was as wide as a standard room and as long as...well, it looked eternally long. Like markers, tall Hungarian vampires were planted all over the place. Guards, obviously. The power humming around them indicated that, although they were merely guards, they were actually master vampires.

Behind us, one of the servants elegantly strolled with my bulging duffel bag. He was extremely tall and had an Egyptian look about him. Occasionally as we walked, I'd see a small sitting area branching off the corridor. Everything gleamed and reflected. Even with clean hands I'd be frightened to touch anything in case I dirtied it.

Sebastian finally stopped at another sitting area, which had a huge sofa-slash-bench in front of a set of extravagant patio doors. "I'll be back momentarily," was all he said. The servant placed my bag near the bench, nodded once and then strode off. Too restless to sit down – being in strange places made me edgy – I strolled over to the patio doors. The small balcony overlooked a large swimming pool which was, uniquely, the shape of a bat with its wings outstretched. It was nice to know that the Big Man wasn't without a sense of humour. Unless your vampiric gift was shape-shifting, morphing into bats didn't come with vampirism.

Noticing that one of the doors was slightly ajar, I quietly stepped out and absorbed the night-time. Beyond the pool was a beautiful beach decorated with palm trees. So he really did live in the Caribbean. I imagined that the place would look all the more inviting in the sun. Although sunlight didn't affect us in any way, we were nocturnal and naturally preferred the cover of darkness for hunting.

A lover of swimming, I was unable to resist a trip down the small set of steps to the pool where the water twinkled in the moonlight. I was just about to dip my fingers in when there was a huge splash and the water began lapping against the edges. My gaze found a delicious sight that sparked a rush in my blood. Burly shoulders and arms seemed to glide across the surface of the water as the swimmer moved with total ease. Even from the opposite end of the pool, his gorgeousness was apparent. His chiselled facial features and perfect bone structure made me think of the statues inside the mansion. The way his jaw was set gave him a very determined look. His hair was short, but not so short that I couldn't run my hands through it. Bloody hell, where had that sleazy thought come from?

And then he caught me staring.

And I couldn't think of anything to say to excuse myself.

He didn't speak as he climbed out of the pool, all the while looking at me suspiciously; probably contemplating the idea that I could be some kind of stalker. As he approached me, dabbing himself with a towel, I tried to concentrate on his intense hazel eyes rather than his alluring pale skin or his mostly naked body which was as defined as they came. Heat shot through me as a heavy throb of desire settled low in my stomach. Up close, I could see that not only did he have a red tint to his irises, marking him as a Pagori vampire, but that those irises were glowing. He was either a pissed, horny, or thirsty Pagori vampire. Not good.

"What're you doing out here?"

What a welcome. Not that I would expect a Pagori to ever be anything but moody. They were naturally irritable and easily became aggressive. So would I be if my irises flashed red. The Pagori strength came with a price. So did the Keja beauty; they had fangs. "I'm just —"

"Are you a friend of Joy's?" He was appraising me from head to toe now, making me feel self-conscious. His nostrils flared as he took in my scent. "Or a servant?"

"No, I—"

"Only a select number of servants are permitted to have access to this section of the house."

"Well that's great for them, but I'm—"

"This pool is especially off limits."

I huffed. "Do you always interrupt people mid-sentence?"

His mouth curved up on one side. "British," he observed in an approving tone. I quite liked the south Californian twang to his American accent too. After a short pause, made uncomfortable by how much he was staring, he said, "You're new here. Who is it you're working for?"

"Depends how the try-out goes."

"Try-out?"

"For the legion."

He looked taken aback but didn't miss a beat. "Tell me you're kidding." His grin was mocking. "Tell me you're not here hoping to try for a place in the legion." When I didn't say anything, he laughed. "Let me give you some advice: run along home."

"Why? Because I'm a girl?"

"Yes."

What an arrogant little sod. I folded my arms across my chest and snorted. "Are you for real?"

"Listen, this isn't a cheerleading squad. You don't get points for being pretty. It's some serious shit, which is why a girl has never been accepted, and never will be. There's no place for a female in the legion."

Sebastian had failed to mention the past lack of success for females. I had to wonder just how widespread this misogynistic view was in this place. "You do know it's not 1735, don't you?"

"I'm just stating a fact."

"No, you're blurting out a prejudiced opinion."

He shook his head. "Even if you were a guy, I'd be telling you to go home right now. For one thing, going by the fact that your skin tone isn't very pale, I'd say you're only a few years old; that's just not enough experience as a vampire for you to have a chance at landing a spot in the legion. For another, no Sventé vampire has ever had any success with the try-out."

Sebastian had failed to mention that as well. A man of few words, apparently. "So you're prejudiced against women, young vampires, and against another breed of vampire. I bet you're a delight to have around."

"Take my advice; don't put yourself through the embarrassment of going to the try-out, just go home."

Before I could yell at him for being a sexist sod, he had walked around me and disappeared through the patio doors. A little shocked, I slowly returned inside just as Sebastian was coming to summon me.

"Ready?"

I considered telling him to stuff it, that it wasn't worth it, but I knew I could handle myself and my gift well. It was too tempting to attend the try-out just to irritate the bigot Pagori. "Ready."

I marched behind Sebastian down the corridor again until we reached another set of patio doors, much more extravagant than the last. We then walked along a narrow cobbled path that zigzagged through the well maintained garden en-route to an outbuilding which, I soon realised, was actually an enclosed arena. Inside, the ground resembled a large horse paddock: a sandy floor with the letters A – D representing north, east, south and west.

Also inside was a line of blokes. About fifteen in all.

"Sam, you need to join the line," said Sebastian. "I'll be observing from there." He pointed to what looked like a glass VIP spectators' box. "Good luck."

And then Sebastian was gone, and I was alone. Alone because each and every one of the fifteen vampires looked at me like I was a leper when I joined the line. There were sniggers, and snorts, and whispers, and gasps of amusement. I ignored it all and stood still, calming my irritated self and trying to anticipate what the test might be. Probably duelling, I decided.

The only advice that Sebastian had given me was to wear something that would promote flexibility — hence why I was dressed in my black sweatpants, a white t-shirt with a white sports bra underneath, and my cross trainers. I'd tied my long, dark hair back in a high ponytail to keep it from falling around my face.

While I tried to get my head in the right place, another four blokes entered. They joined in on the 'laugh at the girl' crap. All in all, there were now twenty of us. And I was the smallest. And the only female. And the only Sventé. Oh joy. Five were Kejas, the rest were Pagoris.

After a further ten minutes or so, three male vampires strolled in — all carrying an air of authority and power, and everyone immediately went silent. The assessors, I guessed.

The first was a Keja, extremely tall and bald with dark skin that had paled slightly due to the vampirism; he was all elegance and composure. The second was a well-built Pagori with a studious gaze and tousled auburn hair. At total variance to the first vampire, he was casually dressed in jeans and a 'Life Sucks Then You Become a Vamp' t-shirt. The third was also a Pagori...and the sexist sod from earlier. He spotted me and smirked evilly. Ah, bollocks. If the final decision came down to him, I was definitely going back home.

But I refused to be intimidated or made to feel unsure of myself, so I straightened my posture and arched a sardonic brow at him. He didn't like that; he looked away, sniggering.

Folding his arms, he began pacing in front of the line of potential recruits as he spoke in a clear, authoritative voice. "All right, everyone, listen up. I'm Commander Jared Michaels. Beside me are Commander Will Norton," – he gestured to the casually dressed Pagori who nodded, wearing a half-smile – "and Commander Lou Sherman." The Keja also nodded.

Jared the Bigot continued, "As has already been explained to you, our Grand High Master wishes to replace his squad of ten that was recently annihilated. I will be commanding that squad." He looked hard at me with those words. It turned out that he was just as appealing dressed as semi-naked. He was made even more alluring by that black, knee-length, Matrix-style leather jacket he was wearing. Why couldn't he be ugly? Then maybe need wouldn't be tugging at me. Now that his hair was dry, I could see that it was a lovely shade of chestnut. I'd love to yank every strand of it out.

"There have been four other try-outs before this one," he told us, "and I now have three spaces left to fill. Hopefully three of you will meet the criteria for the squad." He halted in front of me as his gaze flicked over each vampire in the line except for me. "You've all been selected for one reason or another. Maybe it's your strength, maybe it's your fighting skills, or maybe it's your gift. But if you can't control your bloodlust, all of that means nothing to me."

He signalled to someone sat above the spectators' box and then suddenly gas began pouring out of hoses that were protruding from the roof. No...not gas. Worse. Various scents of blood now circulated around us, shooting up my nostrils and making my head swirl. And now, even though I usually didn't have an overpowering bloodlust, I was incredibly thirsty.

"In any kind of battle, blood will be spilled," said Jared. "This is what it will feel like to be on a battlefield, varying blood scents will be swirling around you. It is important that you can still be focused, alert, and controlled, and that you can resist your bloodlust."

I didn't glance along the line of vampires, but I could feel the nervousness and anxiety among them − feelings that amplified as Jared brought over a human. I didn't even see where he came from. He had thin lines of blood slowly dripping down from a bite mark on his neck, heading toward his bare chest.

"You," called Jared, signalling to one of the blokes in the line. He ushered him over and had him stand in front of the human. It was apparent that the Pagori was mesmerized by the sight, but he did nothing other than tremble a little. After about thirty seconds, Jared nodded at him to move away. The Pagori exhaled heavily as he went. Jared then selected another from the line, then another, and another.

I, unsurprisingly, was left till last.

By the time Jared called me forward to stand before the human, the blood was dripping down his legs. A year ago, I would have been as mesmerised as some of the others had been. I might even have stepped toward the human for a quick taste, just like two of the other vampires had. Needless to say they were now on their way home. But with Victor as your Sire, life was gory. You got used to it or you went insane.

Jared didn't look pleased by my perfect composure – I wasn't trembling, or swallowing hard, or squeezing my eyes closed, or trying to hold my breath like some of the others had. A mischievous smirk surfaced on his face as he used his forefinger to collect a little blood from one of the ribbons trailing down the human. He tried teasing my nostrils; wafting his finger right under my nose. The teasing didn't work, which clearly irritated him. He brought the finger toward my lips, hoping to tempt me to at least try to lick it off. But I didn't. Even though my body was curious and thirsty, I gave no reaction to Jared's teasing. Instead, I held his gorgeous hazel eyes with a defiant stare. At last he dropped his hand, sighing loudly.

"The next part of the try-out is going to test you physically," he announced to us as I returned to the line. He signalled with his hand for us to all follow behind him. He led us outside and over to a small forest which was made up of trees that were various shades of green and looked beautifully exotic. Scents of wildlife immediately hit me. I wondered if the vampires here ever hunted the animals. I'd never tried them myself.

"Hey...you really think you can pass this?" asked a Pagori who was now walking alongside me. He'd said it as though he believed I was mentally challenged. Apparently he found my presence here just as ridiculous as Jared did, which was a shame really because he was actually good looking and I didn't want to think of him as a wanker. His mousey hair had been shaven to stubble, and the style suited him really well, giving him quite an intense look. His blue eyes were shining in amusement as they appraised my slender figure, which didn't even have a muscle to pull.

"Don't tell me you feel threatened by a woman."

"Hey I believe in equality and all that, but there's no way you'll pass this."

"Enough talking," snapped Jared, stopping where the trees began. A group of vampires – all male, typical! – were waiting there. Going by their militant posture and the respectful bow of the head that they each gave to Jared, I guessed that they were members of the legion.

Jared informed us, "Your aim in this task is to reach the end of the forest in the fastest time that you can. Three things you need to know. One: you can't step on the floor. You can use the trees, logs, rocks...but not even once can you step foot on the ground. Two: you are not permitted to use your own unique gifts; this is all about your strength, speed, and agility. Yes, before you ask, I do have people watching. The third thing you need to know is that you will have someone chasing you the entire time. If they catch you — task over."

Anxious with anticipation, I watched as each vampire took their turn at the task. Each had a ten second head start before a member of the legion was on their tail. Most seemed to be completing the task within forty seconds, providing they weren't first caught. Of course, from outside the forest I couldn't see a thing. It wasn't until they returned through the forest that Jared would be told of the applicant's success, or lack thereof.

Standing there waiting for my own turn was agonising. I couldn't even plan a strategy as I had no view of what the forest was like inside. Worse still, the members of the legion that were stood here were all Pagoris. There was no way to outrun a Pagori unless you were one yourself. Sure Sventés were stronger and faster than the fittest human, but it didn't compare to Pagori strength and speed.

However, there was one thing that could go in my favour: Pagoris lacked agility. Sventé vampires, on the other hand, had the dexterity and sprightliness of a jungle cat. If these legion members weren't used to working alongside Sventés, they might not be prepared for it. So if I tapped into that and also made good use of my head start, there was a chance – I didn't like how slim that chance was – of succeeding.

Was it any wonder that I was left till last to do the task? Or that Jared paired me up with the stockiest legion member of the lot to chase after me?

Jared gave me the fakest, most patronising 'good luck' that I'd ever heard, so I gave him the fakest, most patronising 'thank you' that he had ever heard.

It felt like forever before Jared finally said 'Go!'

I sprung forward with as much force as I could, grabbing hold of the nearest branch for only a fleeting moment before then swinging to the next one ahead of me. Never letting myself forget that soon I would be pursued, I zoomed through the forest with such grace and litheness, like a feather in the wind.

Plenty of logs and boulders scattered the ground, but for now I was relying only on tree branches. Bouncing from branches to boulders and back again would be nice and creative, but would slow my speed. That was the last thing I needed. Before long I could hear my pursuer...and there was no sign yet of the end of the forest.

I put more force behind my swings, but the Pagori behind me was fast and I knew that I couldn't stay out of his reach for much longer.

"I is a comin'," he called out in a fake, and somewhat odd, accent. Clearly he considered himself playful and believed this was a game that he was going to win.

Ah, crap! He may just win it. Up ahead there was a wide river. Plenty of rocks stuck out of it, and although I could easily dash across them that would slow me down. I almost felt dispirited until I saw what was beyond the river: the end of the forest. As I noticed the fallen tree in front of the river, an idea entered my head.

"Don't hurt yourself now," the Pagori was shouting in a patronising voice. Arsewipe.

As I reached the river, I landed nimbly on the fallen tree and pushed hard on my legs as I leaped into the air...almost there...almost there. Down. Ha. I'd cleared the river.

"Fuck me!" exclaimed the Pagori in surprise.

I'd rather not. Swinging from branches again, I could hear the Pagori stomping across the rocks. Apparently he couldn't match my leap.

One more swing. *Yes!* I celebrated in my head as my feet met the ground outside of the forest. Three seconds later, the blond Pagori was beside me. He shook his head at me, his smile filled with surprise and his eyes glowing with respect.

"What's your name?" The Australian had dropped his playful accent now.

"Sam."

"Well, Sam, I think I've just fallen in love." His state of disbelief now had him chuckling. "Come on."

We ran back through the forest at vampire speed, finding Jared waiting at the mouth of it. He seemed amused. Until the Pagori spoke.

"She's like a wood nymph or something!" He shook his head. "I can't believe she did it."

The look on Jared's face was priceless. "Green, are you saying she outran you?"

He nodded. "You should have seen her leap over the river, she completely cleared it!" He patted me on the back and then waltzed over to his comrades, telling them about the chase.

Whereas Green was dazed yet excited, Jared was dazed but irritated. The other blokes weren't laughing anymore, but they were still looking at me oddly and whispering. Then I got extremely cheesed off when I heard one of them suggesting to another that I must have given Green a blow job to get him to say I'd outrun him. I stomped hard on his foot and shot him a scowl. He didn't seem confident enough to scowl back. Were they all arsewipes?

The Pagori who'd earlier assured me that I wouldn't pass the try-out stared at me curiously. "You sure you're not a disguised Pagori vampire on crack?"

"Oh shut it, Slaphead."

He just chuckled.

"For the final stage, we'll return inside." Jared's walk was filled with that much frustration that he was almost marching.

I knew as I entered the building and joined the line in front of Jared that my smugness must be apparent on my face because he was glowering madly at me. I snorted.

"The final stage," he drawled, "is combat. This is where you get to use your gifts. In the legion, we train to avoid up-close and personal combat as this only tires a vampire and leads to more injuries. Instead we like to rely mostly on our gifts, aiding us to attack from afar. For this stage, the effectiveness of your gift will be just as important as your control of it. There are now only seven of you left. From what I have seen so far, I'm confident that the three spaces I have left in the squad will be filled today. Which means four of you will be going home."

Jared first matched up one of the two remaining Kejas with a Pagori. "Your aim is to outmatch your opponent, not to kill or cause any harm that can't be fixed by our self-healing."

Contrary to mythology, vampires could be killed in lots of ways. A stab to the heart would do the trick purely because we needed it beating just as much as a human. We could also be bled out if our injuries were too extensive. Being starved of blood for more than four weeks was another way to go. In addition, a lot of vampires had deadly gifts that would just as effectively kill us as they would a human.

Both the Keja and the Pagori were good. They stayed clear of each other, as instructed. Their powers were impressive. Although the Keja was a conjurer and was materialising weapons, the Pagori could secrete smoke from his hands, making the room hazy and thus preventing the Keja from finding his target. As such, the Pagori seized a weapon on a bad throw and used it against the conjurer. Combat done and dusted.

Jared then paired up the other Keja with another of the Pagoris. The Keja was exhaling tiny thorns which I guessed were poisonous to some degree. However, as his opponent had the power to deflect or negate anything thrown at him with just the wave of his hand, the thorns simply hit the floor each time. I never got to see what effect exactly the thorns could have as Jared stopped the duel on realising they were both as good as each other.

The last two Pagoris were next – one being the annoying but cute Slaphead. He winked at me before confidently heading to the northern point of the building. His gift was so extraordinary that the whole thing was over in seconds. He had the power to cause temporary sensory paralysis, rendering his opponent blind, deaf, and mute. As such, he was shooting his superhuman breath blindly – literally.

I was next. And I lacked an opponent.

Jared sighed and stared at me through narrowed eyes. I half expected him to say 'I'm afraid there's no one to duel with you, you'll have to run along home.' But instead, he started removing his jacket.

"I guess I'll have to be your duelling partner."

CHAPTER TWO

(Sam)

A giggle almost choked me. "You're joking, right?"
He arched his brow and gave me an 'are you scared?' look. I hadn't been giggling with nerves or fear. I just couldn't believe my luck. Even if it turned out that he had the most amazing gift in the history of the universe and beat me within a second, I'd still be a happy girl just to get one shot in.

He positioned himself at the northern point while I took the southern. Still he was mistaking my giddiness for nerves. "I already told you there're no points for being a pretty girl. You really should've run along home. I tell you what, I'll give you one more chance to leave with your pride still intact."

"And while I appreciate the warning, I'm afraid I'm going to have to ignore it."

"Fine then. We duel until one of us is floored."

"Sounds like fun."

"Well if you really must embarrass yourself..." The movement was so fast that it was a blur. But my mind registered his left hand rise and his fingers twitch, and admired as beautiful blue sparks of electricity came predatorily toward me. Still, I didn't move out of the way. The sparks invaded my body with such aggression that I was suddenly zooming backwards and landed awkwardly on my back. God, it hurt. Like a burning hot sizzling fire spreading through my veins. It took a lot for me not to cry out.

Seconds later I bounced to my feet, feeling a little frazzled and slightly unsteady. Jared was laughing like a giddy kid in a fairground.

"Thanks for that," I said.

"For putting you on your ass?"

"No. For this." In a movement faster than what his had been, I expelled the sizzling energy from my body, sending blue electric sparks identical to his soaring at him. Although he made a dive to the right, his shoulder was briefly caught.

"What the hell?" he exclaimed. He then watched carefully as my fingers prickled at the air around me, drawing and manipulating energy to manifest my favourite weapon. A silvery-blue energy whip materialised in my hand.

"You're a Feeder," Jared realised.

"And you're electrokinetic."

He seemed to be talking more to himself as he added, "You can feed on the energy around you; absorb it and control it. Very rare."

"Again let me thank you for allowing me to absorb that power of yours. I have to say, I prefer this though." I teasingly flicked my whip in his direction. "I can shape the energy into lots of different weapons. Bolts, beams, balls…but I like the whip best. It's more fun."

"It is," he agreed with a nervous smile. "But it's not going to do you much good against high voltage electricity."

I snorted. "As you Americans say – duh! You're forgetting that *I* can practice electrokinesis now as well."

"So you're planning on defeating me by using my own power against me? Sounds a little like cheating."

"Oh I've no time for pretty sparks. I can do something much more interesting than that."

"Oh yeah?" Doubtful, his expression said.

"Yeah." I let the whip fade away. "Feeding on energy means that I can tap into the natural energies, which means…I can do this." I absorbed more energy into my palms and then sharply released it as a blast of air. The gust of wind swept him up like he was no more than a leaf on the ground and sent him crashing into the wall behind him. "By natural energies, I meant the classical elements – air, water, fire and earth."

Jared was on his feet in seconds, looking somewhat bemused and confounded.

"That wasn't even full force," I told him. "Are you sure you want to do this? I tell you what, I'll give you one more chance to leave with your pride still intact."

He wasn't pleased to hear his own words coming back at him. Unsurprisingly, the blue sparks headed for me again. The strong sizzles in the air told me that this discharge was double the voltage of the last.

One single, sharp step to the left took me out of reach of the electrical discharge. I enjoyed the sensation of my palms sucking in more energy, which I used to generate a blast of fire. It tingled as it left my hands. I could have burned him alive, but I settled on simply setting his clothes alight. Then I took a brief, morbid moment to enjoy his dismay before easing more energy into me and sending a long swish of water at him, calming the flames…and drenching him.

"You all right, Commander?" My tone was mocking. "You're looking like something off an appeal poster."

Totally pissed now, Jared growled as he raised his hand high and projected a massive lightning bolt. The voltage was so high that there was a ripple in the air. But I'd pre-empted him.

I squatted on the floor, slapped my palm to the ground on my right side, and raised my arm over me to then slap my palm on my left side. Simultaneously I had tugged at the surrounding energy, making a beautiful silvery-blue energy shield appear over me like a tent. The lightning ricocheted off the force field, slamming into the eastern wall.

Before Jared could act again, I sprung up in less than a blink, remoulding the energy from the shield into a silvery-blue ball. I hurled it at him. He moved fast, but not fast enough. It struck his arm, making him jerk with the impact.

Trying to appear unfazed, he raised both hands this time and emitted more streams of blue sparks. Wow, he really wanted to hurt me. And that really would hurt.

I pounded my foot twice on the ground, absorbed the energy of the Earth into me and let it sprout out as a mound of earth that rose speedily in front of me. Jared, relentless, was zapping the protective boulder when I darted out from behind it – my energy whip back in hand. I cracked the whip around him, pinning his arms to his sides, and yanked hard to bring a tied-up Jared toward me. Just for fun, I cracked the whip again, making him slam once to the ground before I then let the whip fade away.

I looked down at a coughing Jared and arched a brow. "Now who's the pretty girl?"

Although he appeared a mixture of nettled, flabbergasted, and stupefied, his mouth twitched slightly in some form of dark amusement.

I offered my hand to him but he bounced independently to his feet, still staring at me. He seemed undecided whether to be extremely exasperated or pleasantly surprised. Either way, there was some respect there in his gaze. It was hard for me not to look smug, considering the way he had dismissed me earlier. But I didn't give him an 'I told you so' look or a quirky grin. Disconcertingly, I was actually more caught up in this little silent exchange of respect than I was in the glory of having won the duel. He might be a chauvinist, but he was a gorgeous one.

"Didn't I tell you she was fast?" said Green as he joined Jared.

Slaphead came next. "Definitely a disguised Pagori on crack," he decided as he clucked me. "Know that you can practice on me with that whip anytime."

Jared didn't look amused by that and squared his shoulders. "Please all return to the line while I consult with Commander Sherman and Commander Norton."

"And I thought *my* gift was cool," said Slaphead as we joined the end of the reforming line below the spectators' box.

I glanced up at Sebastian. Grinning with satisfaction and pride, he saluted me. I smiled.

"I'm Max, by the way," Slaphead told me as he held out his hand.

I took it. "Sam. I prefer to call you Slaphead, though."

He laughed. "Whatever turns you on. Hey, Feeders are really rare. I heard that most Feeders go crazy and die after a few years because all the energy overwhelms them."

Distracting me from responding, I caught Jared swerve and meet my eyes. His expression was thoughtful. For a moment, I considered smiling at him. I'm actually not much of a smiler, so that was odd.

"Good luck," said the thorn-exhaling Keja vampire as he appeared on my right.

I win a duel and suddenly everyone's nicey-nicey. I simply nodded.

Finally the three commanders came to stand before the line. Jared's gaze settled on each of the recruits, including me this time, for a few seconds before he spoke. "Between us, we have selected three of you to join my squad. The rest of you will be required to return home immediately."

He began a slow walk along the line of recruits. Halting in front of the Pagori with the power to deflect, he pointed at him with a congratulatory look on his face. "Well done." Next he stopped at Max and pointed. No surprise there – Max's power was exceptional. Then Jared came to the end of the line, standing between myself and the thorn-exhaling Keja. He looked at each of us, then slowly raised his hand, extended his index finger...and pointed at the Keja.

What a fucking little shit.

Instantly there were murmurs and gasps, whether those were of surprise or disagreement I didn't know. I didn't care to find out. "Congratulations," I said to Max and the Keja beside me. Then I twirled sharply and paced away.

"Sam!" Max caught up with me and sighed. "You should have gotten a place. You deserved it more than any of us."

"It's all right," I said, though my tone made it very clear that it wasn't. I let my eyes track Jared, who was staring at me with a crease between his eyebrows. As I spoke to Max, I continued to look hard at Jared. "I wouldn't want to work for a sexist twat anyway."

As I stormed away, I couldn't decide what incensed me more – the fact that I hadn't been given a place in the legion even after proving myself, or the fact that this bothered me so much. It was only then that I realised that I hadn't just wanted a place to spite Victor, or to escape him, or even to annoy Jared. The truth was that I'd wanted to be a part of the picture that Sebastian had tried selling me, to make the most out of the life I now had whether it had been my choosing or not. I wanted to be part of something important, to have a purpose beyond Victor's plans for me.

Sebastian travelled with vampire speed to my side. "Sam, I—"

"It's fine. Really." But I'd said it too sharply; I didn't sound in the least bit convincing.

"I intend to dispute Jared's decision. His judgement was impaired by his—"

"Really Sebastian, don't bother," I advised him gently as we entered the museum-like house. "If I had to see Jared's ugly mug every day, I'd probably stake him."

"Yes, I imagine you would," agreed an amused, unfamiliar voice before me. It belonged to a Latino-looking Keja – though he spoke in a very clear American accent – with shoulder length, thick, coal-black hair and the widest eyes. Everything about the way he conducted himself while he slowly circled me spoke of pure power. This had to be the Grand High Master himself. Flanking him were two Pagori vampires, both looking robotic and fearless.

Sebastian whispered down my ear, "This is the Grand High—"

"Oh I know," I said, irritated. "I'm not thick." I simply gave the Big Man a half-smile. I knew I wasn't being very respectful, but he couldn't do anything worse to me than what Victor would do when he found out I'd taken part in the try-out. No doubt my good ole Sire would taunt me about how I hadn't been successful.

"Miss Samantha Parker," he greeted. "I am Antonio."

"Well, hi…and bye." I proceeded to walk passed him.

"Might I have a few moments of your time?" Antonio asked.

I twirled round intending to tell him no, he could do a run and jump because I was getting out of this place that was stuck in the 1700s. But then he smiled at me and his eyes held tightly to mine. Suddenly I didn't feel so angry anymore. *That bloody Keja hypnotic beauty!* "Look, I don't mean to be rude, it's just that I have to be getting back."

"To Victor? I have to say that I don't much approve of your Sire. Everything I've heard about him from my researchers has indicated him to be a vampire of cruelty."

At that, I stiffened. I felt defensive at the thought of people checking up on my personal business, especially considering what my life with Victor was like.

"You intrigue me, Miss Parker. Your presence. Your self-expression. Your determination. Fascinating." He gestured for me to follow him. "I promise not to keep you long." Instantly he began walking, all elegance and grace, down the everlasting hallway.

Sebastian nodded encouragingly at me. Rolling my eyes, I followed Antonio and his hefty bodyguards. Antonio didn't halt until we reached the most eastern point of what was proving to be a gigantic mansion. The room he ushered us into was bigger than my flat. Some sort of parlour — very posh. The walls were lined with books and there was beautiful, marble fireplace. In the corner sat a grand piano, and in the centre were two black leather sofas that framed a glass coffee table.

Suddenly two dogs dashed toward us, growling and barking.

"Quiet," said Antonio simply. They quieted.

"I love Pit Bull Terriers," I told him. One was reddish brown while the other was brindle.

"I would not approach them if I were you, they can be quite—" Antonio watched, stunned, as the two dogs approached me and nuzzled my hands, hinting for a stroke. "Oh. They are usually only so friendly with me. That is how I like it." He frowned at the dogs.

Well it made sense that he'd want them to only be loyal to him. "I think it's because I can absorb any excess energy they've got, it makes them more relaxed."

His frown morphed into a smile. "Please sit," he invited, gesturing to one of the sofas.

Feeling completely out of place among all the luxury, I gingerly sat. Sebastian lounged beside me, fitting the atmosphere like he was an ornament.

Holding my gaze the entire time, Antonio sat opposite me and crossed one leg over the other. "You're a Feeder," he eventually said, his tone soft and curious.

"Yes."

"Did you know that the gift has only ever run through Pagori bloodlines before you? This means that not only are you the first female Feeder, you are the first Sventé Feeder."

"So I've been told." Victor had been thrilled about it. I was his key to more territory.

"I observed the try-out from the spectators' box. I deeply enjoyed your duel with Jared."

I snorted on hearing that name.

Antonio smiled in amusement. "You're not a fan of his? I do not think I have ever before met a female who was not." The guards laughed at that – oh, so they weren't robots.

I snorted again. "I can't think why. If you observed the try-out, you must have seen the way he acted."

Antonio jiggled his head. "Admittedly, he was a little discourteous."

"Oh let's just call it what it is, shall we? He's an ignorant, arrogant, narrow-minded bigot."

Again Antonio seemed amused. "He's also my Heir. Out of hundreds, I made him my Heir six years ago."

"Bad decision on your part." I could feel Sebastian's eyes drilling into me, cautioning me.

"It is fine, Sebastian," Antonio told him, waving a hand, "I like her frankness." Antonio looked at me again. "I know that Jared does still have things to learn. In fact, his biggest weakness is that he does not realise that there are still things for him to learn. But pride aside, he is an asset to me. He is very devoted to me and to my legion. He, much like you, has great drive about him. And he is an excellent trainer. I could hand him a newborn vampire and within a month Jared would make him a model warrior."

Antonio seemed to be waiting for me to respond, maybe concede that there was more to Jared than what I'd seen. Hardly likely. "That's great," I said in a flippant tone.

"I want my new squad trained quickly. Physically, they will be prepared. I am confident that Jared will ensure this. However, with regards to learning the new recruits how to control and best utilise their gifts, I believe that Jared may…struggle to have them prepared so quickly. He's an excellent motivator, but not the best teacher. You, on the other hand…I believe that you are just what I need. I want you to work with Jared."

Oh this had been a surreal twenty-four hours. "Say again?"

His laugh was silent. "You will be thought of as an employee, a commander in your own right, an equal to Jared and the other commanders."

I waited for the punch line, but there didn't appear to be one. "You think I'd make a good commander because I'm a Feeder?"

"No, because you have tremendous control of your gift. Not many can boast of that. For a Feeder – a type of vampire known for being too overwhelmed by their own gift to live much longer than a couple of years – to have such tremendous control is astonishing. Yes, I am confident that you would be an asset to me and my legion."

I cast a look at Sebastian. His face was all 'go for it'. I turned back to Antonio. "You know that Jared would hate this, right?"

Antonio raised his brows. "You would allow that to influence your decision about accepting such a position?"

"No. But I don't want to accept your offer and then later be told to go back home because Heir Boy had a tantrum."

"Jared may be my Heir, but I cast all final decisions on every matter. He knows this. He respects this."

The brindle Pit Bull Terrier laid his head on my lap and stared up at me with an almost pleading expression on his face. Not that I thought the dog understood what was going on and was begging me to take up Antonio's offer. But I felt like it was a sign – hopefully that sounded less psychotic.

(Jared)

I had my ass kicked. I had my ass kicked by a Sventé vampire. I had my ass kicked by a *woman*. The guys would never let me live this down. Neither would my brother or Antonio. Neither would she if she had stayed. *Sam*. It suited her.

I had to laugh inwardly at myself: the whole thing was so weird. She had kicked my ass, embarrassed me in front of God knows how many people, and even called me a pretty girl...and all I'd wanted to do was grab her, kiss her, and bite her.

Why couldn't she have come here to ask to be one of my consorts? When I'd saw her at the pool, I'd thought that might have been why she was there. Oh I'd have said yes. Who wouldn't have? There was that amazing body, that great accent, that husky voice. Even her smart-ass attitude was a turn-on. I wouldn't have cared if she was like the other women around here; not interested in me, just wanting to be 'the Heir's' consort. If it was the power and authority that they liked, fine, whatever. Just as long as they were there when I needed them, all was good.

But she would never have done what I told her to. Never have bowed down. Never have batted her eyelids. She hadn't been impressed or intimidated by my authority. Sure, she wouldn't have known that I was the Heir. But she'd known that I was a commander, and potentially her boss. Had she cared? No. She'd kicked my ass. All of that made her different. It made her interesting.

Nothing could have stopped me from offering for her to be another of my consorts. Nothing except for that look on her face when she realised I hadn't chosen her for the squad. Pure hatred. And strangely, that had got to me. So had the idea that I wouldn't see her again. What had got to me even more was that it had felt so...I don't know, *wrong*...to watch her go. Like I was watching something go that was mine.

Well, whatever. Maybe I was just horny. I'd go see Joy once I was done in the office. Or maybe Daniela. Or Tammy. Or maybe even all of them. Only one thing stopped all that from being the turn-on that it should be: I could make it happen so easily.

I shrugged it all off as I teleported from the Squads' Quarters to my own personal office in the Command Centre. As I appeared at the desk, movement in my peripheral vision snatched my attention. A weird feeling circulated through me when I turned my head to the left. It was a feeling that made me feel sickly and energized at the same time.

It was *her*.

She was sat on the oak desk, swinging her crossed legs slightly. A tiny part of my brain registered that the furniture was new, and liked how it was situated to my left so that the desks together formed an 'L' shape. The rest of my brain joined my body in being totally preoccupied with the sight of her. It was weird how good it was to just see her, especially since I hadn't expected to ever again. God, she was too tempting. Like a trap. And I'd already stepped in it. With both feet.

She had her head tilted to the side as she returned my stare, but her expression was blank. I could guess why she was there. "Come to contest my decision?" I asked as I leaned casually against the front of my desk. "I thought you wouldn't want to work for a sexist twat."

"I earned a spot. And you know it. I suppose whipping you into place didn't do anything for my chances, seeing as you obviously have an ego as swollen as a horse's rigid dick."

The laugh just burst out of me. "You're powerful, I'll give you that. But there's a lot more to being in the legion than being agile and gifted."

"Explain it to me."

I sighed. "Some of the things that the recruits will be required to do...let's just say they're not for the faint-hearted. There's no space for compassion or even guilt."

"So...because I'm a woman, I must be faint-hearted, compassionate, and prone to guilt-trips?"

My smile widened a little. She couldn't have any idea how much her attitude was making me want her right now.

"You know what, Commander Michaels," – there was no respect in the title, it was patronising, and I loved it – "I would have thought that today might have at least taught you one thing; women might just be able to handle things better than you give them credit for.

You held blood to my lips," – I'd wanted her to lick my finger badly – "and I didn't even so much as twitch. You had me playing Tarzan in the forest with that giant ogre chasing me and I delivered on that task as well. Then you purposely left me until last for the third task so that I'd have to duel with you...and let's not butter up the fact that I put you on your backside."

"Yes, you did. But those tasks aren't nearly as bad as the tasks you get once you're in the legion. Some will keep you up at night. Stick with you forever."

Narrowing her eyes, she slowly slid off the desk with the smoothness of a snake and approached me in a predatory manner. With only a footstep between us, she spoke, "Well let me tell you something. I've done things in my time that would make the curly hairs in your pants go straight. Female or not, I reckon I've got bigger balls than you have."

Her voice went even raspier when she was irritated and that just made me want her even more. I found myself wondering what it would be like to bury my fingers in that dark hair or claim her mouth. I didn't bother masking my desire for her. I let my eyes wander to her full lips. I let the red tint to my irises flare. Then I watched her face as she noticed. She didn't shrink away. Instead, more defiance entered her expression as she shot me a 'not a chance' look. I strongly disagreed.

"So, you want me to give you a trial-run in my squad?"

She tilted her head again. "No."

The office doors opened and in strode Antonio with his bodyguards and Pit Bulls flanking him. The dogs, to my complete shock, trotted over to Sam, sniffing and nuzzling her. Antonio didn't seem surprised, which also shocked me.

"You have told him the news?" Antonio asked Sam.

"News?" I queried. Something told me that I wasn't going to like this. Mostly it was her smug expression.

"You will both be working together."

"We'll both be what?"

"I've offered Miss Parker—"

"For the *gazillionth* time will you just call me Sam?" she stressed.

Antonio smiled at her indulgently, like a father. What the hell had been going on? "You've offered her...?" I prompted.

"The role of aiding you with training your squad to control their gifts."

"Isn't that great?" she said with fake enthusiasm.

Antonio looked as though he was stifling a chuckle. Great, the joke was on me. "You made this decision without first speaking to me," I said in a low voice, feeling overlooked.

He sighed. "Jared, you know that I hold you in the highest esteem. You know how valuable I consider you to be. You know that I trust in your capability—"

"But I'm apparently not capable enough."

"I have my reasons for needing the squad properly prepared without delay. I will be holding a meeting tomorrow during which all will be explained to you, Sam, and the other commanders. What I will assure you of now is that my employing Sam is not a reflection on you, or my faith in you."

"Yeah, right." That was when I walked out.

(Sam)

"Well that went well," I said after Jared slammed the door shut behind him.

Antonio sighed. "After a little time alone with his thoughts, he will be fine."

"I certainly hope he isn't."

"In the meantime, please acquaint yourself with your personal assistant."

"I have a personal assistant?"

"Fletcher has been Jared's assistant for the past three years, and now he is also yours. A fellow Brit, too. Fletcher?"

In a blink, Fletcher appeared, his hands clasped together and his eyes shining with enthusiasm. I realised that I had seen him at what looked like a reception desk outside the room. The feminine way with which he held himself, and the fact that he was so colour coordinated to the extent that he sported designer glasses that had a navy frame to match his navy suit, all told me one thing: Fletcher was homosexual. And so cute. He had the cutest baby face that looked almost perfectly circular and was framed by short, tight, mahogany curls. The most adorable dimples decorated his naturally pouty lips. I just wanted to pinch his cheeks like a grandmother would do to a child.

"Yes your Grandness?" He was a Londoner too? Even better. I could tell just by looking at him that we were going to have such a laugh.

"Fletcher, I'd like you to meet *Commander* Sam Parker. You may have noticed a new desk and leather chair being brought in here. Sam will be working with Jared, so I hope you will be just as valuable to her as you are to him."

Nodding, Fletcher said, "That goes without saying, your Grandness."

Antonio returned his focus to me. "Sebastian will ensure that your Sire is notified of your employment here. I'm sure he'll be delighted about it." Wearing a sly smile, he left the room with his entourage.

Fletcher approached me and held out his hand, "'Ello Commander, I'm—"

"Let me stop you right there," I said, smiling. "No *Commander Parker* – I beg you. Just call me Sam."

"Oh my God, you're a Cockney like me! D'ya know, I was the only Brit in The Hollow until now."

"The Hollow?"

"That's what we call the place, luv. Hmm, I suppose the teleportation process didn't give you a great view. Come with me."

It turned out that Fletcher had a feminine walk too. This Keja just got cuter and cuter. He led me up two flights of stairs to the roof of the building. "There," he said, pointing down. "See?"

"My God." The place was humungous. Like a holiday camp or something. Several buildings were scattered around, forming a rectangular shape around a man-made, white-sanded beach that had a bridge in the middle. It had a relaxed Caribbean feel about it. "Where are we exactly?"

"A little island just south of St. Lucia, luv. You won't find it on any map. This here, as you know, is The Command Centre. It has ten offices, one for each Commander. You're now the eleventh, but of course you share an office with Jared."

"So there are ten squads in the legion?"

"Yes, with ten vamps in each one." He gestured to the main mansion, which was to our left. "That's Antonio's residence. The only other vamps who reside there are his consorts – the greedy git's got about fourteen of them – Sebastian, and his Advisor. Oh and his personal guards, you might have noticed he's got plenty of them. He mostly stays there.

"Then to the left of the mansion is the Guest House. We don't get many guests, as Antonio likes his privacy. Then there are two Residence Halls for his general staff like the chefs, and maids, and maintenance people, and what-have-ya. The row of buildings directly facing us are shops, cafes, restaurants, and bars. Oh, and there's a cinema, a bowling alley, and even a nightclub."

"You're kidding?"

Fletcher grinned. "I'm glad I'm not. With all those bars and shops, this is my Graceland."

"Is there a clothes shop? I've only got enough stuff to last me till tomorrow. Something tells me that my Sire won't pass along my belongings," I grumbled.

"Oh yeah, there's nothing those stores don't have. The idea behind Antonio's design of The Hollow was so that he wouldn't have to leave. As the Grand High Master, he has to worry about attempts on his life. If someone was to kill him, they would have the right to fight the Heir for the position of the Grand High Master. So, Antonio built himself, his bloodline, and his staff a nice little community. Or a world within a world, as he likes to call it."

"So...anyone who works here can't leave?"

"Oh don't worry, luv, it's not like a prison," he chuckled. "People can venture out if Antonio gives them permission. I've never met anyone who wants to leave, though. All the staff gets full use of that lovely beach there, and plenty of time off, and the pay's good. Most important to them, they have the best vampiric protection they could possibly have. There's no securer place to be."

I gazed around me, astonished and in awe of Antonio's little community. "What are these buildings to our right?"

"That's the Residence Hall for commanders, their consorts, and personal assistants. Then you've got the Residence Hall for all the members of the legion, and another one for any humans. And that last building in the corner by the nightclub is the security lodge." He twirled on the spot and then ushered me to the opposite edge of the roof. "Last but not least, we have all this."

The view overlooked the pool and the gardens of Antonio's mansion, the arena where the try-out had taken place, the small forest that I had not long ago been chased through, and also a beach. It was absolutely breath-taking with the azure blue sea and white sand. So inviting.

"Only Antonio, the commanders, and the legion have access to this beach," Fletcher told me. "That's why he has the man-made beach for the other vamps. So...what d'ya think?"

I smiled at him. "It's all right, I suppose."

He elbowed me gently. "Give over. It's *fabulous*."

Back at the office, Fletcher handed me document upon document about the history of The Hollow and the legion. I made myself comfy on my leather chair, balancing my feet on the desk, as I settled with the files. Meanwhile, Fletcher was gathering as much available personal information as possible on the new squad members to create their personnel files. I was eager to read them and get a proper idea of who I would be coaching – a job that was in effect from tomorrow.

"Reading up on the history of the legion, huh," said Jared, leaning against his desk, gazing at me. He was getting a good look at my legs, like he was trying to see through my pants. Self-conscious – not many people ever made me feel self-conscious – I was itching to drop my legs from the table. But then he would know that he had made me feel uncomfortable, and he would get off on that.

Then a thought came to me: how had I not heard him or sensed him enter the room?

As if guessing my train of thought, he said, "I can teleport."

"You have two gifts? How is that possible?"

"I have three, actually. My natural gift is electrokinesis, but Antonio has the power to pass on gifts. Twice he singled me out to receive two others as rewards."

"So what's the third?"

Telepathy, I heard in my head. It was like hearing him talk through a phone.

"You can read thoughts?" I sounded horrified by the idea, which made him smile.

No, but I can communicate using my mind, he replied.

I was extremely relieved that he couldn't read my thoughts. No way did I want him to know how gorgeous I thought he was, or that I was trying so hard not to ogle, or that I was hoping to get a good look at his backside the next time he turned around. "Good for you."

I tried to sound uninterested, and returned my attention to the documents.

"You could have said that with your mind, you know."

"I thought you said you couldn't read thoughts."

"I can't. But if you direct a thought at me, I'll hear it."

I looked up at him and smirked. *I'd like to slice off your salami and shove it up your sexist arse.*

His smile became a mischievous grin as he arched a brow. *So you've been thinking about my salami?*

I scowled at him and went back to the documents, but apparently he wasn't finished teasing me yet.

Well, you've been thinking about my salami, so I suppose I could think about you naked, and then we'd be even.

"No, no, I do not want you thinking about me naked."

You really should've said something sooner.

I meant to scowl at him again, but the intense red glow in his eyes froze me for a second. It was almost impossible not to get a kick out of someone as gorgeous as him wanting you, even if they were a sod. Recovering quickly, I asked, "Where are our new recruits?"

"*My* new recruits are having a tour of The Hollow, and then they'll get settled into their accommodation before dawn."

"Oh they're *your* new recruits, are they? So you're still intent on being childish."

He sighed. "Actually, I've been thinking."

"*Sulking* would be more accurate."

"Did you honestly think that I'd be thrilled that Antonio thought I needed help?"

"I knew you'd hate it. I knew you'd think you don't need my help. And I knew you'd try to make my life difficult, hoping I'd jib it. But here's the thing, Commander: you can't possibly hate this more than I hate working for my Sire, and there's nothing you could do that could be worse than what he'd do if I went back to him. So if I were you, I'd stop the sulking and get over it."

He tilted his head. "Is that why you took the job? To get away from your Sire?" He didn't say it judgementally.

"That played a factor in it. But I wouldn't have taken up Antonio's offer if I didn't think I could make a difference. If you're that immature that you can't bring yourself to work with a woman, we'll split the time. You can have the recruits from dusk till before lunch break, and I'll have them from after lunch for a few hours."

"Sounds fair. But I still say I don't need the help."

"Anyone who's so narrow-minded needs help; being prejudiced just holds people back."

"Is that right?" he asked, smiling and crossing his arms over his chest.

"I can guarantee you that, within seven nights, you'll see a difference with *our* new recruits' control of their gifts. When that happens, you'll owe me an apology. A public one."

He strolled over, stopping only when he reached my desk. The challenge in his eyes made me stand up. "Care to make that bet interesting?"

"Bets are always interesting."

"*If* you manage to improve their control in five nights—"

"Five? I said seven."

"What, you don't think you could make a difference within five nights?" His smirk was triumphant as he knew I wouldn't show any weakness.

"Fine. Five nights."

"As I was saying, *if* you manage to improve their control in five nights, I'll apologise. I'll even make a public apology if that's what you want. But if you *don't* make any difference," – he leaned across the table, leaving only inches between our faces – "I get to taste you." His gaze wandered down to my throat and his irises began to glow red again. I had to admit – reluctantly, of course – that I liked that tasting my blood was so appealing to him.

My instinct was to say 'You can *sod off*.' But that would be the equivalent of me saying that I wasn't one hundred percent confident in my ability to help the squad. His grin was smug – he knew he had completely cornered me. "Fine."

"I'll look forward to collecting on my bet."

"Why would you want to give yourself false hope?"

Suddenly, there was a tiny knock on the office door, a female voice called out 'It's only me, sweetie!' and then a girl barged into the office. Immediately I didn't like her, because she was obviously Jared's girlfriend. With her shoulder-length pitch-black hair, her penetrating Keja-amber irises, chunky scarlet lips, and coal-black dress, she made me think of a witch. She was beautiful, yeah, but she was also so skinny to the extent that she was all bony. Her skimpy dress perfectly illuminated this fact.

I sent a thought to Jared. *Oh come on, there's no meat whatsoever on those bones. And she doesn't even make up for it in the boob department – they're like bee stings. I really thought you'd have better taste than that.*

He looked amused. *Jealous?*

Of a stick insect? Yeah, right.

He didn't look convinced, and well he shouldn't. I *was* jealous, which surprised me.

Her eyes narrowed slightly as she saw Jared leaning across my desk, but she quickly pasted a wide smile on her face and walked over to him. She held my gaze as she planted a kiss on his cheek. Possessiveness twinkled in those eyes. I really didn't like that. I was pretty sure that I'd later question why on earth it had bothered me so much.

I smiled pleasantly at her. "Hi, you must be Nancy." Damn if I knew any Nancy. I just wanted to enjoy seeing the possessive twinkle become paranoia.

Her own smile faded. "I'm Joy," she said emphatically before turning to Jared. "Who's Nancy?" Although she had clearly tried to sound aloof, she hadn't pulled it off at all.

Jared gave me a knowing smile. "One of the human girls." No idea why he was playing along. "Joy, this is Commander Parker."

She sniggered. "Since when does a woman – or a Sventé, for that matter – work *here*?"

"Since she kicked my ass."

"So *she's* the one who did that. But she looks so, well, ordinary."

Before I could snap her head off her twig-like body, Jared told her, "Joy, it's really not smart to irritate someone who could kill you easier than she can breathe."

The phone on my desk rang, snapping me out of my planning what would be the most rewarding way to watch her die. I answered quickly, "Hello?"

"Sam, luv, Sebastian's here to see you," Fletcher informed me.

"Send him in, Fletch. Thanks." No sooner had I hung up the phone than Sebastian was stood before my desk. Jared backed away with Joy nibbling on his ear. He was more interested in what Sebastian had to say, though, by the look on his face. I already had a pretty good idea what this was about.

"One of my assistants managed to reach Victor and inform him of your new circumstances." I guessed right. Sebastian puffed. "He more or less indicated that—"

"I should get back there or he'll hunt me down and drag me back himself?" I supplied. That was the kind of stupid thing Victor would say, considering he had always viewed me as a possession. Losing me also meant losing his consort and his main weapon.

"Something like that."

Is Victor your Sire? Jared asked. I gave him a curt nod.

"The threat is pointless, of course," continued Sebastian. "There is no way that Antonio will hand you over to Victor unless you wish to go of your own free will. However, Victor insisted on you being personally given the message and for you to respond immediately as to whether you will be going back to him."

With all seriousness, I replied, "I'd rather lick my own arse hole." Sebastian, apparently now accustomed to my occasional harsh language, only smiled. "You be sure he gets that message, word-for-word."

Sebastian nodded his head obligingly. "I shall do so, Commander. With extreme pleasure. Oh, I almost forgot to inform you that your apartment is ready for you."

"My a-what?"

"You didn't think Antonio was going to ask you to stay in shabby accommodations, did you?" He threw me a key card. "I'm sure Fletcher will take you when you're ready."

"Thanks." And I sincerely meant it.

Before leaving, Sebastian shot Jared a look of distaste, just as nauseated as me by how Joy was moaning while dabbing Jared's neck with noisy kisses. I decided to take a leaf out of Sebastian's book and get out of there. Hearing Victor's name had made my skin crawl, and I just wasn't in the mood to listen to some twig drool all over my colleague, who I inconveniently found so tempting.

Tidying the documents on my desk, I spoke to Jared as one professional to another. "Fletcher said he'll have the personnel files on the recruits done by dusk, so could you leave them on my desk once you're finished with them? I'll need them before lunch break."

"Where're you going?"

He'd asked that as though he actually thought he had a right to know. "Why? Do you need me for something?"

His brow arched suggestively as a devious smirk surfaced on his devastatingly attractive face.

I corrected, *do you need me for something that doesn't involve tasting my blood?*

Five nights, and I'll be tasting you, whether you like it or not.

I snorted. *You keep telling yourself that if it helps you sleep in the day.*

CHAPTER THREE

(Sam)

Fletcher, the gem, insisted on accompanying me to the Residence Hall. In front of the building, there was a spacious garden with a pebbly path that wound toward the entrance. The main doors were black and bulky yet easy to open thanks to my vampire strength.

It was even quieter inside than it was outside. Quieter than I thought anything could be. You know that feeling when everything's so quiet that you can actually hear a weird little buzzing sound in your ear?

Fletcher's voice was like a boom in the silence. "All of the commanders' personal assistants live on the ground floor and the basement. Our apartments aren't as big as yours, but they're nice and cosy; that's all I ask of life."

"Have you always been a personal assistant here?"

"Oh yeah. When my Sire got the position of one of the security guards about forty years ago, he brought some of his vampires with him – one being me. I've only been Jared's assistant for a few years. Before that, he had a dozen different women. I think Antonio appointed me for Jared because he just wanted him to have an assistant he couldn't shag."

I giggled. "Something tells me you would shag Jared given half the chance."

"Am I that easy to read?"

Together we ventured up the soft, regal-blue carpeted staircase until we came to the eighth level. We walked along a beige-painted corridor, passing two or three black doors until we finally stopped at a door that sported the sign 'Commander Samantha Parker'.

Earlier, I'd pictured myself dashing inside that apartment, content as a pig in shit. Call me odd, I know I would, but I now found myself procrastinating. I'd spent the past three years sharing a flat with

Victor and having him and his guards spying on my every move. Now I would not only have privacy, I'd have things that were *mine* and just mine. That title on the door was mine. This apartment was mine. The new job I had and the wages that would come from it would all be mine. Furthermore, I didn't belong to anyone now except myself. There was a lot that my slow brain needed to absorb, so many changes happening so quickly.

"You're gonna love this, I just know it," said Fletcher excitedly as I finally unlocked the door with my key card. "The walls are even vampire sound-proof. How great's that!"

Noiselessly the door swung open and presented me with my new home. Wow. It was much more stylish than what I'd been expecting. I walked along the soft luxury beige carpet of my living area. The walls were brilliant white, as were the window frames, the curtains, and the balcony doors.

"Oh yes I have a balcony," I drawled, passing a crescent-moon shaped sofa in the centre of the living area. The sofa was angled toward a large wide screen TV that was hanging on the wall. *Ooh nice.* Between the two was an oval pine coffee table that was positioned comfortably on a white fur (fake fur, I could tell) rug. In one corner was a large dish lamp, while in the other corner there was a CD player and a collection of CDs. As I swerved back to flash a delighted smile at Fletcher, I noticed that my duffel bag had been placed near the door.

"Come see your kitchen," he urged.

The carpet ended at a small glossy-cream kitchenette which was tiled the same glossy-cream. Although it was miniature, it was all there: cupboards, oven, hob, sink, refrigerator, microwave, kettle, washing machine, and tumble dryer. Fletcher did a Vogue-worthy pose against the fridge before opening it and making a '*voilà*' sound. "In here, they've stocked you a load of NSTs—"

"NSTs?"

"Sounds like a sexually transmitted disease, doesn't it? No, luv, I mean Nutritive Supplemental Tonics. They've got blood in them and a load of other funky vitamins. Antonio has them made so we don't have to move thousands of humans into The Hollow to feed on." He took one of the glass bottles out and sniffed. "They're not bad, actually. They get to your thirst quick enough and they give you a good boost. This one's supposed to have a vanilla flavour to it, but I wouldn't know if it's nice or not, I've never tried it. I think these ones are the best." He pulled out another bottle. "Honey flavoured. Go on, have a sip."

Mainly because I knew Fletcher wouldn't shut up until I tried some, I took the honey flavoured NST and removed the cap. The aroma that escaped the bottle was alluring and hypnotic, drawing me to the liquid. It was the kind of smell that would make you feel hungry even if you weren't. But I was hungry – well, thirsty – so I aggressively chugged it down. I probably looked like an animal, but I couldn't have cared even if you'd paid me to. "That's all right that."

"Good Lord, you must've been parched. Why didn't you say something?"

The feeling that came from devouring the drink was strange. I felt relaxed the way I did after a mug of hot chocolate, but I also felt giddy and hypo the way I did after a can of Red Bull. There was such a silky feel to the liquid that it soothed my throat and made me feel refreshed rather than groggy. But although it got to work on the thirst pretty quickly like Fletcher had said it would, it also left me wanting more. Nothing really quenched the thirst except pure blood itself.

Fletcher tugged on my arm. "Come on, come see the bedroom suite."

The beige fluffy carpet began again after the kitchenette, leading into a gorgeous bedroom where there was a queen-sized bed adorned with rose-pink satin bed sheets. Fletcher and I exchanged a knowing look and then both dived on the bed.

"My word, this is comfy," he purred. "I think you'll struggle to get out of this bed in the evenings. I know I'd never leave it if it was mine."

"And it's *all* mine!"

"You're not getting yourself a consort?"

The word always gave me a chill. I'd been Victor's consort against my will for the past three years. Having sex with someone who you despised had a way of making you feel ill inside. I had to question whether sex itself had ever really been that thrilling. "Not a chance in hell. Do you have one?"

"Better. I have a boyf: Norm. We've been together 'bout a year now. But maybe you should think about getting a consort for a little while. Pardon my saying this, but it looks to me like you could do with a good shag. I mean, it might help with the aggressiveness, and then maybe you wouldn't get so hot around Jared all the time."

Completely taken aback by the comment and the way Fletcher had said it so casually, I guffawed. "What?"

"Oh don't muck about, it's obvious you want him, and him you. You might have decked him at the try-out, but those red irises tell me he's gotten over it quick enough. I've heard he's well hung, if that helps."

"I do *not* get hot around him."

"That's a little thing called *denial*." He waved a hand. "Anyway, if you're not going to get a consort, at least get yourself a vessel, luv." A vessel was a human readily available to you, and only you, for biting anytime. "There are plenty of NSTs, but nothing compares to the act of biting and drinking blood, does it? Maybe you could have a little nibble on Jared's—"

"Right, that's it." I reluctantly rose from the bed. "If you persist on mentioning that sod, I'm continuing my look of the apartment without you."

Fletcher gasped. "You can't do that, I'm your tour guide."

On either side of the bed were fitted, triple wardrobes that had long mirrors on the doors. I was now looking forward to going shopping just so I could fill them. God, it would feel good to go shopping and pick my own things as opposed to having Victor picking everything for me.

Hanging above the top of the bed, adjoined to the wardrobes, was a row of six cupboards. I fully intended to fill them with books. I'd always liked reading, mostly Stephen King or James Patterson books. You couldn't go wrong with those authors.

On the opposite side of the bedroom was a white chest of drawers on which stood an elegantly framed oval mirror. Last but not least, in the corner of the room were a black leather desk chair and a smaller version of the desk in my office. Better still, on the desk sat a laptop computer and printer.

I guessed that my astonishment must have been clear on my face, because Fletcher elbowed me and said, "Overwhelmed?"

I nodded. "But in a good way."

"Well you're about to get even more overwhelmed, because in that en-suite bathroom you'll find a large corner bath that doubles as a Jacuzzi."

"What? You're joking."

"See for yourself, woman."

No, it hadn't been a joke. The bathroom was immaculate. The walls were painted spearmint green till halfway down and then had large white tiles decorating the bottom half. A turbo shower was hung on the wall over the Jacuzzi bath.

"Well...what d'ya think of your new home?"

"I'm in love." In theory, the predominantly white decor should have been quite plain and boring, considering that this colour scheme ran throughout the apartment, but it was actually very beautiful. It made the place feel pure and heavenly. But even if it had had a dull, gloomy appearance, I still would have adored it because it was mine.

(Jared)

It was getting so easy to sense her. I couldn't explain how I did it, though. It was almost like there was a part of me that remained dormant until her husky voice or intoxicating scent was near; then that part of me woke up and completely took over. At that point, all I could think about was her.

I didn't even suspect that she was aware of me hanging over my balcony watching her hanging over her own, two levels down from me, until she sent a thought to me.

What? Her gaze didn't move from her balcony view. *I can feel you staring so don't say 'nothing'.*

So she was intensely aware of me too. I couldn't resist teasing her. *If you really want to know, I was getting a good look at your ass.*

That made her pivot on the spot, her mouth gaping open as she glared hard at me. I could've sworn she looked a little self-conscious.

The truth is I was thinking about what that blood of yours tastes like.

She scowled. *You should know that you're setting yourself up for disappointment.*

You know you've wondered what it would feel like to have me sink my teeth into your skin.

Oh yes. Sarcasm. *I want you, Jared, I need you.* Eye roll. *Haven't you got a twig to go snuggle up to?*

Joy doesn't sleep in my apartment. Come see for yourself if you want.

Another eye roll. *Good night.* Looking a little flushed, she retreated into her apartment.

As much as I teased her about our little bet, the truth was that I didn't really want to win it. Did I want to taste her? Hell, yes. But I wanted to taste her because she wanted me to, not because of some bet. And I knew that wasn't going to happen if I started giving her leeway or showing signs of weakness. Sam was spirited, and it was letting her exercise that spiritedness that got her going. Whether she realised it yet or not, this betting stuff and the constant conflict between us was foreplay.

(Sam)

I should have sliced off his salami. I should have. Then I wouldn't feel all flushed right now, imagining him biting and tasting me. God, this was ridiculous. How could you be attracted to someone who made you so pissed off that you'd considered burning their balls with a lighter? I wanted to twat myself over the head for being so relieved that he didn't share his apartment with the twig. I didn't *want* to want him, or think about him, or be jealous about the twig. Maybe it was nothing to do with Jared, maybe Fletcher was right and I needed a good shag to set me straight. Maybe getting a little once-over by a stranger would help me burn off those stupid feelings. With horniness out of the equation, I wouldn't want Jared anymore…right?

I'd think on that a little more at dusk. For now, as much as I was curious to know if I also had internet access and satellite channels, I was way too tired for that or anything else. Without undressing, I plonked myself on the bed and immediately entered dreamland. I slept like, well, the dead…until about fifteen minutes after dusk had settled.

I dug out the last of my clothes from the duffel bag – a pair of black denim, slim-fitting jeans and a white long sleeved top that hung loosely over one shoulder – and dressed with vampire speed. Then I enjoyed three NSTs (greedy, I know, but I'd burned off a lot of calories yesterday and I'd have a busy evening ahead) before heading out my door.

As I descended the final set of stairs, I saw a blond bloke coming my way that I'd never met, but who at the same time I found familiar. It wasn't his tallness that was familiar, or his athletic yet slim build, or his cocky strut which I really liked. I'd remember someone that appealing. But there was something about his smile and his eyes...hazel eyes.

"You must be Commander Parker," he said in a friendly, chirpy tone.

"Sam."

"Commander Michaels – the other one – but just call me Evan."

I took the hand that he offered. He had a firm handshake. "You're...Jared's brother?" I hadn't known he had one.

"We're twins. Both got Turned into vamps at the same time. I heard you're a Feeder."

"Yep."

"And you use an energy whip...?" His smile turned a little roguish.

"Not in a dominatrix kind of way." What was it with blokes and whips?

"Shame." His eyes ran over me, but not in a slimy way…It was more of a studious look. "See you at the meeting."

The meeting was being held in the mansion in one of Antonio's many conference rooms. Arriving fifteen minutes early, I found a long table that seated thirty people. Only Jared and a few other vampires were there.

"Evening, Commander Parker," said Jared with a smirk – totally taking the piss – as I sat opposite him near the head of the table. We'd be the nearest to Antonio, by the looks of things. Jared was wearing that same expression he'd worn when he'd proposed his little bet. A bet that I was having a hard time not thinking about.

"Stop calling me that, you know it does my head in."

"Does your head in?" Unfamiliar with the terminology, it would seem.

"It annoys me," I amended.

"Sam, this is Commander Dawson." Jared gestured to the vampire beside him who had quite a gangly look and buck teeth.

"Hi," I said. I wasn't much of a conversationalist after just waking up.

"I heard about your performance at the try-out." Dawson's voice was gruff, making him sound aggravated, which perfectly suited a Pagori vampire. "Controlling the elements is a hard thing to do."

"And this is Commander Marsh," said Jared as he pointed to the vampire beside Dawson. Marsh flashed me a smile that was obscured by a badly-in-need-of-a-trim moustache. Both his moustache and his hair were bushy and silver.

"And I'm Donnie," said a wide-eyed, incredibly cute vampire in a flirtatious voice, "or Commander Rodney."

Just then, more vampires piled into the room, laughing and joking amongst themselves. I recognised two of them as the blokes who'd judged at the try-out with Jared. If I remembered rightly, the dark-skinned Keja was Commander Lou Sherman and the auburn Pagori was Commander Will Norton. Both nodded at me, looking a little awkward.

I knew it was childish that I didn't nod back, but both of them should have done the fair thing and told Jared not to be so biased against women and given me the place I'd earned in the squad. *Well, here I am sitting in a meeting with them as their equal so who's laughing now?*

Jared introduced me to three more commanders: McGowan (a tall, miserable-looking Pagori), Baker (a dark Pagori who laughed like a hyena) and Rowan (another Pagori who turned out to be a whistler).

"And, of course, there's me," said a familiar voice. I turned to find Evan doing his cocky strut into the room. "Hello again," he said to me before turning to the bloke beside me, Commander Baker. "Move along, Laugh-a-lot." After a short game of musical chairs, Evan was seated next to me.

"I see you two have met." If I didn't know any better, I'd think Jared sounded sour about it.

"I tell ya something, bro, that consort of yours – Joyce, or whatever her name is – is *weird*. She's just pulled me aside and asked me to keep you away from Sam."

"Why?" I asked, amused.

"Because she's weird," Evan repeated. "Not that I mind keeping you company."

Going by the odd looks being exchanged between the brothers, I'd say they were having a telepathic conversation. And it wasn't altogether pleasant.

"But won't that upset your consort?" I said to Evan, teasingly.

"Oh I don't have one." He waved a hand as if the whole concept was dumb. I liked Evan.

Just then, Antonio entered with his two guards, Pit Bulls. Behind them were Sebastian and a strange, tall Keja with long white-grey hair and a matching long beard.

That's Luther, Jared informed me. *He's Antonio's Advisor.*

Someone should tell him that he's not living in the film Lord of the Rings.

Jared coughed to hide his chuckle.

The brindle dog, Nero, nuzzled my hand then lay by my feet almost protectively. Instantly there was whispering in the room. My God, these blokes were like little old women – gasping and gossiping about every little thing.

Antonio only rolled his eyes at Nero's behaviour. "You will all no doubt be wondering why I was in such a great rush to have this latest squad prepared so quickly," he said as he gracefully sank into the chair at the head of the table. Apparently he didn't like to beat about the bush. The red Pit, Achilles, sat up straight beside his chair. "You will also be curious as to why I have ordered for the other squads to be pushed to their limits these past few weeks." After a long pause, which I assumed was for dramatic effect, Antonio explained, "Luther had a vision."

With those words, all eyes fell on the Gandalf lookalike – who happened to be staring at me.

"He foresaw that The Hollow's walls would be attacked in the near future. It was not possible at the time to be sure of when, but two nights ago, he had another vision. It was clearer and Luther saw a great number of vampires preparing for battle, lead...by the Sventé High Master, Bennington."

Bennington, who was British like me, had quite a reputation for collecting gifted vampires. I'd met him a few times. He had tried to buy me from Victor, but even though Victor barely had any money, he'd refused to hand me over for any price.

"As you are all aware, Bennington is a Sventé vampire with no impressive gift to boast of. But using his gift to measure the power voltage coming from other vampires, he has compensated for his own weak defence by selecting extremely gifted vampires to build himself a team of bodyguards. We are now thinking that perhaps it was not a security team he was building, but an army to aid him in overtaking The Hollow. We must be ready in every sense of the word, which is why I have employed Commander Parker to assist with training the new recruits in controlling their gifts."

"How many did Luther see?" asked Evan, all seriousness now.

"Approximately three hundred, which leads us to believe that Bennington will add more and more to his own numbers as he makes his way here. I would imagine that he will try and rally supporters during Rupert Connelly's gathering in a few weeks' time. I am hoping that some of those High Master vampires will refuse his offer and then journey here and aid us in guarding the exterior of the walls. We can only be glad that Luther's vision has enabled us to have the time to properly prepare."

"You said you wanted the new squad ready in a month," said Jared. "You don't think they'll be here before then?"

It was Luther who answered. "No. In my vision, during the attack I was rounding up the humans to take them into hiding, and there were 'summer sales' signs up in one of the clothes' stores. After I'd had the vision, I asked the manager of the store when those signs would be put up. That is not for another four weeks. So I would say that it will be a minimum of one month before the attack is made." Again, Luther's eyes found me. His gaze was searching...like he was trying to see through me.

Uncomfortable, I looked away quickly. "Antonio, you say you're going to protect the walls...?"

"Yes, we will attempt to stop them before they enter."

"I'm sorry but it sounds like the battle for Troy all over again."

"You want to leave the walls unprotected?" sniggered Commander Hyena Baker — who had severely tested my patience already with the Sventé jibes he'd made shortly before Antonio arrived.

I rolled my eyes. "How about you pipe down and try not to crack a *not funny* joke for just a few minutes?" I turned back to Antonio. "I don't see why you're going to let them get so close to The Hollow's walls. They'll probably guess that you've got someone who has the gift of precognition. They'll expect you to be lined up outside the walls, waiting like Trojans. I mean, think about it, you've got rainforests surrounding the entire place – rainforests that the squads train in and probably know inside and out. This is your front and back yard, which gives you an advantage. Use it."

"Ordinarily, vampires and animals give each other a wide berth."

"And that is exactly why no one will be expecting you all to be planted around the rainforest, waiting."

Evan nodded. "I like it."

"As do I," said Luther. His eyes still spooked me out so I didn't meet his gaze for more than a few seconds.

"If nothing else," began Commander White, "at least we'll be able to minimise the number of vampires reaching the actual walls."

"I don't mind going on the front line," I told Antonio, "I know—" I stopped short at the sound of a snigger. Turning in my seat, I found that it wasn't Baker this time.

Commander Dawson was shaking his head at me from across the table. "Sweetness, you help coach the new squad, but that's where it should end for you." Up until then, I'd thought he wasn't so bad.

"How many more of you are sexist?" I said through my teeth.

"This is not about you being a female, sweetness. You might be a Feeder and have the ability to produce a nice little whip, but being part of the legion requires more than that."

"A nice little whip," I echoed. He sounded like Jared.

"You ever killed someone, sweetness?" His tone made it clear that he was expecting the answer to be 'no'.

"Yes," I answered honestly and with no guilt. They'd all had it coming – especially the bastards who kidnapped the little kids to sell as vessels, or even as consorts to those who were sick in the head. One thing I could say for Victor was that he never gave me a mark that was innocent.

Dawson quickly rephrased, "You ever killed them *purposely*?"

"Yes."

"How did that make you feel, to kill in cold blood?" He clearly wasn't happy about my answers so far.

"With all that adrenalin pumping away, I felt great."

They were a few muffled chuckles. Some were from Jared, Evan, and Sebastian, I noticed.

"Ever led a squad before?" he asked, grimacing.

"Yes."

"Are you saying you—?"

I growled. "God, give me strength," I begged as I looked upwards. "I'm bored with Question Time now, *Dickson*."

"It's Dawson."

"I know."

I heard Antonio mutter to Luther in amusement and approval, "She brings life to these meetings, doesn't she?"

I returned Dawson's scowl as I continued. "Let's save us both some time. My bloodthirsty Sire sent me on a hell of a lot of assignments – some on my own, some with a squad of eight. I always got my target, and I always brought all eight back."

Sebastian nodded, huffing at Dawson.

"Then I assume Commander Dawson's concerns are now addressed," said Antonio. Dawson, looking a little sheepish now, nodded. Antonio then included everyone as he continued. "I agree with Sam that we should capitalize on our knowledge of the surrounding area and attack Bennington's force before they have a chance to attack us. I trust that you can decide amongst yourselves which squads should concentrate on defending the walls and which should be positioned within the rainforest. I give permission for squads to leave The Hollow's walls to train within the forests. That will be all. Thank you."

Nero gave my hand a slobbery lick, which almost seemed like a goodbye gesture, as I rose from my seat.

"What a flirt," Evan said jokingly, referring to Nero, as he also stood.

"Well you'd know all about that, wouldn't you?" Jared was glaring at Evan again in that weird way.

"Hey, don't forget to leave the personnel files of the recruits on my desk," I told Jared.

"Sure," he replied, walking speedily out of the room. I gave Evan a questioning look.

Evan shrugged at his brother's behaviour. "He never was quite right upstairs."

"Commander Parker…sorry, Sam?" called Antonio. "Could you spare a moment?"

"Yeah, course." I gave Evan a farewell smile, which he returned.

Once the room was empty of commanders, Antonio gestured to the Keja who had spent much of the meeting staring at me. "I do not believe you have formally met my Advisor, Luther."

Luther's handshake was gentle. "It is a pleasure to meet you at last." The soft bugger shook the hand that was covered in Nero's slobber. He wasn't too pleased about that and wiped it on his grey trousers.

What he said suddenly sank in: a pleasure to meet me at last? I hadn't even been here for seventy-two hours yet. Not really knowing what to say to that, I replied simply, "And you." His smile seemed to indicate that he had picked up on my confusion.

Antonio spoke again. "Sam, as you know, Luther's gift is precognition. He sporadically has visions. Whenever I appoint someone to have a high position within The Hollow, I offer them a glimpse of their own future. This helps them with either avoiding something or working towards it, which in turn is good for The Hollow."

"A glimpse of my future?"

"Part of Luther's gift is that he can allow another person to have a vision of their own merely through touch. He would not see your vision, only you would. And you would not be obliged to reveal anything of what you see. It can be for you and you alone to know."

Luther quickly said, "Many have decided that they do not wish to know anything of their future. Some believe that having the vision is what causes the event. I cannot comment on that as I do not know for certain. But most of my visions do come true."

Antonio placed a hand on my shoulder. "It is your choice, Sam." He said it like a question.

"What kind of vision would it be? I mean, will it be a positive one or a negative one? I don't want to see my own death, but if I'm going to win the lotto that would be interesting to know."

Luther smiled, shrugging. "There is no way of knowing."

Not a great answer. "When you say 'a glimpse of the future', do you mean *my* future or the future itself? I'd rather not see other people's future — it'd feel like spying or something."

"The vision may indeed contain other people, but only if they are interlinked with that time in *your* future."

"Are the visions clear or more like brief flashing images? I don't see much point in getting a glimpse if it's going to be like looking through fog."

"Sometimes they are very clear, sometimes clear enough, and other times they are so vague that I will be awake all day trying to decipher what I saw."

Not what I was hoping to hear. "Are we talking near future or really distant future?"

Luther chuckled. "Do you know, Sam, that not one person has ever considered this offer so deeply. You have asked some very wise questions. To answer your last question, I have no way of knowing. I cannot control the content of the visions. I can only guarantee that it will concern your own future."

One side of me was wondering what the hell I was waiting for – a vision would be brilliant. But another side of me was thinking that things were weird enough right now without throwing something else into the mix. Luther had said that they were not always very clear.

Eventually, curiosity won over. "All right, what do I have to do?"

Luther offered me his hand. "It is very simple. You need only hold onto my hand until the vision is over. They are not very long. Thirty seconds has been the longest I've ever experienced."

Nodding, I took his hand. The vision didn't waste any time coming at me, it was like being sucked into a vacuum. For a moment, all I saw was darkness. Then, as if a light had suddenly been switched on, my eyesight was clear.

I wasn't in the room anymore with Antonio and Luther. I was in a rainforest, alone…and yet not. I *felt* different inside. Like I was…squashed, maybe. But at the same time, I felt stronger – so much stronger, so unbelievably powerful – and more alive than I had ever felt. Every nerve ending was buzzing. And in the strangest way I also felt complete and sure of something. I was looking at my hands. They both looked different – bigger, even. In fact, my entire body seemed different. Stockier. Taller. A voice in my head screamed, *Sam no!*

And then I was back.

I heaved in a breath, treble-blinking with the feeling of being spat out of something. I half expected to find myself on the floor flat on my back, but as much as I felt as though I had done a round trip into outer space, my body had stayed right where it was. I released Luther's hand and took a second to centre myself.

"Sam? How do you feel?" Antonio searched my eyes. "Dizzy at all?"

"Baffled beyond belief."

Luther sighed. "Yes…I can sympathise."

"You really didn't see what I saw?" I asked him.

"No. Remember that you need not share the vision with anyone unless you wish to."

"I don't think I could even if I wanted to," I said, rubbing the back of my neck, which now seemed to have a crick in it.

"Why?" enquired Antonio.

"Because I didn't understand a bloody second of it; I wouldn't know how to explain it."

"Maybe in time it will come to make sense," suggested Luther.

"I doubt it."

CHAPTER FOUR

(Sam)

As I knew I had a few hours before my time with the new recruits, I thought it was a good a time as any to go clothes hunting around the shops within The Hollow. Sebastian had given me a month's wages in advance so I could afford to; he was beginning to feel more like a doting uncle.

I wasn't surprised when Fletcher begged to come along, pressing forward the argument that seeing as Jared was busy with the recruits and I wouldn't be in the office, he wasn't needed right now. He'd even arranged for his boyfriend, Norm, who was just as cute as him, to take over on Fletcher's desk. Basically, Norm would serve as an office guard, though I couldn't imagine who would have any wish to root through our files.

I was extremely impressed with the shops. There were at least five that specialised in clothing alone.

"It's a good job I'm here to help," said Fletcher, "or you'd be walking round looking like a tomboy, and we just can't have that. You need something that compliments your figure."

"I still need casual stuff for while I'm coaching the recruits."

"Oh don't be daft. A nice show of cleavage will make them better behaved."

Fletcher's advice was more like pressure selling, but I had to admit it would have taken me a lot longer to shop if he hadn't been my 'wardrobe assistant', as he called himself. He didn't tot around having a gander; instead he seemed to know exactly what he was looking for, and I swear he was like an animal in the jungle. It was like he could sniff out the clothing and my sizes. It was fascinating to watch.

Then before I knew it, I'd have an armful of stuff to try on. His input wouldn't end there. He would then pass judgement on what suited me and what didn't; he was brutally honest. I actually learned a few things about myself that, truthfully, I couldn't have cared less about. Apparently I have calves that would go with any skirt or shoes, a bust so 'fantastic' that skin-tight or flimsy tops should be my priority, a bum so 'luscious' that tight jeans were 'a must', and hips that had 'the softest flare' so I should wear pants that fasten beneath them.

He also selected me some really nice dresses, but if I hadn't specified beforehand that they could not be shorter than just above knee-length, he'd have had me looking like a stripper. I drew the line when he wanted to help me pick out my underwear.

At first I was surprised to see that the stores sold things like make-up and shampoo and stuff, but then I realised that those must be for the humans. Personal hygiene wasn't an issue for vampires. Brushing my teeth or hair wasn't necessary. Nor was the use of body lotions or perfumes. We each had our own alluring scent. And the texture of our skin was beyond perfect, with no freckles or scars or moles. My skin would become paler over time due to my nocturnal lifestyle and lack of exposure to sunlight.

For the purpose of luring in prey, vampirism granted sexual appeal by illuminating a person's best features. That means, for me, that my long dark hair was never unruly or greasy or tangled; it instead had a silky appearance and was extremely soft to the touch. My lips were constantly glossy and a plum-pink colour. My aquamarine eyes always looked bright and inviting, like I'd used eye drops, and they had the darkest, thickest eyelashes to frame them. Still, I was no Keja.

Once the shopping was over, Fletcher and I had pasta for lunch at one of the cafés. Although vampires didn't *need* solid food to survive, we could certainly eat and enjoy it. He introduced me to a grape flavoured NST, which tasted like red wine – very nice and now officially my favourite. By the time I'd arrived back at my apartment, there was no time for me to unpack all my shopping bags, so I put my new batch of NSTs in the fridge and darted down to my office in the Command Centre.

Were the recruits' personnel files on my desk as I'd expected them to be? No.

I knew it was rude, but I searched Jared's desk since he was intent on playing games. It would seem that he'd anticipated that I might do that, however, as all his drawers were locked and nothing of interest was on the surface of the desk. Plonker. Well he really didn't know me at all if he thought that this would be enough to rock my resolve. I'd just have to learn about the recruits on meeting them.

Were they in the training arena waiting for me? No. Not even one of them. Were they all plonkers as well?

I ventured around the squads' grounds, but there was no sign of any of them. Nor were they in the gymnasium, or training with the other squads in the rainforests, or even lounging lazily at the beach. After twenty minutes of wandering aimlessly, I tried the canteen. There they were having a freaking food fight. Yes, they really were plonkers as well.

"Oi!" I hollered. "There better be a very good reason why you're all in here instead of in the training arena."

Some of them sighed, some of them whined, some of them snorted, and the others whistled as they suddenly found the décor to be fascinating.

"Well?" I demanded.

"Easy there, Commander," said Max the Slaphead. "It's nothing personal, okay; we just don't think we need tutoring on our powers. Commander Michaels told us that usually when squads are assembled, the recruits' gifts are raw, so they need a lot of training. *We* were selected for having such good control of our gifts already, as Antonio needs us ready soon. Commander Michaels said it's up to us whether we go to training with you or not."

"I'll bet he did," I said through gritted teeth. I *so* wanted to put Jared on his backside again.

Max flashed me a flirtatious smile. "Why don't you come and join us, me and you could—"

"Don't even finish that sentence, Slaphead."

"Hey, I told you, call me Max."

"While you're being a wanker, you're Slaphead." I glanced at each of the squad. "So that's how you all feel?" Again I was talking through gritted teeth.

Some of them nodded, while others said 'yes' – but none of them met my eyes. Bloody cowards.

"It's lucky for you lot that I'm fuming more with Commander Michaels than anyone else. But I'm warning you all now – and don't take this lightly – if you're not at the training arena tomorrow, I swear to God I'll put every one of you on your lazy arses."

I could have kicked their backsides right that minute, but all I could think about was snapping Jared in half. It was one thing to mislay the files or other menial crap like that, but it was another thing altogether to undermine my authority to the recruits. Besides, kicking their backsides wouldn't make them think of me as an authority figure while they were in that mood.

Lucky for me, but terribly unfortunate for him, Jared was in the office fumbling through papers when I entered. Enraged to the point of feeling homicidal, I hadn't even bothered bidding Fletcher 'hi'. "What do you think you're playing at?" I growled loudly at Jared as I barged in.

Even though he had his face down in the papers, I could see his mouth twitching as he strained to contain a smile. Oh he knew what this was about, and he'd been looking forward to this dispute. "Training session not go well?"

"You think you're being clever? You think it's funny?"

"Sorry, Sam, but I've no idea what you're—"

Sucking the energy around me into my palms, I sent a gust of wind at him, blowing the papers from his hands. "You look at me while I'm talking to you."

He lifted his head, meeting my gaze. "I wouldn't call this talking."

"You told them they didn't have to come to training!"

"That's not what I said. I told the guys that I thought they had good control of their gifts and that if they didn't think they needed extra training, then that was up to them; they're mature enough to decide for themselves."

"Mature? Know where they were? The canteen, having a food fight! You gonna try to tell me they're models of maturity?"

His mouth curved into a smile; he didn't even try to hide it.

"You know, I expected you to make things difficult, but I really didn't think you'd go as far as to undermine my authority like that. Now is not the time for fun and games. The Hollow's walls are going to be attacked! Doesn't that mean anything to you?"

"I already told you that I didn't think I needed your help, you already knew that."

"Is this still about your pride? After what you did today, you shouldn't have any."

"Look, Sam, here's how you've got to look at it: if the guys had respected your authority, it wouldn't have mattered what I said to undermine it, they'd have been in that arena waiting for you. If you can't control them enough to even get them to show up, you've got no chance of managing them in a training arena."

I took a long breath. "You're right. They don't respect my authority. They respect you more than they respect me."

"Yeah."

"Then that leaves me only one option."

"What's that?"

"I'll just have to whip you silly so they see exactly who they should respect." Instantly I absorbed the energy around me and moulded it into my energy whip.

Jared raised his arms, palms out. "Now, Sam, hang on a minute."

"Fletcher!" I called out.

Looking like a bag of nerves, he peeked through the door. "Yes?"

"Shut that door and lock it."

"Right, luv," he said nervously.

As soon as I heard the telling *click*, I began to run my whip through my fingers, enjoying the feel of the energy buzzing against my skin.

"Sam, don't do this."

"Why, Commander Michaels? You fucked me over. You don't want equality in this business relationship. I'm giving you what you want – just not the way around that you were hoping for." I cracked the whip at him, catching his bottom lip.

"Son of a bitch," he cursed, wiping at the blood just before the wound healed.

I cracked the whip again, catching his left ear.

"Sam, stop! I don't want to fight you again."

"Well you're gonna." The whip split the top of his right ear open this time.

"*Sam.*" The word dripped with warning.

I snickered and lashed the whip again. He yelped as it ripped through the sleeve of his jacket and sliced the skin of his forearm. His expression said 'fine then'.

A spray of electric sparks abruptly came at me from shaking fingers. I held my palm out straight, slamming a protective shield in place. The sparks bounced back at Jared but he leaped in the air and did a perfect summersault over me. By the time he had landed on his feet, however, I was facing him with an energy ball in hand. He ducked, causing the ball to hit the filing cabinet behind him.

My wrists suddenly sizzled with pain; Jared had gripped them tight and was sending electric shocks through my hands and up my arms. Which would have been clever had it not been for the fact that the source of my gift wasn't my hands – they were just my preferred outlet. Closing my eyes I inhaled deeply, concentrating hard on breathing in the energy around me, and I then whistled out a current of air strong enough to send him crashing into the already broken filing cabinets. Again he cursed at me.

In less time than it took to blink, Jared had teleported behind me and was pinning my arms to my sides. Not as clever as he'd thought it was. I absorbed more energy into my palms and then wiggled my trapped arms enough to allow my hands to slide behind my back. If it had been anyone but Jared, I might have felt guilty about what I was about to do. But I was sick of him being so sexist, sick of the way he looked down on me, and sick of how I still found him to be the most gorgeous bloke I'd ever seen. I slapped my hands over his crotch and emitted the energy I'd absorbed in the form of boiling heat.

Jared cried out and released me. When I turned, he was on all fours, coughing and making noises that were a mixture of pain and total aggravation. Finally he peered up at me, his irises red. I expected him to try to electrocute me again, or curse at me, or growl at me, or maybe even strike me. Instead, he abruptly grabbed my leg and yanked. Suddenly I was lying on my back, my head the only thing not connecting with the floor, and being slid toward him. And then he was on top of me and his mouth had closed over mine.

I might have fought him if there hadn't been a blast of heat inside me the very second that his lips touched mine. And then *bang* – self-control gone. Conscious thought gone. Rest of the world gone. All I was aware of was that moment.

The kiss was hungry, dominant, possessive; demanding everything from me. His hands slithered into my hair and tugged and pulled, causing the sweetest pain. Each time his tongue stroked mine, the heat just intensified until my whole body was burning. The feel of him was entirely too much but at the same time was nowhere near enough. I slid my arms around his neck and pulled him tighter against me, and he growled into my mouth.

It had been so long, too long, since anyone had touched me like this. But nothing in my vampire life or my human life came remotely close to this moment. His hips rocked against mine, feeding the ache that was ruling my body and making me arch into him. And, God, the way he was kissing me...it was like he was claiming me, and the kiss just kept deepening and deepening, taking me down to a place where nothing but Jared and the feel of him mattered. I was ready to moan in protest when his lips left mine, but then they began to kiss their way down my throat and my body practically turned to liquid.

Sam, I heard in my head as he scraped his teeth over the pulse in my neck. *I want you.*

And God I wanted him too, but suddenly I had the sensation of someone splashing cold water on me and of another voice in my head. A browbeating voice: my conscience. Then a face flashed in my mind and I remembered that none of this should feel right.

"Joy." That was all I managed to say. I breathed it more than I said it. I might see her as a twig-witch, but Jared was *her* boyfriend, and there I was kissing him while she was wherever she was, none the wiser. That was so unlike me, but reason and rationality had just gone the second his mouth touched mine.

"She's just a consort," he said against my neck, kissing it attentively. "I'm not committed to her, just like I'm not committed to Daniela or Tammy."

Daniela and Tammy? There wasn't just Joy? I didn't know what was worse — the idea of sleeping with someone who I thought was already claimed, or the idea of sleeping with someone who would consider me nothing more than a notch on his already very busy bedpost.

He must have felt me tense beneath him, because his mouth paused. "Sam?"

"Sounds like your dance card is already full." I wriggled under him and pushed on his chest. Reluctantly he moved away.

He gazed at me incredulously as we stood facing each other. "I don't get it."

Men! If he was a woman he'd be considered a bit of a slut, but apparently because he was a male it was completely normal and acceptable. "I suppose you probably don't."

"Look, if you're offended that I haven't asked you to be one of my consorts yet then, believe me, I was going to ask. I've wanted you since I first saw you." He said it as though I should be so unbelievably flattered that I'd be bouncing on the spot with excitement like someone who had just won X-Factor.

"Well then you won't like this: the answer's 'no'."

"You are definitely one of the most confusing women I've ever met in all my human and vampire years." His tone didn't suggest this was a bad thing.

"Seriously, Jared, did you honestly expect to hear 'yes, yes, a thousand times yes' to being a live-in prostitute – who does it for *free*, to make things more insulting." I waved him away from me. "If you're horny, you have three women on call for sex whenever you need them, so you know where to go."

"You want me, I want you. I don't see what they have to do with what just happened. They're just consorts. They don't even share my apartment with me. They share a separate one together."

That made me laugh.

"What?"

"It's just the idea of it. You having three women all living together just waiting for you to come along. I'm actually offended that you think I'd be up for anything like that. Well, I don't work well as part of a group, sorry."

"Lots of vampires have consorts."

"I know," I said bitterly.

"You were one," he realised.

"I won't be again. If I slept with you when you're the kind of person who has three women at your beck and call for sex, I'd feel no better than them."

Jared ran a hand through his chestnut hair, releasing a breath with a long puff. "Sam, I—"

"Let's just not talk about it anymore, all right. It would have been stupid to shag when we've got to work together anyway."

Jared shrugged. "Okay, we won't talk about it."

I nodded and paced toward the door. Just as I reached it, I heard Jared's voice in my head.

But you'll still want me. And I'll still want you. That won't change.

Life's full of changes, I replied as Fletcher unlocked the office door and I waltzed out.

(Jared)

A loud grunt escaped me when I sank into my chair. I looked around the office at the mess that the scuffle, to put it lightly, had left in its path. Broken cabinets. Cracks in the plaster of the walls. Documents scattered everywhere.

Then my gaze fell on the spot on the floor where only moments ago I'd had Sam underneath me; my mouth on hers, my hands in her hair, teasing her tongue with my own, and tasting her skin. I had no idea how I'd managed to reign myself in and not skate my hands over every single part of her. My control had completely shredded when that blast of heat circulated through me on just kissing her. It'd felt even better than I'd imagined it would. *She* had felt even better than I'd imagined.

Then she had pushed me away.

Obviously she'd had to put up with a lot of shit from her Sire – that got me pissed. *Fucking jerk*. I double-blinked at the vehemence in that thought. It was kind of weird to feel protective of someone other than Evan or Antonio. It also weird to be around a woman who wasn't wowed by the whole Heir thing – refreshing, too.

It made sense that she wouldn't want to be a consort again if things had been that bad for her in the past. But I had the feeling that there was more to it than that. The emotion in her voice...It was like she didn't want there to be anyone else. So did that mean that she wanted me to herself? Maybe. *I* wouldn't want to share *her* with anyone else whether it was casual sex or not. See, this was another weird thing that I was being forced to deal with – an element of possessiveness. And I had no clue how to deal with it. Unfortunately, my twin would be more likely to laugh his tits off than give me any advice.

Mentally I slapped myself, wanting to stop stressing over a woman and hoping to just blank it all out for a while. But I could still smell her on me. Still feel the silk of her hair between my fingers. Still feel the burning that the heat of the moment had left behind. Still taste her skin on my tongue. And I knew then that I'd never be able to be around her without wanting her. Not great.

(Sam)

Fuck. Twat. Shit. Crap. Bollocks.

Each profanity burst through my mind as I clambered out of bed. I'd only been awake for ten seconds and a flashback of what had happened with Jared was all over me! Wasn't everything supposed to feel better and clearer after a good sleep? If that was a rule, I was clearly an exception to it.

Two red grape flavoured NSTs later, I still felt like I'd spontaneously self-combust any second. Maybe I should go back to bed. It wasn't like the recruits had any intention of showing up at the arena anyway. I'd then have to set their backsides alight, and I seriously doubted that Antonio would be okay with that.

Three pounding knocks on the door made me jump. "Sam, luv, it's me."

Fletcher. If anyone was capable of pulling me out of my irate state it was Fletch with his relaxed personality and funny ways. I opened the door to find him stood there with his hands on his hips and an eyebrow arched. "Um-hmm."

"What?"

"I knew you'd procrastinate," he said as he barged in and marched through the apartment. Not exactly the relaxed, humorous bloke I was expecting.

Confused, I raced after him and found him in my bedroom flicking through one of my now full wardrobes. I'd unpacked my bags last night in pretty much a daze, so I doubted that it was well organised.

Seconds later, Fletcher thrust an outfit into my arms. "Dressed now, lady."

"I'm quite capable of picking myself something to wear, thanks. And since when do you have this right to order me about?"

"Since you and Jared had a fumble and you now want to hide in your room." His expression dared me to deny it.

"We did *not* have a fumble. It was just a kiss."

"So that's why you're so uptight? You didn't actually get to the fumbling?"

"I'm *not* uptight." We both chuckled since my tone had contradicted my words. "Believe me when I say that I do not want a fumble with Jared, I think he's a sexist pig."

"That's the thing, luv, I *don't* believe you. There's really no point in telling me porky pies, because I'm an Empath."

Oh. Empaths could sense the emotions of people near to them, which meant he'd been able to sense how much I'd wanted Jared last night. Suddenly I felt extremely vulnerable and embarrassed.

"Look, luv, I know it's not my place to say, but I'm going to say it anyway – and I say this with love – you're being a silly little mare if you're going to hide from some bloke."

"It's not just Jared, all right," I said tiredly as my bottom sunk into the bed. "The recruits wouldn't come to training yesterday. They don't think they need my help."

"They're Jared's arrogant spawn, that's why. Listen, you can't take it personally. Blokes never like taking orders off women, especially if those women are more powerful than they are. Like you, they've escaped the hold of their Sires and their past, and they're making the most of it. Plus, they're probably stuck up their own arses too just because they got picked for the legion, thinking they're too sexy for their shirts."

Fletcher said more, but I'd stopped listening; certain things he had said were stringing together in my mind and an idea was slowly forming. A triumphant grin must have surfaced on my face, because Fletcher looked at me oddly.

"What?" he said dubiously. At some point, he'd sat beside me on the bed while I was in deep thought.

I kissed his cheek. "You're a genius, that's what."

I relayed my little plan to him while I slipped on the outfit he had selected for me: a tight pink vest and pair of tight white khakis (most things he had picked out for me were tight). As the vest didn't quite reach my hips and the khakis hung just below them, this left a belt of bare skin on show – enough so that my silver diamond belly button ring could be seen.

"Well you'll certainly get the recruits' attention," said Fletcher approvingly as he examined my appearance. "And once you put your creative plan in place, they'll be on their knees begging for forgiveness and your help."

"I wouldn't go *that* far," I chuckled.

"Luv, you're gorgeous and they don't see a lot of women around here. Trust me when I say they'll be drooling."

When I entered my office, I was confused for a few seconds to find some male vampires inside wearing white coveralls that were stained with paint. Then I realised they'd probably spent hours in here fixing the plasterwork and replacing the broken filing cabinets. Oops. They seemed to be repressing snorts of laughter as they left. I supposed it wasn't hard to gather that Jared and I had been duelling again.

While Fletcher was busy doing the research that I'd requested, I carefully examined the personnel files of the recruits. They had been waiting nicely on my desk for me. Maybe Jared had had an attack of conscience.

Unlikely.

The first file belonged to a Pagori vampire named Reuben, who was originally French. He'd been Turned at the age of thirty and been a vampire for sixty years. Aptitude tests showed him to not be the brightest bulb, but he certainly made up for it in the physical department; he was by far the strongest of the squad and was built like a body builder. He had shoulder-length brown hair and a beard of stubble that added to the wild look. His gift was power augmentation, meaning that he could weaken or strengthen the gift of another.

The second file showed a half-American half-Australian Pagori vampire, Stuart, who had been eighteen when Turned over thirty years ago. His curly, fair hair tickled his broad shoulders and he had a wide, clown-like smile. Average intelligence, average height, and average weight. You might then conclude 'so, *he's* average', but Stuart's gift made him far from it. Like an old vampire friend of mine, he was a Shredder: his gift allowed him to disband until he was nothing but molecules and then reform again at will.

Next was the thorn-exhaling vampire from the try-out, Chico. The dark haired, moustache-wearing Keja was Spanish in origin and, by far, the smartest of the squad. Even in his photo, you could see the intelligence in his eyes. Apparently the poison in his thorns caused the victim to instantly lose consciousness for a period of up to five hours. How delightful. He obviously wasn't a good person to piss off, but that was what I'd be doing very shortly.

File number four was of a Pagori vampire – also at my try-out – from Miami, Robert Richardson, who went by the name Butch. His photograph showed him to have an extremely smart appearance, especially with his slicked back bronze hair. But his dark eyes and crooked grin spelled wildness. He was well built in the upper body area and had notable speed. Butch was a Negator: he could completely cancel out any power aimed at him.

Next was Slaphead; an army brat who had spent his childhood moving constantly round the US. At the age of twenty-six, he had been Turned and had been a vampire for just over twenty years. Like Butch, he was notably fast. His weakness, however, was in his agility. On his photograph he had the same cheeky, warm smile that he'd flashed me at the try-out – oh and a nicely defined upper body. I could remember how he had completely paralysed the senses of his opponent in the try-out.

Recruit number six was especially interesting, and not just because he was British like me. David was a Keja vampire and the youngest of the squad; Turned at seventeen and had only been a vampire for three years (same vampire life-span as me). He was tall and grey-eyed with copper, dishevelled hair. He didn't have much to boast of with regards to strength and speed, but he had an amazing power to attack an opponent with: a psionic boom, something which caused extreme pressure on the skull and completely overwhelmed the brain, leading to either a temporary coma or death depending on the strength of the blast.

The seventh file concerned an excessively muscled, African-American Pagori named Damien. He was only a year older in vampire years than David and I, and had been Turned when twenty-four. He was apparently the fastest of the squad and excellent at one-to-one combat. Damien's gift was astral projection, but apparently his consciousness wasn't able to travel far from his body.

Eighth in the squad was a blond Pagori who was born in Ireland and went by the nickname Salem. I'd be interested to know how he came by that. Turned at the age of thirty-six just over forty-eight years ago, Salem was tall and brown-eyed. He had incredible strength despite that his physique wasn't a statue of pure defined muscle. His gift enabled him to emit an invisible blast of psychic energy that could render an opponent completely unconscious. Basically, he had a psychic punch.

Next was a very exotic looking American Pagori, Harvey, who I thought was over-muscled for his short size. He'd been just nineteen when Turned almost twelve years ago. His strength was higher than average, but his intelligence left something to be desired. He was quite cute with his child-like smile and short dark hair that looked more like pure silk. Harvey was telekinetic, which meant that he would be able to move something without physically touching it.

Lastly was Denny, who was an American Pagori vampire from a tiny rural town with a very innocent appearance; scruffy dark hair, blue guiltless eyes, and a dimply smile. His athletic physique didn't do his strength and speed justice. He also had the best reflexes of all the recruits. A vampire for over seventy years, Denny had been twenty when Turned. I'd never encountered anyone with the gift of animal mimicry before, so I was eager to see which abilities he had up his sleeve.

Fletcher proved to be fantastic with researching. No sooner had I finished consulting the files than he had handed me the list of contacts that I had asked him to find. I then made call after call to conduct my own research on the recruits as part of my little plan, jotting down plenty of notes. Before lunch had even begun, I had all the information I wanted and was feeling very optimistic and very relaxed. Until Jared teleported to the office.

"You went through the files," he observed, nodding toward the untidy pile on my desk.

"Yeah," I replied simply. He was looking much too good in that knee-length leather jacket. And he knew that I thought so – going by the smug smirk he wore. God, I had to leave this room. "Fletch?" I called out while I gathered my notes together.

His adorable face popped through the door seconds later. "Yes, luv?"

"I'm off to get some NSTs. You want me to pick you up anything?"

Fletcher squinted. "Shouldn't I be asking you that?"

"Yes or no, Fletch?"

"Honey flavoured ones please, luv. Oh and could you get me some snacks as well?"

"Yeah, course." I folded my notes and tucked them into the pocket of my khakis. Not that I thought I'd need them. I was reasonably sure that I had all the details memorised.

"You're not going to ask me if I want anything?" griped Jared.

"Nope."

He sighed. "Listen, if you want I can have a word with the guys and tell them to get their acts together and start listening to you."

"No need. They will." He heard the confidence in my voice and his eyes immediately narrowed.

"What plan are you cooking up?" he asked suspiciously but with a smile.

"It's already cooked, and it's crispy round the edges."

Still going to pretend you don't want me? he asked as I advanced toward the door. *I just thought you should know it's not working too well. You're far from Hollywood material.*

At least I don't shag a twig!

Your interest in my sex life adds further support to my argument.

Well file this away with all the info: you're a prick.

It was far from shocking to find that the recruits were not waiting for me in the arena. Ten minutes later, I found them all on the basketball court. Chico, Butch, David, Max, Stuart and Damien were playing basketball while Reuben was observing. Denny and Harvey were deep in conversation, and Salem was moonlight-bathing on one of the benches.

Max noticed me first and signalled to the others that I was coming. Most of them shrugged, unaffected. The others were pretending they hadn't heard him.

"So, you still think you don't need me." I folded my arms across my chest, squashing my bust so that my cleavage was more prominent. As I'd expected, they all gave me their full attention. I wanted to see their faces when I acted on my plan.

"It's just that we think we're okay as we are," said Reuben.

Max's face beamed with a cheeky smile. "Come on, Sam, it's not *you*. We just—"

"Don't want to take orders off some chick," finished Harvey in an arrogant tone. Damien and Stuart nodded in agreement. Wow, Jared had really been to work on this lot.

"It's like Max said, it's not you," repeated Denny in a very soft, sensitive voice. "Why don't you come hang out with us?"

"Yeah, hang out with us." David seemed to have an inability to keep still.

I smiled at them and jiggled my head as if considering their offer. "Well I would...but I'm not convinced you plonkers don't need some coaching."

Salem laughed, as if he thought 'plonkers' only applied to the others.

"Look, you've seen me in combat at the try-out." Chico sounded bored. "Did I look like I needed help?"

"Same here," said Butch.

"Help? No. But do I think you could both be better? Yes."

Chico sniggered. "I exhale *thorns*. How much better can you get?"

I puffed. "Oh I don't know...Can you emit them from your palms?"

"The thorns come from *within* me." His tone was stressing his opinion that I was dumb.

"You really think little poisonous thorns are embedded inside you? Wrong. Your body produces toxins. These toxins travel in your blood, your entire body. They harden into thorns the second that they meet the outside air. You can emit the toxins from your pores in just the same way. Your palms can be an outlet just the same as your breath can. Try it."

Chico sniggered again and waved a hand at me dismissively before going to collect the ball.

"You won't even *try*? You're that scared to fail? No wonder you never made Sergeant when you were in the police force. Got passed down for your brother too, didn't you?"

Chico immediately stiffened. Slowly he turned to look at me, his face grim and his jaw taut. "Where'd you hear that?"

"Oh I'm sorry, did I touch a nerve?" I *knew* I had. Preparing for a violent response, I absorbed the immediate energy, feeling it tingle and tickle as if eager to be released.

"You need to get away from here now, do you understand me?" His tone was deadly.

"Or you'll spit some measly thorns at me?"

Without hesitation, he forced out a heavy breath of poisonous thorns. Quickly I manipulated the energy I'd absorbed into the form of a hungry flame, burning the thorns to nothing.

"What about you, Butch? Think you can take me on?" I asked. I was a sponge of energy at that point, anticipating attacks from all angles.

"You can fling all the flames you want at me, I'll just negate them."

"Negate *this*." Before Butch could blink, I had my energy whip in hand and slashed open his cheek with it. I knew that the crack of the whip would be too speedy for him to act in time. "You could have protected yourself, you know. All you'd have had to do was use the counteracting force you have to form a deflecting shield."

"Negators can't form shields."

"Oh yes they can, Butch. I bet you'd love a shield that would help against emotional pain. Maybe then you wouldn't still be feeling so raw about your mummy leaving you on the doorstep of a church."

His eyes blazed red instantly and he came at me without thought. I let my hands shoot out in front of me and then spread them wide, pulling the energy to pop up my own shield. Butch ricocheted off it like a bouncy ball.

"Wouldn't you like one of these, Butch? I can show you how to do it."

He was too busy panting and sneering at me to answer.

"I've had an interesting afternoon talking to all your Sires and vampy friends. Turns out they were quite happy to divulge dark secrets. It must be jealousy because you were picked for the legion and they weren't. Should I just carry on revealing them, or shall we go to the arena now?"

"My Sire would never have told you anything," said Stuart.

"Oh is that right? Would you bet your pride on that?" He seemed confident, how silly of him. "Come on, Stuart, shred yourself into nothing and come all the way over here and then I'll only whisper to you what I was told. No one else has to know." He laughed, but there was no humour there – and I knew why. "You can't move from where you are when you shred?" I said, is if echoing him. "Not even when I'm telling everyone how you couldn't protect your little sister and she became a drug addict and then a prostitute to pay for her addiction?" God, he was pissed now: if looks could kill...

"And what about you, Damien?" I said. "Shall we share with everyone how, just because your rich daddy left you bugger all in his will, you beat your brother half to death like an ignorant, bitter shit?"

"Bitch," he cursed through his teeth.

"Sorry, didn't catch that. Why don't you astral project all the way over here and say it to my face? Oh that's right, you *can't*. Just like

Reuben can't weaken my power unless he holds on to me, not even when I tease him about how his Sire abandoned him and he woke up to find nobody there to help him control his bloodlust and he more or less *ate* three people."

Reuben started to charge at me, but I raised a hand and released a tiny breeze at him as a promise of what would come if he proceeded. Wisely, he stopped.

"Slaphead, Slaphead, Slaphead." I sighed at him. "Aren't you gonna silence me with that nifty power of yours before I blab about how you were abducted as a kid by a nut who couldn't have a baby of her own? Stuck with her for three weeks, weren't you?" There was plenty of cursing going on now. "Why not shut us all up and save yourself the earache? Or can you only attack one person at a time with your gift?" It was a rhetorical question. Max inhaled deeply but attempted no attack on me. Probably because he knew I'd just put my shield up.

I noticed that Denny and David didn't appear challenging in anyway, as if they thought they might deserve a little payback. So I decided not to tease animal mimic Denny about not knowing his biological parents or psionic blaster David about being Turned against his will.

When I looked at Salem, he knew what was coming and arched a brow in warning.

"What?" I said innocently. "You don't want people to know how your gambling debts ended up getting your parents burned alive while they slept in their bed?" I felt the ripple in the air as he aimed his invisible psychic punch at me to knock me out cold. My shield came in handy again. The punch almost hit Harvey as it bounced off the shield.

Growling, Harvey waved a hand my way, sending a force in the air that was intended to send me zooming backwards. I stamped twice on the ground and let the energy of the Earth fill me and then grow into a mound of dirt that rose before me. "What's the matter, Harv?" I called from behind the boulder. "Still upset that your girlfriend left you for your Sire even though you became a vampire for her? Then why don't you send a force strong enough to move this big rock out the way so you can get to me?"

Sucking the energy from out of the mound in front of me, I watched as it crumbled to pieces. "Or better still, why don't you all attack me together...?"

They glanced at each other as if assessing who might be willing. Then the energy in the air intensified as I felt Harvey preparing to use his telekinesis, Chico ready to exhale more thorns, and Salem ready to aim his psychic punch at me. Simultaneously, Reuben, Butch, Damien, and Stuart made moves to charge at me.

The massive dosage of absorbed energy within me was now begging to be released. I obliged. Drawing on every ounce of it, I expelled a concentrated air blast from my palms that was powerful enough to sweep every single recruit off their feet and send them crashing hard into the railings of the basketball court. That felt good.

Impressive, said a voice in my head.

A fleeting glance to my left confirmed that Jared was nearby. He was lounging against the railings at the far end of the court. I wondered how long he'd been there, watching.

"Keep denying you need help if you want," I told the recruits as they scooped themselves up off the floor. "Or drop the ignorance long enough to realise that I can actually help you; that there is more to learn. I'm not trying to be a twat by bringing up your past. The point of all this was to show you that you need to snap out of this little zone you're in. Yes, you got picked for the legion and, yes, that's a big thing, but it doesn't mean you're faultless or that you have the right to have rods stuck up your backsides. And it doesn't mean you get to be arrogant or forget all the experiences that made you what you are, that gave you your strengths in the first place."

Having seen how much everyone seemed to look to Chico for clues of what to do next, I concluded that if I was going to get through to the others, I had to drive the situation home to him primarily. I looked mostly at him as I continued. "Like it or not, every one of you has excess energy swirling around you, which means that you're not using your gift to its full potential and you're not controlling it either."

Chico sighed. "Even if we said we'd listen and come to training, it'd do no good. Your expectations of us are too high. You're asking us to do things with our gifts that we can't do. There are limitations, there's no way I can shoot thorns from my palms."

"Wrong. Let me show you." I walked over to Chico and circled him.

He was looking at me curiously. "What're you doing?"

"Absorbing the energy that's leaking from you so I can have your power for a little while." With that, I shot a dozen poisonous thorns from one palm in Jared's direction. He dodged them, unfortunately.

Hey! His scowl was cute.

Chico gazed in astonishment at me. "You can teach me how to do that?"

I nodded slowly. "And if the energy hadn't been leaking from you like that, I would have had to touch you or get shot by the thorns to get the power. In other words, you're vulnerable like this." I turned to Butch. "You don't think you can make your counteracting force into a shield? Watch." Like with Chico, I let my pores drink in the energy that seeped from him. "Chico, thorns."

Nodding once, Chico puffed out a spray of thorns. I drew a circle in the air in front of me with my hand. The recruits all gasped as the thorns hit an invisible wall and fell to the floor.

Butch's eyes darted from me to the thorns repeatedly. "But...I didn't see any shield. The thorns didn't bounce."

"It's different from the shield that I can generate with my own gift. Mine's visible and vibrant because I feed off all the energy surrounding me; kinetic energy, solar energy – it all combines and mingles together crazily. The energy that generated your shield was your own energy, not a clash of varying energies. Want one?"

Butch laughed out of his nose. Not attractive, don't try it. "Maybe."

Next I looked at David. "The excess energy around you is absolutely wild. Your power is strong, but right now it seems almost completely out of your control." His expression was glum. "Ever hurt anyone by accident?"

He nodded, the picture of remorse. "You can help me keep a lid on it?"

It wasn't difficult to sense that he resented having it. "Yes."

So suddenly that I gasped, a draft spread through my entire body. My extremities went cold. My head ached. My stomach lurched. Only one thing had ever had this effect on me. Subconsciously I turned my head toward the mansion.

What is it? Jared asked, sounding almost as unnerved as I was.

Without a word to anyone, I moved with vampire speed as I darted out of the court, passed the training arena, across the gardens and into the mansion, almost colliding into Sebastian in the hallway.

His expression was grim and filled with annoyance as he confirmed what I already knew. "He's here."

CHAPTER FIVE

(Sam)

"Who's here?" asked Jared. I didn't realise he'd followed me.

"Sam's Sire." Sebastian sighed as he looked at me. "He appealed against your leave of his hold on the grounds that your request to be free of him was not made in person. Antonio had him brought here some twenty minutes or so ago, hoping to have this over with once and for all. We suspected that he would not let you go easily. He has requested an audience with you, asking for Antonio be present; he's confident that you will return with him and wants Antonio to witness your decision to leave."

"Where is he?" My voice dripped with agitation.

"With Antonio in one of his parlours."

"Why would he think you'd go with him?" asked Jared.

I puffed. "Victor's a master at manipulation."

"He will not be allowed to threaten you," Sebastian assured me. "You can refuse to see him if you wish, but I suspect that he will only press the matter until you agree to see him."

I nodded in agreement and inhaled deeply. "All right, take me to the bugger."

"I'm coming." Jared's tone left no room for negotiation.

As much as the moral support was nice, I didn't want Jared there. I didn't want him to see the weak person that Victor had the power to reduce me to. "No."

"Why?"

"If a bloke walks in there with me, it'll piss him right off. He never liked other males around me, it made him paranoid. He'll think you and I are together, and he'll be even more difficult."

Jared shrugged. "That's a good thing. If he loses it, Antonio's got an excuse to throw him out – no conversations necessary."

"He has a point," said Sebastian.

Before I could speak, Jared added, "I'm Antonio's Heir *and* you're my co-worker—"

"Co-worker?" I echoed with a smile.

"Yeah, co-worker. I've a right to be there, and I'm going with you – end of discussion."

"If I can't even get you off my back, how in the hell am I going to stand up against Victor?" I grumbled.

Jared grabbed my lower arm gently. "Look, all you have to do is go in there and tell him you don't want to go back to him."

Sounded easy enough. But it wasn't. "Victor's power...he can gauge and alter your emotions."

"Alter your emotions?"

"In other words, if he wants you to feel or want something, it can be very hard to resist. I've had plenty of practice, and I reckon I can block him better than most. But not for long. It has this crushing effect on you, until you feel like your head will explode."

"He'll try to make you want him."

I nodded. "Won't this be fun."

"So then we need to get you in and out the room as quickly as possible."

Jared had made it sound so simple. Maybe it could be. Maybe I was fretting for nothing. It hadn't been long since I'd left Victor, and already I felt like a different person. For the first time since becoming a vampire, I'd experienced freedom, friendship, passion, and the feel of having a life of my own with my own job, my own home, my own money, my own belongings. Just the very idea of Victor wanting to make me lose all that was enough to make me boil with resentment. "Let's get this over with."

With each step I made nearer to the parlour, that cold draft within me got chillier. I easily sensed that Victor was well and truly pissed. Vampires always had close emotional links to their Sires, whether they wanted them or not. Being a mixture of both eager to get it over with and tempted to procrastinate, I had that dreamy feeling of walking on the spot and not actually getting anywhere. Determined to be strong or else I'd never resist Victor's influence, I squashed the sense of panic, and focused on the graceful, elegant, leisurely stroll of Sebastian as he led Jared and me to the parlour.

He's already trying to reach your emotions, isn't he? said Jared as Sebastian opened the parlour room door. *I can feel the weight of his power in the air.*

My head's pounding already.

I'll get you out of there fast, I promise.

This parlour was much the same as the one Antonio had taken me to when he'd offered me the position of commander, except that there was no piano in here. Antonio was sitting on a beige sofa with Luther. His guards were standing either side of the piece of furniture, glaring at Victor.

Both Nero and Achilles dashed over to me protectively. The snarls they hurled at the very unwanted visitor were silent. Victor was stood between the two sofas in a smart black trouser suit, staring at me as if we were the only people in the room. Several emotions flashed in his squinty grey eyes. Relief. Pleasure. Desire. Betrayal. Fury.

Instantly I had the feeling of being hit hard with a heavy object, but it wasn't an object. It was pressure — pressurising sense of guilt.

"Sam," he drawled, his thin lips forming a warm smile. "You don't know how much I've missed you, luv." He had a way of being able to sound friendly, polite, reasonable and compassionate; totally concealing the other side to his nature. As his eyes scanned my appearance, he clenched his fists. I got the feeling that he wasn't too happy about the skin-tight clothing. "Looking well."

I didn't speak. I was afraid of what I'd say. One part of me had an instinct to yell a string of profanities at him and tell him to go jump up his own arse. But another part of me wanted to run to him, beg him to forgive me for leaving him and ask him to take me home – thanks to the weight of the guilt that he was throwing at me. The more I tried to fight it, the more my head hurt.

Knowing that the closer I physically was to him the easier it would be for him to rule my emotional state, I stopped about five feet away. Jared halted beside me. It seemed it was only then that Victor noticed him. I watched as Victor read Jared's emotions. A smile appeared, which surprised me.

"Aren't you going to come and give your old hubby a hug?" he asked me.

The strength and sharpness in my voice surprised me. "You're not my husband."

"There's no need to lie."

But I wasn't lying. And Victor knew that. Just like he knew that I hated being called something that I wasn't, especially a liar. "I know what you're trying to do," I told him. "Trying to piss me off so my composure will crack and you can more easily control my emotions." I shook my head. "It won't work."

Suddenly the force of the guilt was overwhelming, and there was a new emotion too: self-loathing. I had the sensation of being stuck in a pit with emotions that weren't my own clinging to me and trying to devour me.

"You agreed not to manipulate her emotions," warned Antonio.

"And I'm not." Victor was utterly unaffected by Antonio's air of authority, I realised. That was probably a lot to do with the fact that he was a fruitcake. "You must have noticed by now that my Sam can be temperamental. One minute she's furious, the next minute she's calm, and then all of a sudden she develops a sense of humour."

As usual, he was coming across as reasonable and fair while making me out to be the pain in the backside. Planting the seed of suspicion was a speciality of his. Plus, he knew that falsely accusing me of doing things or being things was likely to crack me.

"She did a runner because she was angry with me, not because she doesn't love me or want to be with me. Isn't that right, Sam, luv?"

God, I wanted to smack him. I wanted to scream out to Antonio that Victor was a lying, manipulative twat and not to listen to a word he said. Victor knew this. But I didn't do those things, because I knew that the more energy I spent trying to defend myself, the weaker I would be to his power. "What is it you want?"

Victor's smile disappeared, but his friendly, caring tone remained. "I just want you to come home, luv. What else would I want?"

"No." The word was no more than a whisper. It hurt to get it out, especially since a part of me hated myself for saying something so awful – all thanks to the heavy dose of self-loathing.

Good girl. I could almost feel Jared's pride.

"No?" chuckled Victor without humour. As he took a few steps toward me, another emotion came crashing down on me. Desire. It stirred low in my stomach, sending a bolt of warmth through me. My thighs instantly clenched and I had to swallow back a moan.

"Don't be daft, luv. Come to me." He opened his arms, and it was a struggle to not walk straight into them.

What's he trying to make you feel now?
He wants me to want *him.*

A second later, Victor's head whipped to face Jared, and I felt a million times lighter as the saddle of emotions slipped away from me. I could guess that Jared must have sent a telepathic thought to Victor that he really didn't like.

I spoke quickly, "You've come to hear it from me so here it is: I'm not going back with you, Victor. I'm asking you to free me from your hold."

Victor snickered. "I bet you're very pleased with yourself, aren't you: getting picked to partake in the legion's try-out and then being hired by Antonio as a commander. You just remember that *I'm* the one who made you, and *I'm* the one who taught you how to use your gift—"

"*Taught* isn't the word I'd use," I spat.

"—and every single strength you have, you owe to *me*. You wouldn't be where you are now if it wasn't for *me*."

I smiled. "Then you only have yourself to blame for Antonio offering me a position, don't you?"

His snarl was loud and feral, making Nero and Achilles bark.

"Victor, will you release me from your hold?"

"Never," he growled. No surprise there. "You're mine."

I turned my attention to the powerful vampire sitting on the sofa. "Antonio, you've witnessed me say I don't want to leave with him, will you grant me release from his hold?"

Victor pivoted on the spot and bared his teeth at him. Had he been a Keja vampire and had fangs, it would have been an unnerving sight. "She's mine." The guards were beside their Grand High Master instantly.

Antonio, completely unfazed by Victor's behaviour, said calmly, "Samantha Parker, I release you from your Sire's hold with immediate effect."

No one else felt it but me. That surge of black, bottomless hatred, that seething need to cause pain. I could sense it coursing through Victor. Then there was a snap within him. Antonio's guards were quick and would have easily apprehended Victor before he reached Antonio, but I didn't think about that when I saw him ready to pounce. All I thought about was defending Antonio.

Soaking up the energy around me, I felt it swirl in my grasp and I blasted it out of my palm in the form of a thermal beam. The long, silver ray of hot energy buried itself into Victor's abdomen and burned him from the inside out: his favourite thing for me to do to his marks.

He cried and writhed and fell to his knees, and I felt that same pain…like being torn open and sliced by a boiling hot knife. Heat shot through my body, singeing my extremities. And then, with one last loud cry, he disintegrated completely. Then it was my turn to cry out.

(Jared)

I couldn't believe she'd done it. Not many vampires would kill their Sires. It was the same feeling of killing a parent: even if they were a total ass, you respected that they created you, and you had a special link with them – well, in most cases, anyway. Plus, the physical pain of destroying that link and killing your Sire was, from everything I'd heard, unbearable. It could even make vampires ill. It was the only thing that could.

So there Sam was on her knees, gritting her teeth against an agony that I could only imagine.

I was the first to react. It was pure instinct to kneel beside her and pull her to me, locking my arms around her. I'd half-expected her to push me away – what with her being as stubborn as she was. But instead, she buried her face in my chest while her hands clamped down tightly on my arms. An ear-piercing whine still escaped her mouth, despite how much she was grinding her teeth together. She was shaking so hard, she was more or less convulsing. I couldn't even tell where the pain was coming from.

"What hurts?" I asked Luther and Antonio as they rushed over to her. The dogs were making slight howling sounds. "Will it be her stomach, her head – what?"

Luther gazed down at her with sympathy. "The pain supposedly hits every single part of your body."

I exhaled heavily, feeling the urge to punch something. "How long will it last?"

"She could be like this for minutes or hours," replied Antonio, running a hand over her hair. She didn't seem to feel it. I wasn't even sure if she knew who was holding her.

Sam? Sam?

It BURNS! The pain was obvious in her mental voice.

Where?

EVERYWHERE!

"Brave little thing, isn't she," said one of the guards.

"A very extraordinary young lady," commented Luther.

Just then, her body shook hard and blood poured out of her mouth, drenching my t-shirt.

I glanced up at Antonio and Luther. "Is there anything that'll make it stop?" I already knew the answer would be *no*.

"You have to think of it as her body grieving," said Luther. "As vampires, our links with our Sires are based on the exchange of blood that occurred during the creation process. Victor drank her to near death and then fed her his own blood. Her body no longer has a living, breathing blood-link, and it is grieving it. Grieving is a process – painful, draining, overbearing. It must run its course. For vampires who have ended the life of their own Sire, the agony will be no less than excruciating. I'm told that the pain is bad enough that it makes you want to die."

Jared? She sounded weak, but there was something else in her mental voice. Hope, maybe? *Hold me still.*

What?

Just hold me still.

So I did. I tightened my arms around her until she was as still as I could get her. Then I watched, completely baffled, as she moved one of her hands from my arm to her chest. A slight zing went through her body. Mere seconds later, she was limp in my arms.

"What's wrong with her?" Seized by panic, I set her back slightly and examined her body with my eyes. The hand she had against her chest flopped down to her lap, revealing something small lodged there. Holding her securely with one arm, I used my free hand to pluck the little thing out from between her breasts.

"Is that a thorn?" asked Antonio.

I laughed a little. "I would never have thought of that."

"What is it?"

"When she was coaching the guys, she absorbed Chico's power to exhale poisonous thorns. Thorns that knock you unconscious for a couple of hours."

"Smart," said Luther. "By the time she wakes up, the effects of severing the link may well have worn off."

"Perhaps you should teleport her to her apartment," suggested Antonio. "I think it will be better for her to wake in her own bed. Oh, and leave her a note to the effect that she should avoid work for the remainder of the night."

Standing upright with her in my arms, I nodded.

In a blink, we were in the centre of the living area in her apartment. I'd been curious to know what it was like inside; whether she'd tried to put her own mark on it, or whether she'd left it to look like a show home. With books stacked on the shelves, a glass bowl of filled with sweets on the little table, and a fleecy throw hanging over the sofa, it had a homey feel to it.

I noticed the tiny, pink, decorate cushions on the sofa and suspected that Fletcher may have had something to do with them. Sam just didn't seem that girly. As I carried her through the apartment, heading for her bedroom, I noticed that she wasn't the type who had a specific place for everything. The apartment wasn't disorderly or cluttered, but nor was it obsessively and freakishly tidy. It was lived in. Like mine.

Unfortunately there was no underwear lying around. Whoa, did I really just wonder about that? Shaking off my dirty thoughts, I laid her carefully down onto her bed and covered her with the satin bedspread.

And now I should probably leave. I really should. I really, really should. Especially since she'd be absolutely irate to wake up and see me sitting here next to her. Yes, I was now sitting next to her. I could stay for a while and then just teleport out the second she woke up, though, right? She'd never have known I was there.

Tentatively – *I know, since when was I tentative?* – I brushed that gorgeous curtain of dark hair away from her face and ran my knuckles from her temple to her jaw. I was pretty sure that I'd never done that to a woman before. Not in my eighteen years as a vampire, or in my twenty-four years as a human. But, then, there had never been anyone like Sam around me in all those years. She intrigued me on every level.

I saw then that I had dried blood on my finger. Her blood. It was all over my shirt too from when she'd had a coughing fit. Well that explained why subconsciously my eyes kept dancing to her throat, and why I'd gotten so incredibly thirsty out of nowhere. It was that enchanting scent. Christ, even the potent scent of her blood all over me hadn't been enough to distract me from how worried I was about her.

But as much as I was yearning to taste that blood on my finger and had almost brought it to my mouth, I didn't want to taste her until she wanted me to. And she *would* want me to. I'd make sure of that.

At least now I had a good enough reason that would motivate me to leave; I needed to change out of this shirt that was soaked in her blood before I lost it. Tentatively – again the tentativeness – I kissed her forehead and ran my hand through her hair one last time.

It was when I stood upright that I heard her.

Jared.

Of course I had to question whether I'd only heard it because I'd wanted to. And I'd have to question my sanity if things were so bad that I wanted to hear her voice in my head for no apparent reason.

Jared.

I smiled down at her. Supposedly, when a person was unconscious they could still hear stuff, right? Maybe, on some level, she'd sensed me around her. Or maybe she was dreaming about me. If it was the second, I'd be interested to know just what was going on in that dream.

And now, just because I'd heard that husky voice saying my name in my head, I couldn't leave. Sighing in defeat, I shrugged off my leather jacket – which I knew she loved a little too much so I wore it all the more – and hung it over the wardrobe door that was wide open. A lot of skin-tight stuff in there. Good. I'd bet that they had been pushed on her by Fletcher, though.

I peeled off the bloody t-shirt, wiped my hands with it, and balled it up before plonking it in the kitchen bin. Returning to the bedroom, I sat down on the bed. Yeah, she was going to crack every one of my ribs for this. It was a good thing that I had accelerated healing.

Keeping a respectable distance between us seemed like the decent thing to do, considering that she was unconscious and my hands wanted to wander – just like they always did when she was around.

So I positioned myself on my back with my arms behind my head, and just watched her sleep…wondering if she'd say my name again.

(Sam)

I was in that hazy, faraway state that was one stop away from being awake when I felt the body beside me. A chest that was firm and hard, covered in the softest skin. The scent that flavoured it was spicy and masculine – a scent that I'd know anywhere and would happily inhale all day long. So what I did next I did without any real thought. I snuggled into him, laying my head on his shoulder and draping my arm over his chest. God, this was comfortable.

A hand appeared on my arm, fingers tickling my skin soothingly. Another hand was then in my hair, stroking through a patch of it ever so gently. I sighed, content. The skin-to-skin contact was interesting. A kiss would be nice. Really, really nice.

Opening my eyes, I began to raise my head…and that was when I left the faraway land and found myself totally awake, and realised my little predicament. My body immediately tensed. Oh shit.

There was rumbling in the chest underneath me and a laugh came soon after. I sat up with the bedspread more or less glued to me. A second later, it registered in my brain that I was fully clothed, but I didn't release the sheet. Gaping, I looked down at a laughing, bare-chested Jared. It was a strain to keep my eyes away from the chest, but I did it.

He laughed out the words: "Ah, I wondered how long it'd take before you woke all the way up and realised what you were doing. I bet you hate yourself now. Shame I didn't get a kiss."

"What're you doing in my bed?! In my apartment, for that matter?"

"Relax." He was still laughing.

"And *why* are you half naked?"

"You got blood all over my shirt, remember?" He sobered up then. "I guess you probably don't. How are you feeling? Pain gone?"

"Um, yeah." The words came out quiet. Wow, I'd really killed Victor. My own Sire.

"After you put yourself unconscious – which was good thinking, by the way – I brought you here."

"And stayed with me half-naked because...?"

He rolled his eyes. "I *was* going to go to my room and change, but..."

When he hesitated to continue, I pressed, "But, what?"

"You don't wanna know."

I tensed again. "Why don't I want to know? *What* don't I want to know?"

"Seriously, you'll get embarrassed, you don't want to know."

"No, I really, really do. Cough up."

He sighed and sat up. "I stayed because...you said my name."

"I was unconscious. Unconscious people don't gab."

"Not with their mouths. You must have been dreaming about me or something. Was it a *good* dream? Kinky? I'll bet it was kinky. Tell me about it, I'll analyse it." His smile and arched brow gave him the most impish look ever.

I knew my cheeks were an unattractive beetroot shade at that point, which just made me even more embarrassed. A change of subject was urgently required. "How long was I out?"

He shrugged. "A couple of hours. Not as long as I'd expected."

"So, what, you just lay there all that time?"

"Yeah," he said quietly. "I don't think I've ever seen anyone in that much pain. I don't think I've ever met anyone who killed their Sire either."

A little guilt nipped at me then. My *Sire*. I'd killed my own Sire. Victor had been right about one thing: he'd made me...and I'd just gone and killed him.

"Hey," said Jared as he gently pinched my chin with his thumb and forefinger. "Don't go feeling bad about it. He deserved it. I know they say not to speak ill of the dead, but that Victor was one evil son of a bitch. Did he really try to make you *want* him? As in, like, desire him?" I nodded. "So he could make you horny, make you want to have sex with him?"

"It's his idea of foreplay. *Was*. But it was the only way he could ever get me in his bed."

"That's sick. It's basically psychological rape."

Now I didn't feel so guilty. But I was still surprised at myself. I hadn't hesitated in killing my own Sire. Antonio didn't need my protection. He had enough by the way of guards and two Pit Bulls. But it had been like a reflex to protect him. I hadn't even realised I liked him all that much. I tended to get along best with outgoing people, and Antonio wasn't exactly the life and soul of the party.

But he'd freed me from a crazy, cruel, psychological rapist. To think I'd come so close to folding under all the pressurizing emotions... "By the way, what did you say to Victor? I was about to snap, and you telepathically said something to him that made him lose all focus on me."

"Oh I, um, told him that I didn't want him to take you back because I wanted to screw you a couple more times first."

My jaw dropped. "You made him think you'd been shagging me?"

"It distracted him, didn't it?"

I sighed, conceding that he was right. "God, I'm thirsty." In the time I'd taken to sling the bedspread off me, Jared had moved with vampire speed to the fridge and back again; now sitting beside me with a red grape flavoured NST. "Thanks," I muttered, a little taken aback. Feeling unbelievably drained, I gulped down the drink. My stomach felt better within seconds, but my body had the enthusiasm of a decaying leaf.

"Antonio said to tell you to take the rest of the night off. And I really think you should, you look half dead."

"But then the squad will end up having another evening of lounging around."

"I won't let them lounge. I'll have them repeat the training they were doing with me earlier. Then tomorrow night, you can blast them into the railings again if they don't turn up at the arena."

"They'd better."

His chuckle was silent. He stared at me for a minute. Not as though he had something to say, but as though it was perfectly normal to just stare at someone. I didn't know how he could be so at ease about it. Before I could comment, he bounced off the bed and retrieved his leather jacket that was hanging over the wardrobe door. My treacherous eyes scrolled down from his face to get an eyeful of the lines, curves, and sinews of his chest.

Jared – I couldn't have expected him to not notice really, could I? – raised a brow.

There was no point in trying to deny it or letting myself fall into a pit of embarrassment, especially when ogling was a favourite pastime of his too. "*You* look."

"Hey, I don't mind you looking. When you're ready to stop pretending you don't want to do more than that, let me know."

"Will do," I said sarcastically.

Losing his light-hearted air, he sighed as he gazed down at me. "You really don't look great."

"Thanks," I mumbled dryly.

"Take some energy from me."

"What?"

He sat on the bed again. "Take some energy from me. I know you can easily absorb the natural energy around you, but it can't be as good for your body as energy from a living thing." He was right. The human body was like a battery. "Come on, the process of severing the link between you and Victor probably sapped nearly every last bit of your energy."

I shook my head. "It's okay, but thanks."

"You must have done it before to someone."

I nodded. "Yeah...but it's weird."

"Weird how?"

"Well...you know when you're *really* thirsty, for any fluid, and you start swigging down a drink but then you keep going even when you're not really thirsty anymore – just because it feels so good and soothing against your throat?"

"Yeah. Don't tell me you get, like, an energy-lust?" He smiled at that.

"I've been known to take more than I need to. I could wipe you out; you'd be just as exhausted as I am now."

"I won't let you wipe me out."

"You won't stop me; you won't *want* me to stop. It's almost like when you're drinking blood... It won't make you horny, but it'll make you feel a bit high."

"Really? Go for it, then. I'm way too intrigued to let this go. How do you do it?"

"Well, you don't have much excess energy around you, so the best and quickest way to do it would be for me to put my hands on your head, but that'll probably make you dizzy."

"That's okay."

I didn't like the idea of repaying him by sending him off all wobbly. "You sure you want to do this?"

"Sam, just do it."

"Hands." I held out mine, palms facing upwards, and he took them. "Right. You don't have to do anything, but it'll work better if you don't resist when you feel the pull."

"I won't," he assured me in a whisper as he twined his fingers in mine and shuffled closer to me.

"When I say stop, you have to pull away or the connection won't totally break." I didn't actually need to close my eyes, but I did. It was just too distracting to look at him when he was doing that obvious staring thing. It felt as though my entire body was a lung as it sucked in his energy as if it was vapour. Instantly Jared shuddered, but he didn't resist.

Sam. It was a gasp of pleasant surprise. Clearly it felt good to him already.

Hungry for more of that force, my body drew in more and more. I felt Jared's hands tighten on my fingers and then his forehead was suddenly pressed against mine. I opened my eyes to find that his own were closed. I could feel what he was feeling: that he was outside of reality, that he was at peace, and that nothing else mattered but this moment. Well he was certainly enjoying himself.

It was as my body began to grow desperate for more of his energy that I knew I had to stop – it was like heading toward a cliff at high speed, knowing that if you stopped now you'd be okay but if you kept upping that speed… "Stop."

I tried to pull my hands away but Jared held them even tighter. "No, don't stop."

"I have to." But his hold was unyielding. "Jared, you have to let go." But he didn't, he wasn't even having some sort of inner struggle about whether to release my hands or not. He was completely caught up in the feeling. I thought about butting him, but in his state of bliss, the pain wouldn't even register.

Jared!?!

If he didn't let go of my hands now, I'd fall off that cliff.

An idea came to mind – something that was sure to snap him out of it. I kissed him. A firm, greedy kiss. His eyelids shot open and, sure enough, he kissed me back. His hands instantly went to my face and held it to his, as if he was expecting me to pull away any second now. I should pull away. But that was easier thought about than done. That blast of heat that I'd felt last time flowed through me again, making a shudder ripple down my spine.

I'd have been lying if I said I wasn't enjoying his tongue exploring the crevice of my mouth, or if I said that my hands were clutching the skin of his back of their own accord. Just like I'd have been lying if I said I hadn't wanted him since first meeting him, or that him being misogynistic had made me want him any less. That was why, when he dragged me onto his lap, I curled my legs around his waist instead of pulling away.

He ground me against his erection, growling into my mouth, as he intensified the kiss ten-fold; it was raw, and primal, and drugging. Then he was skating his hands all over me as I threaded my fingers through his hair, just like I'd imagined doing that first night when I saw him at the pool. Shoving up my vest, his hand splayed possessively over my breast, clutching and kneading, while his mouth latched onto a nipple through my bra and plucked at it with his teeth.

Suddenly my head hit a hard surface, and there was a strong smell of earth. Jared released my nipple and looked around us just as I did. Then he laughed.

"Why are we in the arena?" I asked, spooked.

"You must have teleported us here."

"Say again?"

"When you took some of my energy, you must have absorbed a little of my power."

"But I didn't try to teleport us. I certainly wasn't thinking about the arena." Thank God it was empty of people.

"It can be a little temperamental until you get used to it. The arena's been on your mind the past couple of days, right? So, here we are."

Yes, here we were — bodies pressed together, my hands in his hair, my legs tangled around his waist, hearts hammering away.

"Um..." I had no idea what to say. Whatever Jared saw on my face made him release an aggravated sigh and move from above me. I got to my feet, more mentally off balance than I could ever recall feeling. As we stared at each other wearing dubious expressions, it made me think of last night after we had broken away from each other.

"I know you only kissed me because you couldn't get through to me before. I know that. But you didn't stop, Sam. You could have, because sure enough the kiss served its purpose. Not only did you *not* stop, but you got so carried away that you teleported us without trying to. So I'm thinking that maybe you want me a lot more than you're letting on."

I honestly wasn't sure what he wanted from me. Yeah, a shag. But I didn't get why it was so important. "Jared, why are you pushing this? What is it you want to hear?"

"I just need to understand why you pull away from me."

Oh, he wasn't used to rejection. Blokes and their egos!

"I know you said that you find me having three consorts a bit weird…but, I mean, what is it that you're saying exactly? Is it that you want me to get rid of them? That you want to be my only consort? That you want more from me than just sex?"

He did seem genuinely confused, and my first thought was that he must be one vain bastard. But I couldn't help but notice how much confusion had coated that last question. It seemed that he wasn't so much confused that I didn't want him as he was confused that I wouldn't be perfectly happy to simply use him for sex.

Just like all the other women – including his consorts – used him, I mused.

Huh. I sure as hell knew what being used felt like. But whereas I was determined for it not to happen again, it seemed that Jared had simply become accustomed to it. The world had to be a lonely place for Jared then, didn't it? It made me feel a pang of empathy for him.

I held up my index finger. "All right, first of all, I'll never be anyone's consort ever again in my life. I thought I made that clear. And I don't want some fairy-tale relationship – I couldn't give that much of myself anyway when I've only just got *me* back."

"*I* don't want a relationship either, so what's the problem?"

Yep, he genuinely didn't understand why I wouldn't be content to use him just like those others did. But *he* was using *them*, too, and therein lay my problem. "Jared, I can't sleep with someone who sees women as possessions. I've been doing that for the past three years."

"I see women as possessions?"

"You have three tucked in a little apartment."

He sighed and shook his head, still looking baffled. "So you're saying that you ignore that you want me because I have consorts? So then you *do* want me to get rid of them."

"You're not listening to me. You see women as possessions – *that* is the problem."

He started pacing in front of me. "Why are you being so judgemental about this? I'm not the only one who has consorts. Antonio has them, do you judge him?"

"Antonio isn't asking me to sleep with him."

"Half of the commanders have them. Most of the security guards have them."

"Yeah, and some of them don't. Sebastian doesn't. Your brother doesn't."

He halted his pacing and his irises glowed red. "Whoa, wait a minute. What does my brother have to do with this?"

"I'm just saying—"

"Comparing me to my brother? Who's scoring the most points so far?"

"Oh don't be a dick."

His gaze suddenly turned studious, like he was trying to see through me. And then a smile – it wasn't a nice one – crept onto his face. "Know what I think, Sam?" He walked toward me stealthily, his eyes narrowed. "I think it's just been that long for you since your body and your mind responded to someone without any manipulating involved from anybody else, that you don't know what to do. It scares the hell out of you, doesn't it?"

I'd never seen him angry before. He was unnerving, to be truthful. At the same time as wanting to reach out and calm him, I also wanted to slap him for making me see something about myself that I really hadn't wanted to see. I was – human and vampire years added together – twenty-three years old...and I didn't know how to handle something as basic as desire anymore.

"Maybe," I allowed. It didn't seem worth denying it. "Can you honestly blame me for that? Can you blame me for not wanting to feel like someone's possession anymore? Every single time he touched me I felt sick, dirty, and sometimes I wanted to die. So excuse me if I don't want to sleep with someone who sees women as nothing but sexual outlets just the same as *he* did!"

Jared pointed hard at me and spoke through his teeth. "Hey, I am *nothing* like him. Don't ever compare me to him again. I'll tell you what, Sam," – he raised his hands – "I'll make things easy for you: right now is the last time we'll ever talk about this. I'll never come onto you ever again. The bet's off. You can just get on with your celibate lifestyle, and I'll get on with *shagging* my *sexual outlets*."

He then teleported away, leaving me alone with thoughts that I didn't want at the forefront of my mind, and feelings that I didn't want to feel. If I, a vampire — a creature that was naturally sensual — couldn't even cope with desire, then I was basically broken, wasn't I? I hated Victor so much right now. And Jared. Actually, no, I didn't hate him. I *hated* that he was so infuriated with me. I *hated* that he was somewhere thinking bad of me. I *hated* that I'd hurt him.

How could I have compared him to Victor? I hadn't been comparing him to Evan, or at least not in the way that he was thinking; I wasn't weighing up who was the better brother to be with. I didn't want to be with either of them. I honestly just wanted to belong only to myself and not have to be concerned with pleasing other people.

Well, I got what I wanted. So why didn't it feel as liberating and comforting as it should?

CHAPTER SIX

(Jared)

I hadn't been kidding when I told Sam to go enjoy her celibate life while I went to screw one of my possessions. That was exactly what I was about to do right now, even if it did make me feel sick.

I watched as Joy writhed underneath me, begging me to enter her. She looked beautiful when she was like this. She had no problem with losing all self-control. She was eager when it came to experimenting. She said – moaned – all the right words. She knew exactly what I liked and exactly how I liked it, and she did it without even being asked to. All of that made her my favourite of the three.

But that wasn't why it was her who I'd come to. I wanted her because right now – even though I hated myself for feeling it – I wanted to hurt Sam, and I knew she really disliked Joy 'the twig'. It didn't make sense that I'd do this, considering that I wasn't exactly going to tell Sam about it. Surprisingly, her rejection had hurt, so maybe all I was really trying to do was make myself feel better.

Yeah, that wasn't working too well.

Because as much as Joy was beautiful and seemed to have this innate gift for sex, she wasn't Sam. With that thought, my hands halted at the snap of my jeans. My heavy sigh made a slight whistle as it escaped through my gritted teeth.

"What is it?" asked Joy in a whiny voice, looking up at me with a sulky expression.

"Nothing."

"Well it must be something, you've just *stopped*."

"I'm just a little worn out, that's all." I *was* drained. Sam had taken a fair bit of my energy in more ways than one.

"Okay, well lay on your back and I'll ride you. I'll even do the reverse cowgirl if you want." Her grin was seductive. "We haven't done that in a while."

Not a bad idea, actually. Then I wouldn't have to look at her. Every time I looked at her face, I was just reminded that hers wasn't the face that I wanted to see. There didn't seem any sense in cutting short sex with her just because I was thinking about someone else — someone who I'd never have like this anyway — but all I wanted to do was leave.

Then an idea popped into my head. It was totally immoral and unethical, but appealing all the same. I could ask Joy to do the thing I loved most out of all the things she could do…I could ask her to use her gift of Physical Imitation.

Plenty of times she had morphed into someone else for me. She'd do it now, no questions asked. Sam could be underneath me just like that. Then maybe all this frustration would go away. Maybe half my problem was that I was just too curious about what it would be like with her. Maybe if I got that curiosity cured, I'd be all right again.

The thought left my mind pretty much as fast as it came. Having Joy transfigure was always fun; what guy wouldn't want to sometimes have Jennifer Aniston or Cameron Diaz suddenly underneath them? But in this instance, it just wouldn't work. I didn't just want Sam's body. I wanted *her*.

I wanted her mind, her blood, her voice, her scent…everything. The whole package. Not that I wanted a relationship — I wasn't built for those — but I wanted all of her to belong to me and only me while she was with me. Joy could look like her, but she'd never be her. Whether I liked it or not, it wasn't just curiosity that made me want Sam. I hated both her and me for that.

So I did the only thing I could really do: I left Joy on the bed, gaping, while I grabbed my jacket and, without a word, teleported to the bathroom of my apartment. A cold shower had a way of making me less stressed, and I actually did feel better after it — less frustrated, less dreary.

Since I would soon be in dreamland, there wasn't any point in picking out an energising drink. Instead, I retrieved two lager flavoured NSTs from the refrigerator. The first barely touched the sides as it went down. I was a little more civilised with the second, taking little swigs as I left the kitchen and entered the living area.

That was when I felt it — that familiar tug in my stomach. Every one of my senses seemed to be having a sing and a dance, leading me straight to the balcony. Without opening the doors, I looked down to see just what I'd known I'd to see: Sam. She was in the pool. Fully clothed? As she rested against one of the walls of the pool, she was gazing up at the moon as though it might answer a question that she wished she didn't have. Snort. I knew how that felt.

I didn't go out onto the balcony. I didn't want her to sense me watching her like she had last time. Besides, I'd meant what I'd said...I'd never come onto her again.

Sucking in a long breath, I started to move away from the window. But then a vision of something snagged my full attention, and I wanted to punch that something's lights out. *Slaphead.*

(Sam)

Why couldn't I have just said a big resounding *no* when Jared asked me to feed off his energy? Then I wouldn't be in this mess at all. I wouldn't have kissed him again, I wouldn't have teleported us both to the training arena so we would never have had a big blow out, and he wouldn't hate me. Amazing how one little decision could have such an effect.

Right now, I really wasn't impressed. I'd been in my apartment totally brassed off and thinking that I just needed to cool off, and the next thing I'd found myself at the bottom of the pool! Damn this teleporting shit. I didn't bother getting out. I'd wanted to have a dip in the pool the minute I'd spotted it. Only problem was that when I thought of the first time I'd seen it, I remembered the vision of Jared swimming in it.

Tonight had been one of the worst nights ever. First I'd had my squad being absolute sods to the point that I'd had to send a blast of air to knock them off their feet. Then I'd had to see Victor again. Then I'd killed Victor. Then there'd been that horrible, indescribable agony while my body grieved. Then there'd been all that stuff with Jared. And now I was stuck worrying where this teleporting power was going to take me to next.

I definitely had to stop thinking about Jared in case it took me to him. That'd be bad.

So I thought about the pool, the feeling of the cool water lapping up against my skin. Technically then I should stay where I was. I thought of how weird it had felt swimming just minutes ago. That had been my first time since becoming a vampire, and God it was effortless. I didn't struggle to stay fully afloat no matter how tired I was. I didn't have to dig deep in myself for the energy to keep going, and nor did I have to wait long before my hair dried.

Closing my eyes, I thought about how peaceful it was here in the water alone, and how relaxed my body was becoming, and how—

SPLASH!

I opened my eyes to find Max the Slaphead in the pool. He hollered a noise of exhilaration.

"I'll say this only once," I told him. "Fuck off."

"Now, now," he said, wagging a finger. "Sure you have your authority when it's training time. But right now, I'm on my own time. And I'm staying."

"Tosser," I cursed, too brassed off to take much notice of his bare chest. There had been a lot of bare chests going around tonight.

He came a little closer. "I heard what happened."

I tensed. A lot had happened tonight, so what exactly did he mean?

"Killing your Sire must have been a hard thing to do." There was a lot of sensitivity in his voice. I hadn't thought of Slaphead as the type to have a sensitive side.

"Yeah, well, he was a dickhead."

"I heard that too." His smile was only small, but it held all its usual cheekiness. "At the risk of sounding like a pervert, why are you fully clothed in the pool?"

"Ah, you sound so disappointed. Had you been hoping that jumping in here would get you a better look at what lies beneath?"

"Oh, I can see your assets just fine, don't worry about it. In *fact*, with your wet clothes clinging to your skin, it's a really good view."

I splashed a handful of water at him. He shook it off like a wet dog and then edged closer – but not too close, which I appreciated.

"I wanted to ask you something." His tone was serious now. "If you knew that rumours were getting spread round about someone...would you tell them?"

It couldn't have been more obvious what he was getting at. "What have people been saying about me now?"

"The messengers get shot a lot," he continued, "so if you were the messenger, would you risk getting shot?"

"Slaphead, tell me now," I ground out.

His eyebrows shot up and a smile crept onto his face. "I'm not telling you a thing until you drop the Slaphead thing. We're not working now, we're on our own time, and my name is Max."

"Either get out of the bleeding pool and leave me in peace, or cough up."

"Is it really that hard for you to say my name? Does it make you shudder or something?" He was even closer to me now. "Or maybe I just make you nervous."

"You make me want to slap you."

"All right, fair enough. People have been saying that something's going on between you and Commander Michaels."

I stiffened. Had someone been in the arena who we hadn't noticed? I played aloof. "And this rumour is based on...?"

He gave me an incredulous look, like he thought the answer should be obvious. "Well, um, there's how he looks at you. There's how you look at him. There's the fact that there's that much sexual tension between you that it gets us *all* horny. I mean, come on, you guys can't even work together."

"Thanks for the heads-up about the rumour," I said simply.

"Well? Do you wish to confirm or deny these rumours?"

"You know what? No comment. And I'll tell you why: you lot need to grasp the fact that I'm your superior, not your equal, not your mate. That means my business is my own."

Max grinned. He'd taken that as a denial, by the looks of things. There was the smallest space between us now. I had to question why I was allowing him to get so close. It wasn't like I had any intention of kissing him. But, contrary to what he believed, I wasn't nervous around him. He was easy to be around, because he didn't want to play games, or make bets, or push me on things. He just wanted to have a laugh.

"Okay. But like I said, we're on our own time now. This is just one single person talking to another."

"What does this single person want?"

He pursed his lips for a second. "Hmm. I guess what I want is to know if, when we're on our own time...we can cancel out each other's single status."

His cuteness, smooth voice, and the fact that he wasn't being pushy almost made me consider it. But I had plenty of reasons not to. "Mates is the best I can do. And by mates, I mean friends."

Max nodded but didn't lose his smile. "There's one thing you'll learn about me in training tomorrow."

"What's that?"

"I don't give up easily."

"I'm not playing hard to get," I told him as he hopped out the pool. "Mates — that's it."

"I know you're not playing. But babe, that just makes you even more of a challenge. You've no idea how much I like challenges. You might not have meant to, but you just turned me on big style."

I had a feeling that he didn't walk away with vampire speed because he was hoping I'd take a sneaky look at his arse as he strutted off. I didn't look. I'd already gotten a good look at it at the try-out. It was a nice behind if ever there was one. Biteable.

You've just saved his life by saying no, I heard in my head. Jared.

My head immediately snapped up to look at his balcony. He wasn't out, but I could see him at the window. Seconds later he was out of view, but I'd seen his expression long enough to notice that he was absolutely livid with me.

That bothered me as I lay there later that morning, trying desperately to get some sleep. But after a day's sleep in the comfiest bed ever, I actually didn't feel so bad. Yeah, I still felt crappy over everything that had happened with Jared. And I still had mixed feelings over killing my maker. But there were bigger problems — like the fact that The Hollow might be attacked soon and the squad had to be prepared. So although I was again a little tempted to hide away in my room, I ignored it.

I thought about trying to teleport to the office but immediately decided against it. God knew where I'd end up. It was odd. Usually when I absorbed someone's power, I could handle it just as easily as I handled my own — I knew exactly how to harness and channel energy, and that was all you needed in order to control and effectively use a power. But I couldn't seem to grasp how to use this teleporting thing. Thankfully it would fade as soon as I used up all of the energy that Jared had passed on to me.

Before I was even halfway down the corridor to the office, I knew that Jared wasn't in there. Not simply because I hadn't picked up his scent, but because I couldn't sense him near. The fact that I *shouldn't* be able to sense when he was near totally galled me.

"All right, Fletch," I greeted as I reached the reception desk outside my office.

"Oh, luv, come here." Before I could say a word, he was on his feet and his arms were clamped around me. I guessed he'd heard about Victor meeting his doom at my hands. "It's all right, luv. It's *all right*," he crooned, as though I was crying. "I know, I know."

"Fletch, I'm fine honestly."

"You don't have to act for me, luv." He was patting my back now.

"Oh bugger off ya big Nancy," I giggled, stepping out of his arms. "I'm fine."

"Your emotions say different."

Oh crap, yeah, I'd forgotten he was an Empath. "Okay, I'm a bit mixed up."

"Mixed up? You're all over the place. You're like a broth of conflicting emotions." He cradled his head as if the impact of it all hurt – bloody drama queen. "Ooh I can feel a migraine coming on."

"Then I'll leave you be."

"Ah, bless ya. Bless ya."

Once settled at my desk, I retrieved my notepad, intent on doing flow charts on the recruits for me to document what their ability was now and what goal I had for each of them. That was, of course, if they bothered turning up later at the arena. I got the feeling that some of them might. Max, David and Denny would. Maybe Chico and Butch. I wouldn't go chasing after the others as that would cut into the training time of those that *did* show, which wasn't fair to them. As for afterwards…I might make cook up a mini tornado and stick the lazy, absent gits inside it. That would be satisfying to watch.

On completing the flow charts, I stuck each one in the relevant recruit's file. I still had an hour to kill before it was time to meet the recruits at the arena when Evan strolled in the office, wearing a cheery grin.

"You're here. I knew you would be." He looked edible in those tank-green pants and t-shirt, but I wouldn't have thought they'd suit him if I hadn't seen the evidence for myself.

Confused, I said, "Where else would I be?"

"Well, some people thought you might want more time alone. *I* said you'd have bounced back by now. Right, come on."

"Say again?"

"Antonio wants to see you. In the mansion." With that, he turned and waltzed cockily out the office, confident that I'd follow. Which I did.

Fletcher's face was a question mark as Evan and I started down the corridor together. Wanting to be careful not to start rumours that I was shagging both brothers, I told my assistant, "Fletch, I'm just going to see Antonio, and after that I'll be at the arena if you need me."

"Right, luv." He looked less suspicious now, but still curious.

"What does he want to see me about?" I asked Evan as we left the Command Centre, heading toward the mansion. I wouldn't be surprised if some of the recruits had gone whining to him that I'd thrown bits of their past at them.

"Don't look so worried," chuckled Evan.

"I'm not worried. It's just that I feel like I've been sent for by the School Head Master and I'm now being escorted to his office to get a rollicking for something."

"Oh, no, I don't think it's anything like that." He held the door open for me, and we stepped into the grand hallway of the mansion. "He probably just wants to make sure you're okay after what happened last night." After a moment of walking in silence along the hallway, he said, "So, *are* you okay?"

"No offence, but I'd rather not keep going with this conversation, considering that I know exactly what course it'll take."

"It'll take a course?" he asked, amused.

"I'll say I'm fine, then you'll say I can't really be fine, then I'll try to convince you I am, then you'll say how it must have been really hard for me kill him."

"Well, it must have been."

"Jared, Max, and Fletcher said the same thing, and all three times it made me feel like shit."

"Why?"

"Because it *wasn't* hard. I did it without thinking."

"You did it to protect Antonio, that's nothing to feel bad about." Gently Evan squeezed my shoulder, giving me the sort of smile that begs you to smile yourself. So I did. And that was the moment – while Evan had his hand on my shoulder and we were smiling at each other widely – that fate decided it would be fun for Jared to walk down the same hallway, heading in our direction. His face was a picture of fury. Oh bugger.

Where're you taking her? I heard in my head. Did Jared realise he'd sent that thought to me instead of Evan?

Antonio wants to see her. Why are we talking about this telepathically? Evan's confusion didn't show on his face.

Then I understood what was happening. Absorbing a little of Jared's power must have made it possible for me to listen to telepathic conversations around me. I didn't let it show that I could hear.

Jared, nearly at us: *Why are* you *taking her to him?*

Evan: *I was asked to go get her, what's the problem?*

Jared: *No problem. You can both do what you want; it's none of my business.*

Evan, amused: *Oh, I get it — she won't let you screw her, will she?*

"Hi," said Jared to both Evan and me as he stopped before us. If I hadn't been able to hear the frustration in his telepathic voice, I might have bought his aloof expression.

"All right," I greeted, trying for aloof too.

"Where you off to, bro?" Evan asked him.

Evan: *Oh I bet this is all new for you. I was starting to think there wasn't a girl out there who wouldn't spread her legs for you. She just gets more and more interesting.*

Jared: *Evan, I'm not in the mood for this. Oh, and don't think she'll let you in her panties either.*

"Going back to the squad," replied Jared. "Dawson supervised them for me while I came to speak to Antonio and Luther." He gestured with his head to the room across the hallway.

Evan, still amused: *Oh my God, this has really gotten to you, hasn't it? It's not just killing your pride, you're—*

Jared: *Luther's just told me there'll be trouble ahead, he obviously meant you.*

Evan, even more amused, began singing the chorus of Irving Berlin's 'Face the Music and Dance' in his head, the idiot.

Jared turned to me, all business but still friendly. "I need to update the recruits' files. You done with them for tonight?"

"Yeah, they're on my desk," I replied in the same tone, close to laughing at how Evan was singing in his head about moonlight and music and romance. Just to fuck with them, I sang aloud the last line of the chorus, drawing out the word "dance."

They both gawked at me unattractively.

"I'll see you both later." And then I strolled off, whistling the tune of the song that might very well end up stuck in my head all night long. I could feel their eyes still on me as I advanced into the room that Jared had come out of only a minute ago.

"All right," I said to Antonio and Luther who offered me greeting smiles. I then nodded to the guards who nodded back as I was licked half to death by the dogs. Nero was especially attentive.

This room was absolutely huge and amazing. I'd been expecting another parlour, given that Antonio seemed to love them, but this was different from anything I'd seen. In the centre was a large rectangular aviary; inside were canaries, rabbits, guinea pigs, and some other types of birds that I didn't know the names to.

The aviary was made of glass and had a tiny stream covering the perimeter of it. Antonio and Luther were standing side by side, staring through the glass of the aviary at the trees, and animals, and other plants. I was already thinking what Antonio was thinking before he said it.

"It's such a peaceful place." He was still gazing through the glass. "I come here whenever an emotion overwhelms me. So I thought this would be an extremely good place for me to speak with you tonight. I can imagine you might be quite overwhelmed."

Reaching his side, I grumbled, "Not you as well."

He laughed at that, as did Luther. "You know, if a number of people are interested in your emotional state, maybe you should consider this a good thing: it shows that you are finally accepted and cared about."

"It might be a good thing to someone else, but I'm not really a 'let's hold hands, cuddle, and share all' person."

He laughed again. "Maybe one day you will learn that it is not a fault to care." Turning to face me – his expression all business now – he continued, "My guards have never failed to protect me. They would have reached Victor before he was able to reach me."

"I know."

"And yet, you intervened in spite of that." It was half-question, half-statement.

"I did."

"I would not go as far as to say that I owe you my life, because I do not believe that it was ever truly in danger. But your intervention was much appreciated, and I thank you for it."

"You also have my appreciation," said Luther. The guards mumbled something like 'and ours'.

Sighing, I admitted, "I wouldn't bother thanking me, I didn't really think about it, if I'm honest. I just did it."

"Do you not see that for this to be your natural reaction to my safety being jeopardised is a tremendous thing?" Antonio regarded me curiously. "There have only ever been three other people to intervene in such a way; Sebastian, and the brothers. None of them intervened by harming their Sires. You have known me for all of a few nights, and yet you not only instinctually protected me, but you killed your own Sire in order to do so."

I smiled. "Maybe you didn't notice that he was a prick who I had no time or respect for."

"He was still your Sire, Sam. And just like any human would have that small moment of doubt before harming either of their parents, any vampire experiences this before trying to harm their Sire. Most vampires never do it, no matter the circumstances. A blood-bond is overpowering for the mind. And yet, you did not experience that moment of hesitation."

I bowed my head. "Cold-hearted, I suppose."

"No," he insisted gently. "You are not cold-hearted. Harsh at times, yes – but only if you believe it is necessary. Foul-mouthed on occasion, yes – but we don't mind that so much. Capable of brutal honesty, *oh* yes – but sometimes the absolute truth is what people need to hear. You are *not* cold, Sam. Do not ever think that about yourself. Consider that an order."

"Sir, yes, Sir," I said light-heartedly, to which he rolled his eyes.

"I did not call you here just to enquire about your well-being or to thank you." He made his way to a bench beside on one of the walls – I hadn't even noticed that it until then, the beauty of the aviary had taken up all of my focus – and invited me to sit beside him.

"Are you giving me a raise?" I teased.

"You could say that." I wasn't expecting that to be his response. "As I told you before, you are not the only individual to have intervened to protect me. In each of those cases, I called them to me just as I have called you now. I believe in thanking people with actions more than with words. Rewards, you might say."

"Okay." Did he mean, like, a medal or something?

"I am a Bestower, Sam – that is my vampiric gift. Have you ever encountered a Bestower before?"

"No, but I've heard of them. You can pass on gifts to other vampires."

"Not exactly. I can impart power to a vampire, not a gift of my choice – that is different. It can only be done at my control, but I cannot control what reaction the power has to your own innate concentration of power. In other words, I do not know what gift you will then develop, but it will most likely not be my own."

Wow, I hadn't seen that coming.

"It is your decision, Sam. I know that you already have a substantial gift to control, so it is understandable if you do not want another. But if you would like to accept my offer, I would be very happy to reward you in such a way."

The idea of having another gift was exciting. Even the idea that I'd have no idea what it would be was exciting. But it had taken me a while to have the control that I now had over my gift…This wasn't exactly the best time to be struggling with another one, considering that The Hollow's walls would be attacked in a few weeks.

"Will I be able to control it? I mean, I can control other vampires' gifts easily enough, because it's just about channelling energy and I'm a master at that – I have to be. But when I absorbed some of Jared's energy," – Antonio raised his brows at that, but he didn't comment – "I couldn't get a grip on the teleporting thing."

"That is not because you couldn't control it," explained Antonio. "Teleporting is not as simple as people might think. It is a lot like being a satellite. Your mind picks up and commits to memory the signals and coordinates of places or people – all on a totally subconscious level. For Jared, his initial struggles were due to his inexperience at channelling energy. For you, the problem is obviously that you did not absorb the amount of his energy required to receive enough of the concentration of that power. As such, you are, through no fault of your own, an incomplete satellite."

"Oh. Right." Well that was good news.

"So, do you wish to accept my offer?" He was eager, I could tell. Probably curious as to what gift I'd end up with.

I had to admit I was extremely curious myself, and curiosity killed the kitten in this instance. "What do I have to do?"

Antonio smiled pleasantly and exchanged a pleased expression with Luther before returning his attention to me. "You will need to join your forehead to mine. It might feel a little strange, sort of like a sizzling sensation, but do not withdraw from it. The process is not something I can control; it depends on the reaction that the power I impart has on you. It can take anything from thirty seconds to an entire minute."

I nodded. "Okay." Although I was a little hesitant due to the shock and weirdness of it all, I didn't let it show.

Antonio closed his eyes. Seconds later he spoke, "I am ready for you."

I almost laughed as that unintentionally sounded a little kinky. Slowly I leaned in. When my forehead met his, there was the strangest bang inside my body. I guessed that Antonio felt it too, because he gasped.

"Antonio?" said Luther, sounding concerned. I took it that the bang wasn't normal.

"All is well, Luther," he assured him. "Sam, do not fear, be still."

Remaining still had to be one of the hardest things I'd ever done. It was the freakiest thing. It felt as though bugs were crawling under the skin of Antonio's forehead and bursting out, scraping their way through the skin of my own. Then there was this almost unbearable feeling of bubbles bursting inside my skull. My limbs burned. My heart went ten to the dozen. My lungs pained. My stomach ached. And God, I was so thirsty all of a sudden.

It felt like forever before all of it, as abruptly as it had started, ended with one more bang which made us break apart.

"Oh. My. God. What was all that?" I was wheezing. Luther thrust NSTs in mine and Antonio's hands. So efficient. I gulped it down so quickly, I didn't even taste it. My throat stopped aching then.

"It would be fair to say that my power has never had such an enthusiastic reaction before to the process of bestowing," explained Antonio after reservedly drinking his NST.

"That was *enthusiastic*?"

"The pain and the discomfort are normal. The explosion-type sensation we had at the beginning was not. That was my power literally bursting with enthusiasm to enter you."

"Why so enthusiastic?"

Antonio looked to Luther who, for once, seemed to have no answer.

Eventually Antonio theorised, "Perhaps because your own concentration of power was so great, it massively attracted my own."

I took an inventory of my entire self. "I don't feel any different."

"It may actually take a few weeks for the gift to manifest itself, just as it does for a vampire's natural gift to emerge," said Luther. "I must say, I am eager to see what it will be."

Antonio smiled at him. "As am I." Turning back to me, he asked, "Do you feel able to return to work this evening?"

"That's where I'm going now." I rose from the bench. "Hopefully the gift doesn't pop up then, or God knows what I might end up doing to the boys." An evil smile surfaced. "That would be the most perfect excuse to beat them senseless, though, wouldn't it?"

"Oh and Sam, there is one last thing before you go," called Antonio casually as I reached the door.

"What's that?"

"When the attack happens on The Hollow, I'd like you and Jared to lead the squad together."

I spun on the spot. "Say again?"

CHAPTER SEVEN

(Sam)

Entering the training arena, I almost dropped dead with shock – which would be a hard thing for an immortal to do. Inside, stretching and gabbing and laughing at dirty jokes, was every single one of the recruits. No sulky or irritated expressions. No lazy postures. No yawns or groans. Not even any signs that they were angry with me after I dug into their past and hit them with it. In fact, they all seemed eager and raring to start.

I giggled, which made them all turn. "Did someone mistakenly tell you lot that I'll be doing this topless or something?"

"Naked, I heard," joked one of them. It might have been Harvey.

Max flashed me his usual smile – no hint of last night's flirtatiousness in it, which was good. Like most people, I wanted my personal life and work life separate as far as possible. "We're big boys; we can admit that we were wrong about you."

Chico nodded and gave me a look that was both apologetic and respectful. "If you're someone who can kill your Sire to protect Antonio, then there are things I can learn from you. And you're the kind of person I would listen to."

There were murmurs of agreement from Denny, David, Salem and Reuben.

"Plus, you've got a great body and I'm starting to get sexually confused being around guys all the time," said Damien, appreciating my navy jeans and my pink top that came attached to a white vest, covering my cleavage a little better. Needless to say, *I'd* picked this when Fletcher and I went shopping. He had begged me not to buy it.

"And you were right," said Butch, "we let ourselves get caught up in the high of being picked for the legion and thought we were the best thing since sliced bread."

"So, where do you want us, and what do you want us to do?" asked Stuart.

I snorted. "Well first of all, the lot of you can stop the friendliness and flirting. I'm not your mate, I'm not here for you to ogle at, and I'm not here to joke with you. I'm here to train you."

They all nodded and, in unison, said, "Yes, Commander." Was I dreaming?

"Oh no, you can drop the 'Commander', I can't stand it." But I wasn't going to let them call me by my first name either.

"How about Coach?" suggested Denny. The others seemed to approve of that.

I considered it for a moment. In terms of being someone who people would listen to, it was kind of the middle ground. People tended to respect coaches or trainers and have better relationships with them than what they did with people who marched around and barked orders.

"Coach, it is," I decided. "I won't be sending you off doing cross country or any physical exercises – that's Commander Michaels' department. All I will be concentrating on is aiding you with your gifts. Now...considering that you're all lazy sods, it'd be stupid of me to assume any of you have been practicing on your own time." They didn't deny it. "Right then, let's deal with all that excess energy, because until you learn to channel it, I can't teach you how to use your full potential and make use of it in combat."

They reminded me of a rugby team getting ready to play with the way they were getting rid of any cricks in their necks and bouncing a little on the spot.

"I'm going to give you all individual coaching, but do *not* mistake this as an insinuation that you only look out for number one. The point is to all become stronger as a squad, but you can only do this by first improving yourselves individually.

"Also, you will need to know each other's gifts inside and out – there might be a situation one of you can't handle but another can by, for instance, paralysing an enemy's senses or by mimicking a certain animal. It'll also mean that if you see one of you in deep shit with an enemy, you'll know whether their gift will mean they can protect themselves or whether someone needs to intervene. What's more, you'll know exactly who the best person to intervene would be. All of that clear to you?"

"Yes, Coach," they all said.

God, their compliance was weird. "Just to be sure that having your eyes almost glued to my cleavage isn't making everything I've said fly right over your heads, someone tell me the first goal."

Max immediately said, "To work out how to channel all the energy so there's none leaking out."

I nodded. "Good. Someone give me the next one."

"To improve our use of our powers, so we can improve as a squad," shouted Butch.

"Good. One more..."

"To know each other's powers in and out," offered Reuben.

"Well what do you know, you lot actually do listen," I said, smiling wide. "After you've reached all those goals, we can start looking at formations. But for now, let's tackle the first goal. Denny?"

Instantly the animal mimic stepped forward. His baby face made me want to take it easy on him – it wouldn't have the same effect on an enemy, but it might very well make them underestimate him.

I stood opposite him, arms folded over my chest. "Right, what animal-like tricks have you got?"

"Well, um, I have a sting. At will, I can make a poisonous needle appear out of the top of my right index finger."

"Okay, what effect does that have?"

"It doesn't really cause much harm, but it can make you itch like crazy. And I mean *crazy*."

"So in combat, would you say it would be distracting?"

"Definitely," he assured me, widening his eyes to emphasise his answer. "All you can think about is the itching."

"That's good. What else?"

"I can make my body go as soft as liquid, and then obviously back to hard again. Like the sea cucumber. So I can be mush and wiggle through little cracks or anything like that."

"Interesting," I drawled. "So it's slightly similar to how Stuart can shred into molecules and then reassemble himself."

Denny nodded. "I can ooze slime out of my pores, too. It's the most amazing slime – I can wrap someone in it and suffocate them. A little like with Hagfish."

"I'm impressed. Anything else?"

"He can jump higher than you can *believe*," Harvey spouted out.

I twirled and raised a brow at Harvey. "I can't remember asking *you* anything, so pipe down. You'll get your minute in the spotlight in a sec, big boy." I had to think of this as a classroom of students: let one get away with something and they'll all try it, and then before you know it, you're at risk of losing total control of the students. I turned back to Denny. "As you were saying..."

"Yeah I can jump really high. Better than a frog – about as good as a copepod."

"You can accelerate as fast as five-hundred body-lengths per sec when you jump?" He nodded. "Wow."

"I'm not too crazy about the last one…" All the blokes started chuckling quietly, so I knew this had to be embarrassing for Denny. He closed his eyes as he confessed, "I can release an anal musk. Like a skunk."

I couldn't help *wanting* to laugh. Not *at* Denny, it was just the shock of what he'd said. I didn't laugh, of course. But the other recruits all did, which was a shitty thing to do as they already knew about it, just as they knew just how embarrassed he felt. It was hard not to be protective of the baby-faced boy. So I got an idea. "Show me."

"Sorry?" said Denny.

"I just want to know how bad it is. You can test it on your friends there."

I heard an 'Oh hell no' and a 'No way' and a 'Not a chance'.

I turned to look at them. "It wasn't a request. Every one of you has just been giggling like a school girl at Denny here. So why shouldn't he get to have a good laugh? Tit for tat."

"Oh, come on, Coach, we were just laughing," said Damien. "You gotta admit it's funny."

"All of you line up by the eastern wall," I ordered.

"Coach, please, don't be tight!" begged Max.

"We laugh no more," promised Reuben.

"Unfortunately for you lot, I am unmoved. Either you walk over there yourselves, or I'll air-blast all of you over there."

Grumbling and whining and holding their noses, they all lined up.

Chuckling, Denny said to me quietly, "You're just kidding, right? You don't really want me to do it?"

"Oh, I do. See, I had a skunk do it to me once, and I know it's bad. I promise you Denny, if you do this now, they'll never laugh about this again. Think of it as a learning experience for them."

"Yeah, a learning experience," he agreed, working up the nerve to go do it. Sucking in a mound of air, he added, "It's for their own good."

I nodded. "Exactly." Then I patted him on the back. "Go, boy, go. And don't be shy about how much musk you let go." All the other recruits were sending me pleading expressions, begging for mercy. "I'll just stand right over here, I think." I backed up against the wall opposite them.

"Come on, Coach," said Max, "we won't laugh again, we swear."

"Too right you won't," I assured him. "Not after this."

Denny was now in front of them, facing me. Smiling, he…well, farted I suppose. And then every single recruit – other than Denny, who it seemed could take the smell of his own lethal fart – were on their knees, coughing and gagging and scrubbing their eyes. I could get a whiff of it from where I was, but as I hadn't been in the…line of fire, you could say…I was able to take it standing.

Denny was giddy when he came back to my side. "Cool or what?"

"Very." We both stared at the grown men on their knees studiously, as though they were a science experiment. "I have to admit that after the way they all behaved toward me, I'm really enjoying this."

"Me, too," he chuckled. "You know, I really am sorry about the way we were."

I just smiled at him. Eventually they all recovered and walked dozily back over to myself and Denny. "Hi, welcome back." Their expressions were priceless. "Now, I think you're all expertly familiar with what Denny can do. What I want to know, Denny, is which of your gifts you have a problem controlling or you find to be a bit temperamental."

"I'm okay with the jumping and using the sting and the musk and the ooze, but making my body go soft can be a bit time-consuming. I'm not sure if I'd be able to do it faster, but if it's possible I'd like to."

"Well let's find out." I fed off the energy around him, letting my system breathe it in and revel in it. I could then feel Denny's energy as separate from my own: his was wilder and more potent. Still, I knew exactly how to channel and control it. I let it travel throughout my body until it filled me, hitting even my extremities, and then I let it go. In the space of a second my body was mush, and then just as quickly I was solid again. "Yeah, you could do it a lot faster."

Denny's mouth was hanging open rather unattractively. "Um…how…how do I do it faster? What am I doing wrong?"

"You're not doing anything *wrong* with your gift." I spoke to them all then. "You're all making the mistake of thinking that this is the same as physical energy, but it's not. It's an *un*natural energy that started being produced when you Turned and your body evolved. It's produced up here," – I poked my head – "and that's where you have to dig for it."

"But *your* power comes from your hands," said Stuart.

"No, it doesn't. You have to think of a water tank and a hose." I poked my head again. "This is the water tank. Your hands, *or* your breath" – I pointed at Chico – "can be the hose. Whatever hose you want. I even use my feet when I'm drawing energy from the earth beneath me. Denny uses his arse hole sometimes." Nobody laughed – they didn't want more skunk musk up their noses. "The outlet and the water tank are two different things."

I saw a few of the recruits exchanging looks that said this made sense, that they couldn't believe it was that obvious and yet they had never considered it.

"Commander Michaels never told us that," griped David, like a kid looking to blame a teacher for his lack of knowledge.

"Don't worry, you'll still get your gold star sticker at the end of the session," I told him. He laughed just as the others did.

"What about people like me and David?" said Stuart. "We don't use outlets, we just kind of will it to happen."

"And that's exactly where your problems stem from. You're limiting yourselves. Vampiric gifts don't work off will power. You don't *wish* it would happen and then it just *does*. David, you concentrate hard with your eyes when you send out that blast, right?" David nodded. "There's the outlet you've been using without even realising it. Stuart, didn't it occur to you that when you shred into tiny little molecules that *that* is how the energy is being released? That it bursts out of you?"

He tilted his head. "Huh."

"Didn't it occur to you that shredding could also serve to teleport you around? You can go from place to place as molecules." I turned back to Denny. "Now, I want you to close your eyes." He did. "Think about nothing but that water tank – all the water swilling around in there, wanting to get out so that more can replace it. All it needs is a hose.

"Remember, this is similar to Stuart's gift. But whereas he has to feel the water bursting out of him, *you* have to think of it bursting *inside* you; filling you and filling you, drowning you into nothing but—" And then he was like a puddle in the space of a second. "Mush," I finished. Everyone clapped for him. "Now, Denny, you need to think of the water filling you again, stretching you and stretching you until you might burst again. But this time, you don't burst. You turn off that hose and leave the water in the tank."

It was strange talking to a puddle, and even more strange to think that the puddle could fully understand me. He was mush for a good ten seconds before speedily reforming – I took that as him concentrating on the water/tank metaphor.

Whole again, Denny gazed at me with a cocktail of astonishment, gratitude and respect in his eyes. "Oh my God, I did it. For years I've been trying to control it. I could just kiss you right now." His face turned serious. "I won't."

All the others reacted in much the same way when I took them aside individually as I had done with Denny. Chico learned that he could in fact use his palms to emit thorns; he just needed to work on emitting more than one thorn at a time and having a better aim. Butch was able to pop up his shield a couple of times, he just needed to learn how to form it at will and how to keep the shield up for the length of time that he wanted. Stuart was now able to shred in the space of three seconds and reform again just as quickly – his goal was to learn how to do it within the space of a second in order to avoid any power directed his way. He also wanted to master how to move around while he was only molecules.

Salem, being quite violent, decided that it would be much more fun and dramatic if the outlet for his psychic blow – that could knock you unconscious – could be his fist. After Reuben had weakened his gift so that the blow felt more like a slap, I let him practice on Damien, who was being a lazy little sod. Damien's low concentration span meant he was still having trouble with trying to project his astral self any further than a few feet. But after a while of getting psychic slaps from Salem, he – in utter desperation – was able to astral project away from the impact. Sometimes learning the hard way was the only way to learn.

David had decided that he wanted his outlet to be his palms, not his eyes, so he was working on that and doing excellently – Reuben had weakened his power in advance to ensure that the blast couldn't do any more than give his victim a minor shock. He practiced mostly on Denny, who had said he would happily practice with his own powers in his own time so he could help David. I'd noticed that Denny looked out for him a lot, which was good as I came to realize that David was very nervous of his power.

It turned out that Reuben had a little trouble with controlling whether he strengthened someone's gift or weakened it, but by the end of the session he had a better hang of it. He was working toward increasing the degree to which he could affect someone's gift and with being able to affect it with minimal bodily contact as opposed to holding onto them for up to eight seconds.

Max and Harvey were hard work because both believed that they had nothing left to learn…so I paired them up, which they soon regretted. I first let Slaphead – he was back to that now that he was being a wanker – explore whether he could choose exactly what senses he wanted to affect. He didn't believe this was possible until, one by one, I took each of his senses away and left him to silently whine about it to the wall. It transpired that although Harvey was able to send something zooming away with his telekinesis, he couldn't make something rotate, or levitate, or come toward him. So I allowed him to practice on a practically defenceless Slaphead. He of course stole every one of Harvey's senses once he recovered his own, just as payback.

Each time the recruits were successful in their attempts, I would give them a nod of approval, but after that would holler, 'Again!' And, to their credit, they did it over and over and over. I was tempted to loudly express how pleased I was with their efforts, but they'd most likely interpret signs of kindness as weaknesses and then start taking the piss. I felt that if I didn't keep a tough exterior, they'd all end up being wankers again. Besides, as Max had said, they were big boys.

By the end of the night, they were all exhausted…but they were proud to be tired because they were proud of their efforts. I was actually proud of them, too. I showed this by simply saying in a flat tone, "You did good. You worked hard. But it doesn't end here. You've got goals to hit, don't lose sight of them." As motivation, I made them a promise. "Once you meet those goals and can master the formations that I have in mind for you to learn, I'll let you practice an attack on one of the other squads."

Every one of them grinned. I knew that the other squads teased the newest recruits. It was tradition. It was part of the tough love of the place; soldier sense of humour was somewhat different. But it pissed these blokes off all the same, just as it would piss me off.

"Oh yeah, I'll send those shitheads flying through the air," said Harvey. "Then we'll see if they still want to throw eggs at my door."

The recruits all seemed to be cooking up revenge plots as they left the arena, each sure to shout, "See you tomorrow night, Coach."

And they did see me tomorrow night. And the next night. And the next. Each time they put in maximum effort, never complained at the constant holler of 'Again', and the improvement was immediate. Jared never knew this, as he never came to observe. Not even when I took them out to the rainforest to familiarise themselves with it and do some training there.

The night of the 'bet' came and went. Jared made no mention of it at all. Nor did he mention Antonio's order that Jared and I lead the squad together during the attack on The Hollow. Antonio had assured me that he was aware of his 'order', so I'd decided to wait until Jared brought up the subject before speaking of it. But he didn't broach the subject. He barely mentioned *anything* to me. Toneless, polite greetings and farewells were all I got these days.

"You're going to have to tell me what's going on, because all the emotions swirling around that office are giving me migraines," whined Fletcher one evening as he barged past me and into my apartment. As always, he was looking like he had just stepped out of a fashion magazine.

"Well hello to you too, Fletch. I'm fine thanks."

He spotted the three empty bottles of vodka flavoured NSTs on my table in front of the sofa and sighed. His words were gentle but firm. "Spill the beans, lady."

I sat beside him on the sofa. Well, I flopped down onto it. "Remember the night when Jared and I nearly had a fumble?"

"How could I forget? The pair of you were throwing that much heated passion around that I was sweating cobs and downright bloody horny. Not that Norm was complaining when I got back to the room, mind. I was like a bleeding jungle cat the way I—"

"Fletch, I love you, but could the record please show that I do not want to visualise my friends *doing it*. Feel free to withhold details like that in future."

He rolled his eyes. "Prude." In vampire speed, he retrieved a bundle of NSTs from my refrigerator and returned to the sofa. "So, you were saying..."

"He told me about his consort collection...and then asked me if I'd like to join it."

Fletcher's mouth fell open. "No!" As of this moment, he was absorbed in the conversation.

"Yes."

"The randy bastard. You'd think three were enough. Well don't keep me in suspense, tell me what you said."

"I told him I didn't want to be a consort again, and that I couldn't sleep with someone who collected women – who all live in the same apartment, by the way."

"No!"

"Yes." I didn't realise until now just how much this had all got to me. "He couldn't seem to wrap his head around that, and he wouldn't let it drop. Then we had another kiss. I'd been absorbing his energy because I was wiped out from the blood-link with Victor being broken, but I couldn't get him to let go of me before I took too much of his energy. So the idea of the kiss was to distract him."

"That'd definitely distract randy ole Jared. I'm guessing from that look on your lovely face that it didn't end there."

"Oh no it did. I mean, we didn't do anything more than kiss. But the kiss had gotten a bit..."

"Tongue-tastic," he supplied.

"Yeah. So then Jared made his proposition again. I said no again. And we ended up arguing. I don't even know how it got so bad. I mentioned that his brother didn't have a consort, and he seemed to take that as I liked Evan as well. And when I said he saw women as possessions like my Sire had, he got all pissed off. Then he told me he'd let it all go, and I could get on with my 'celibate lifestyle'."

Fletcher tilted his head as he considered it all. "So, basically, he's sulking over a bonk."

"A bonk that I won't have with him, yeah."

He snorted and adjusted his glasses. "Half his problem is he's too used to getting whatever he wants."

"Have you noticed that Joy's been turning up at the office at least once a night?"

"What? Who? Oh you mean that cross between a whippet and a witch. Personally, I don't know how he can shag something that looks like it's just escaped from Azkaban."

I instantly burst into laughter. Thank God Fletcher had turned up. He always had a way of making everything not seem so bad. The truth was that it had annoyed the hell out of me that Joy had been turning up the past few nights. She and I did the 'hello' and 'bye' thing, but that was all.

Once, she had brought along the other two consorts. Both were Kejas too and almost as gorgeous as Joy. Daniela had a very Mexican look about her and a bust that any woman would envy, which completely compensated for the fact that she was dopey beyond comprehension. Tammy was dark-skinned and very voluptuous, but the devious expression that seemed to be fixed on her face kind of negated her beauty. They also 'hello-ed' and 'goodbye-ed' me. Daniela actually seemed sincere about it, as opposed to the other two. Their dark grins always made it feel as though they were really saying, 'We hate you, please die'.

Jared would watch me closely when they were around. No idea why. I took to focusing on whatever documents were in front of me, no matter what they were. I would sooner have left the office altogether, but then it would have looked as though their presence bothered me in some way and I was not about to let Jared believe that. Even though it was true. I had to admit to having a lack of rationality where Jared was concerned, though it made no sense. As such, the whip nearly materialized in my hands a few times when Joy gave him some of those noisy kisses of hers. Whipping her into insensibility would have felt good.

"I wouldn't let her or him bother you, luv. Spit him out of your mind. What about that Max bloke? He's all right, and he likes you well enough. Luscious too."

"Yep, he is," I admitted. Max had continued his flirting and always on his own time, to his credit. I was actually beginning to think that the wanker wasn't all that bad. The way he didn't take life too seriously made him an attractive person to be around. I laughed a lot when he was there.

"Can I ask…I've noticed Evan goes to the office a lot these days, who is it he goes to see? I would've thought it was Jared, but whenever I pop my head through the door to speak to you he's perched on *your* table."

"I know how it might look, but I swear we've never flirted or anything. When he comes, it's always to see Jared, but then Evan and I end up laughing about something or other. I think he just finds it easy to talk to me because, unlike every other woman in The Hollow, I don't mistake it for flirting and then try it on with him."

For some reason Evan had rejected every girl who showed interest in him, but he always turned them down gently; he was sweet in spite of the cockiness. Quite the opposite of his brother in that respect. One thing that really impressed me about him was that although his twin brother had been made Heir and was highly thought of and involved in absolutely everything, Evan wasn't a bit jealous. He had told me that all that stuff wasn't important to him; that he liked being just a commander and that he thought his brother deserved the attention he received.

"You know, I get the feeling that he's a bit lonely sometimes, but I can't work out why he seems to prefer it that way."

"Oooh, maybe he's secretly gay," Fletcher crooned, excited. Then he suddenly sobered. "Oh luv, please don't tell Norm about the 'oooh', he'll kill me."

I chuckled. "I'll take it to the grave."

"You're *immortal*. What grave?" He picked up another of the NSTs, a curry flavoured one, and eyed it suspiciously. "Why is it that this looks more like a burst abscess?"

Again I laughed. And that was pretty much how the evening with Fletcher went. I couldn't help but absolutely adore him. Every home should have a Fletcher.

CHAPTER EIGHT

(Jared)

Although Joy was whispering something in my ear about plans for tonight involving chocolate mousse, handcuffs and a whip, my eyes were on Sam. I guessed that Joy's loud whispering was for Sam's benefit. She felt threatened by Sam, I now knew, which was why she persistently appeared at the office. I had to wonder if Joy's mention of a whip was just to ensure that she got Sam the Whip-Queen's attention. If Joy had succeeded, Sam wasn't showing it.

She was at her desk staring at the documents in front of her, looking completely engrossed in what she was reading. She was twining a stray strand of her hair around her finger, reminding me of the time when I had *my* fingers in that hair. Her other hand was cupping her neck as she leaned her head into it, reminding me of the time when I was leaving a trail of kisses along that neck. She was running her tongue along the inside of her bottom lip, reminding me of how that tongue had knotted with mine and how those lips had felt on mine. She was a greedy kisser, and I'd loved it.

The gentle rise and fall of her chest as she breathed was repeatedly drawing my attention to her cleavage, which was already accentuated enough by that low-cut vest. God bless Fletcher and his clothing advice. Every time she twirled her ankle, my attention drifted to those legs that had felt so good curled around me.

She could have no idea how much she, by doing *nothing*, was making me want her.

I almost hated her for it.

Hating her would be a good thing. She was the only woman ever to make me feel bad about myself. As soon as I'd calmed down after our fight, I'd wanted to slap myself. She hadn't meant that thing about her Sire the way it had come out. I knew that. But I'd been an ass to her, and I regretted it. Would I tell her that? No. Pride and all that.

It was stupid that I'd accused her of having a thing for my brother. She hadn't. I knew that. But it was likely that she *now* did. Evan was just as bad as Joy for coming to the office all the time. Sam and he would then always end up talking. He always seemed to have something to say to her. It felt like I was being sliced at every time I watched her laugh at something he said, or greet him with that big smile which she had never once shown me.

Because of that, I liked that Joy came to the office. This way, both Sam and I felt awkward sometimes. She could pretend to be engrossed in those documents all she wanted, just as she always did, but I'd bet she was well aware of everything that Joy said and did.

The night when Joy had brought along Daniela and Tammy hadn't been a good night for me. I knew seeing the three of them would remind Sam of just why she had refused me, would make her conclude that she had made the right decision. I'd been hoping that in time she would come to change her mind, open her eyes more to the idea of what I'd offered. If she had, the three of them turning up together like sisters would have cancelled that right out, because Sam was right; she could never be a part of anything like that. She was more than that. I respected her for it. I wanted her for it. I almost hated her for it.

It was always that I *almost* hated her. I could never get past the wanting her. Could never shake her off. Could never find anything about her that made me want her less. The wanting was quickly becoming aching. I didn't want to be like this anymore; constantly thinking about and wanting someone that I couldn't have but who my soul seemed to think was mine.

Christ, now she was just making it worse...she had left her chair and was stretching up to reach the top shelf of one of the filing cabinets, returning some documents. Her top had risen up and the small of her back was showing, flashing me some kind of swirly tattoo. To make it even worse, but at the same time better, I could see the top of her panties...red silk with a band of lace at the top. I was seriously at risk of becoming painfully hard.

"Hey bro." Oh great, Evan's here.

I nodded briefly. It was all I could manage because I knew what was coming next...

"Hey Coach," he greeted Sam, grinning. Most of the commanders were calling her that now, though they said it as a pet name whereas the recruits' said it with an air of respect. She had come a long way with them, completely turned things around.

Her head swivelled, revealing that smile that she always had for him. I wished I could say that I thought she did it to get a rise out of me. But it was so obvious that the smile was authentic. "All right, Ev."

I stiffened. I wasn't sure why it got to me so much when she abbreviated his name like that. Joy seemed much more relaxed now that he was here. No prizes for guessing why. She loosened her hold on my neck, but I still felt like I had a chimp hanging off my body.

Evan stood by Sam's desk, tapping it with his fingers. "I was hoping you'd still be here."

She seemed just as surprised by that as I was. He had never come specifically to see her before. I won't lie, I wanted to punch him.

"I'm just leaving for the arena," she said apologetically as she returned to the desk and tidied the pile of papers on it.

"Actually, that's why I'm here. I was thinking I could come along and watch. I'll sit in the spectators' box out the way and I won't say a word, I swear."

"Aren't you working with your own squad?"

"I decided to give them half the evening off because it's one of the guy's birthdays."

"You're too sweet," – Did she want me to punch *her* too? – "I said I'd let mine leave early if, and only if, they did good. Why the sudden interest in my squad?"

"Well it turns out that, um, some pranks have been getting played on the other squads, particularly mine. The guys swear it's payback from your squad, that a certain telekinetic individual called Harvey was responsible. But I thought they can't possibly be right about that because you've only been training Harvey for, like, a week."

"Huh, weird." There was just as much humour in her voice as in his.

"And now I'm all curious. So, can I?" His grin was charming, he'd get his way.

"All right, but I need a favour from you."

He shrugged. "Whatever you want."

"I'd like to borrow your squad some time to spar with mine. It won't be for another week."

"Do you think they'll really be ready for that?"

"Well you can decide that for yourself, can't you?"

I couldn't bring myself to say anything to his "Later, bro" or her "See you later". At least, not anything that wouldn't be a threat, curse, or insult.

Sam? Hell, I hadn't even meant to call her. The last time I had spoken telepathically to her was when I saw Max flirting with her at the pool. I wasn't expecting a response now, just like I hadn't then — especially since she had continued walking out of the office.

Yep? Forced friendliness.

Now I was going to have to come up with a reason why I had called her. *I'll be coming to watch too.*

I'm surprised you haven't sooner — they're your recruits as well.

Joy grinned at me. "It's only a matter of time."

"What?"

"That's if they're not already."

I sighed. "Joy, when have I ever liked riddles?"

"I was saying it's only a matter of time before those two get together."

A blazing heat of half-anger half-panic shot through me and I felt like I'd explode. No. I couldn't let that happen. I couldn't let them be together. If she was to ever be with Evan for even one night, there would never be any chance of there ever being anything between Sam and me. I couldn't be with someone, for even one night, who had been with my brother. Too weird for me. And the idea of there never being a chance sparked a dull ache in me. All this over a goddamn fuck?

"Are we going up now?" said Joy sweetly.

"You are. I've got somewhere I need to be." I moved so fast around the table that she lost her monkey grip on me.

"Where are you going?"

"Why don't you get the chocolate mousse ready," I suggested in an irritated voice. Not that I had any intention of following her up there.

"It's chocolate *ice cream*."

Oh. Turned out I'd been paying even less attention to her than I'd thought. "That too." I went at vampire speed to the arena, expecting to see Sam and Evan along the way, but it seemed that they had travelled at vampire speed too.

I joined Evan in the front row of the spectators' box. He had his arms folded and a hand holding his chin, intensely interested. So was I. But only in Sam.

"Hey bro, I didn't know you were coming."

I only nodded at him.

He sighed. "Jared, I could be wrong, but I could swear that I'm supposed to have done something, and if I have, I truly have no idea what it is."

I forced a mini smile and patted his back. "I've got a lot on my mind right now." That was true. The upcoming attack on The Hollow's walls wasn't something that just slipped from your brain.

"I'm guessing that it's mostly Sam."

"No," I denied. "Squad stuff."

"Yeah. Right." He shook his head, grinning, before returning his attention to the scene below us.

Sam was pacing in front of the guys, who were all stood side by side in an almost perfectly straight line. None of them were smirking or fidgeting or whistling – which was more than I could say for when they were training with me. Even Damien was focused. Wow, she ran a pretty tight ship. It was when she said the first few words that I realised exactly what they were focusing so much on doing.

(Sam)

"Harvey, there's a tiny bit of excess energy around you, suck it in," I said.

"Yes, Coach." His expression was aggravated, as always. Harvey still hadn't rid himself of his arrogant streak, so he always got touchy whenever he was singled out for one reason or another. For once, however, he didn't grunt before doing as I'd asked. I took that as progress. It was a case of baby steps with Harvey.

"Last session, you each met your goal of channelling all your energy. That's an achievement, but it's not yet the time to do a sing and a dance about it unless you can channel all that energy under pressure. During an attack, you won't be in a nice, quiet arena, secure in your safety, with me right here to tell you if you're doing it right.

You'll be out in the open, you'll be surrounded by stimuli, you'll have enemies hunting you down, and you'll have me to answer to if you don't move your arse."

They each smiled at the latter part, knowing better than to laugh. This was a serious matter and they were expected to treat it seriously.

"So, here's where we get a hint of just how well you'll do. Tonight, we'll be doing two exercises. The first will involve me testing you all individually to see how well and how quickly you can respond to an oncoming threat. I'm sure you'll all be pleased to know that *I* will be that threat," I added, to which they smiled. "I know you'll definitely be pleased to hear that I don't want you to just defend, I want you to attack."

Enthusiasm seeped out of every one of them; they wanted desperately to let go and abuse those powers. Boys and their toys.

A few of them suddenly noticed that the spectators' box wasn't empty tonight. I guessed that there must have been some movement from up there.

"Yes, yes, you have observers. Get over it. Note that my intention in this exercise isn't to hurt you and see how well you can ignore the pain, we'll leave that for another night." More smiles. "During this exercise, all I am interested in is your reaction to an attack. Only if I can be sure that you're handling your gifts as you need to can we move on to the second exercise. All that understood?"

"Yes, Coach!" they shouted soldier-style. Dramatic, but whatever. I thought that they were probably showing off to Evan and Jared. I could swear that Jared's eyes were on me. I had to expel that thought from my mind before becoming self-conscious and losing focus here. But it was hard, especially when only minutes ago he had spoken to me telepathically for the first time in days. Funny how you don't realise you ever liked something until all of a sudden it happened when you weren't expecting it.

Blocking out Jared for now, I moved at vampire speed toward the southern wall, stopping just short of five feet. Letting my body feel part of the ground beneath me as though my feet were roots of a tree, I stood firm and sucked in the natural energy of the Earth. Ready, I then stamped twice with one foot, directing to energy to shape itself in the form of a decent sized boulder which suddenly rose in front of me. It was big, sturdy and bulky enough for each one of them to individually hide behind it one-at-a-time, even tall David.

Returning to my spot near to the northern wall I repeated the action, creating myself an almost identical boulder. I then randomly called out a name.

"Harvey?"

"Coach?" He seemed eager for this. Harvey was eager during most exercises, but not so much enthusiastic...it was that he wanted to prove himself – prove that he didn't need as much coaching as the others did. But all he proved time and time again was what I was already telling him − he was not ready to take on the world yet. But Harvey could nonetheless be reckless and arrogant, which meant he was not the best team player. If he could only get past that, I could properly consider the ideas that he was full of. But until then, as I said before, it was a case of baby steps with him.

"I want you to go to that boulder over there." I gestured with my head to the one at the southern point. "Use it as cover when you need it, but don't hide behind it. Remember, I want you to attack *and* defend. But the intention isn't for anyone to be hurt. Oh, and nobody moves from the boulder unless I allow it."

Harvey wiggled his head as if loosening any tension in his neck, making his black silky hair dance around. "Sure thing, Coach." However, behind that childlike grin laid a hint of mischief. His reckless side might just manifest here. If he believed that hurting me would make him seem power-tastic, that would be exactly what he would do. Then I'd have to twat him.

After I'd ushered the others to gather in the corner of the wall behind me, both Harvey and I stood behind our boulder. Wiggling my fingers, I drew in the energy surrounding me, especially the natural energies and held it in reserve, feeling it thrash about like a caged animal struggling to get free.

I then reached out with my enhanced hearing, listening for any movement from Harvey. He was fidgeting crazily – wouldn't be a good thing in combat as he'd be sounded out immediately. "Harvey, keep your movements to a minimum, remember."

Instead, I've-something-to-prove Harvey attacked first; striving to move the boulder with his telekinesis. Idiot – did he really think I'd build something flimsy? Converting some of the absorbed energy into my beloved silvery-blue whip, I − in the swiftest movement − let half of my body peek around the boulder and cracked the whip at Harvey. He cried out, cursing.

"Don't be a whelp, I didn't whip you hard," I called out. "But I will whip you senseless if you don't give up trying to move the boulder and come up with something else. Come on, where are all those ideas of yours?"

I listened for him again. No movement. Wow, he'd actually listened to me.

I enjoyed the sizzling in my hands as I converted the whip into an energy ball. Vampire-swift again, I peeked around only long enough to fling the ball at the boulder before then retreating behind my own. I knew perfectly well what Harvey would do in response. Sure enough, he used his telekinesis to deviate the energy ball. It crashed into my boulder, but the mound didn't crumble.

"Oh come on, you can do better than that!" I told him. "Stop trying to attack the boulder, that's not what has a power to fling at you. If an enemy is really that intent on finding cover, they'll simply find something else if you *do* manage to damage their cover."

Again I threw an energy ball, but this time I kept my eye on Harvey. I then watched as he levitated the ball up into the air and then sent it zooming down, hoping to catch me behind the boulder. Instantly I called on my energy shield, which made the ball rebound and hit the wall.

"Better!" I told him as I held up a hand as a gesture that the exercise was over. We both then came out from behind our boulder.

"Oh Coach, I was just getting into it," he complained.

"Sorry, but I've got nine other people to get through before we can move on to the next exercise. Did you not want to get out of the session early tonight...?"

His frown was replaced by a grin. "You'll really let us?"

"I already told you that I will – *if* you all do good. David, you're next."

As I'd expected, David did excellently. He waited patiently for his chance, and then peeked out and sent a psionic blast from his fingertips – my shield stopped the blast before it got to me. He was extremely pleased with himself because the nervousness that he had originally felt while handling his gift – not knowing exactly how to control the strength of the blast – had all but gone. I knew that because the youngest had done so well at the exercise, all the other recruits would now try harder; not wanting the youngest to do better than them.

I then challenged Salem. His psychic punch wasn't all that dissimilar from David's blast, however Salem didn't wait for an opening as David had – he didn't have David's patience. Instead, violence-lover Salem repeatedly tried penetrating my shield. Ballsy, but stupid. The psychic punch ricocheted both times and he narrowly avoided it, cursing 'Fucker' at the punch each time. His fumbling around gave me the opening I needed, and pretty soon a gush of water sent him sliding backwards toward the wall. He didn't care – the adrenalin was pumping, so he was happy. Learning from his mistake, however, he took a leaf out of David's book and waited for his chance. Soon enough, he got his opening. My shield protected me, of course, or I'd have been unconscious on the floor.

Damien did a lot better at the task than I'd been expecting. He peeped out one side, then the other and then above, but it turned out that he was tricking the shit out of me. In fact, it was his astral self that had peeped out – meaning that his physical body was safe and sound. If he did that during an attack, he could keep his body safe while still baiting the enemy.

Next was Chico. As his aim still needed to be improved on, he couldn't emit the thorns from his hands without actually having a visual of where I was. It took a few tries, but he eventually got his opening – again my shield came in handy. He wasn't too pleased when I used a teensy bolt of fire to singe his moustache, but it served to make him concentrate better on *me* rather than on the fact that everyone was watching him. His fear was exhibiting weakness, because he was kind of like the alpha of the squad. I could empathise slightly.

Denny farted some musk at me, the sod. So I zapped his butt with an energy blast. After that, he decided that taking his eyes off me was a bad idea and took to becoming mush every time I attacked. This aggravated me, though, because he wasn't using his full potential; he needed to realise that 'attacking' was just as important as 'defending', so I sent his mushy form swirling around using a nice gush of water. He got the point that being mush wouldn't necessarily protect him and then began spraying ooze at me.

As Reuben's gift depended on physical contact, I allowed him to leave his boulder and try to reach me. Even with my taking it easy on him he didn't get the hang of it, because he was too busy concentrating on dodging my gifts to concentrate on *my* movements and pre-empt where I was going. As he believed that it wasn't possible for him to pre-empt me and reach me, I absorbed some of his energy to temporarily give me his gift. I then had Denny repeatedly spray ooze at me so that I could show Reuben how focusing on an enemy's movements would both help him pre-empt their movements and notice when an enemy was about to attack with their gift. It took under thirty seconds for me to physically touch Denny, which made Reuben more optimistic. I also suggested that maybe he could tie back his lovely brown shoulder-length hair so it did not disturb his vision.

Butch did well with negating anything I flung at him. But when he got a little cocky and kept flashing that crooked grin of his, challenging me with those unbelievably dark eyes, I put more force behind one of my fire blasts to illustrate to him that he couldn't negate everything and would need to learn to bring up his shield better. We had practiced this last session, but Butch had only managed to do it once. Not because he wasn't a capable person or in very good control of his gift, but because Butch was only just getting used to the idea that he could use his defensive negating power in different ways.

Max was absolutely delighted when I called him up. He was extremely chuffed with his gift and kept promising me that one day he'd rob me of my senses and then kiss me hard, to which he received a small punch in the gut. Each time I felt him reaching out, I popped my shield up, however I was impressed by how well he was able to dodge my gift. His agility had dramatically improved, which he owed to Jared's training.

God, Jared. I hadn't once forgotten that he was up there. I couldn't. Not when those eyes were drilling into me. I daren't look up at him in case my brain shut off for a second; that's what it felt like would happen if we made proper eye contact for the first time in days.

Out of all of the recruits, Stuart was the least enthusiastic. Mainly because he was still sore about not being able to do much else other than shred. He was sometimes able to explode into molecules before my gift hit him. But the *almost* part pissed him off. As did the fact that he was finding it extremely difficult to move from place to place as molecules. But he did move a step. Progress.

"You all did good," I told them. "Good enough to move on to the second exercise. I'm going to ask you all to line up; five of you against the eastern wall, the other five at the western wall. I want at least three car-spaces between each of you."

"Yes, Coach," was said in unison.

Without delay, they found themselves a spot. Chico, Butch, David, Denny, and Stuart lined up against the eastern wall while the others stood against the western wall. Damien was facing Chico, Salem was facing Butch, Reuben was facing David, Harvey was facing Denny, and Max was facing Stuart.

Pacing between the lines of blokes, I spoke. "Take a good look at who's opposite you. Remember everything you can about their gifts, because in a moment those gifts will be heading right at you." As I'd anticipated, there was some discomfort in the lines. I'd never set them against each other before. "I'll shout your names individually. As soon as you hear it, I want you to do your thing. And I want you to do it fast. Because that's what it will be like out there: me barking your name or an order, and you acting without hesitation. If you panic now, if you buckle under *this* pressure, then you know you've got some learning left to do.

"Do *not* turn this into a spar. Only when I shout your name do you act. Those who have a gift coming at you, block it if you can, or dodge it. But do not retaliate. That all understood?"

"Yes, Coach."

Turning and pacing back the way I'd come, I added, "You'll remember that your second goal was to memorise as much as you can about the gifts of the rest of your squad. This exercise should also give you an idea of just how near, or far, you are to that goal. Right, first I need Reuben to weaken Max, Chico and Salem's powers."

"Coach," obeyed Reuben. He touched each of them for only three seconds. Then his face twisted in confusion. "Coach, what about David?"

"Well David's who you're facing in the line-up. You'll get your chance to weaken him when I call you – but you're going to need to do it in quicker than three seconds. An enemy won't let you hold onto their shoulder and wait. For anyone who can move at vampire speed, three seconds is more like ten."

"Coach," he said, bowing his head, before then scooting back to his spot.

Once I was back at my own spot against the northern wall, I let a moment of silence drag on. This served two purposes. One: it created a hint of the suspense that they could expect during an attack, and two: my call would sound exceptionally loud against the heavy silence. While some of them stood tall and still, others shuffled their weight from foot to foot, and others were repeatedly clenching their hands.

I was terribly proud to see that each and every one of them was doing the one thing that I had instructed them to in past sessions: they were keeping their eyes on their opponent.

"Chico!"

At the sound of his name, Chico abruptly lifted one hand and shot out several thorns from his palm. They embedded themselves in Damien's chest, which would have made him cry out in pain at the sting had he not astral projected a few feet away in less than the time it took to blink – a handy way to dodge.

Without missing a beat, I called out, "Salem!"

Fixed where he stood, the blond vampire threw an uppercut toward Butch. I could see the ripple in the air that the psychic energy had produced as it flew from Salem. More determined than I had ever seen him, Butch placed his hands in front of his chest, palms out. The effect was like watching the sun shine on glass. The boom hit the flat, glass-like shield and collapsed to the ground.

"Harvey!"

Wearing a cocky grin, Harvey made a quick movement that resembled someone throwing a small ball upwards – I guessed he intended on sending Denny levitating upwards. Before the impact could hit Denny, he instantly liquidised into green mush. Two seconds later, he was himself again. Harvey made an animal tssssk noise in frustration.

"Max!"

He always wore the same tough-bloke expression when he was reaching out to paralyse someone's senses – his eyes would narrow, his mouth would twist, and his eyebrows would dip. With the simple gesture of closing his open hand, he attempted to temporarily quash Stuart's senses. But Stuart had literally exploded into molecules – nice dodging! Resembling quickly, he flashed Max a smug grin.

"Reuben!"

Ooh, good ole Reub was nervous. I would be too if I knew that David's power would shortly be heading for me. God that bloke was fast: vampire speed had him at David in under a second. He touched his shoulder briefly before returning to his spot.

"David!"

David, standing tall and determined, exhaled heavily and splayed his fingers. The blast rushed toward Reuben, who was frozen — there was simply no way to dodge David's gift. Every one of us watched intently, hoping that Reuben had successfully weakened it enough for the impact to feel merely like a thump over the head. If Reuben hadn't weakened it enough, he'd end up unconscious. If he had accidentally strengthened the blast...he would die.

I think all of us released a brief sigh of relief when Reuben simply flinched and brought his hand to his head. I didn't give them time to celebrate, though.

"Stuart!"

This was the big test for Stuart. I watched as he stiffened and then, like before, exploded. I continued to watch as the molecules rushed toward the vampire opposite him. Max jerked backwards as Stuart, in under a second, reassembled in front of him. "Hi there," he said to Max, winking. He had every reason to be chuffed with himself.

"Denny!"

I wondered if Denny might use his anal musk on Harvey. It wasn't that he didn't like him, but Harvey picked on David a lot – who happened to be Denny's best friend. Instead, Denny flexed his hands, making them appear more like claws, and then sprayed yellow-green ooze from his thumbs and little fingers. The times when he attacked were the only moments that his baby face looked, in any way, threatening. The ooze was sturdy and stringy, wrapping around Harvey like a web in spite of his telekinetic efforts to divert it – there was just too much of it. Denny's dimply smile surfaced instantly.

"Butch!"

Knowing what I wanted him to do, Butch placed his hands in front of his chest, palms out, in the same way that he had before. This time, instead of leaving them there he forcefully extended his arms in front of him and spread them to the side, pushing his invisible shield outwards and surrounding himself with it.

"Chico, David, Salem – get him now!"

Thorns, a psionic blast, and a psychic punch came at Butch from different directions...but all of it hit the shield.

Last but not least...

"Damien!"

I was very surprised when he didn't hesitate or lick his lips nervously. This was the first time I had seen him sure of himself. He blinked hard and then, suddenly, his astral self was lounging on the floor in front of Chico, chuckling.

With that, the eyes of every recruit concentrated on me, all of them keen to jump for joy but desperately wanting my approval first. I made them sweat by keeping silent a few seconds. "*Now* you can do a sing and a dance," I said with a smile.

They practically did. Some bounced on the spot, arms shot up toward the sky, and I heard plenty of celebratory noises.

Then they were all heading toward me.

"Oh no, you don't," I warned them, one finger pointed at them. They appeared to be ignoring it, however, as they were still coming at me. "Don't you dare!" Too late. I was scooped up by Reuben and hung over his shoulder while he bounced. "This is a bit dramatic!"

I ended up with some of Denny's ooze that had been dripping from Harvey now in my hair. Not so happy about that.

I heard cheering and clapping from the spectators' box. I looked up. Evan was smiling and clapping. He was also alone.

"I don't know what to say," Evan said as he reached me and we began a slow walk out of the arena. The recruits were still celebrating their glory further on ahead of us, heading to their apartment block by the looks of things.

"You could say something flattering," I suggested light-heartedly.

"I just...I never expected them to be in such control. It took my squad a long time before they reached that point. Don't take that the wrong way, I'm not saying that I didn't think you were capable—"

I interrupted before he tripped over his words. "It's all right. I know what you were trying to say."

"I've got to ask: you've been around my squad, right? Did you pick up any excess energy around them?"

I bit my bottom lip. "Yeah," I finally admitted. "And there's a little around you too, if I'm honest."

"Really?" He looked mortified, though he was smiling. "I guess you'll have to give me and my squad a lesson some time. You know, you're a good coach. I take it you had a good coach to pick that up from."

My smile faded. "Not exactly. So did Jared decide not to stay and watch?"

"He stayed to the end but then scampered pretty quickly; said he had somewhere to be." His tone suggested he hadn't believed that excuse. "Have you two had a falling out or something?"

"Jared and I have never had a friendship to fall out of. Even our business relationship is beyond strained. Antonio employing me hurt his ego. You must know how your brother cherishes that ego."

There was silence for a moment. "I don't think it's just that."

"You mean the fact that I 'wouldn't let him screw me', as you so aptly put it during your telepathic conversation with him."

His cheeks reddened. "I can't believe you heard that. Jared said absorbing some of his energy must have made you tune into it. He wouldn't say much about the absorbing his energy part." His tone was probing.

"There's nothing to tell. I was in a bad way after killing Victor, and Jared let me absorb some of his energy." I shrugged as if to emphasise the simplicity of it all.

"Well that confirms my suspicions."

"Suspicions?"

"Jared doesn't give anyone anything, let alone his energy. Like I said before, I don't think his problem is just a wounded ego. I think he likes you — a lot, actually."

I gave him a doubtful look. "I fail to see how you could make that conclusion when he barely speaks or looks at me. He asked me to join his consort collection, yeah, but that's just about sex. He's been sulking ever since I said no."

Evan pointed a finger at me. "But, see, that's the thing with Jared. Although he thought he had at one time, he's never truly liked a woman in more than a physical sense, so he doesn't know how to handle it. He just knows that he wants you, and he probably thinks that if he screws you it'll all make sense."

"So you're attuned to him, are you," I mocked playfully.

"When we were human, we were really close. There wasn't a part of his life that I didn't know about, and vice versa. We did almost everything together."

"What changed?"

"Jared." He didn't say it with bitterness or even disappointment, but understanding. "As soon as he was made Heir, he totally changed. He loved the attention, the respect, the rewards, and the power that came with it all."

"So he forgot about you, kind of left you behind?"

"Oh no, nothing like that. He wanted me to live the high life with him. He had the power to give it to me, he had the girls to share...but I wasn't interested. He never took it personally, he respected that I didn't want that kind of life, even though he didn't understand why."

"You *are* a bit of an enigma."

"I am?" He sounded amused.

"I get that power and attention isn't what you feel you need in life. But everybody feels that they need something; little or big. And yet you just plod along, but always smiling. Even though you've never been short of offers from women, you've turned them down – although I'm told that in the very beginning, you were almost as bad as Jared. I've never once seen you even harmlessly flirt with anyone. Should I assume that there was a woman from your human life who you can't forget?"

He smiled, scrutinising my face. I got the idea that he was wondering how much or how little to say on the subject, whether or not he could trust me. I tried to assure him with my smile that he could.

Finally he made a puffing sound and sat down on the lawn outside the rear of the mansion. "You know Luther has visions, right?" he asked. I nodded and sat beside him. "Has Antonio ever asked you if you wanted to have one via Luther?"

"Yeah. I didn't understand it, though."

"In mine I was in the rainforest, and I was waiting really anxiously for someone; worried they were in danger. Then Jared and two women appeared, and I almost collapsed in relief. One of them had blazing red hair and pale blue eyes and the most amazing smile you've ever seen. My emotions in the vision weren't very clear, but I could feel that she was mine. Since then, I couldn't bring myself to be with another woman, it would have felt like I was being unfaithful. That might sound weird."

"No, no it doesn't at all. You're waiting for her. It's really sweet."

"After time just kept dragging on and she never showed, I was starting to think that maybe she was never going to. That maybe I'd made some sort of decision somewhere along the line that had changed the future. But then you came, and you can't imagine how much optimism flowed through me."

"What do you mean?"

"You were the other woman in my vision. You and Jared brought her to me."

My eyebrows jumped up. "Oh."

He laughed. "Yeah, *oh*."

Well I really didn't know how I felt about that.

"Spooked?" he asked, amused.

"Sort of. You've never told Jared about her," I realised.

"He wouldn't understand." He was so close to Jared and yet so far apart. It made me sad. "I knew that if I told him, he'd laugh about it and say she must be a really good screw for me to feel that way. I didn't want to hear that, I didn't want him to taint it."

"Don't worry. I'm not going to tell him, or anyone else."

"I know." It was said with utter confidence and trust. "You know that Jared's a little unhappy about how much we talk and stuff, don't you?"

"My guess is he's worried you'll manage to get in my pants when he couldn't. That would be a huge blow to his ego."

Evan laughed. "Yeah, it certainly would."

"But I've never once felt like you were coming onto me."

"In my vision, I could feel that I was relieved you were okay. That I cared about you just like a sister, the sister I never had. And I do, already."

"And I think of you as a brother."

His expression was so cheery. I guessed that hearing me say I felt that way was making everything click into place for him, giving him even more optimism that this girl would soon be in his life.

"You didn't say the brother you *never* had. So you had a brother? Any sisters?"

"Nope. My mum and dad were workaholics; totally obsessed with the business they ran that didn't even make any money. They barely had time for me, let alone any other kids. I was a big disappointment to them because I wasn't driven to follow in their footsteps and join the crappy family business. I have to say, though, it seems like an appealing future now…but no sense in dwelling.

"Hey, you've done okay for yourself in your new life. So far you've got the big job, the flashy apartment, the hefty salary. All that's missing is the husband. Anyone wanting to be your husband would either have to be incredibly turned on by being challenged, or quite content to be submissive in every way."

"The latter wouldn't be interesting."

"Well I know of one person who fits the first."

"Say your brother's name and I'll whip you senseless."

"I was going to say Max," he laughed. "I'm not going to root for Jared when I know what he wants is for you to be a consort, you're better than that."

"That's what *I* said." It was nice to hear someone tell me that there had been reason and rhyme to my choice. After the way Jared had overreacted, I had occasionally wondered if I was being fussy or stupid, because whether I was his consort or just a casual shag, the result was still the same; sex and nothing else.

Of course Fletcher had supported my position, but he also believed that I needed a good one-off shag to burn off all the aggression and horniness. As such, he wasn't all that bothered who that shag was, even if it was Jared. If Jared's own brother thought he was being idiotic, then maybe I wasn't being as harsh as Jared thought.

CHAPTER NINE

(Sam)

The hammering at my apartment door switched my posture to confrontational. I could only think of one person who would be so pissed off with me that he would knock like the rent man. But when I swung the door open, my face a mask of aggravation, I was met with a scene that I would never have guessed at.

"Coach!" crooned Denny.

"Hey," greeted Stuart.

"I was kind of hoping we'd got you at a bad time – like a *naked* time." Typical Harvey. Max dug an elbow into Harvey's ribs, who grunted.

"What're you all doing here?" I asked.

"Coming to get you," said Max as if it was obvious. "All of us are going down to the Barcelona bar, and you're coming with us."

"Isn't the Barcelona a 'men only' bar?"

"Tonight was a big achievement for us, and we couldn't have done it without all your training. We're going out to celebrate, you're our Coach, and so you're coming with us." Max had said it like it was a mathematical equation.

"I'm not sure whether I should be offended that you see me as one of the boys."

"Don't tell us you don't want to get out of this apartment for one night," said Denny.

"We could always carry you there..." Max let the idea taunt me.

"You wouldn't dare," I said.

Max arched a brow. "Wouldn't I? I've told you before, you have your authority during training, but when we're on our time it means squat." He made a move toward me.

"Okay, okay, I'll go, I'll go," I said quickly.

Max gave me a curious look, as if he couldn't understand why I had caved so easily. The answer? I was naked under my nightgown. Not that I thought Max would cart me all the way to the bar in just my nightgown, but he would certainly pick me up just to prove the point that he was willing to do that if push came to shove.

So I got dressed. I didn't put much thought into it really. I just stepped into the black halter-neck dress and the matching shoes that Fletcher had picked, and then slipped on some fashion jewellery. With my hair left loose, I stepped out into the hallway. All of the squad were stood waiting. Each one stared and swallowed hard. Poor buggers didn't have many female vampires around them on a regular basis.

I couldn't really understand why they wanted to go to an all-male bar as I'd always thought that part of the fun for blokes was to get themselves a girl. Denny explained that the drinks were cheapest at that bar, so they always went there first to get hammered and then they'd move on to the unisex bars.

I didn't have any trouble getting in the bar; one look at my cleavage and the sound of the word 'Coach' and the fact that I was female faded into nonexistence for the doormen. The inside was actually all right. It looked more like a club with its strobe lights, packed dance-floor and booming music. Despite it being chocker, it was easy enough to get a drink since the bar was eternally long.

Max stayed close, a hand always on my elbow or my back. Chico repeatedly rolled his eyes at the sight, as if Max was trying too hard and making himself look desperate. I didn't see it that way. Max was trying hard, sure, but what he was trying hard at was to show me that there could be a completely different relationship between us outside of work hours; that it wouldn't make anything awkward. I wasn't sure if the fact that I didn't want anything more than casual sex would be a let-down for him or the biggest turn-on ever. I wasn't sure if I wanted to find out.

I was overjoyed when I came across Fletcher and Norm. Tonight they had been again colourful in their choice of clothes.

Fletcher hugged me tightly. "How the bleeding hell did you get in here, it's men only? Me and Norm just about get in."

"How do you think I got in?" I gave my boobs a little push.

Fletcher laughed. "I told you a bit of cleavage works wonders, didn't I?"

"It certainly works for me," said a voice into my ear. Max.

"Hey Coach," sang another voice. Evan. He assessed the dress and frowned playfully, giving me the 'big brother' look. "I should send you home to get some clothes on."

"Oh I *beg* you not to do that," said Harvey. "The view is perfect."

Evan shot him a warning look. "Note that she is much too good for you."

"Harvey's right, though, she looks absolutely gorgeous," said Fletcher. "The only girl who has ever tempted me to go straight."

Max ushered me closer, but I shrugged him off. "Sorry, Slaphead, but I'm going."

"Where?" he asked, deflating.

"To the dance-floor, of course. And anyone here who isn't on that dance-floor won't see me all night."

"Don't think you're leaving me behind," said Fletcher.

At first I was surprised that the entire squad came to the dance-floor with me, but after a while I realised it was because I was getting approached by a lot of blokes since I was the only female in there. Evan's warning gaze served as a great deterrent to the would-be-drink-offering-blokes as well.

I was dancing with Max when Evan spoke down my ear, "You probably won't be pleased to know that Jared's here."

My heart did a little jump at the sound of his name. Maybe it was faulty. "I don't care. He can go where he pleases; it's nothing to do with me."

"Do you realise that that's near enough the same thing he said to me telepathically that night when you eavesdropped?"

I spun on my heel, giggling but offended. "I did not eavesdrop." In truth, I hadn't turned so that I could jokingly confront Evan. I wanted to get an idea of where Jared was. My senses reached out, alerting me that he was somewhere to my right near the bar. And not happy.

"I was just letting you know he's here."

I knew what he meant: be aware that Jared's here and tone it down with Max or Jared might snap. I'd have disagreed, but Jared had told me telepathically that I'd saved Max's life by saying no to him, though I never really understood why he was so mental over a bonk.

"Look," began Evan, "maybe you should pretend you're going to the bar for a drink and let him approach you."

"Why would I do that?"

"Because I can feel that he's riled."

So could I. That was the thing that got to me: I shouldn't be able to sense his emotions so well. "It's not my fault that Antonio wants me to lead the squad alongside Jared. I told Antonio I didn't want to, he made it clear that it was an order."

"So let Jared approach you, let him bring it up, and then tell him that. Let him get it off his chest."

"Why should I reassure the plonker?"

Evan sighed. "Please, Sam?" He very rarely called me that. "Yeah he's a pain in the ass sometimes, but he's also my twin brother. Maybe once he's got it off his chest, you two can start behaving civilly to each other again…you know, like grown-ups do?"

I couldn't help smiling at that. I supposed it wasn't very mature to snub your colleague when you have to see them and work with them every day. Plus, if we didn't somehow sort this out, how would we ever successfully lead the squad together? How could we ever protect The Hollow the way we were required to?

Evan kissed my cheek when I sighed in defeat. I then left it to Evan to keep Max out of the way while we tested this theory that Jared had something to say. As Evan suggested, I went to the bar and ordered a drink. I then leaned my back against the bar as if having a brief rest, and kept my gaze forward as I sipped on the red grape NST. Only moments later I felt Jared approaching. Felt his eyes, felt his annoyance…and God that scent.

"I never thought you'd manage to pass as a guy." His humour didn't disguise his irritation very well.

"I never thought you'd manage to gain entry either, considering you have to be an adult. Sulking is more a toddler thing." I heard him take a long breath. It pleasantly tickled my skin as he exhaled.

"The squad was impressive at the arena."

There was a slight emphasis on the word squad — the interpretation being that he believed it was them that deserved the glory, not me. I didn't rise to that. The fact was they had been impressive, and they wouldn't have been unless they had listened well and tried hard. I was proud of them and I wouldn't take that away from them.

"I've noticed that they're improving physically too," I said. "Especially Max. You're obviously training them right."

He hissed slightly on hearing Max's name. "You sound surprised that I am."

I hadn't sounded surprised at all. My tone had been completely flat. I realised then that he was trying to get an argument out of me. Oh he wanted to get things off his chest all right, but he wanted to argue while he did it.

"Antonio thinks highly of you, so why would I be surprised?"

"Antonio thinks highly of you, but I was surprised tonight."

"Like you said, the squad was impressive."

Another long, heavy breath. "Look at me." It was said softly.

So I looked at him and, as I'd earlier expected might happen, my brain clapped out for a second. It had felt like so long since we'd actually properly made eye contact. He was doing his shameless staring thing again. I didn't look away this time, but I couldn't help that my pulse was racing madly.

"Antonio must have told you that he wants you to help me lead the squad when The Hollow is attacked."

I nodded. "He did."

"But you never brought it up? I thought you'd have been dying to throw it into conversation and tease me about it."

"Then you don't know me very well." I had taken it as Antonio thinking I was good at what I did, not that he thought that Jared was crap.

"So tell me why you didn't bring it up."

"We weren't exactly having conversations that anything could have been brought up in. And, besides, I had a pretty good idea of how that conversation would go, especially since Antonio had admitted that you weren't happy about it."

"I don't think I need you as co-leader."

"Ooh, now that's a shocker right there," I said sarcastically. "Antonio ordered it; it's out of my control. You can confront me, or sulk, or whatever else, but none of it will change that. Talk to Antonio." I looked away from him again.

"Why is it you can't seem to look at me for long without squirming or turning away?" he said tauntingly. "Surely you're not feeling self-conscious." His tone dared me to object.

My peripheral vision alerted me to the fact that he had taken a slow step toward me, leaving only one step between us. I watched as his eyes drifted to my lips a few times. Yes, I'll admit my libido thought this was great and I was tempted to give his lips a look or two…or even a kiss or two. I was also tempted to put more space between us. I did neither. "Trying to aggravate Max, are you?" No doubt he was glaring at us.

"I don't give a shit about Max." He said it in a way that implied that there was something else he gave a shit about.

"So then you just want to make me feel uncomfortable, you want to aggravate me. Come as close as you want, it won't work." He did come closer, which I hadn't actually expected him to do. My body was now pining for him, aching even more because he was close enough to touch and I was doing nothing about it.

He looked pleased with himself, so I gathered he'd picked up on it – maybe by the fact that I'd stiffened a little and clenched my fists. "So, you were saying it won't work…"

I turned so that I was facing him, and covered a little of the space left between us. Oh he was taken aback. Good. My tone and posture and expression were all confrontational. "I can't work out what I did that's pissed you off this much. You certainly want to get me just as riled as you are, and you're wasting no time at all in doing it. Just tell me, Jared." I placed my face even closer to his. "Be a big boy and tell me what it is that's really making you be a prick."

His irises began to glow red. But he didn't look angry. "Don't push me, Sam, or I swear to God I'll kiss you right here, right now with everyone around to watch, and we both know you won't stop me."

Why did disputing get this bloke horny? "I won't stop you?" I probably wouldn't, actually. I doubted I'd be able to. As soon as his lips touched mine, the same thing always happened: fire.

"No." His eyes dropped to my lips again. "And I seriously doubt that your boyfriend will like it. Does he know we've kissed before? Twice?"

"What's up, Jared? Worried one of your recruits might just get to shag me while you can't? That's a worryingly big ego you have there." I demolished the remainder of my NST, plonked the empty bottle on the bar and went to walk away. His hand seized my wrist. His grip was possessive, and my traitorous body sort of liked it.

"I'm not finished."

"Take your hand off me or I'll snap it off."

He snorted. "I'm not hurting you, you probably like it." Plonker. "I want you to stop leading my brother on."

All right that was the last thing I had expected to hear, hence why my response was, "Say again?"

"Evan's not like me." Too right he wasn't, that was why Evan and I got along so well. "When he likes a woman, he wants the whole thing. Seeing as you're not interested in a relationship with anyone, all you're doing is leading him on."

"You think you're brother and me are interested in each other?"

His jaw went tight. "Don't be cute with me, Sam. It's obvious with the amount of time you spend with him."

"You should try it some time."

"Meaning what exactly?"

"Meaning that he's your brother, your twin, and you're barely a part of his life. I know more about what's going in his life than you do."

"I don't need advice about my brother from you, all right. Now stop trying to change the subject. I won't watch while you lead him on, not when he likes you."

I half-snorted half-chuckled. "Do you know that what you've just said adds further support to the argument that you don't know anything about what goes on in his life?" I went to walk away again, but although I'd tugged hard to free my wrist, he'd tugged harder to keep it.

He was speaking so close to my ear that he was almost nibbling on it. "You can wander off back to Max and Evan, but we both know that you don't really want either of them. You think that's fair to Evan? Or to Max? I wonder what they'd think if they knew about our little encounters."

I snickered and faced him again. "If you honestly thought that having this little info that we'd kissed gave you some power, then you're thick as pig shit. It gives you nothing. Just because I haven't told them doesn't mean I care if they know. If you really want to find out what Evan and Max would think, go ahead and tell them. Better still, we'll go together." I grabbed his free hand with mine and pulled. "Come on, let's see what they say."

I could almost sense Jared's ego screaming at him not to back down. Jared eventually listened to it – typical. He released my seized wrist and allowed me to pull him with my other hand to the dancefloor where Max and Evan stood amongst the rest of the squad, Fletcher and Norm.

"Hey," greeted Evan, smiling. "Everything sorted between you two now?"

"What was all that about?" Max asked me discreetly.

I looked to Jared, daring him to tell them, totally unconcerned if they knew.

"I can't have my bro and my honorary little sister fighting," said Evan, ruffling my hair exactly like a brother would.

Jared's expression suddenly changed. His eyes danced between Evan and me, studying us, as if truly seeing us together for the first time. Realisation of the truth seemed to hit him, and then he nodded. "It's sorted." His smile faded slightly when his glance slid to Max.

Max, being Max, moved slightly closer to me and grinned at Jared sort of evilly. Then he said to me, "I thought I saw him grab you...?"

Jared, having heard, laughed. "You don't need to worry. I'd never hurt her. We just like to play rough, don't we?" I would have responded with a sour scowl but his crooked smile just made me want to laugh. Evan seemed amused too. "Getting my ass kicked by Sam is my idea of foreplay, and she's very good at foreplay."

Jared might have thought he was being clever, but he'd misjudged Max; rather than being discouraged, Max attached himself to me. Any closer and he'd have passed for my Siamese twin. At first Jared had seemed agitated by it, but then he took to repeatedly saying things down my ear – inconsequential things that could have even been said telepathically, but it was all part of winding Max up. It seemed that Jared was intent on making Max either storm off in frustration or snap. He did neither. The more something became a challenge for Max, the more he wanted it. They weren't actually all that different.

Chico had been watching Max cling to me all night and got increasingly annoyed about it to the point where he came over and said something to Max about needing his help with an extremely drunk Butch. Being the good friend that he was, Max left my side to help with Butch – a little hesitant, but still he went. Chico winked and nodded at me. I gave him an appreciative smile. It was nice to have some breathing room.

"Here's my darlin' girl," said Fletcher as he approached with Norm. Standing behind me and holding onto my shoulders, he asked, "So, who will you be shagging tonight?"

I almost choked on my drink. "Say again?"

"Oh come on, you can't tell me you're not horned-up to death. I can sense it coming off you like fumes."

"Max will definitely be up for it," said Norm.

Fletcher nodded. "The way he's glued his body to you all night, he practically has shagged you."

"Sam's got a complex about being someone's consort," said Jared, not seeming to like the topic of conversation.

"Doesn't mean she can't have one of her own," insisted Fletcher with a giggle. He squeezed my shoulders. "Or just a nice jump to keep you going for another week."

A jump with Max sounded good to my body, but not good enough. It completely ached for someone else. However, with Jared not being an option that meant a night with Max was on the cards. Why did the idea of it make me feel off inside? "I need alcohol," I told Fletcher. "None of these alcohol flavoured NSTs, I need real alcohol."

"Good idea," he said. "It'll settle your body a bit and then you won't end up assaulting the bloke." Fletcher patted my upper arm and then disappeared, returning seconds later with one gorgeous, muscled, brown-haired human who had several teeth marks in him. Drinking blood from intoxicated people was how we vampires got drunk. "Here we are."

The bloke looked at me and grinned. "A Sventé? I haven't been bitten by a Sventé in years. I'm going to enjoy this."

Well of course he would. Our saliva did a good job of getting our prey all hot and bothered and could make them orgasm on the spot if we drank from them for more than ten seconds.

"You'll have to hold my hands still," he told me, high on anticipation.

"Why?" snorted Jared.

"Because it's that good, I'll end up fondling her if she doesn't. I'm used to getting bitten and standing the pleasure, but when it's a Sventé bite there's no way of keeping still."

I grabbed his hands and held them firmly behind his back. I was more or less embracing him. Although some vampires were content to drink from the same bite mark that others had made, I wasn't. It was like sharing a cup that had been passed around a load of strangers. Not for me, thanks. As I ran my lips down the curve of his neck, he shuddered. Content with a certain spot on his neck, I paused.

A vampire bite was a lot like a kiss; there were different styles. For instance, there was the firm bite; clamping the eyeteeth abruptly down and making the suction fast, hard and greedy. Then there was the softer approach; tenderly popping the skin with the tips of the eyeteeth and then feeling the blood rush into your mouth, keeping the suction gentle and slow. Of course there was also a bite that was somewhere between the firm and the soft style that some vampires preferred to do.

My personal favourite was a style I'd developed myself. First I nicked the skin with my eyeteeth, which tickled the human, and then I lapped up any blood that surfaced. It was more or less teasing, but Sventés were like that. Then I always did a double bite; letting one of my eyeteeth pierce the skin slightly first, and then sliding them both down into the neck.

When I nicked his neck, the human instantly quivered. Then he felt the double bite and moaned in pleasure. I hadn't even started sucking yet. When I did, gulping slow but taking long pulls, his arms strained against my hold and he tried grinding against me. I had to ensure to keep it shorter than ten seconds or else I'd probably make him come in his pants – something that wouldn't be great for either of us. Not right here, right now anyway.

Opening my eyes as I began to draw back from him, I noticed that Jared was watching intently. The human wasn't so easy to shake off so Evan and Jared helped.

He shook his head as if clearing his foggy thoughts and smiled. "It's on the house. I'll come back later."

I returned his smile. "You do that." When I turned my focus back to the vampires around me, I found four sets of eyes fixed on me, two glinting red, and two glinting amber. "What?"

Fletcher swallowed hard then said to Norm, "Now I'm even more curious."

The others nodded, and suddenly I understood. "None of you have ever been bitten by a Sventé? Oh come on, you can't be serious."

"You're a Sventé so you travelled in Sventé circles, none of us did," explained Evan.

"There has to be some Sventés here."

"Only a few," said Fletcher. "Antonio and Luther have them as consorts."

The curiosity was still shining from their eyes. Their mouths were twisting to the side and they seemed to be debating whether to say something, looking to each other for cues.

"You want me to bite you?" I asked all of them. Their smiles and arched brows all said 'hell yes'. "You can all sod off. I'm not biting any of you."

"Why not?" whined Fletcher.

"Because it would turn you all on."

"That's *why* we want you to do it," said Norm, sounding horny already.

I grimaced. "I am not biting my best friend, my best friend's boyfriend, someone who I consider a brother, or my co-worker who I have to work close with every day." Suddenly my head felt a little heavy and I almost swayed. Oh yes, I was now tipsy! It'd been a while. A hand caught my elbow. Oh, I *had* swayed. It was Jared's hand. My body automatically reacted, pining for him again, and I found myself automatically clenching my thighs. I had to move away from his touch, and now.

I did. But his hand only moved to my back as if ready and waiting to steady me again if necessary. Making matters a gazillion times worse, he spoke down my ear again, close enough that he was nibbling on it as he spoke. I just about managed to hold back a shudder.

"You've got the Dutch courage now. Shall I go get Max?" His tongue lightly flicked my earlobe. "Or are you ready to admit that it's not him you really want?" Discretely his hand teasingly travelled slowly and lightly down to the small of my back, fingers splayed.

Oh God. Another shudder began to crest. I tried holding it back, but a tremor still ventured through me. Jared felt it and chuckled softly. It wasn't so much the contact that was causing the shudders. It was more to do with the fact that it was Jared who was touching me.

Desperate for some kind of distraction, I glanced around the club; concentrating on how bright the flashing, colourful lights were, and how drunk humans were prancing about waiting to be bitten, and how—

Oh my God. The sight my eyes found made my brain fail for a second. My cheeks and hands burned — something they always did when I was irate. My breathing became short pants as I felt the anger swirl around my lungs. The contents of my stomach curdled and my pulse was practically out of control.

Familiar voices were talking to me, but my brain didn't interpret the words; every part of me was far too fixated on the spectacle before me. Approximately eight feet away from me, dancing and laughing like he had a right to walk the Earth, was someone I never thought I'd see again. Someone I swore to one day find. And now he had more or less fallen in my lap.

At that moment, his eyes found me through his fuzzy, red, unruly hair — as if he'd sensed he was being watched. He tensed and his eyes widened. Abruptly he swung his arm in my direction and a ball of black fire came zooming at me. Without even waiting to see if his aim had been successful, he darted toward the exit. I drew in the energy around me and released a gush of water from my palms to cancel out the black flames. Then I chased after him, ignoring the complaints of the people around me who were now a bit wet.

Outside the club I halted and scanned the street. The tall, scruffy bugger was zooming passed each of the stores with admirable speed. Sucking in more energy, I manipulated it into the form of my whip and cracked it like I'd never cracked it before. It wrapped around his ankle. I yanked the whip hard, dragging him along the pavement and over to me.

Looming over him, I *ts*ked. "Throwing fire balls at me; that's not very nice, is it." He didn't struggle or try to free himself. He just gazed up at me, a mixture of shocked and incredibly anxious. I realised something then. "You thought I was dead, didn't you. I hate to disappoint you, but Victor spared me."

"I should have known that the Sventé Feeder everyone's been talking about was you," he said in a shaky voice.

"Yes, you should've. You never were very bright." I became aware that there were crowds of people around. I picked up the scents of Jared, Evan, Chico and Max close behind me. But I didn't care to answer their questions. "Is this where you've been hiding for the past few years then, Clark, hoping Victor wouldn't still come after you just for the fun of it? Turns out that Victor was the least of your worries, eh. No wonder I couldn't find you. Just how did you get accepted here?"

"My Sire got a position as a security guard here. He was permitted to bring along two of his guards."

"And the stupid bastard thought you'd be loyal? Well I hope he's not going to miss you too much, because your life has now reached its expiry date."

Clark held up his hands, palms out. "Now hang on a minute, Sam. Let's talk about this."

I straightened up and sniggered. "Trying to negotiate? This isn't a hostage situation. It's called *retribution.*"

"Come on now. Killing me won't bring Bryce back."

"Oh, I know that. But it'll feel bloody fantastic." It wouldn't bring me peace, but it was the next best thing. "Just how does it feel to know you're the reason your best mate's *dead?*"

"He wouldn't want this. He wouldn't want you bitter like this, he loved you, he—"

"Oh do me a favour and stop with all that." I shook my head; amazed at his nerve. "Do you know what, Clark? I told Bryce not to go to you for help. I told him I didn't trust you. You know what he said to that? He said he'd known you all his years as a vampire, that you were his best mate and you'd never betray him, and that he trusted you *with his life.*"

Clark's face was even paler than before. I doubted I'd ever reach the tiny conscience he had, but he was getting the lecture all the same. Clark was like Victor in many ways; he was good at politics and manipulating people. He would know exactly what you would want to hear and then he would tell you just that. If you had a compassionate side, he would appeal to it. If you had a weakness, he would pounce on it. If all else failed, he would barter.

"I didn't betray him. It wasn't like that."

"He went to you for help, for somewhere to hide out for a couple of days, and you handed him and me over to Victor on a silver bloody platter!"

"I had no choice, Victor would've killed me if he'd found out I was hiding you and Bryce."

"Bryce wouldn't have gone to you if he'd thought you'd have been in danger because that's the kind of person he was. *Was.*" I spat the last word. "Now get up." I allowed my whip to fade away, freeing his ankle, and watched as he struggled to get up.

"What're you going to do?"

"We're going to duel. There's no sport in just killing you outright."

"I can't fight you, Sam," he said, shaking his head.

"Why's that?"

"I can't hurt you. Bryce loved you, I can't hurt you." The words couldn't have been more false. The people around me sensed that too, a part of my brain registered.

I snorted. "It wasn't five minutes ago that you threw a fireball at me, and then you legged it like a rat up a drainpipe. I think what you really mean is that you don't think you can defeat me, and now you're just saying all this shite in the cause of self-preservation. Well you're only stalling the inevitable."

Backing up a little, he said, "Sam, it won't bring him back."

"Yeah, I believe you already said that."

"I'll leave here. We don't have to duel, I'll leave The Hollow and I won't come back. You'll never see me again, I swear to you."

I had to laugh as we reached the bartering stage. "I know that if I let you walk off now the *second* I turn my back there'll be more fireballs coming at me."

He looked exasperated now. "Okay, we duel," Clark finally said, snarling. His expression was so different now that he had dropped the fake crap. The innocence and fear had vanished from his eyes only to be replaced by the callousness and spite that usually resided there.

Apparently Clark had no intention of duelling, however. He hadn't even fully turned before he abruptly swerved, hoping to catch me off-guard, and launched more deadly fireballs at me. I absorbed the energy of the natural element air, releasing it as a forceful wind that not only sent Clark careening backwards but sent his pretty fireballs with him. When his back reached the wall of one of the buildings he fell to the floor. His fireballs then crashed into him and he disappeared, screaming, in a large ball of black fire. A black fire that was meant for me.

Both mine and Clark's suspicions were right; his death hadn't made much difference to how I felt inside. Bryce was still gone, he had still been betrayed, and it still hurt to even think about it. But the whole thing now seemed more balanced. The people responsible for his death weren't living the life that *he* should have had.

Victor had once told me that it wasn't anything personal to Bryce; that he'd just had to die because he loved me. 'Wrong girl, wrong time,' Victor had said. But Bryce had met me and loved me before Victor even knew me. By loving me and wanting to be with me, Bryce had been living exactly as he should have been, and exactly when he should have. It was Victor who had wanted the wrong girl at the wrong time, and it was Clark who had made it possible for Victor to get what he wanted.

The memory of Bryce's last seconds flashed in my mind so forcefully that it was almost like being slapped. It was all as clear as if it was happening right that moment. I could perfectly remember his contorted expression, his cries of pain, and the way his eyes had shot me a 'goodbye' glance.

A hand gently rested on my shoulder, and I suddenly realised that my name was being softly repeated. The touch, the voice, and the scent alerted me to the fact that it was Jared. And although there were plenty of people around and several of them seemed to be trying to reach me through my daze, it was Jared I needed. I turned into him, burying my face in his chest and gripping his shirt. His arms instantly went around me.

"Will you just leave her alone for a minute," he said to someone. That someone seemed to persist, and Jared responded with, "This isn't a game of who can get closest to her. Just give her a minute." Louder now, that someone persisted. Max.

Jared spoke down my ear, "Want me to teleport you away from here?"

I nodded against him. There was fluttering in my stomach and then the ground beneath me was softer. Opening my eyes, I saw that we were standing in the living area of my apartment. But I didn't move away from Jared, and he didn't drop his arms. He didn't ask me questions, which I appreciated. He just let me have a moment to collect myself.

After a few minutes I stepped out of his embrace and, without meeting his gaze, uttered a barely comprehensible, "Thanks." I then headed straight for the refrigerator. Sure vodka flavoured NST couldn't get me drunk, but the taste would be enough for a little comfort.

Jared didn't leave. He followed me into the kitchen and leaned against the counter, mirroring my stance. "I don't know what to say." He was speaking softly. "I was going to ask if you're okay, but that would be a stupid question."

"I'm fine. Seeing Clark just dragged up a lot of memories, that's all."

"Memories of someone called Bryce."

I nodded. "Yep."

"Who was your boyfriend…?"

"Yep."

"What happened to him?"

"Victor killed him right in front of me."

(Jared)

There was no emotion on her face, or in her eyes, or in her tone as she spoke those chilling words. But I sensed that underneath all that, Sam was screaming. I could feel the ache in her chest like it was mine. I wanted to hold her – not that that was anything new – but the air around her was so tense that it was almost like she was inside an impenetrable, invisible dome.

"Tell me about it."

She studied my face. "You don't have to stay with me. I'm not going to breakdown or anything."

"I'm not asking you to tell me as an excuse to stay and keep an eye on you. I genuinely want to know."

Sighing, she opened her refrigerator door and gestured to the contents. I took a Cola flavoured NST and leaned against the counter again, a little closer to her this time.

"I'd been in a relationship with Bryce for about six months when I first met Victor; we bumped into him at a club. I hadn't known Bryce was a vampire, and he told me that Victor was his boss at work. I noticed that he didn't seem to like having to introduce me to him, and then they started arguing because Victor said I'd make a good consort for him – I had no idea what he was talking about, of course – and he wanted Bryce to give me up. Bryce wouldn't. And when Victor came onto me, I said no."

She paused as she drank the last of the contents of her bottle before then grabbing herself another. "I was attacked that night outside the club, left for dead, and Victor Turned me into a vampire. I think that maybe Victor was the one who attacked me. He had plans for me to be his consort. He was my Sire so he had rights to me that Bryce didn't have...But then he realised I was a Feeder, and his plans for me grew immensely.

"Like any newborn Feeder, I was out of control. I was absorbing energy without meaning to and then shooting fire, or water, or energy balls here, there and everywhere. Victor had to lock me up in a little room by myself. He didn't let me feed much so that my energy levels wouldn't be too high and my power would be diluted. But every day, three times a day, he took me out of the room and tried to get me to control my gift. He'd have a line of humans waiting, and for every time I failed to do whatever task he gave me, he'd kill one of them."

"Bastard."

"Yeah. Bastard." She took a long swig out of her bottle before continuing, emotion creeping into her voice. "Bryce had been appointed as one of my guards, and he promised me that as soon as I could control my gift and there was no chance of me hurting myself, we'd make a run for it. We did. We went undetected for a whole week, but then Clark gave us up. Victor tortured Bryce before slitting his throat. I couldn't stop him, I wasn't as controlled as I am now, and Victor had me drugged and completely bound and gagged while I was forced to watch."

If I'd known all of this before meeting Victor and Clark, I'd have killed them both myself. I couldn't imagine having to watch someone I cared about go through something like that, especially while I could do nothing to stop it. Something like that would stay with you forever.

"I tried to run away from Victor by myself after that," she said, her voice steady again now. "He'd told me that if I ever tried it, he'd kill one human every day until I was returned to him. I hadn't believed him. I was caught two weeks later by a Pagori who had a similar gift to Salem's. When I was conscious again I was back with Victor, and at the other side of the room were fourteen dead human bodies; most of them just kids. I didn't try it again after that. At least not until Sebastian showed up. I knew Victor would be too busy following me here to be bothered killing humans."

It was only now that I was getting a true idea of just why it was so important to her to be her own person. She had spent the past few years under the total control of another person, someone she despised, someone who had killed a person she'd loved. I admired her for being stood in front of me now; a lot of people would have tried to end their own existence rather than live the kind of life she'd lived. "That's what you meant when you said to the guys that they had no right to forget their pasts."

She nodded. "In a nutshell, Bryce died because he loved me. Trying to forget that would be the biggest insult to him and his memory."

"You really did love him." As unreasonable, strange, and seemingly idiotic as it was, I felt a twinge of jealousy at the idea.

"I'm not going to lie and say I thought we were going to be together forever. Sometimes people simply love each other for a little while. But I did love him, yeah. Look where it got him."

"Hey, the blame doesn't lie with you. You have to know that."

"Do you know what the saddest part of it all is? Bryce hadn't wanted to go to the club that night that we saw Victor. I'd been all packed ready to move into a new flat the next morning, one that was at the other end of London. I'd said I wanted to go to that club one last time. Funny how one decision can lead to so many different things. I might never have been Turned into a vampire, Bryce might still be alive—"

"Or you could have met Victor at a later date and had the same thing still happen." I advanced toward her, but didn't attempt to penetrate that dome she had created around herself. "You can't go thinking stupid shit like that. They're the kind of things that Victor might have said to you. I'll bet he's looking up at you right now, listening to this and laughing about it. This would be exactly what he wants."

She smiled a grim smile. "Victor already got what he wanted; he said the 'experience' should teach me not to want to love someone ever again. It did. I've never wanted anything like that since. It hurts to love someone. I couldn't ever again watch someone I loved die."

I couldn't watch her in pain anymore. For the second time that night, I held her. Tight. She didn't resist like I'd thought she might. With her palms flat against my chest, she tucked her head under my chin. How could it feel this good just to have your arms around someone? I'd say I was getting just as much comfort from it as she was.

I'd never seen Sam look vulnerable before. Even now, though, there was still an air of strength about her. She was the last person I knew who would need protecting, but she made me want to shield her from everything. She brought out this protective side of me that I hadn't even known I had. I lightly kissed her hair and squeezed her even tighter.

The moment was shattered by the heavy knock on her apartment door. "Sam, it's Max."

Oh, great. Had I ever wanted to smash his face in as much as I did right then? I loosened my hold on her, expecting her to dash to greet him.

Sam sighed as she took a single step backwards. "I know he means well, but I just can't deal with him fussing right now."

If she had any clue as to how happy I was to hear her say that, she'd laugh her ass off. "Then don't answer. He'll get the idea." I held her tight again. And again, there was no resistance from her. Max knocked once more but, as I'd suggested, she ignored him. At that, he went away. Happy days.

"You're good at hugging," she said after a minute or so of silence.

I chuckled. "Thanks, I can't say I've had much practice at it. You're comfortable to hug."

"You seem to like my hair as well."

Subconsciously I had begun stroking her hair. In my defence, it was *so* soft and beautiful. Like her. "Want me to stop?" She shook her head. So I didn't stop. I combed through it with my fingers, enjoying the silky feel of it against my skin. I'd swear she was close to purring. But then she squirmed a little, and I thought she was about to free herself. I was wrong. In fact, she was sliding her hands up my chest and reaching for the collar of my shirt.

One button open. Another button open. And then there was the unbelievable feeling of her lips on my skin. Not kissing, just lingering there. That was enough to make me hitch in a breath. She kissed the spot beneath the hollow of my throat and I shuddered a little. Her lips then slowly began to work up the column of my throat, dabbing it with light kisses. She then gave it a little lick, and exhaled heavily over the wet spot before scraping her teeth over it. My downstairs department rose to attention.

I wasn't much of a person for ethics and morals when it came to sex, but a feeling struck me just then that had me questioning whether I wanted this now. It wasn't so much *me* that she wanted, it was comfort that she was looking for, and I didn't want us sleeping together to be about that. Voicing this view, however, was proving to be a struggle as I was sort of caught up in the sensation of her lips, and tongue, and teeth on my skin. Then she ground against me. Not helpful.

As such, all that came out was: "Sam, you have to stop." I couldn't say that I sounded all that convincing, especially since I was clutching her close to me.

"Why?" she murmured against my neck. "You want me." As if to emphasise her point, she ground against my raging erection again, and a low moan escaped me.

Her lips worked their way around my entire neck, her tongue lightly flicking out each time, her teeth nibbling. There wasn't one part of it that she didn't tease. Christ, I had to make her stop. I was too close to thinking 'comfort sex it is'.

"Sam, really, you need to stop." Again there wasn't much force behind my words, and considering that I had one hand tangled in her hair while the other was cupping her ass, she wasn't likely to take much notice of me.

"Why?" her husky voice said into my ear before she kissed the hollow beneath it while grinding against me again, harder this time.

"If I kiss you, I won't stop."

"And that's a bad thing?"

I want you, you've no idea how much, but I don't want it to be about comforting you. Can you honestly say that you would've kissed me like this tonight if it hadn't been for what happened with that guy out there?

Her mouth left my skin and I felt her release a small sigh. As she stepped out of my arms, she gave me a half-smile. "Fair enough." At that, she slowly headed to her bedroom. "Good night," she said quietly over her shoulder.

It took every ounce of my self-will not to follow her into that room and into that bed. *God, why am I being such a fucking girl?* If she wanted to use me, she could use me, what was so bad about that? Wasn't that what I'd wanted all along? The end result would be the same whether it was tonight or another night: sex.

And yet, it was oddly important to me that she wanted to sleep with me for no other reason than that she wanted me. It wouldn't have felt balanced if it was any different.

Since when did I care about things being balanced?

This whole thing was too weird.

I was stood staring at the closed door of her bedroom with my hands slapped against the sides of my head, releasing sigh after sigh after sigh after sigh. Occasionally I'd step toward the door only to then take a step back. I couldn't help thinking about how she was in there, in bed, – naked? – finally willing to sleep with me. Seriously what the hell was I doing out here?

But then, like a smack to the face, the importance of her wanting me just for me, not comfort, hit home. True, this wasn't like me. True, being used for sex had never been a problem for me before. But, for whatever reason, it mattered to me now with *this* woman. So, with a strength I honestly hadn't known that I had, I ignored the protesting coming from the bulge in my pants and teleported to my own room.

CHAPTER TEN

(Sam)

All right, so I wasn't exactly enthusiastic about leaving my apartment. I'd cursed the setting sun as I rose and dressed. I had no doubt that news had spread of my duelling with Clark and that people would be putting two and two together to theorise what it was all about. They'd definitely be coming up with five. I wasn't sure what would bother me more – leaving people to believe rumours that weren't true, or explaining the entire truth which was something personal to me. I'd already explained it to Jared, but I knew he wouldn't go blabbing about it.

God, Jared.

I wasn't eager to see him either. I'd spent God knows *how long* insisting I didn't want him that badly, and then I'd gone and tried to seduce him...? I mean, seriously, I was turning into my own worst enemy.

I blamed him. It was the hug that did me in. I'd relaxed against him, and then suddenly I'd felt...well. Engulfed by warmth. Sheltered. His arms had become some kind of refuge. No one had ever held me like that before – so securely, so comfortingly, so possessively. Then after a few minutes, even in spite of everything else I'd been feeling, there had been a thirst for something more, a violent throb of desire low in my stomach.

Thinking about everything as a whole, as I made my way to the Command Centre, I had to wonder if he had rejected me to make things *even* between us, to get his own back. It just didn't make sense that he would care what had made me want to have sex with him. He was a bloke, a woman-obsessed bloke, and he'd spent most of any time we were together doing that staring thing and suggesting we have sex.

And men said that women were confusing!

Regardless of his rejection, I wasn't embarrassed by my behaviour. Okay, maybe I was a little. No doubt I'd have been mortified if I hadn't known he wanted me and the whole seduction thing had been a gamble. But it was obvious that neither of us had walked away satisfied. No way would I blush or act all weird when I saw him. He'd love that. I refused to allow Jared to reduce me to a nervous, rambling blusher. If it wasn't for my raging hormones, he probably wouldn't have had much of an effect on me anyway.

Oh, who was I kidding? I wasn't even at my office and I was reaching out with my senses to ascertain whether or not he was inside it. I was both glad and disappointed to find that he wasn't.

Fletcher spotted me approaching and rose from his seat. If I was in a better mood, I would have laughed at his peach cashmere sweater, which hugged his body in a very feminine style. In fact, the sweater wasn't too unlike my own. "All right, luv, how you feeling?"

"Fine," I said, nodding. "You?"

"I always suspected you kept your distance from Jared because you'd been in a proper relationship and it went pear-shaped." He offered me a sympathetic smile. "Although I must say, I hadn't thought the bloke had died."

I ignored the nonsense about any of that affecting my lack-of-a-relationship with Jared. It was Bryce who was the important part of the conversation. "He was great. You'd have liked him."

"Well if you ever want to have a good gab about it, you just let me know. All right?"

"Will do."

"Now, I've been instructed to send you straight to Antonio. He wants to see you in the aviary."

"About what?"

Fletcher shrugged. "I'm just the messenger luv, don't shoot."

Antonio had obviously got wind of what happened outside the bar. Had Clark been one of his top security guards? If yes, I was in for one hell of a rollicking. Wonderful. Just what I needed two minutes after waking up.

His own point of view might be that it was irrelevant what Clark had done in the past; that if I had wanted to duel with him – one of his employees – I should have gone to Antonio first for permission. Hopefully it would work in my favour that Clark was the first to attack. If I hadn't defended myself against that fireball inside the club, I might not be here now.

It wasn't surprising that people stared as I passed them in the hallway of the mansion. There was no wariness or disgust on their faces. They looked fascinated and approving. I supposed that since not an awful lot happened round here, it was probably the most excitement they'd had in a while.

Like last time, Antonio was staring through the glass of the aviary, admiring the little animals with a glowing smile. Sebastian and Luther were stood slightly behind him, mimicking his own position. They all gave me a nod as I entered, as did Antonio's two usual bodyguards. The dogs dashed over to nuzzle and sniff me to death.

When I reached Antonio's side – who was now admiring the animals again – I spoke, "Will I be being sent to bed without dinner, or are you just going to ground me for a while?"

His mouth twitched. "Do you know why I always enjoy our conversations, Sam?"

"Because I'm such a charmer?"

"Because I never know what it is you will say next. You never fail to surprise me." Luther and Sebastian murmured words of agreement. "I have not called you here to discuss your actions of last night. I knew when I employed you that you were a livewire, and I knew that your reflex to a challenge is to accept it. I am told that the vampire in question attacked first, so I will look upon the incident as a matter of self-defence. This time."

The message was loud and clear: *I'm letting you off with a warning, but don't go challenging my vampires again unless truly necessary.* "Got it."

"Good."

"As much as *I* also enjoy our riveting conversations, I have to ask, what's with the summons if it's not to talk about Clark's unfortunate demise?"

His mouth twitched again. "Has your new gift manifested yet?"

"No, not yet."

"The suspense is painful," said Luther.

I turned to look at him. "Are you really that intrigued?"

"No Feeder has ever been given additional power before, no one would have dreamt of it. You are therefore somewhat of a..."

"Science experiment," I supplied.

"We are keen to observe you, yes. You must appreciate that when one has so much time on their hands and not much to entertain them, the smallest thing can become intriguing."

The creaking of the door behind me stole everyone's attention. I swerved to see Jared swanning inside and strolling gracefully toward us. As always, it took a lot of control to not gape at him. Especially when he had that leather jacket on. Feeling a little intimidated, I suddenly became incredibly aware of my own appearance. I didn't exactly look very appealing in my simple white tank top and my hip-hugging sapphire-blue denim jeans with my hair in a high ponytail. Sigh. Oh well.

It was a good ten seconds before I stopped ogling, which meant he'd probably noticed. I would not blush. I would not blush. I would not blush. I didn't — more so because I was distracted by his confused expression, which mirrored my own. He repeatedly studied my face as if for some clue as to what this meeting was all about. I gave a shrug.

"Sorry I'm late," he told Antonio after exchanging brief greetings with everyone. His dubiousness was apparent in his tone. "I had to find someone to cover the squad."

"It's quite all right," replied Antonio.

Feeling any better today? asked Jared as he positioned himself on Antonio's opposite side, facing me.

I went for nonchalant. *Fine thanks.*

He responded with a tiny nod.

"I wanted to speak with you about the Connelly gathering," Antonio said to Jared.

"What about it?" Jared stuffed his hands in the pockets of his jacket, which drew my attention back to it and, thus, to him. It wasn't fair that he looked so good in it, that he could so easily affect me. He'd probably look even better without it and any other clothes on. Not that I wasn't interested in finding out or anything now that I was thinking straight again. Honest.

Maybe I could go at the jacket with a razor blade or something. That would help.

"It is tomorrow night, is it not?"

"Yeah," confirmed Jared, still dubious.

"And you will be attending, I assume."

"I do every year."

Antonio nodded. "I want you to take Sam along with you."

"What?" asked Jared, almost overriding my "Say again?"

I didn't even know what this gathering was supposed to be, or who the hell Connelly was.

"All those invited are welcome to take a guest," said Antonio. "From what I remember, you always do so."

"Why do you want me to take Sam?" Agitation streamed through his veins at the idea; I felt it as if it was my own. Oh, cheers Jared. I couldn't help snorting.

"It is a very worrying time. Soon The Hollow's walls will be attacked. You can appreciate why I would wish to take precautions with regards to your safety. And as you do not usually take a personal bodyguard with you, people would find it rather odd if you were to do so this year. If there are any would-be-traitors amongst the guests, this might tip them off to our alertness of the upcoming attack.

"Up to now, although they may suspect that someone within my counsel has had a vision, they will not be sure. So, I propose that you take Sam along as your guest, let her pose as your consort" – I snorted again, to which Antonio smiled – "or your partner, whichever. Then if you do encounter any trouble, you have her as back-up."

"*Again* you're insisting I need back-up, and help, and protection," grumbled Jared. "Antonio, I'm a Master vampire. I have a reputation that ensures most vampires wouldn't dream of bothering me. And any that have tried taking me on have only ended up a pile of ashes."

"Except me, of course." I couldn't resist.

Jared ignored me. "It's one thing to be concerned about me being targeted; it's another thing altogether to imply that I can't handle it myself."

"This is not about what you can or cannot handle," insisted Antonio. "This is about taking precautions. You are my Heir. I will do as I must to ensure your safety."

"Ensure my safety? So you're saying a young, female Sventé vampire is all that's needed to ensure my safety. Hey, why not get rid of me and make her the Heir then."

"Oh we're back to that crap, I see," I spat. "Honestly, Jared, you're like a little kid who doesn't want to hold Mummy's hand."

"It's nothing personal to you," said Jared.

"Your last words sort of contradict that. What's wrong – you don't want to be seen out with a Sventé?"

Antonio interrupted our dispute. "What if this was Evan, Jared? You know he can protect himself from any threat. But would you want him to go alone while such a threat is live?"

"That's different," argued Jared.

I snorted. "Oh, you know what? I'm gone. Antonio, if you want me to go tomorrow night I will. But I'm not staying here to listen to him sulk any more than I have to."

"Understandable," muttered Sebastian.

I was in such a desperate need to put distance between me and Jared that human velocity just wasn't good enough. Vampire speed had me at the office within seconds. I slumped down onto my seat. God, what was so wrong with me in Jared's eyes that made him so horrified by any idea that involved us working closely together? Oh I was good enough to shag, though, wasn't I? So should I take that to mean that he'd shag absolutely anything, even if he loathed it?

Worse still, I couldn't seem to shrug my shoulders about it all. I *told* myself I didn't like him that much. I *told* myself that what little attraction I had to him was purely physical. But if that was the case, why was I so bothered by what he thought of me as a person? Why did I suddenly care about what he thought of my appearance? Why was I jealous of his relationship, if you could call it that, with his consorts? Why, when I needed comfort, was he the only one I wanted around me? Why, when Max was so cute and sweet and made an effort to spend time with me, did I find myself thinking about Jared instead?

Maybe Jared was right; maybe it wasn't fair to Max that I responded to his flirtatiousness if it was Jared I wanted more. Well, time to remedy that. And not by pushing Max away or attempting any further seductions with Jared. No. Time to rid myself of this craving I had for Jared. Yes, it had somehow, without my even realising it until now, developed into a craving. How was I going to rid myself of that? Easy, because I wasn't a shallow person and I didn't believe that looks were more important than personality. So now all I had to do was remind myself of all his bad traits.

Of course there was the obvious one: he was outrageously sexist, even to the extent that he hadn't been prepared to give me the job I deserved merely because I was female. Hell, he wouldn't even work with me, so we had to split the training hours for the squad and train them separately.

Number two: he was prejudiced against Sventés, seeing them as inferior to him and horrified at the thought of being seen outside the walls with one. Arsewipe.

Number three: he placed so little significance in women that they were simply objects to him – objects that he could claim, and possess, and tuck away in an apartment.

Number four: he was such a spoilt brat that he sulked whenever things didn't go his way, even going as far as to barely speak to me for days at a time.

Number five: he was so unbelievably vain, he couldn't grasp the concept that a woman might not want to be his consort.

To sum up, he's a dickhead.

And now my head felt so much clearer.

Objective: Forget Jared, concentrate on Max.

(Jared)

Sam wasn't in the office when I teleported there. She was always in her office during lunch hour, flicking through files and charting the progress of the recruits. It wasn't exactly cause for alarm that she wasn't there now, but I didn't like it. I had apparently gotten so used to knowing where she would be that this simple detail threw me off. It shouldn't matter that I didn't know where she was, but I really didn't like that at all.

It would make sense that she wouldn't be enthusiastic about talking to me right now. I knew I'd hurt her feelings by protesting about taking her to the gathering tomorrow evening. It hadn't really registered until now that it was possible to hurt her. It should've done, as I'd glimpsed what she hid behind that frosty exterior – the pain, the anger, and the shame at what her dick of a Sire had done to her. And now I was the dick too.

It wasn't that I was ashamed to be seen with her, like she thought. Okay, I admit, I didn't like the idea of everyone staring, and whispering, and judging, and if it was any other Sventé I'd have point-blank refused to take her. But I didn't look at Sam and see a

Sventé. I saw a strong, determined, wilful, gorgeous, good-hearted person. A good-hearted person who I'd just hurt.

I had to see her. Not that I was going to say sorry or grovel. Pride and all that. But the idea that she was somewhere thinking horrible shit about me or upset because of what I'd said...I just didn't like it. It was probably just that I knew it would make getting her to admit that she wanted me even harder. Yeah, that was all it was. It wasn't like it could be anything else.

Feelings weren't something I experienced when it came to women. Maybe that was because the only ones I'd ever had in my life had let me down in ways I didn't even want to think about, maybe that was why I no longer seemed to function that way with women. In all honesty, I didn't even see the point in relationships anyway. After watching the way my parents were – arguing, brawling, cheating – I didn't see the attraction in having a relationship and I definitely wasn't built for it.

Evan was the opposite of me. Witnessing the messed up marriage that our parents had had only made him want to seek out the *right* woman and not just settle for someone, the way our parents had. Personally, I didn't think there was a right woman for each and every guy. You either cared about them or you didn't, and it either lasted or it didn't. Like Sam said, sometimes you love someone for a little while and then it was over.

Odd how much it bothered me that she once loved someone. I wouldn't have thought it was possible to be jealous of a dead person. I couldn't even work out why I was experiencing jealousy over it at all. Nothing I felt or did when it came to Sam made much sense. I still couldn't believe I'd walked away from her offer of sex last night. Evan would laugh his tits off if he knew. That was why I wasn't planning on telling him.

Shaking my head at myself and my inability to explain my weird responses to this woman, I picked up the phone and called Fletcher using the internal line.

He answered immediately. "Yes, Commander?"

"Fletcher, do you have any idea where Sam is?"

"Sam?" He sounded uncomfortable. "Well, er, Max came to take her out for something to eat for lunch."

My jaw suddenly hurt, and I realised I was grinding my teeth together. "Okay, thanks Fletcher."

Max had taken her out for lunch? *Motherfucker.* I was really going to end up seriously hurting that guy. I'd never before felt threatened by another guy when it came to women. Mostly because it didn't really matter to me if the woman wasn't interested, there were plenty more strutting around. It wasn't really much different from me browsing through a shopping mall with a vague idea of what I might like and then choosing an outfit to try on for size.

This time it was different. Sam was different. I didn't want a woman like her, I wanted *that* woman. But if all I was doing was just trying her on for size and had no sense of ownership, it meant other people could try her on for size too. And that nettled more than I'd have expected it to. In which case, Max really needed to get the hell out of the picture. Could she be right: was my ego really that swollen that I couldn't stand the idea of someone else beating me to it? It had to be that.

And now all I could do was wonder what they were doing, if she was enjoying herself, whether his little lunch date would amount to anything. I didn't believe that Sam was the type to be dazzled by dates or anything soppy, but she would appreciate the fact that he was making an effort. I really didn't appreciate his efforts at all. In fact, I'd like to shove them up his ass along with any objects I could find.

But as much as curiosity was chewing on me, there was no way I was going to walk around looking for the two of them. I wouldn't let things get that bad that I needed sectioning. Common sense told me that seeing as she'd be at the arena within the hour, I might as well just sit, eat, drink, and then head over there shortly.

Needless to say, the time dragged. It was worse because I had nothing to do to occupy my thoughts. It only occurred to me as I was making my way to the arena that I didn't actually have anything to say to Sam that would seem important enough to warrant me walking over there. I'd have to say I was there to observe the training again. I'd actually enjoyed watching last time. Instead of wounding my ego that I'd been wrong about her capabilities, it made me proud of her.

When I arrived at the arena, only a few of the recruits were there, laughing and joking like a bunch of high school kids in a locker room. I waited in the spectators' box. A few minutes went by before she walked in. I'd have been mesmerised by how snug her simple clothes were against her body, hinting at her toned figure, if it wasn't for the fact that Max was walking beside her and they were laughing loudly – you know the kind of laugh that tells you that the joke was private between the laughers and you'd never get it?

Sam was two recruits short and the training session wasn't due to start for a further ten minutes but, to her credit, she ushered Max away; conveying the message that now she was his superior and he'd get the same treatment as everyone else whether he'd taken her to lunch or not.

I was about to telepathically alert her to my presence when she did something that again had me mesmerised: she removed the bobble from her hair, letting her dark hair fall loose from the ponytail, and then smoothed it back before gathering it together to style it into a higher, tighter ponytail.

Now I was stuck thinking about how soft those strands were and how good it felt to scrunch them in my hand last night. Just as it had felt good having her lips, tongue, and teeth on my neck. If she'd sunk those teeth into my skin, I'd have been inside her before she could even swallow one gulp of my blood.

Didn't expect to see you here. Her tone was flat and emotionless. I guessed that she had sensed me.

It's called keeping a close eye on the progress of our squad. I almost said 'my squad', but I figured that wouldn't help me get back into her good books.

As long as you don't interfere, that's fine.

That was exactly what I would have said to her had our positions been reversed, so although I'd had no intention of interfering, I resisted being defensive. Just as I was about to make a throw away comment about her lunch date with Max, the final two recruits entered and she quickly rounded them all up like sheep.

Throughout the entire session, I watched her. I couldn't take my eyes off her; she conducted herself so confidently and had such control over her gift that I was in total awe of her. She basically commanded the entire arena and everything in it just with her presence. Not once did she become unsure of herself. Not once did she lose control of the situation. Her husky voice echoed and teased my ears, hypnotising me almost.

She had the recruits repeat the same exercises of last session, making them practise their gifts on one another. But this time she acted as a distraction; she threw energy balls or thermal beams or tapped into the natural elements.

"During any kind of battle, the odds of you getting a fair spar with another vampire are slimmer than Commander Michaels' favourite consort," she said to them. I had to laugh a little. "There'll be other vampires coming at you from all angles. It's important that you're able to defend yourselves and attack despite these distractions. I've been serving as that distraction, but I haven't attempted to hurt any of you.

"In a battle, it will be different; the vampires coming at you will have every intention of hurting you. So, we try this again. This time I will aim at you – don't start whining like girls, I won't be too harsh. No, this isn't fair, but battles aren't fair. The only way you'll learn to dodge is if you experience what will happen if you don't. So, let's go."

Damn, she was amazing to watch. The way they all hung off her every word...It was a situation that only an extremely good leader could create and sustain. I had to agree with Antonio – albeit begrudgingly – that she would make a good co-leader in a battle, and that the squad would benefit from having her there. I'd benefit from having her there.

Was I in any way surprised that the second the session was over Max dashed toward her like a puppy to its master? No. By the looks of it, neither was Sam. When uncertainty flashed on her face, I strained my hearing to listen to their conversation.

"You said you'd never tried eating there and that we could go together some time," Max was saying to her. "So I just thought, hey no time like the present."

"You're not content with whisking me off to eat lunch; you now want to commandeer my entire night as well?" She was laughing, but there was awkwardness in it.

"Oh come on, it's gotta be better than sitting in your apartment munching on crap while Fletcher turns up to eat half of it."

She smiled in surprise. "How do you know he does that?"

"Sam, please," – oh he's begging her now? Pitiful – "put me out of my misery, come out with me later. Please?"

She rolled her gorgeous eyes. "All right, fine, we'll go out. You'll have to give me an hour to change clothes and stuff."

Motherfucker. I was down there in a second before he could propose anything else like, oh I don't know, him going to her apartment for 'coffee' after the meal. This was so like the feeling of someone trying to take something that was mine. She'd whip me to death if she knew that. She looked up at me, waiting for some kind of comment. I tried really hard to gather the words together to form a compliment about her coaching, but nothing would come out. I just wasn't practiced at compliments. Her growing smile indicated that she noticed my inner struggle. I could actually *feel* her amusement.

"So, I'll come to your apartment in an hour then," Max said to her. His eyes then darted to me and he shot me a self-satisfied smirk. Yeah, he knew I wanted her and he was sending me a message that it was too late. He really believed that? I almost felt sorry for the guy. Almost.

"I'll just meet you in the lobby," Sam told him.

Then it was my turn to shoot smirks at him. He couldn't be doing that well with her if she wasn't taking up the opportunity to have him in her apartment. If I was childish, I might have mouthed '*I've* been in there'. Maybe I could be childish just this once.

She turned to me, pulling me out of my thoughts. "I'm assuming you noticed that I didn't leave the files on your desk like I usually do." I hadn't noticed. "I actually didn't get a chance to finish updating them—"

"That was my fault, I took her to lunch." Could he have made it more obvious that he was trying to mark his territory?

"—but I'll sort it at dusk." She had ignored Max, which he didn't seem to like.

"It's okay."

"Say again?" She seemed astonished. Did she wonder if I'd come here just to make snide remarks about trivial things? Well, I had done trivial stuff in the past.

"It's okay," I repeated.

"You're being reasonable." Suspicion entered her eyes. "You've either done something you shouldn't have, or you're after something."

I gave her a devilish grin. *I'm only after the same thing I always want.*

What would that be? My blood, or my body?

Put those two together.

She shook her head at me, stifling a giggle.

Max snickered. "I'd say he's done something and feeling guilty about it."

"Jared doesn't do guilt," she told him.

Except with you, I almost said. Christ, I'm losing it.

The playful banter continued as we all strolled to the apartment building. Max got increasingly agitated about it and tried further marking his territory by touching her or complimenting her. She only laughed each time. I was pretty sure that she knew what he was trying to do and she was just humouring him. But even that didn't make me want to pound him any less. Max saw that and so he did it all the more.

Therefore, I was already beyond incensed when he turned up at my apartment door forty-five minutes later. "What?" was all I said.

He pushed past me, took a quick glimpse at the interior of my apartment and then exhaled heavily. "I want you to leave her alone." The nervous tremor in his voice disappeared as he continued to speak. "I'm not here as a squad member talking to his superior, I'm here talking to you as one guy to another. Leave her alone."

As a gesture of boredom, I stuffed my free hand in my pants pocket while using the other to swirl the contents of my NST bottle. "I'm afraid I can't do that."

"All she'd be is another notch on your bedpost. You can get sex anywhere, you've got three consorts to give you it whenever you want, just leave this one woman alone."

"What would you know about what I want?"

"I've heard all about how you treat women; that you're only out to get laid. Fine, that's your business. But Sam's worth more than that."

Inwardly I groaned before shooting a rhetorical question at him. "Are you and her together?"

"No."

"Then I don't see how what Sam and I do, or don't do, has anything at all to do with you." I gestured toward the door with my head, but he remained still. Like an idiot.

"Okay, let's look at it this way. We both want her. But you don't care about her, I do. So don't you think it's only fair that you just leave her be?"

"Let's look at it another way. Sam doesn't want someone to care about her; she wants to keep it simple."

He frowned. "How would you know?"

"She told me. After everything she's been through, I don't blame her." Yes, that was me making a point to him that there were things about her and her past that he didn't know and that she had trusted me with. "I'd seriously think before you go declaring your undying love for her. She'll run a mile."

"Yeah, right, like I'd listen to your advice. You'd say anything that'd mess up my chances with her. What's the matter? Feeling threatened?"

"*You* obviously are, or we wouldn't be having this conversation."

"I – I – Oh fuck you, Michaels. Be smart and leave her alone. You'll be sorry if you don't." His tone was sharp and clipped.

In vampire speed, I was nose to nose with him. "I really hope you can follow up on that threat 'cause you're going to need to." What bothered me more than the threat was the way he talked about Sam like he had rights to her. "Let me ask you, she ever let you kiss her?" His silence answered that. "You mean you're making all this effort and not even getting any action?" I shook my head and whistled. "You're missing out. She's one really good kisser."

His eyes widened and lots of veins and tendons in his face and neck were bulging. It could have been mistaken for envy, but it was more to do with anger. He had realised that he was only embarrassing himself by coming here with this all high and mighty attitude only to find out that he wasn't the expert on Sam that he thought he was.

Once his face was no longer contorted, he flashed me an ugly smirk. "I better go. I don't want to be late for my dinner with Sam."

"Don't choke on your food now, will you," I called over my shoulder as he passed and left the apartment.

What a son of a bitch. Barging into my apartment. Confronting me. Threatening me. Acting like he had any rights where Sam was concerned. I should've just decked him. Full points for me for not losing it. But did that mean I was going to just let this go, that I *could* let this go? Oh no. Not a chance. His evening was going to be cut short.

(Sam)

I stared hard at the menu, not really reading it, trying my hardest to ignore the anger that was steaming off Max and making him unbelievably uncomfortable to be around. I'd already asked four times if he was okay, each time getting a 'yeah, great'. Only he wasn't great – far from it. And now *I* was brassed off. *He* was the one who'd wanted to come here. How was it that I'd become the one keeping a conversation going to fill the silence? I'd given up on that now, meeting the silence with silence, fully intending to walk right back out if he didn't perk up within the next ten minutes.

At last, he spoke. "I never got a chance to ask you what all the crap was about with that guy last night." He sounded like a deflated version of himself, like someone had sucked the enthusiasm out of him. "Something about him being responsible for the death of his best friend...?"

I nodded. "Who also happened to be my boyfriend at the time." I consulted the menu again, hoping for a subject change. "What're you ordering?"

"I tried to see if you were okay. Last night, I mean. I went over to see you, but Jared was holding you. He wouldn't budge."

"Oh." Well of course I knew that, but Max wouldn't understand that I just couldn't deal with talking to everyone about it. He was the type of person who could talk about anything. Anything at all, no matter how personal, and not feel awkward or embarrassed. He never seemed to ever experience the feeling of needing to keep anything private.

"And then I came by your room. You didn't answer."

I hoped I was imagining the element of suspicion in his voice. "I must've been asleep when you knocked."

"How long did Jared stay with you? Or did he just leave straight after teleporting you there?"

"What's with the round of twenty questions?"

"I'm just asking."

"Where's that waiter?" I didn't need the waiter, I needed the exit.

"Have you and Jared ever..." He started playing with his own fingers, keeping his glare fixed on the table. "I mean, I wouldn't blame you for falling for his bullshit."

"I haven't *fallen* for anything, or haven't you noticed that he's not here?" It came out much snappier than I'd intended. Max didn't seem fazed by my change in tone. His mind was very much elsewhere. "Has Jared said something to you?"

"Has Jared said something to me?" He laughed – a miserable laugh with a cutting edge to it. "Jared says a lot of things. Are you referring to how he made it obvious you talk to him about personal stuff, or that he told me you and him had kissed?"

The first seemed to bother him most. Like I'd said, Max didn't feel the need to keep things private, so for him to hear that not only did I keep things private from him – realistically, though, that wasn't exactly uncommon with people you barely knew, was it? – but the fact that I had no problem sharing those things with someone else was just incomprehensible to him.

"I can understand why you might like him," he said before I could respond to his question. "But you have to see that all he wants is to use you."

"Max—"

"He'd drop you straight after it easier than a bad habit."

"Max—"

"Did you know he never screws the same woman twice unless it's one of his consorts?"

"*Max*, will you just stop with the ranting." I might have been annoyed with Jared for what he'd said to Max, but he'd only spoken the truth. It wasn't like Max and I were together or anything. And I had to wonder if Max had ranted at Jared and that was why Jared had then disclosed the info. I would've wanted to shut him up as well.

"So what he said was true?"

"Jared and I have kissed, yes."

"You didn't tell me."

"You didn't ask until now. I never had any intention of hiding it, but I've got no reason to go round jabbering on about it either, have I? Now can we stop talking about inconsequential crap and just order the food, please."

Before the hand even appeared on my elbow seconds later, I knew he was there. My senses had screamed it at me. Such a simple thing to have someone gently hold my elbow, and yet every nerve ending in my body was now extremely alert.

"What the hell are you doing here?" spat Max.

Jared shrugged. "I'm going to have to take her, sorry." He looked down at me, his alluring hazel eyes glinting slightly with humour. "Antonio wants me to show you the file containing the information on all the High Master vampires who'll be at the gathering."

"What gathering?" demanded Max.

Jared smiled at him. "Oh we're going together to a gathering of one the High Master Vampires tomorrow night."

"And looking at this file just couldn't wait until tomorrow night?" Max sneered at him.

"You aren't suggesting I'd interrupt your meal unless I had a really important reason, are you?"

"The things I said really got to you, did they?"

Yes, I'd been right; Max must have ranted at Jared not so long ago and now he was getting a little payback. I wouldn't have let the game continue except that it was a fantastic excuse to get me out of there. Before they started pounding on their chests like gorillas, I pushed out my chair and rose. "Sorry about this, Max. Another night."

Jared shot me a curious glance. *I thought you were going to be difficult. Let's just go.*

Max cursed and scowled. "Sam, wait, will you just—"

Jared held onto my lower arms and smiled triumphantly at Max. "Sorry to leave you stranded."

CHAPTER ELEVEN

(Sam)

The second that the queasy feeling in my stomach, courtesy of teleporting, eased and we arrived at Jared's apartment I ripped my arms from his grasp. He was already laughing, rather pleased with himself. I wasn't sure what I felt most: annoyed at him for thinking he had the right to interfere with my plans, or flattered that he was so affected by the idea of me having plans with someone else. It was always nice to have a little power over someone who tended to consider themselves to be all big and bad.

"Next time you feel like winding up some bloke who you know I'll be going out with, you might want to warn me in advance."

"*I* wound *him* up?" He snorted. "I wasn't the one who turned up at someone else's apartment threatening them to stay away from you."

I gaped. "He did that?"

"Must be love in its purest form."

I went to slap his arm but in a blurred motion he was out of my sight. That was when I took notice of the apartment. It was, like, double the size of mine. And incredible. The colour scheme was a perfect mixture of warm gold, cream and ivory. Dark oak flooring was a feature throughout.

His living area was bigger than my bedroom and en-suite bathroom combined. He had one of those leather corner sofas that seated like eight people and was so bulky that when you sat on it your feet just about touched the floor. The rectangular coffee table had pillar-like legs and matched the oak flooring so perfectly that I wondered if the table was made out of the same wood. Typical of blokes, his platinum T.V. was unnecessarily wide. And wow he had a fish-tank somehow built into the wall. Posh bugger.

Past the living room was a large space with a conference table in the centre, and following on from that was the kitchen. Even from here, the beginning of the living area, I could tell that the large square kitchen was extremely modern: rich woods, chrome appliances, and marble counters.

I suddenly became conscious that Jared was stood at the outer edge of the kitchen staring at me, as he tackled a NST. He raised an eyebrow. "Like it?"

Oh so this was usually all it took to have women on their backs with their legs spread. I casually shrugged one shoulder. "It's all right."

He laughed. The gruff sound of it was alluring. God, *he* was alluring. Even more so when he wore those black Armani jeans and that very complimentary white Armani t-shirt, the best feature of course being that knee-length leather jacket. I was starting to suspect that he hadn't removed it because he knew how much I liked it on him.

Raising both brows now, he used his thumb to gesture behind him. "The bedroom's that way, if that's what you're looking for."

I gestured to behind me. "And the front door's that way, and unless you want me to walk right on out of it, you can behave yourself."

He smiled. "I'll try to behave."

"On a more serious note, doesn't it get weird having all this space to yourself?"

The humour in his eyes dimmed a little for a split second. Then he shot me a roguish smile. "I need all the space for my big swollen ego."

"I never thought of that."

He nodded toward the kitchen. "Want anything? I take it you haven't eaten." His mouth twitched. Clearly he was delighted about the situation he had created.

"Got any alcohol flavoured NSTs?"

"I might have Budweiser flavoured ones."

"They'll do."

"You like Budweiser?"

I gave him an impatient look. "Let me guess, you find that so surprising because I'm a girl and we girls generally drink wines and cocktails."

He held his hands up in an apologetic gesture. "I'll take my sexist ass to the refrigerator and bring you back some Bud flavoured NSTs."

"Yeah, you do that."

He laughed again and nodded toward the conference table before disappearing into the kitchen. On the surface of the long, glass table was a thick file. So he was telling the truth about there being information for me to look at, he wasn't just trying to get me away from Max. A small part of me was stupidly disappointed that he hadn't simply acted on a need to end my night with Max.

Placing my small white handbag on the table, I called out, "What is this gathering anyway? And who's Connelly?"

Jared swiftly appeared beside me with a handful of NSTs that he plonked on the table, making them noisily clink against the glass surface. "Connelly is a High Master vampire. He's about three centuries old and he's got a rod stuck up his ass, but he's devoted to Antonio."

"So then why invite *you* to the gathering and not Antonio?"

"Antonio never leaves The Hollow. Ever. By going to the gathering, I'm kind of his representative."

"And this gathering is an annual thing?" I took the opened NST he was offering and took a swig. Not bad.

"Yep."

"For what?"

"It's the anniversary of the day that Connelly became a vampire. He has this huge party every year, but really it's just an excuse for everyone to get together and get smashed. *But*, the reason people go is because Connelly's very select about who he invites. He never exceeds a certain number either. So to get invited is thought of as an honour; a statement that you're considered important in the vampire world."

"So basically it's an opportunity for all of you 'select' people to get together and shine your swollen egos."

He jiggled his head. "More or less. Unless a vampire is a master vampire, they don't get invited. The only ones who aren't masters are the High Masters." He patted the file. "Antonio wants you to have an idea of who they are before you go. We know that Bennington will be invited, and Antonio's concerned that if Bennington attends he will use the opportunity to approach the other High Masters with his plans to attack The Hollow. It's doubtful that he'll just come straight out with it, but he might hint at it to test the water; so Antonio wants us both to be on the alert."

I cast him a suspicious look. "I could have just gone through this at dusk before we left."

He smiled. "So you could've."

So he *was* eager to get me away from Max. Hmm. And now he was doing his staring thing again, taking in my white satin strapless dress and my white stilettos. Slowly his eyes skated over every inch of my body, boring into me to the point that his gaze was almost a caress. I could literally feel his need for me and had to repress a shudder. Twisting his lips and raising a brow suggestively, he met my gaze.

I warned him with my eyes before I spoke. "Oi, you can stop that right now."

"What?"

"You know bloody well what, so don't muck about."

"I like looking at you." He shrugged, all innocence.

"Well I don't like you looking at me."

He edged a little closer. "You wanted me last night."

"And you said no."

"It wasn't a rejection, I told you why." His hungry gaze travelled over me again. "I wouldn't say no now." He ran the rim of his bottle down the length of my bare arm. I held back a quiver. "Sam."

"No."

"No? Why?" He was amused.

My God, he had to know that even if I was up for shagging someone who suffered from Obsessive Consort Disorder – which I definitely wasn't, honest – I would never have given in to him so easily after the way he had snubbed my offer last night. Feminine pride was a big thing. "A girl can change her mind."

"Then change it back again." He edged closer again but still didn't touch me. Thank God. It was hard enough just having him that close and feeling his breath at my ear.

"Can we go through this file please?" I said impatiently.

He looked about to object, but then his grin became crooked and he narrowed his eyes. "If that's what you want, then that's what we'll do."

I picked up the file and sat on one of the leather-cushioned table chairs. At the forefront of the contents was an A4 photograph of a middle-aged bloke – although he could be centuries old in vampire years – with quite a friendly face. His shoulder-length sleek hair was almost white and his deep-set amber eyes were framed by sparse black lashes. He had a child-like button nose which was probably the main factor in giving him such a friendly appearance.

"That's Connelly. Rupert Connelly," added Jared as he sat on the chair next to mine. "He's the High Master of the entire Caribbean and other places like Hawaii and Brazil. He's a Keja. As I said, he worships Antonio. Any time he's ever visited The Hollow, he's stuck to Antonio like a fly to shit."

"Is he as friendly as he looks?"

"I've honestly never met anyone so giddy. Very sociable. Laughs a lot. One thing I know for certain is that he'd never betray Antonio. If an attack does happen, he'll align himself with Antonio and do everything he can to help protect The Hollow."

"Will his gift do much good in an attack?"

"That depends how involved he is during the defence. He has infrared vision, so if he was leading his own legion as opposed to having someone else do it then he'd be able to point them in the right direction of where the invaders are."

I took a moment to memorise Connelly's face before then moving on. The vampire on the next photograph didn't look much older in human years than me, but his almond blue eyes held a twinkle of wisdom so I guessed he'd been around for a while. His facial structure was sculpture-worthy and made all the more appealing by the hood of sandy tight curls that hung down to his cheekbones. Very broad shoulders, I noticed.

"That's Carlos – he doesn't use a surname. A Pagori. High Master of quite a few places like Spain, the Canary Islands, Morocco, Portugal...He doesn't reside anywhere in particular, he likes to travel. Sociable enough, but only interested in serving his own interests."

"So, if he deduces that Bennington's plan of attacking The Hollow has a high chance of succeeding, he could easily align himself with Bennington."

"Oh yeah."

"His gift?"

"He's Psychometric. By touching something, he can give details about its past, present, future – that kind of thing."

"Just objects, or people too?"

"Not sure, actually." He snickered at the next photograph as I moved on from Carlos. "Rowan Murdock," he drawled. "Not the nicest of vampires."

Rowan looked as though he had been Turned when he was in his late forties. He had long, dark, incredibly straight hair and the largest eyes, largely glinting amber. Clearly a Keja. With his chunky lips pursed and one dark eyebrow arched, he gave off an arrogant vibe. "He looks stuck up."

Jared chuckled. "He mainly lives in Italy, but he's High Master over Greece, all the Greek islands, Turkey, Algeria, Egypt and more. He's got an extensive bloodline."

"So he's quite the biter."

"You could say that. He always takes his life-partner with him to the gatherings. Marcia, I think her name is. She's very...prim and proper."

"A snob?" I offered.

"But she won't be snobbish to you, because she'll think you're my consort and she's never snobbish toward the consorts, which I think is weird."

"She obviously just doesn't feel threatened by them."

"You mean the way Joy feels threatened by you?" His smile was cute, inviting, and playful. His eyes raked over me again.

I gave him a pointed look. "Oi, we're talking about these High Master vampires, nothing else."

"I know," he said innocently, like butter wouldn't melt in his mouth.

I tapped the photograph. "So what's this Rowan like with regards to Antonio? A fan or...?"

"He's not exactly chummy with him, but I can't see him ever betraying Antonio. He thinks that highly of himself, he'd never associate or align himself with any vampires who were challenging Antonio. He'd see that kind of thing as beneath him. His gift is pretty cool. He can mimic any non-living substance just by touching it."

Although I could feel Jared's eyes on me, I forced my concentration onto the photograph, memorising the face, before flipping to the following one. The first thing I noticed about this vampire was his nose — long, wide and turned up. His cropped hair was a reddish gold and his tiny beard was a few shades darker than his hair. There was a large ring of red around his grey eyes, marking him as a Pagori.

"Curran. Don't know his first name." Jared paused to open another NST. "He kind of keeps himself to himself at any gatherings, but he's all right once you get him talking. He's not High Master over many places. Mostly just Canada and Alaska."

"That could go in our favour. He'll figure that after the battle, there'll be enough casualties to mean that some countries are without a High Master. If he wants more territory, he might join Antonio."

Jared nodded. "Very likely. But I'd say that the other side will try to coax him to betray Antonio because his gift is pretty impressive. Duplication."

"So...he can create duplicates of himself or others, and scatter them around to join the battle to replace any casualties."

Jared nodded again. "I can't see him betraying Antonio though. I'm not saying he'd definitely join the battle, he might want to sit it out completely."

I knew the vampire in the next photograph. I recognised his chubby face, the thin coal-black moustache, the smarmy expression, and it was impossible to forget the way he combed his dark hair to the side of his head, covering his bald patch (not so well).

"Bennington," I said.

"That's right. You've met him, right?" I nodded. "Creepy guy. He might want to have a catch up if he sees you."

"Or try to employ me."

"He tried to take you off Victor?"

"Yeah, a few times. Out of the two of them, Victor was the lesser evil."

Jared tilted his head, conceding that. "He's High Master over Greenland and Iceland as well as Britain. Out of all the High Masters, he's had the most challenges to his role."

"I'm not surprised, he makes enemies pretty easily. Bennington's gift wouldn't exactly help him in a battle. He can sense people's gifts, but he has to be extremely up close to do it."

"I hope he gets up close to me. Decapitating him would be the highlight of my year."

"Be careful, I might beat you to it."

"Bennington's mine," he insisted with a smile.

I gave him a 'whatever' shrug and then flipped to the next photograph. Whoa, they were the bushiest eyebrows I'd ever seen – they joined in the middle, making the bloke look like he had a caterpillar hanging above his round dark eyes. His coppery hair was quite tousled, sticking out here and there and tickling his long ears.

"That's Winston Jones, but he changes his name almost every time the wind changes course. He's High Master over Australia, New Zealand, and Indonesia and all the little surrounding islands. Older than Antonio by a couple of decades. He's known mostly for having the largest harem."

"Go on, how many consorts?"

"Over eighty."

I grimaced. "That's bad, worse than man-boobs."

Jared laughed. "Don't talk about tits. I'm having a hard time ignoring yours."

"That's because you're perverted."

"No, it's because I want you, and you're making it really hard to resist you when you come here dressed like that."

"Er, excuse me, I did *not* turn up here like this for your benefit. I was at a restaurant, and you snatched me from it, remember. Now let's get back to this file. What's this bloke's gift?"

"Nothing uncommon: Winston can levitate, but he can levitate quite high."

"What side do you think he'll align himself with?"

"It's hard to say. Winston's weird like that. One minute he's laughing and joking with you, but the slightest thing changes his mood."

"Typical Pagori," I muttered.

Jared frowned at the jibe but then his smile quickly returned. "Winston's quite impulsive. I think his decision will just depend on how he's feeling at the exact moment that he realises he has to choose a side or back out."

The next photograph was of a Keja vampire of Japanese origin. He was neither smiling nor frowning; his expression and posture was very relaxed and reserved, and I imagined him to be a very cool, collected person. In that respect, he made me think of Antonio.

"He calls himself Bran," said Jared. "He's always been a close friend of Antonio's, and they have the same Sire. There's no doubt where his allegiance will lie."

"Good."

"He's High Master over Japan, China, and Africa, among other places. Quiet and respectful. He makes me think of a librarian. Doesn't like Connelly much. I think that's because Connelly talks so much."

"And what's in his bag of tricks?"

"He's an Ecological Empath; he has a psychic sensitivity to his surrounding environment." His bad-boy smile was suddenly back. "Want to have a rummage in my bag of tricks? You never know what might pop up."

"*Jared*," I growled in warning, but it didn't have much *humph* behind it since I was giggling at the same time.

Wearing a crooked, sexy grin, he said, "Joke." But his tone and the intensity of his gaze completely contradicted that. I swallowed. The horniness continued...

The next vampire looked a lot like Butch with his neat hairdo and the devilish tint to his eyes. Unlike Butch, he seemed to like facial piercings; his nose, eyebrows, lips and ears all either had hoops or studs decorating them. His smile revealed a couple of gold teeth. He didn't photograph very well. I wasn't very photogenic myself. In human years, he was probably the oldest of all the High Masters.

"Ricardo Maxwell."

"You don't like him," I detected.

Jared shrugged. "He thinks he's a hard-case, but really it's all a big act. I can't stand people like that. He's High Master over the US and Mexico. He will, without a doubt, support Antonio. He likes to think of himself as good friends with Antonio, he's a real bad kiss-ass."

"As long as he fights with us, I don't care if he goes as far as to lodge himself permanently up Antonio's arse. Gift?"

"Shape-shifting. And it's not restricted: he can shift into whatever living thing he touches."

"Maybe Ricardo isn't so bad after all."

"I'm sorry to destroy your fantasy, but you're not his type. He's a fan of plump, curvy females with big butts. You'll see what I mean when you get a glimpse of his consort."

"So, basically, his taste is the opposite of yours." Before he could make an impish comment, I quickly asked, "So at some point you'll speak to every vampire in this file?"

He nodded. "That's right. They'll come over, ask how Antonio's doing and to pass on their regards – that kind of thing. It's just exchanging pleasantries to show respect for Antonio."

"Right."

In the last photograph, a very grim looking vampire was staring back at me. He made me think of an army sergeant or something. His face and neck were covered in scars and tattoos and had a beard of stubble, giving him quite a rugged appearance. He didn't look in the least bit welcoming.

"Kaiser Something-Or-Other. I can't pronounce his surname. He's German and a Pagori. High Master over Germany, Russia, Sweden, Finland and other places round those parts. I'm one hundred percent confident that he'll be the first to offer to join Antonio. He might be miserable and mind-numbingly boring, but he's loyal to Antonio. He's visited The Hollow a few times."

"His gift?"

"He can petrify any plant, animal or even human – totally turning them to stone."

"Well he's just gone up in my estimations."

"He'll probably be very pleased with you. Likes the slender but shapely type. Not approving of Joy."

I couldn't help smiling at that. "Well that's because a lot of blokes like to be able to *hold* what they can see."

His expression became all bad-boyish and spoke of utter mischief. "I'd certainly like to hold what I can see right now." He brushed my hair over my shoulder and grazed my earlobe with his teeth. "Sam," he breathed. "You know you want this."

I rose and took a step to the side so that I was standing in front of the neighbouring seat, taunting him more than anything else.

He left his chair and advanced toward me, perching one butt cheek on the table. Grinning, he held up his index finger. "Now that is something you can't do tomorrow night. You'll be posing as my consort; no one will believe that if you're shifting away from me. Speaking of which, you know consort decorum, right?"

I groaned and rolled my eyes. "I was Victor's for three years, what do you think?"

"I know, but that was when you were travelling in lower-class circles. This gathering will be full of the big boys, there's a certain standard they expect. Number one: you cannot leave my side without asking permission. Where I go, you follow. Number two: you don't speak to anyone unless they speak to you first. They'll speak about you to me – that's different. Unless they address you, you keep it zipped. Number three: you don't argue with anything at all that I say. I know that goes against your very nature, but you have to be a good girl."

I groaned. "All that is going to kill me."

"I should warn you and your feisty little self now that you should expect them to speak about you. You're a Sventé vampire. Me bringing a Sventé as my consort is like the president taking his servant to a royal gathering."

"Oh, really? Well I think you'll be very surprised by their response."

"In what way?"

"Just because Kejas and Pagoris rarely associate with Sventés because of their prejudiced view that we're apparently more human than vampire, don't expect them to frown upon my presence. They'll be just as curious as you are about having me bite them."

He gave me a doubtful look.

"Trust me. At least one will ask if you like to have exclusive rights to my saliva because they'll want a sample, you'll see."

His gaze was hot again, and the heat was contagious. My self-consciousness under his gaze had long ago subsided as my desire grew. Those sensual lips and those masterful hands brought plenty of memories – *really* good ones – to the forefront of my mind. This was not good while he was so close.

"Can I claim those rights now?" He leaned toward me, his eyes trained on my mouth. I took a step backwards but he took my wrist and tugged me lightly to him. Not up close to him. He was just stopping me from getting away.

I swallowed. "No, and you won't be claiming them tomorrow night either. You're going to promise me now that you won't try to take advantage of the situation that I have to do what you say."

His smile widened. "Don't worry, I won't. Know why? For the same reason that I'm not running my hands all over you right now. I'm not interested in doing anything to you that you don't first say you want me to do. When we have sex – and we will, Sam – it won't be because I seduced you, it'll be because you've finally admitted that you want it. That's why I didn't want us to do anything last night. It wasn't really me you wanted, and you'd have just said afterwards that you weren't thinking straight at the time because of what had happened outside the bar."

I didn't argue. I would've done that. The truth was that last night I did want comfort. He gave it to me by holding me, but I'd wanted more. I'd wanted to know just how good he could make me feel. Once my head was clear I probably would have berated myself for shagging a bloke who collected women like they were coupons.

He slowly brought his face to mine but didn't kiss me. The red rings of his irises were glowing. "Why do you fight it so hard, Sam?" His voice was no more than a throaty whisper.

"You know why," I whispered.

"I'll get rid of them, all of them. Just say the word and they're gone. You're all I want."

Taken aback, I studied his face, searching for some indication that he was either joking or lying. But there was no deception or humour there, and I could sense nothing but honesty coming from him. "You'll get rid of your consorts? Just like that?" There was pure disbelief dripping from my words.

"Like I said, you're all I want." His voice was still deep and throaty, indicating a barely controlled hunger. "Not as a consort. You're worth more than that. I'll grant you. it's greedy of me to have three, but just because I like to enjoy the advantages of being Heir doesn't mean I see women as objects or that I'm anything like your Sire was. If getting rid of them proves that to you then that's what I'll do."

I went to say something, but the intensity of his gaze as he ran his knuckles down the column of my throat brought me up short. His gaze dropped to my mouth, which was already dry, and I was restraining from licking it in case he mistook that as a signal for him to kiss me.

"I'll get rid of them," he repeated.

"Oh, really?"

"You don't believe me."

"Of course not."

He smiled, brushing his nose against mine. "Why?"

"What was it you said to me when we had that fight? That I should get on with my celibate lifestyle and you'd get on with shagging your consorts?"

"I haven't slept with any one of them since before our fight. Doesn't seem any point when it's you I'm thinking about."

"While you're on a roll with lies, would you care to tell me anymore?"

His gaze seized mine. Softly, he insisted, "I'm not lying."

I snorted. "You can't expect me to believe that. Joy comes to the office all the time talking about plans for you and her involving whipped cream and handcuffs and all that crap."

His smile grew. "I knew you were listening."

I smiled back, in spite of myself.

"Her version of 'seduction techniques'. All were unsuccessful."

I shook my head. "I'm sorry, but there's no way I can believe that you haven't touched them for weeks because of me. And I definitely can't believe that you'd ditch them for a shag, no matter how much you say you want me."

"Oh I don't want 'a shag'." With his nose, he skimmed the line of my jaw, making me shudder. "Once won't be enough. I want to do it over, and over, and over, and over again. And I intend to do a lot more to you than just that."

Great – now I had a series of graphic images circulating round my head that were dazing my brain with lust. "I heard you don't shag the same woman twice unless it's a consort."

"I don't."

"Yet you're saying 'over and over again'...?"

He softly ran the tip of his finger along my bottom lip, which I very nearly flicked at it with my tongue. "It's...different...with you," he finally said.

Close to overwhelmed by his closeness and teasing touches, I swallowed so hard that I was surprised I found my voice. "Different how?"

He seemed to be searching for words; confusion was splattered across his face. Eventually he shrugged one shoulder slightly. "It just is. I don't just want you, I need you. Crave you so bad that no one else even appeals to me."

The hint of desperation in his voice sent a shiver through me. I might have thought those words were just designed to eat at my defences if I hadn't seen the truth in his eyes. But even as he stood there admitting – something that I could see wasn't easy for him to do – that he wanted, needed, me so badly…he was sure to keep his touches light, simple, non-invasive. He had to see the effect he was having on me, had to be able to sense my arousal, and yet he wasn't leaping on that.

He really wasn't going to until I gave into him, I realised with a shock. Until he heard the words come from my mouth, he wouldn't act on what he wanted – craved – no matter how bad it was for him. How could I have ever thought that there was any similarity whatsoever between him and Victor? They were nothing alike. That old bastard had took what he wanted when he wanted, disregarding anyone else.

Yeah Jared was arrogant and slutty, but taking advantage of his position of Heir and accepting the offers of the women around him wasn't a crime and didn't make him anything like Victor. But then I'd known that all along really, hadn't I? It was like Jared had said; it had just been so long since my body had responded to someone without being manipulated that I hadn't known how to deal with it. So what had I done? Slammed up a shield and ran from it.

"You know how it'll feel, Sam."

I did know. I knew how his hands would feel on my skin. I knew how wildly he would kiss me. I knew how tight he would hold me. There would be that explosion of heat coursing through me, like fire. And if just having him kiss me and touch me would make me feel that, what would the rest be like? My clit was throbbing just thinking about it. Oh God, I really needed to step away from him. Right. Now.

Did my body move? No.

"I'll get rid of them, Sam. I told you I will, I meant it. All you have to do is admit that you want me." He brought his lips to mine and spoke against them. "Just admit it. Tell me you want me and I'll get rid of them."

Suddenly every single fibre of my being was sizzling with alertness, desire, and anticipation. Yeah, he was a sod and, yeah, he was sexist and, yeah, he'd rejected me last night and, yeah, there were probably more reasons than that why I shouldn't want him. But at this point I'd had enough of fighting myself, enough of running away. All I wanted now was to feel that fire again. To have his hands on me again. To have him finish what he started weeks ago.

My body was supportive of that idea. My body also sensed the *but*. Yes, there was a *but*. I just found it way too hard to believe that he would ditch his consorts just to shag me, no matter how many times he was hoping to do it or how much he wanted me.

"Just tell me you want me, and I'll get rid of them," he repeated.

Cloaking my hypersensitivity to him, I smoothed out the collar of his jacket and spoke against his lips, "Get rid of them, and then I'll tell you I want you." He didn't tug me back to him this time when I stepped away. His smile hadn't fallen, but frustration – sexual frustration, mostly – filled his expression. And his pants.

There was also respect in his gaze – a gaze that was exploring my body again. Exploring it so closely that I was tingling all over. I wondered if I'd made him even worse by holding back. He seemed to appreciate a challenge more than most.

"All right," said Jared, smiling. No one should have a smile that sexy. "You don't think I will, do you?"

"Nope."

He came toward me. "I can promise you that when I come for you tomorrow night to leave for Connelly's gathering, I'll be consort-free…and ready to make you scream as soon as we get back from there."

"Oh is that right?"

He nodded, seizing my eyes with a gaze so heated that it scorched my entire body. "And I can't wait to hear that husky voice you've got calling out my name."

"Sorry, I don't call out *any*one's name. It's nothing personal."

His smile was now almost stretched from ear to ear. "You will for me. You will for me."

(Jared)

In the interest of not having the people in the neighbouring apartments gossiping – Sam liked her private business very private, she said – I teleported her to her apartment so she didn't have to leave through the door. I was so close to just snagging a kiss before I left, but I held everything I was feeling in reserve. I meant what I'd said just as seriously as I'd said it: I wanted her to admit that she wanted me before I touched her. Twice we'd kissed before, and twice she had backed away full of excuses. This time there would be none, and no one would be backing away. I'd make sure of it.

And I'd make sure she called my name.

Before any of that was going to be possible, there was something I had to do first.

It was Daniela who answered the door when I went to the apartment. As usual, the inside was a mess: open bottles of nail varnish on the table, clothes hanging over the sofa, shoes here, there and everywhere, empty NST bottles on almost every surface. All three of them were, in a word, slobs. They were so bad that the maid had gone on strike.

"Jared, hi," said Daniela, reaching out to me with those weirdly long acrylic nails. "I've missed you."

I avoided her touch and advanced further into the apartment. Joy and Tammy appeared from the kitchen within seconds, both glowing and ready to start their usual seduction techniques. I held up my hand as a signal to them to stop in their tracks. All three girls were now looking at me with confusion and wariness flashing across their faces, glancing briefly at each other.

No matter how I phrased what I was about to say, their reactions would be the same. As such, I didn't see the point in creeping around the issue. "I'm relieving each of you of your consort position."

There was a brief moment of silence. Shock echoed within it.

"You don't want us anymore?" asked Daniela after a minute or so.

"What did we do?" Tammy was doing her hands on hips thing.

I glanced at the three of them as I explained. "My decision is not something that any of you should take personally, I—"

"You're replacing us," said Joy sharply. She had the look of someone who was considering how to do the perfect murder.

Tammy gasped and then shot Joy a scowl. "If he is, we all know who's to blame."

"Yeah," spat Daniela, glowering at Joy. "It's your fault for being so heavy on him all the time, following him around."

Joy's hands balled into fists. "I wasn't being 'heavy all the time'" – oh she was – "it's not my fault if I'm the favourite and he likes having me around."

None of this was unexpected. We'd been through something similar when I almost added another consort. All of them had suddenly become insecure and repeatedly asked what they had done wrong, if I was punishing them. Daniela had become whiny. Tammy had become full of questions. Joy had become snappy and wouldn't let the issue go. Then they all turned on each other. With that in mind, I knew that this could go on all night long. Time to cut it short.

Before I could speak, Joy turned back to me and demanded, "Who're you replacing us with?"

"I don't need to explain myself to any of you. My decision has been made, that is all you need to know. You have a week to find alternative accommodation."

Ignoring their noises of protest, I proceeded to leave the apartment. I might have let them keep it if it wasn't for the fact that it would look to others – most importantly, to Sam – like I was still using them. I'd originally thought that, since I'd had consorts for so long, it would be weird to suddenly have none. But it wasn't.

As I reached the door, there was a tug on the back of my shirt. I pivoted sharply, ready to reprimand the tugger. I hadn't expected to see the vision that was then in front of me.

Sam.

My initial reaction was to hitch in a breath and insert warmth into my expression. But then reality quickly kicked in. I sighed, irritated. "Joy, what're you doing?"

"This is what you want, isn't it," she said bitterly.

"Joy, that's—"

"I can give you that. You don't need to make her your consort. Yu don't need to do all this. *I* can give you that."

"You have a week to get out," I repeated.

Before I could open the door she threw herself in front of me, still physically a perfect imitation of Sam. Her hands grabbed my t-shirt. "Jared, listen to me. I can give you what you want. If this is what you want to see, *who* you want to see, then this is what I'll do. And I'll be better than she is. You'll be able to see her in front of you like this but you won't have to deal with all the shit she pulls. *I* won't insist on being your only consort. *I* won't talk down to you. *I* won't disrespect you. *I* won't fight you."

I sighed. "I know. That's why you'll never be her."

"So, what, you're saying it's not enough because you *care* about her?"

For a second my mind went blank, but then I deduced that of course I didn't. I couldn't. The only people I cared about were Evan and Antonio. I didn't do 'feelings' when it came to women; hadn't for a very long time. I'd already been over all this once in my head before – just because I wanted her as much as I did, it didn't mean anything. It was just lust on a very grand scale. A very, very grand scale. That was all it could be.

I removed Joy's hands from my shirt. "Have a bit of pride." And then I left.

CHAPTER TWELVE

(Sam)

At eight-thirty in the evening exactly there was a knock on my apartment door. Wow, Jared had actually used the door rather than just teleporting in. He was obviously on his best behaviour. Imagine that. Full points for punctuality.

Our eyes raked over each other as I opened the door. God, there was no denying how gorgeous he looked in his pale blue designer shirt and black designer trousers – such a simple combination and yet he looked edible. I suddenly felt underdressed, even though I was wearing a blood-red cocktail dress that was so thin and clingy it was more like an extra layer of skin. Somehow, though, it didn't look tarty or cheap.

Fletcher had sorted my entire outfit. Three hours he had spent rallying around me asking me to try things on. Eventually he had settled on this dress, a pair of high-heeled strap-up red shoes, and a matching purse.

Jared did exactly what Fletcher had said he would do. He flashed me the sexiest, hungriest smile and sucked in a breath. "I'm so torn right now."

"Torn?"

"As much as I know how important it is to go to this gathering at Connelly's place, all I really want to do is push you back inside and ravish you. What to do..."

"What makes you think I'd let you ravish me?"

He settled his hands softly on my hips. "I held up to my side of the bargain, now it's your turn to deliver."

"You really got rid of them?" I hadn't actually been convinced that he would. Not just for me, just like that.

"I told you I would, didn't I?"

I pursed my lips. "Then *maybe* I'll let you ravish me after Connelly's gathering."

"You're a tease."

"You like that. Now let's go."

"Yes, let's. The sooner it's over, the sooner I can get you back here."

"How are we getting there?"

He smiled. "How do you think?"

There was then that familiar queasy feeling in my stomach and suddenly we were outside a double-glazed. security box that was attached to a large set of black iron gates. One of the two guards inside it was startled by our abrupt appearance but seemed to recognise Jared and dropped his reproachful twist of the lips.

"Evening," he greeted Jared, carefully taking the invitation in Jared's hand that had been addressed to him from Connelly. He hadn't acknowledged my presence at all. Wow, they really were stuck-up round these parts. Stepping aside, he gestured for us to pass through. "Have a good night, Sir."

Jared nodded and then, with a hand at my back, guided me through. Now, I was not one to get overly impressed by big fancy houses, but this one came second to Antonio's mansion. The grey limestone building was three stories high and had stained-glass windows of varying styles and sizes – something I wouldn't have thought would have added to its character. It had a very welcoming, extravagant portico which, right now, was the only part of this angle of the mansion through from light was shining through.

The winding path toward it was a bit annoying, I felt like I was off to see the Wizard of bloody Oz. If I hadn't been wearing my heels, I would have suggested to Jared that we take a small detour and just cross straight over the lawn. He'd have probably said no. Tonight I had to do as I was told. How wonderful.

Having entered through the solid pine porch doors, we came to the Grand Entry Hall. It was crowded with vampires. Obviously the gathering began here. It seemed to then branch out further ahead underneath a chandelier hung from what had to be something like an eight foot high ceiling, with vampires coming and going from rooms on both the left and right. I guessed them to be the living room and the dining room. Far ahead was a curved solid pine staircase that was carpeted golden and had intricate carvings. Connelly was obviously a flashy sod.

Remember not to leave my side, said Jared.

Sir, yes, Sir.

One hand still on my back, Jared guided me through the crowd; his touch burned in the most pleasurable way. The vampires had all congregated into circles, some big and some small. Plenty of those heads turned as we squished through, nodding respectfully at Jared. I got a second look due to being the Heir's consort. Suddenly I felt like I was in school walking down the corridor with the most popular boy, everyone wondering what it was about me that made him pick me.

The blokes seemed to approve of me. I suppose the blood-red dress helped with that. As for the females...well they seemed to be looking for something about me that might make me worth gossiping about. Once they realised I was a Sventé, they'd be in their element. If it wasn't for the warmth coming from Jared's hand, I'd be feeling mightily uncomfortable and a little agitated already.

God, so much excess energy buzzed around the place. Snort. Obviously these master vampires weren't as great as they thought they were if they were leaking energy like that. And to think that they were looking down on me.

The way that Jared once had, I suddenly thought.

For a second, the question of whether he might return to that frame of mind after we had shagged entered my mind. I quickly discarded it. I didn't want to explore that idea, afraid of the answer. Yes, afraid. I concentrated on the feel of Jared, his scent, his proximity, his promise of what was to come later.

The end of this gathering couldn't come soon enough. I'd never liked parties. Not vampire ones, anyway. Going as someone's consort made the night even worse. Not only was I under Jared's control, but I couldn't wander off and socialise or drink from any of the intoxicated humans. And if any vampires did decide to talk to me and it turned out that they were a total bore, I had to stand there and listen to it, nodding in agreement with things I couldn't give a crap about, or laughing at jokes that wouldn't be funny at any time in any place.

Worst of all; if any vampire decided to subtly feel me up a little, I couldn't do anything about it other than tell Jared and hope he told them to get their hands off me. Not that I'd ever stuck to that rule. Victor had usually intervened before I had a chance to react, which was something that I had always been grateful to him for. He never let anyone else ever touch me, or bite me, and he would refuse anyone who proposed that I bite them.

Here comes Connelly, Jared informed me.

Yes, the friendly looking bloke was on his way over, obviously eager to greet any guests who arrived. He seemed even more enthusiastic due to it being Jared.

"Jared," he crooned, shaking his hand. "Always good to see you. You look well."

"And so do you, Rupert." He flashed him a charismatic smile.

"Your charm is still there, I see. May I enquire about Antonio?"

"He's great, thank you. Sends his regards."

"Ah, you must thank him for me. I have hopes to visit The Hollow later this year…"

The conversation faded from my attention as my eyes settled on something else. Bennington. He was stood at the arched entrance to the dining room, sipping a drink…and staring straight at me with a disturbing smile plastered on his smarmy face.

Reminding myself that it was important to play my role, I returned his smile of acknowledgement. He gave me a look that said he would see me later, and then he waltzed off into the dining room. I had no doubt that he would see me later, especially now that he had seen me with Jared. If he planned to attack The Hollow, the last thing he would want was me fighting on Antonio's side.

Three times he had challenged Victor. Bennington's idea of a duel, however, was to set one of his vampires against the one of his adversary's vampires. All three times Victor had used me, and all three times I had won the duel. Bennington knew how well I controlled my gift, and I wouldn't be surprised if he made one last ditch effort to collect me. Luckily, I was secure in the knowledge that Jared would oppose this.

I returned my attention to Jared and Connelly in time to hear Connelly's, "This one is a massive improvement on your last consort."

Could I resist smiling at that? No.

"Yes, she is," agreed Jared.

"A Sventé?"

I felt Jared stiffen. He was obviously waiting to be frowned upon or looked at like he was crazy. He should've listened to me.

Connelly flashed me a smile. "And a beautiful one, too. May I ask your name?"

Say Samantha, not Sam, said Jared. *High Master vampires don't abbreviate their consort's names, it's too informal.*

I know. My expression was shamelessly flirtatious, only missing the wink. "Samantha."

His smile became cheeky and his face was suddenly flushed. He turned back to Jared. "It has been so long since I have had an encounter with a Sventé. This brings back some fantastic memories, I must admit. Dare I ask if your new consort is available only to you?"

Translation: Can I borrow her for a few minutes? I couldn't hold back a smirk. *Told you.*

"I never was very good at sharing," said Jared, sliding his hand from my back to around my waist.

"Ah," murmured Connelly disappointedly but without dropping his smile. "Well, Jared, when you next do a consort spring cleaning, be sure to let me know. I do believe you may set off a trend."

The noise of the Grand Entry doors opening and closing behind us pulled us all out of the conversation. Connelly laid his hand on Jared's forearm. "I have to dash. More guests to greet. Please enjoy your evening. I'm sure we will speak again before you leave." Connelly bowed his head at both of us. "A pleasure to meet you, Samantha."

"Did he really just suggest I pass you on when I'm done?" asked Jared disbelievingly once Connelly had left to greet his new guests.

"What, you've never had anyone do that before?"

"Never. I would never have thought he'd have been so interested when you're a Sventé."

"Look, upper class vampires getting involved with Sventés is a bit like dogging – it happens, but no one let's on that they do it."

His laugh was silent. "And here I am strolling around with one like it's the norm."

"Believe me when I say that if they look shocked, it's only because they wouldn't have expected you to be so out-in-the-open about it, not because they truly think it's degrading. If you decided to pass me round this place like a parcel, they'd all make sure they handled me at some point, I promise you that."

Jared's lips were suddenly at my ear. "The only vampire who'll be manhandling you tonight is me."

"*If* I let you."

"You get such satisfaction out of teasing me, don't you?"

"I still maintain that you like it."

It wasn't long before master vampires came to greet Jared, each with the same questions – How was Antonio? Was Jared well? Was I his new consort and did he like to share? I could sense that Jared was getting more and more aggravated by that last question. His grip on my waist intensified until it was possessive and a blatant display of ownership. Even that didn't discourage people from asking. Of course there were the odd looks of disapproval but never did those snobbish vamps let Jared see their distaste – they probably feared causing offense.

One by one, the High Master vamps from the file also came to greet Jared – except for Bennington. Although I glanced around and feigned disinterest, I was listening intently to every word that was exchanged and the tone in which those words were delivered. I almost laughed aloud at how their consorts, all Kejas, seemed to look down on me. They disliked me even more when the High Masters questioned Jared about me, his new consort. I didn't let it show that I was getting sick of being referred to as a consort. It brought back memories I didn't want to think about.

When Jared discretely gave my hand a supportive, comforting squeeze, I gathered that he had picked up on my irritation. It unnerved me that we could read each other like that. I had slowly gone from being able to sense when he was near to also picking up on what he was feeling at times. If Jared and I had shared blood at some point then I could blame this weird link on that and have the comfort of knowing the link was only temporary. But right now, I had no idea what this link was or how to get rid of it.

What do you think about the High Masters then? asked Jared as we made our way to the patio, which overlooked a large, fancy swimming pool complete with a waterfall.

I'd say Carlos' loyalty is questionable, and I'd say the same about Winston Jones. But I reckon the others would be loyal to Antonio, especially Bran.

You and I are on the same wavelength then.

Oh I knew that, and it was what disturbed me.

Have you noticed Bennington acting odd?

A couple of times I saw him whispering and lingering around the other High Masters. He's been looking over at you quite a bit.

Actually, I think it's you he's been looking at. The idea seemed to piss Jared right off.

If he is, he's probably thinking how best to approach the prospect of you passing me on to him. An idea popped into my head. *How about you go leave me alone for a sec and let him have the opportunity to speak to me on my own?*

Hell no, Sam, I'm not leaving you alone. I told you, you don't leave my side.

Just act as if you're going to answer a call of nature. It's not like I can't defend myself if I have to, but I can't see anyone — not even Bennington — trying to hurt me.

No, I'm not comfortable with having you out of my sight.

I pressed myself up against him, seizing his gaze. Instantly his irises began to glow.

Don't even try seduction to get your way, Sam.

Just give me five minutes.

Hell. No.

With my tongue, I drew a circle on the patch of skin that was exposed by the V of his shirt. He shuddered, gripping my hip so tight that his fingertips were biting into the skin. I scraped my teeth over the patch the way I knew he liked. *Jared, you know this is a good idea.*

Sam, will you quit with the teasing.

Oh this isn't teasing. I've got every intention of biting you tonight. So let's get the business crap out of the way and then we can get out of here. Don't you want that?

He shuddered again. *You're evil.*

Five minutes, Jared.

He sighed, half surrender half frustration. *Three minutes.* He swatted my arse and then pointed a finger at me. "Stay here. I'll be back in a minute." *If anyone hurts you, I swear to God I'll kill the pair of you for it.*

I mentally rolled my eyes. I suspected that it wouldn't be long before Bennington came over — he wouldn't want to chance Jared getting back before he'd had a chance to get whatever it was he had to say out of his system. I was right. Something like thirty seconds later I heard:

"Well hello, Samantha. It's been a while."

I nodded and smiled a little. "Yep, it has."

"I take it that Victor had a price for you after all."

"Oh he didn't sell me, he's dead."

Bennington's thick black brows rose. "Dead? How?"

"I killed him."

"You killed your own Sire?"

"I'd kill anyone who tried to hurt Antonio. And if Victor really thought he could attack Antonio and live to tell the tale, he was a daft sod who was just begging for an immediate death." I saw Bennington's head working away. He probably didn't like that I was clearly very loyal to Antonio.

"It is little wonder, then, that Jared has you as his consort. For now, I should say."

I could guess Bennington's game. He wanted to turn me against Jared. "So he's a bit of a slut?"

"I've never seen him with the same consort twice. It strikes me that he gets bored most easily."

"That works out well for me then as I'm pretty much the same."

He didn't seem to like that answer. "Don't you miss your days as an assassin?"

"What's there to miss? Blood and gore?" I shook my head, my face scrunched up in repugnance. "Don't get me wrong, if Antonio asked me to work for him as an assassin then I'd do it, but I'm quite content as I am."

His expression said he wasn't convinced. "You're a most spirited individual, Samantha. I cannot imagine you being satisfied being nothing more than a consort, even if it is to the Heir of The Hollow. The offer for you to join my team is still open. Then you can exercise that spirit of yours, end your consort days." It wasn't a question. He had every intention of consulting Jared about it and was letting me know in advance, giving me incentives to be cooperative.

"I can't say I've any need to complain. Jared's a good shag. But by all means ask him."

"Ask me what?" I'd already known Jared was approaching. I'd felt it in my bones. He laid a hand on the small of the back and greeted Bennington. To his credit, he was as civil and relaxed as he had been to the other vampires; giving nothing away about his hatred of him.

Bennington spoke, "I was just saying to Samantha that my interest in her is still great. Victor was never open to negotiations about selling her. I wondered about your own willingness to do so." His facial expression and cunning smile told me that he was confident that Jared wouldn't be possessive over a consort.

"I'm afraid my interest in her is just as great," replied Jared as his arm snaked around my waist once again.

"Oh I didn't mean my interest in her is as a consort, no. But if the idea of losing a consort bothers you much, I'm sure we can come to some arrangement." He gestured at his own consort; a blonde Keja who was gazing at Jared like he was a Christmas treat. I had to fight against the urge to cook up a gust of wind that would get her away from Jared and out of my sight.

"No disrespect to you or your consort, but my answer is a resounding 'no'. I'm nowhere near finished with this woman yet," he added in a cheeky voice. "Enjoy your evening." With that, he guided me back into the mansion. *I almost punched the sleazy son of a bitch.*

You're not the only one.

What did he say while I was gone?

Just trying to entice me to become part of his little collection. Typically he'd set up a fight-off between his best assassin and yours, me being the prize. But he hasn't got his team with him so had to use a different tactic. He probably reasoned that I could take you on with my gift and thought that if he could make me want to leave you, I could fight for my freedom or something.

My brows arched as we entered the dining room to find plenty of vamps chomping on their consorts. It seemed that they were making a 'toast' to Connelly for his hospitality. I knew what Jared would say next, and instead of it unnerving me, the idea excited me.

"It would be rude not to join in toasting our good host, don't you think?" Before I could say a word, he'd spun me around and was grazing his teeth over the pulse in my neck. *Sam?*

I couldn't believe that he was actually asking my permission and keeping to his word that he wouldn't do it unless I wanted him to. As his teeth grazed my skin again, I quivered. *Do it.*

I've wanted to taste you for so fucking long. He fisted a hand in my hair, yanked my head back slightly and sank his teeth down hard. As he took a long, greedy gulp he moaned against my skin. The moan vibrated through every fibre of me. Instantly desire began to coil low in my stomach and tingly sensations overtook my body which he kept crushed to his as he continued to drink greedily. *You taste so good, baby.*

The tingling intensified when he called me that, which was dumb really because it wasn't like I hadn't been called that before. And it wasn't as if I hadn't been told that my blood tasted good before now, and yet hearing Jared say those words had a primal, raw desire like nothing I'd ever felt before coursing through me.

I was a little light-headed by the time he had ceased his gluttonous drinking. When he looked up at me his irises were glowing, making me hitch in a breath. What I really, really, really wanted to do was bite down on his neck and have my own little party, but I knew that was against consort etiquette.

Instead, I grabbed the index finger of his left hand and brought it up to my mouth slowly, giving him time to object. He didn't. I sank my teeth into the tip of his finger and sucked eagerly, making him moan and shudder. God, the taste of his blood was amazing; wild and potent with a male spice to it. Conscious that a little too much of my saliva could have him emptying into his pants, I took only a little before stopping.

"It is *so* time to leave." He gripped my hips tightly and then we were gone. I barely noticed the queasy sensation in my stomach this time as I was too hyped up on anticipation and excitement. And on Jared's blood. I definitely had to taste that again sometime soon. He didn't ease his tight hold on my hips even as we arrived at his apartment. His gaze was serious and penetrating, searching mine. "Tell me," he breathed against my lips. "Say it."

"I want you."

And then he was kissing me. Kissing me so hard and so desperately and clutching me to him as though he was half-expecting me to disappear. The very second that those lips touched mine there was that familiar *bang*; an explosion in my veins and the sensation of a hot raging fire spreading through me, just as I knew there would be. I fisted my hands in his shirt, pulling him to me, refusing to accept that there wasn't a way of getting any closer.

His hungry, greedy kisses devoured my lips and overwhelmed my tongue. As I pulled at his shirt with such force that I involuntarily took backward steps, he stalked me predatorily and slid his hands all over me, never parting our lips. We stumbled and staggered and swayed, and then my back slammed against something hard, smooth and cold.

Opening my eyes, I realised with surprise that rather than being halfway through his apartment, we had at one point somehow spun around and now I was crammed against the front door.

Jared, too, opened his eyes and was equally surprised. He braced his hands against the door, forming his own little prison around me, grinning. "I hope you're not trying to escape. But I guess restraining you might be fun."

"I hope this isn't your idea of caging me in. Because if it is, your cage is kind of" – I wiggled his outstretched arms – "flimsy."

He slammed his body against mine, crushing me. I could feel his heart hammering in his chest. I could see those red Pagori irises glowing. "Better?"

I pursed my lips. "Yes. But I could still get away."

"Not a chance." He kissed me so hard and with such intensity that it was as though he meant to back up his words; that he was letting me know that he wouldn't let me pull back this time, that he wouldn't allow me to pretend any longer that I didn't want this as much as he did.

Still, that didn't mean I couldn't play with him a little, did it?

While his hands were preoccupied with scrunching and tugging my hair, I slid my hands down his chest to his waistline and bunched up the bottom of his shirt – which I'd noticed did not button all the way down and so could only be removed by being pulled over his head. Perfect for what I had in mind.

I slowly slid it up and up and then, just as I'd hoped, he raised his arms for me to slide it over his head. God, he was all muscle and sinew. Instead of tugging the shirt off, however, I left it covering his face and trapping his arms slightly as I used the opportunity to escape.

I squeezed out from between his gorgeous body and the door, and bolted, calling over my shoulder, "That was just too easy!"

I heard him mumble something in surprise and then he was pursuing me as I nimbly dashed at human speed around the living area, hopping from the floor to the coffee table to the sofa to the—

Arms seized me abruptly. I was twisted around in those arms, and lips found mine as my legs were simultaneously wrapped around his hips. Again my back collided into something hard and the wind was literally knocked out of me.

Jared chuckled. "I can't believe you just did that." As he resumed kissing me wildly, his hands, fingers splayed, skimmed up my thighs and under my dress. "You won't get away again."

I smiled against his lips. "You have this habit of underestimating me."

He rocked his hips against mine, making me moan and tighten my arms around his neck. "Same goes for you if you still really think you won't be calling out my name."

"Like I said, it's nothing personal. I don't call out anyone's name."

"We'll see." Jared's eyes bore into mine as he let his hands journey further, cupping my arse. While one hand lightly ran over my breast, he slid his other hand, fingers splayed again, further underneath my thigh. It was almost painful when his fingers stopped on reaching my thong, refusing to go any further. Unable to help it, I twisted my hips toward his hand but he only drew his fingers back, smirking.

Fine. Let's play some more, shall we.

It was a squeeze since he was pressed tightly to me, but my hands slid down his naked chest and reached the waistline of his trousers and slowly tackled his belt, my eyes still meeting his. With the belt gone, I took the button and zip out of the equation. Then I tried lowering my legs. He let me, anticipating what I had in mind. I pushed slightly against his chest, creating just enough room for me to slide down the wall. I placed my mouth against the tip of the erection that was straining against his trousers and exhaled heavily, making him groan.

As I planned, he was now off-guard. I tugged on both his trousers and his underwear, pulling them all the way to his ankles. A horse would be envious of what I was looking at right now. I met his eyes and smiled...and then I dived to the side, sprung to my feet and bolted again. "Typical male – the slightest chance of getting sucked off and your mind went blank."

Still at human speed, I rushed passed the conference table. I could hear him struggling behind me; obviously a little delayed by the fact that his ankles were more or less bound by his own pants. Soon, though, he was chasing me again. I leaped onto the counter in the kitchen and ran along the length of it, hopping over the hob and other appliances. Cheating, he came after me at vampire speed and caught me just as I reached the end of the counter. It was a good tackle, I'll give him that. Suddenly we were diving toward the floor.

He twisted his naked body to break my fall and then immediately rolled on top of me, grinning evilly.

"Bitch," he said endearingly. His lips came down onto mine, almost teasing in the way that they moved now. "As it hardly seems fair that I'm naked and you're fully clothed..." He ripped open my dress, tearing the entire length of it. He moaned at the view he then had of my body.

"I liked that dress."

"I'll buy you a new one," he murmured against the column of my throat. Starting there, his lips began working their way down in a straight line; kissing the hollow of my throat, and between my breasts, and along my abdomen until he reached my navel. Then he gazed up at me wearing a knowing smile. He was perfectly aware that I was desperate for him to go further, to remove my thong, to use more than just his lips, but again he seemed intent on teasing the life out of me. Being teased really wasn't my thing, but neither was begging for what I wanted.

Fine. Let the games continue.

I pulled my leg toward my chest and swiftly untied the straps of my shoe before flinging it to the side of me. Jared's eyes had followed the movement closely, sliding a hand along my leg. Correctly anticipating that I would do the same with the other leg, he elevated his body a little to allow me better access to my shoe. That was all I needed. The second my shoe was off I pushed him backwards with my foot, rolled from beneath him and scrambled to my feet. He grabbed an ankle but I wrestled free and bolted again.

I didn't get far this time before he had scooped me up into his arms, laughing. "Okay, fair enough, I did underestimate you." His voice suddenly became deep and rough as we entered another room. "This is where we find out if you underestimated me." Then I was flung onto a soft surface, making me bounce and giggle. The material beneath me was silky-smooth. Silk then, obviously.

Details of the room barely registered. The warm gold, cream and ivory theme continued in here, as did the solid oak flooring. The bed I was on was absolutely huge and the sheets were golden.

Jared slowly crawled up the length of me, bringing his angelically gorgeous face to mine. His lips and tongue overwhelmed my mouth as my torn dress was removed entirely. He gripped my wrists and drew my hands above my head. There was then tearing and fumbling as a strip of my destroyed dress was used to bind my wrists together and secure them to the iron headboard.

"Shall I tell you what's going to happen now?" He moved his mouth to my ear. "First I'm going to play with these gorgeous tits here, suck on these pretty little nipples. Then I'm going to fuck you with my fingers and my tongue until you come in my mouth. Only then will I slide my cock inside you. It's not going to be slow and gentle, Sam. I'm going to fuck you hard and fast until you come so hard you scream. And do you know what you'll scream? My name."

(Jared)

Before she could deny it again, I tugged on her bottom lip with my teeth and slipped my tongue inside her mouth. Sam met it with her own, stroking it and sucking on it while she arched beneath me. A groan escaped me as I palmed and kneaded her full breasts. Christ, the feel of her...No fantasy had lived up to it. I'd almost surged inside her when I had her against the front door. But having waited way too long, I was going to make the most of every minute of it. The way she was protesting with her body wasn't helping me restrain myself from taking her right now, and her burning gaze told me that she knew it.

I swooped down and took a nipple into my mouth, suckling, and nibbling, and licking, and then curling my tongue around it. When her moans became whimpers, I closed my mouth over her other nipple and gave it the same attention, loving every raspy moan she made. That amazing scent of hers – vanilla musk with a hint of honeycomb – was shooting up my nostrils and threatening to splinter my self-control.

Suddenly her legs were around my hips and her thighs were squeezing to bring me closer so she could thrust her hips toward mine. I nearly lost it there and then. Bringing my face to hers, I gave her a reprimanding look. "And here was me thinking that you'd be a good girl."

"Not in my nature."

Smiling a little devilishly, I trailed a hand down, down, down, at what I guessed was a frustratingly slow pace.

"Jared," she growled warningly.

"You can take it, you're tough." On reaching her thong, I tore it and chucked it aside, taking a minute to enjoy the view. Perfect.

"In case you haven't already guessed, I really don't like being teased."

I arched a brow. "It never bothered you when you were doing it to me. Besides, I've been waiting a long time for this, Sam. I'm not rushing it." I chuckled at her low growl and then slid a finger between her wet folds and circled her clit. "Is this what you want?"

She moaned. "Jared, no more teasing."

"Was that a 'please'?"

"What's the matter, aren't you very good with your hands? Seriously, is this the best you can do?"

I had to admire her spirit, but I wasn't going to let her get away with taunting me. I sent that familiar electrical charge through my body and out of my finger onto her clit. She bounced, gasping, as the electricity zinged through her. I smiled evilly. "You decide."

I released another charge. And another. And another. Always watching her, revelling in every moan and groan she made. Then I slipped two fingers inside her. Her gasp was gratitude and pleasure mixed together. "You're so wet, baby," I murmured as I thrust my fingers in and out of her. I released one final electrical charge and then, sensing that she was at the crest of an orgasm, replaced my fingers with my tongue. That pushed her over the edge and four lashes of my tongue later she shattered, her entire body convulsing as the orgasm overtook her.

I wasn't done. The taste of her was addictive. I continued tormenting her with my tongue; alternating between stabbing deeply inside her and suckling on her clit over and over until she exploded once more. Snatching her gaze I crawled back up to her. "Get ready to call out my name for me, Sam."

"Not gonna happen," she panted.

In one quick movement, I hooked her legs over my shoulders and slammed inside her. Her back bowed from the bed as a husky cry tore out of her throat. "Take more, baby." I reared back and then rammed in deep, groaning as her muscles tightened around my cock. "All of me." Again I roughly plunged inside her, forcing her to take every inch. Finally I was buried balls deep in her body. Finally I was where I needed to be. That was it: the little control I'd had left just snapped. Every thrust was deep, fast, hard, urgent, almost violent.

There was a sense of relief mixed in with it all; the urge to do this had been repressed for way too long.

"Oh my God," she rasped.

"Look at me." Aquamarine eyes met mine and a shudder ran through me. "Do you like me fucking you hard? Do you? Tell me." When she didn't answer, I abruptly slowed my movements until they were practically sluggish.

"What're you doing? Don't tease!"

All innocence, I said, "I asked if you liked it hard. When you didn't answer, I figured you wanted it slow."

"Bastard."

"That wasn't nice. Maybe I should just stop." I withdrew from her body completely and smiled at her low growl. "What's the matter, baby? Do you want my cock back inside you?"

"Yes," she bit out.

"You sure?"

"Yes."

I slammed into her, driving deep, but then kept my movements slow as I thrust in and out of her. When she began writhing restlessly I asked, "You want more?" She nodded, moaning. "You want me to fuck you hard again?"

"Yes."

"Then I'm afraid you're going to have to beg for it." I almost laughed as her mouth fell open. Seeing that she was about to curse me, I pounded hard into her once and then went back to soft and slow. Again she growled. "Beg me, baby. Beg me to fuck you hard, and I will." Again I abruptly punched my cock hard inside her before going back to gentle thrusts, every now and then giving her another hard singular thrust.

Soon she was so totally mindless that she was whimpering. "You need to come?" She nodded. "You need it harder?" Another nod. "Then give me what I want." It seemed like forever before she croaked out the one word 'Please'. "Good girl."

I reached up and destroyed the knot binding her wrists, and then I was ruthlessly powering into her and she was clinging to me like I was the only solid thing in her world. She nipped my lips and tongue, lapping up each trickle of blood that came for those short seconds to the surface before the skin healed itself. I did the same, and with the combined bliss of the moment, of the taste of her blood and of her Sventé saliva running through me I was about ready to break.

I upped the speed to vampire momentum, groaning at the sensations that were so agonisingly good that they were at the same time bad and just about bearable. Seeing every feeling she was experiencing shining from her eyes spurred me on – hunger, passion, desire, pleasure, pain – and intensified my own pleasure tenfold.

God, Jared!

"Out loud." I knew I was wearing a boyish, smug grin. "Out loud for me, baby." It went beyond wanting to hear her say it. I needed to hear it, though I didn't bother to try to understand why it was important. I tugged hard on her hair as I demanded, "Sam, *now!*" At last she screamed my name, her muscles clamped around my dick like a vice and I came harder than I ever had before in my life. "Son of a bitch!"

At that very moment she, without warning, sunk her teeth into my neck and drank like an alcoholic would from a whiskey bottle. My hand twisted in her hair and pressed her head closer, and by the time she was done I actually exploded inside her a second time. She matched my smug grin, and she had every damn right to.

Still all tangled together, we then tipped onto our sides. The silk sheets didn't seem so soft now that I had the feel of Sam's skin beneath my hands. We just gazed at each other as the tingly shudders from our orgasms slipped away. The silence wasn't awkward. No feeling that a big, fat pink elephant was dancing and prancing around us. She didn't even squirm under my gaze the way she usually did.

Minutes later, she puffed and glanced at the bedside clock. "Well, I should go. We should forget this happened, needless to say it was a big mistake."

"*What?*" Even as I rolled us over and trapped her beneath me, she was laughing. "You better be kidding."

"You should see your face." The minx was still laughing.

"It wasn't funny. No way will I let you go off into another state of denial." But I was chuckling even as I said it. Mostly with shock; I hadn't thought it would bother me that much if she were to do that. I shook off the issue. "And never has anyone left me straight after sex."

"Oh, but it's okay when blokes do it."

"I'm not doing it. I believe you were warned about the 'over and over and over again' part. Oh and never has anyone run from me before."

She shrugged, smiling sweetly. "Just making you work for it a little."

"A little?"

"I took it easy on you."

"You were like Houdini."

"But I stuck to human velocity. And I never used my gift either."

I brushed a kiss across her lips. "Feel free to conjure your whip some time."

She grinned. "I'm not sure you could handle it. Not if you can't even manage one female Sventé."

"In my defence, this one female Sventé is a hard-ass."

"And you're used to girls throwing themselves *at* you rather than legging it away from you. Speaking of which, how did your consorts take it?"

"As I expected."

"Would I be right in thinking that Joy took it the worst?"

The memory of her plea entered my mind.

"What? You've got a weird look on your face. What did she do?"

"Nothing worth talking about."

"Your expression says otherwise. What happened?"

I sighed. Sam would no doubt find the truth shudder-worthy, but I didn't want to lie to her. I had a feeling that she would know if I did anyway. I rolled off her and onto my side. "Joy, um, guessed that I was getting rid of them because it was you I wanted, though she actually thinks it's to make you my only consort."

"And...?"

"Joy can make herself into a perfect replica of someone, so she offered to morph into you as often as I wanted and then things could stay as they were."

Sam grimaced, but I couldn't read her expression. She twisted her body to face mine. "But you said no?"

"You sound surprised."

"I am. I mean, as creepy as Joy's little offer sounds to me; it's probably a decent one from a bloke's point of view. You could have kept your consorts and still, *sort of*, shagged me."

I kissed her neck as I spoke. "It wouldn't have been you, so it wouldn't have been real. She wouldn't ever kiss me like you do. Or tease me like you do. She wouldn't have had your scent, your voice, your blood, or your mind...And I wanted every part of you." I looked up at her then, shrugging. "I guess that makes me a greedy, spoilt brat."

Again her expression was unreadable. She brought her face to mine and gave me a long, soft, searching kiss. Nothing like any kiss I'd ever had before. And just like that, I wanted her again. I snaked my hands around her and pulled her close, aligning her body to mine. I explored every curve and line all over again, but this time lightly and not so insistently, and never invasive.

Wriggling and squirming in frustration, she said, "I'll tell you what, you don't tease me so much, and I won't fight you this time."

"I'd say 'not a chance', but I did notice that my caging-in techniques need some work. Not surprising since I've never had to use them before." I rolled us so that I was draped over her. "Let's see if we can get you calling out my name again." I brought my mouth down on hers, knotting my tongue with hers over and over. "Sam?"

"Hmmm?" she murmured through another kiss.

"Promise me you won't go back into that state of denial again." She seemed just as surprised to hear me say that as I was to hear me say it. I decided that it should be another one of those things that I knew was important but didn't bother to try to understand. Whatever it was, it meant enough to me to voice it.

Her fingertips traced my cheek. "No more denial. It's too late for that now anyway."

This time when my lips came down to hers, they moved fiercely and urgently. I then trailed my hands down to the backs of her thighs, raised her hips to mine and surged deep inside her.

CHAPTER THIRTEEN

(Sam)

Although I wasn't one for sprawling all over the bed in my sleep and I usually curled up in a foetal position, I still like to have my space. But when I woke up, I found myself nestled into Jared like a bird under the wing. I even had an arm draped over him. Usually I kept my arms huddled against my chest. Sure, I remember us getting into this position – Jared on his back with an arm curled round my waist, holding me to him as reverberations from more orgasms subsided. But how had I *fallen* asleep like this? And how had I actually slept the entire morning like this?

I could try telling myself that I'd just been so wiped after such an eventful encounter with Jared – he had the stamina of a Trojan. Or I could try writing it off as a result of my stomach being so tanked before I fell asleep – I'd swallowed a decent amount of his blood in addition to some NSTs. I could even pin the blame on the bed – it was without a doubt the comfiest bed in the world. But if I was honest, I would admit that the situation was nothing to do with any of those things, and everything to do with the fact that it was Jared who I was with.

But I'd never tell him that. Just like I'd never tell him that he was by far the best shag I'd ever had – his ego was bad enough already. No one had ever touched me the way he had, hands exploring every part of me like he was learning and marking me. No one had ever been so intent on pleasuring me in every way possible or gotten so much satisfaction from that. And then there was the way that he had looked at me...like every tiny flicker of emotion I felt was important. Sometimes something blazed in his eyes that I would have mistaken for possessiveness if it weren't for how certain I was that this was just about sex for him.

God, I'd forgotten what real sex was truly like. Sex with Victor didn't count as real as far as I was concerned. I, *me*, hadn't been part of it. The desire he had made me feel hadn't been real. As such, I hadn't had an orgasm in years. Jared and his teasing had me climaxing again and again.

In truth, I'd loved the teasing just as much as I'd hated it. It was beyond my understanding how he managed to hold back for as long as he had that first time – the hunger had been so evident in his expression. In fact, I couldn't understand why he had felt the need to restrain himself at all. Yeah he'd said he didn't want to rush because he'd waited so long, but I didn't get why that would matter. Then again, Jared didn't operate in the same way that everyone else did.

Like electrifying my clit and G-spot, for instance...That just wasn't normal. But God it had felt *so* good. It had burned and sizzled and sent shooting sensations through me that were the perfect balance of pleasure and pain. As if I hadn't already been on fire just by having him kiss and touch me. Over the edge I'd gone.

Never had I thought he would make me lose control enough to call his name. But taking into account everything he made me feel, how could I *not* have? I hadn't just called it out that one time either. Every single time he had been inside me, without fail, he'd reduced me to such a rapturous state that I would have called out anything he wanted. But after the first time, I hadn't needed asking again anyway. He'd been just as smug about it every time.

The smugness was partly why I'd joked after our first round of sex about it all being a mistake. I'd just wanted to bring him back down to Earth, but I really hadn't expected him to react so badly at the idea of it. Too many things about him I just didn't get. I got *him*, just not all of his reactions concerning me. I mean, *come on*, if Joy could have morphed into me at his leisure then it was a shock that he hadn't even tried it. Surely a girl-obsessed bloke wouldn't be so fussy and would prefer a collection of consorts to this casual shag. I really hadn't, and still didn't, know what to think of it.

In a way, it had somehow managed to sound sweet, especially when he had said that he wanted every part of me. Shrug. Well, now that he'd finally gotten what he wanted, his interest may have expired. It'd be a shame as we seemed to have this weird instinctive understanding of what the other liked and wanted, and it made us good together – in bed, I mean. Just in bed. Honest.

Jared's perfect stillness and even breathing told me that he was still asleep. I'd happily have stayed there, but I was just so thirsty. Quietly and gently, I freed myself from his hold and edged myself further and further along the bed. Finally reaching the end, I gently pushed myself up. I hadn't even taken a step before an arm curled around my waist and I was dragged backwards, colliding with a naked body.

Jared, his chest pressed against my back, nuzzled the crook of my neck. "Hey," he said a little sleepily. "Trying to escape before I woke up?"

"I might have done if you hadn't destroyed my clothes."

"They were in the way."

"So were yours," I said, amused, "but I didn't tear them."

"No, you just used them to get me all tangled while you made a run for it." He repeatedly kissed my neck gently, and almost instantly tingling started between my thighs. I was sure that I had the most sensitive neck in history. "You. Taste. So. Good."

"Are we talking about my skin or my blood?"

A low chuckle tickled my ear. "Both. And I can think of some other parts of you I enjoy tasting. But none of that beats being inside you; I fucking love that." Then he proved that he meant it – in earnest.

He proved it again when he teleported me to my apartment and joined me uninvited in the shower. Needless to say, that wasn't a problem. Then he proved it again in my bedroom once we'd dried off. See what I meant about the Trojan stamina? Little more than ten seconds after our final round, there was knocking on the front door. Considering that both of us were lying on the bed naked and panting, it seemed reasonable to ignore the visitor. But the knocker was relentless.

Groaning, I got up and slipped into my white, silk robe – which made Jared grin in a way that said he wouldn't mind shagging me while I wore it. "I better get that, it might be Sebastian; he and Antonio probably want to know how last night went." Seeing that Jared was making no moves to leave, I pointed at him. "If you're staying then you stay in *here*. I don't want my business spread around."

"Anyone would think you were ashamed of me," he said light-heartedly, gently slapping my butt as I was left the bedroom.

I flipped him the finger, scowling playfully. I was half-expecting the knocker to have gone by now, but they tapped on the door again just before I reached it. Abruptly all the tingly feelings still running through me fell away as I opened the door; it was his pained expression that did it — like a dog walking with its tail between its legs. "Max," I said, surprised.

He smiled as he eyed my appearance, taking in my wet, dishevelled hair. The smile didn't quite reach his eyes. "Sorry, did I disturb your shower?"

"Er, yeah."

"Can I come in?"

Saying no would be wise, but then that would mean that passers-by could do a little eavesdropping. I stepped aside and his smile grew as he entered. He looked good even in just his t-shirt and jeans, like a model from a catalogue or something. "Everything all right?"

"Yeah, I just had to know you were okay after having to go to that gathering last night. I know you can take care of yourself and everything, but..."

"Well thanks, yeah I'm good. There was no trouble or anything."

"Good." After an uncomfortable pause, he cleared his throat. "Listen, about what happened at the restaurant—"

"Max, it's fine."

"No, it's not. I was out of line. I had no right to question you about things that weren't any of my business. It's just...well you already know I like you. I guess I'm just hoping that I haven't messed up any chances I might have had by coming across all paranoid."

I sighed. "The thing is—" I stopped as his eyes moved from mine to something over my shoulder and his expression darkened.

I turned my head to find Jared standing at the edge of the kitchen, casually swigging a NST. At least he'd put his pants on. I rolled my eyes at him. *I thought you might do that,* I grumbled. I might not want Max the way I did Jared, but I had no interest in tormenting him.

Jared offered me an innocent smile and a small shrug of the shoulder.

Dreading Max's reaction, I slowly swerved my head back round. To my surprise he had pasted a fake smile on his face. "So it was *that* kind of night," he said — something that Fletcher would have said, in the exact playful tone that Fletcher would have used.

What could I possibly say? I wasn't going to deny it. I had no reason to other than I felt sorry for Max, but that wasn't a reason to lie to him and it would only insult his intelligence anyway. Acting as though I bought his smile and pretence, I smiled back. "Yep."

"Well I'd better go, got training in about twenty minutes. Although there's a possibility that my trainer" – he nodded toward Jared – "might be late." Again his tone was playful, empty of sourness. But I could detect the slight edge to it.

"See you later at the arena," I said as he let himself out. I then turned to Jared with a 'was that really necessary?' look on my face.

He shrugged again and came toward me. "I did warn him that I wouldn't stay away from you. Not my fault if he didn't listen."

"What happened to you staying in my bedroom out of sight?"

"Max won't do any blabbering. Though he might blubber a little."

I slapped his upper arm as he reached me. "Must you be so mean?"

He curled his arms around my waist. "I just think it's better for him that he knows."

My eyes narrowed. "Or was this about you trying to mark territory that wasn't yours to mark?"

"No."

"Jared."

"All right. I don't want anyone kissing you" – he planted a soft kiss on my mouth – "or touching you" – he slid his hands up to my neck – "the way that I do. Is that really that bad?"

And here I'd been thinking that maybe he was done with me after having his curiosity and horniness taken care of. "No, it's not bad. *But* the whole idea of casual sex is that there aren't any 'strings attached'."

He sucked in a breath. "I think maybe we should get you a new handbook on casual sex because you obviously haven't heard that there are special situations in which exclusivity can be brought into the mix."

"Ah, but that would make me practically your consort, and we've been over this."

Jared inhaled heavily and made an 'hmmm' sound as he released a breath. "Okay, fair enough. I'll just have to make sure you're permanently sated so that you don't have the time or energy for anyone else."

I smiled. "You're very welcome to try." He did try just once more before teleporting back to his apartment to get ready for his session with the squad. That was probably why I had a huge smile on my face as I left my own apartment and headed to the Command Centre.

Instantly Fletcher was on his feet, examining me from head to toe. Then he ushered me into my office and an impish smirk broke free on his face. "You bonked Jared."

"Several times."

He giggled. "How was his performance?"

"You want me to resort to 'kiss and tell'? Let's just say he topped the rest by far."

"What happened to not wanting to be a consort? Not that I'm disapproving of you shagging him or anything."

"I'm not Jared's consort…And nor is Joy, Daniela or Tammy."

Fletcher's brows flew up. "He dumped them?"

"Yep."

"Bloody hell. So are you two seeing each other now then?"

"We're just two adults having fun."

"Fun?"

"Fun."

Fletcher gave me a look that questioned my IQ level. "Sam, luv, a bloke like Jared doesn't change his lifestyle for 'fun'."

I shrugged. "Maybe I'm a lot of fun."

Perceiving Fletcher's theory that maybe Jared saw things a little more serious as totally idiotic, I didn't even consider it. Instead, I got out the recruits' files and made notes on their progress charts. I was confident that they could handle what I had planned for tonight. I was glad that Jared was having a meeting during lunch hour with Sherman, because I seriously doubted he'd have got through that hour in our office without kissing or touching me, and then I would've been one very horny vampire coach at the arena.

When I arrived at the arena, the entire squad was waiting and all were raring to go. Apart from Max – he wouldn't meet my eyes and couldn't have looked less enthusiastic. I might have felt sorry for him if he didn't look like a mutinous, sulky, pouty, five year-old. Instantly they formed a perfect line in front of me and concentrated on sucking in any excess energy.

"I'm impressed," I said as I reached the end of the line. "There wasn't the slightest spark of energy leaking from any of you. I think that means you're ready for what I've got in mind. Chico, I want you to stand with Damien. Stuart, you stand with Denny. Butch, you're with David. Max, you stand with Harvey. And Salem, you're with Reuben. Now, take a look at who's beside you. This is who I'll be pairing you up with not just for now, but during the attack. I'd prefer not to have to separate you during an attack, but if it comes to that then pair up as you are now." Everyone nodded, except for one person.

"You expect me to pair up with Harvey?" griped Max. "You know we don't get along."

I stood directly in front of Slaphead. "I expect you to not be a wanker and to push aside any negative feelings you have for who you're paired up with. Chico and Damien aren't the best of friends either. Do you hear them complaining?"

He spoke through his teeth. "You're doing this to piss me off because of what happened the other night, aren't you? Just like you fucked Jared to piss me off."

The cheeky little bugger! I ignored the gasps coming from the others; they seemed more shocked by Slaphead's behaviour than what he'd divulged. "So you think my life revolves around you, do you? And here was me thinking it was Commander Michaels who had the ego problem." I spoke in a grave, cautioning voice as I continued, "Now you listen to me: personal business has no place in this arena. If you want to make pathetic, sly remarks then you do so out of training time. Not now, not here. You don't waste my time or the time of the rest of the squad. You got that?"

Eventually Slaphead nodded.

Again I addressed the entire squad, who I noticed were looking at Slaphead with disgust. "As I was saying, I want you to pair up as you are now. Each of you have an excellent, powerful gift but some of those are more offensive than others. I've paired you up with people who'll complement your own gift.

"Salem, your punch can be deadly when your power is amplified so I've placed you with Reuben who can amplify it for you. Chico, although your thorns are great, they can be easily dodged. However if Damien is using his ability to astral project, he can have them looking one way while you come up from behind. Stuart and Denny – you can both travel together as mush and molecules, and hopefully get close enough for Stuart to distract the enemy so Denny can then use his ooze or other mimicry. David, once the enemy see how profound your gift is they will want to eliminate you fast. Butch, however, can shield you both and negate any attacks away from you while you do your thing. Also, if Max can steal the senses of any vamps surrounding us, they won't be prepared for Harvey's telekinesis." I looked at Max with the latter sentence, driving home the point of pairing him as I had.

I ushered them aside before strolling to the other end of the arena. "What I'd like you to do is revise in your mind the formations we practised. I'll just be a sec." Tapping into the energy of the element earth, I created several boulders and walls and a few ditches. "Now for the main part of today's training…"

I opened the door to the arena and in strode Evan and his own squad of ten. Instantly my squad turned into a crowd of giddy kids. I gave them a look that told them to take this seriously. They each then straightened their posture and met the gazes of Evan's squad steadily.

"You sure they're ready for this, Coach?" asked Evan as he came to stand beside me.

"Only one way to find out." I stood between the squads, claiming their attention. "I want my squad on the north side, Commander Evan Michael's squad on the south. Invade each other's territory only if you dare. Your object is to annihilate the other squad. First, I want anyone with a deadly or severe gift to come forward so Reuben can weaken it. I don't want people unconscious or dead, but I'll expect that anyone who is struck by these severe gifts to subtract themselves from their squad just as they would have been had Reuben not weakened the effects of these gifts."

Once Reuben was done with that, one of Evan's squad asked, "Coach, will you be letting us know in advance who has what gift?"

"Will the vampires who attack The Hollow stop, smile, and fairly announce what their gift is?" When he looked sheepish, I nodded. "Then don't expect my squad to." Evan and I then went to stand in the spectators' box. Although during the attack we would be there to guide them, we had both agreed that it was best for them to learn not to depend too greatly on our presence. Listen to our orders, yeah, but depend on our guidance, no. So we decided to simply observe for today. I could see that Evan was confident his own squad would win, but I didn't comment.

Just as they'd practiced, Damien, Max, Chico and Harvey covered the front boulder. Denny, Reuben and Stuart covered the boulders behind them, and then Salem, David and Butch covered the rear of the squad. Evan's squad looked as though they were hoping to make the first move, but I'd taught my lot not to give the enemy a chance to do that.

First, Damien astral projected around the first boulder of the enemy which served two purposes; one, he could distract the enemy; two, he could then inform Chico, Max, and Harvey how many were hiding there. Taking advantage of the enemy's distraction, Harvey used his telekinesis to zoom Max to the boulder, and he quickly stole the four members' senses. Chico used this opportunity to aim his thorns at them.

Three other members of Evan's squad from behind a separate boulder aimed their gifts at Chico, but soon they were eliminated when Stuart and Denny travelled to them as mush and molecules: Stuart distracted the vamps and Denny then oozed them while their backs were turned. Meanwhile, Reuben had been hit by the enemy, but not before having weakened some of them so their gifts were pretty useless.

The rest of the enemy – there were only four left – decided to spring forth and get rid of Max and Chico, who were the ultimate threat so far. They were successful, but sadly for them they hadn't known of David's and Salem's gifts. While Butch shielded them both, David sent psionic booms and Salem used his psychic punches. At the same time, Harvey was sending other members of Evan's squad crashing into the walls.

Done and dusted: Evan's squad had been eliminated. There were still seven left of my squad. Evan and his entire squad looked equally stunned. My lot, of course, were looking rather smug and proud. And so was I. But we behaved like adults and didn't jump for joy…until Evan and his squad had left, of course. Then they begin basking in their own greatness, and I somehow ended up in the centre of a huddle while a very odd and crap song was sung in my honour. Max, however, didn't participate. I pulled him aside as the others were leaving.

"You and me need to have a little chat if this is how you're going to behave," I told him.

He shrugged. "What's there to chat about?"

"You're acting like a jilted, betrayed boyfriend and, worse still, you're acting it in the arena. For God's sake, Max, The Hollow's going to be attacked soon."

"Yeah, and I'll be ready. It doesn't mean I have to respect your ass."

I placed my face close to his. "Actually, it means exactly that. Not only do you need to respect me, you need to listen to me and follow instructions. And not just mine, but Commander Michaels' as well. If I can't trust you to do that then, I swear, I'll leave you behind."

He snickered. "Oh you will?"

"Oh I will. So here's what you're going to do. You're going to take fifteen minutes and then you're going to come to my office. After I've been to see Commander Norton, I'll go there for your answer about whether or not you're going to get your act together. If you don't come, I'll take that as a 'no'."

Predictably, he stormed off.

(Jared)

A smile dripping with pride surfaced on my face when I caught up with Evan to tell him about the meeting that was on shortly for the commanders, only to be told that mine and Sam's squad had kicked the ass of Evan's. As much as I hated to admit it – and I really, really hated to admit it – I had been totally wrong. Sam had been indispensable in having the squad in tip-top shape. I doubted I'd ever admit it aloud, but stranger things had happened.

"You're not trying to tell me it's the squad who deserves the glory, not her," observed Evan.

I just shrugged. Yep, I was right: I couldn't admit my mistake aloud.

Evan narrowed his eyes, looking at me curiously and probably wondering why I was smiling like a Cheshire cat. It was a smile that had been on my face all evening. "Don't tell me there's something going on between you two. I mean, I know you wanted there to be. But I kind of got the feeling that she wouldn't be up for the consort lifestyle."

"She's not," was the only answer I gave him, but Evan wasn't dumb. He could guess the rest.

"Why do I get the feeling that you're not going to let it be a one-off thing?"

"Because I'm not."

"I'd say don't hurt her, but I'm sure she's the last person who needs protection and I'm just as sure that she could kick your ass herself if she needed to."

She already had – not a good memory for my ego.

"But I'm asking as someone who considers her a good friend: when you do decide you're done, don't do it harshly the way you usually do when it comes to women."

I didn't like the way he thought he had a right to be protective of her. I felt like that was my job, which made no sense and yet that was how I felt all the same. Just like since the day I'd met her I'd thought of her as mine, no matter how much I'd tried to ignore it. Again it was something that made no sense but it was there. And with that thought, I just had to see her. Immediately I teleported to the office...and the sight that I found made me feel like I'd been hit in the chest with a sledgehammer.

There was Sam sitting on the edge of her desk with her arms and legs locked around Max, who she was kissing so hard and urgently, while he skated his hands down her back. An ache started in my stomach and quickly blossomed until every single part of me hurt. I was in agony both inside and out. I wasn't even sure if I was breathing, it was like I'd been winded.

As much as I wanted to dive on Max and snap every limb off his body I couldn't seem to move. Shock had me rooted to the spot, paralysed. I couldn't tear my eyes away from them. I didn't want to watch, but I couldn't seem to look away. Then the shock and hurt swiftly gave way to anger, and a deep, dark rage surged through me.

Seething, I advanced on them. Both their heads swung to look at me, and then Sam gasped and backed away, hiding behind Max. Instantly I stopped still. Sam was backing away? Sam was hiding behind another person? That didn't ring true.

Another thing occurred to me then. My senses weren't hyper the way they usually were when she was around. I didn't feel that *pull* to go to her that I usually felt.

There was something else I realised too, something that shocked the hell out of me and had me spooked, but I didn't want to think about that yet.

"She's made her choice, Michaels," said Max. "It's me she wants."

"Is that right?" I asked, folding my arms across my chest.

"The only reason she slept with you was because she wanted to get back at me."

"To get back at you?"

He nodded. "That's right."

"I'm afraid I'm going to have to hear this from the horse's mouth." I raised a brow at her. She was still hiding behind Max. As I'd expected, she didn't speak. "If you expect me to believe you want him then I'm going to need to hear you say it." Still she didn't speak.

"Tell him, Sam," urged Max, stroking a hand through her hair, "tell him it's me you want."

She edged closer to Max but still she said nothing.

"Did you rob her ability to speak or something?" I asked Max, who was starting to look a little confused and unsure. "I'm getting pretty agitated now, Sam. Tell me to my face that it's Max you want. What're you hiding for? If you really think I'd ever hurt you then just get out that pretty whip of yours? If you want to defend yourself, you can do it easy. Unless…you're not Sam."

CHAPTER FOURTEEN

(Sam)

I halted mid-stride as I entered the office to find Jared and Max having some kind of face-off. Not only that, but there was a woman cowering behind Max. A woman who was identical to me. "Bloody hell." Three heads turned to look at me. Max looked stunned, my doppelganger looked anxious, and Jared seemed completely unsurprised.

Max spun and glared at the woman behind him. Then his eyes repeatedly darted from her to me, as though he was trying to work out which one was the real me. "What's going on?"

I snorted. "I was hoping one of you three could help me with that."

Jared sighed. "Short version is I teleported here and got to watch while Max had you wrapped around him almost sucking your mouth off. Only it wasn't you, I realised." His eyes bore into the imitation of me. "Game's up, Joy."

"Joy," I echoed with irritation. I was even more irritated by the fact that she was wearing my jacket which I'd left on the chair.

"I think she thought she could cause a nice big rift between us. I told her before that she'd never be you. It's stupid that she didn't just listen."

Joy's entire body seemed to twinkle and then she was back to her old self.

Max stepped away from her, rubbing his mouth as if to rub away any trace of her. He looked over at me. "I came here like you asked me to, and she was sat at your desk. She said she'd made a mistake when she slept with *him* and that it was really me she wanted."

"And you bought her little act? You thought that was me?"

"Well, I mean, I thought you sounded a little weird. Your accent seemed off and your scent wasn't as strong—"

"Probably because it was my jacket that had my scent on it, not her."

"—but I didn't think it was someone else. Why would I?" He turned to Jared then. "How did you know?"

"I just did."

Wearing the scowl from hell, Joy began ranting at Jared. "Maybe now you know what it feels like seeing the person you care about with someone else! Maybe now you have a tiny idea of how *I* feel! Shame you didn't think it was really her and then attack us. I would've liked watching Max steal your senses and then pummel you."

"Bloodthirsty isn't she," I commented to Jared before concentrating my focus on her. "I strongly advise you to scarper out of this office before I seriously end up losing it. I have no time for anyone who thinks it's their right to play with people's lives."

"I'm not afraid of some Sventé."

"Then you're dumber than I thought," said Jared, his voice heavy with impatience and aggravation.

"A good lay, isn't he," she said to me, wearing a cocky smirk. "I quite like his tongue. Does he call *you* baby too? I'll bet he tells you your blood tastes real good too. Feels good when he zaps your clit with that gift of his, doesn't it."

"Are we supposed to be comparing notes? Or is this just your way of telling me that I mean nothing more to him than any other woman?" It wasn't something I hadn't already known. It was dumb that I cared. I shouldn't care about that fact, I shouldn't care that when he called me baby it wasn't because he saw me as more than a shag, I shouldn't care about him. And yet I did. It made me want to slap myself.

"It seems only fair that you know. He has this way of making you think you're special to him when the truth is you're nothing to him but another piece of ass."

I placed my hand over my heart and said mockingly, "Oh, I think I feel it shattering. You've killed the dream." What worried me was that my words were a lot closer to the truth than I was comfortable with. "Now. Get. The. Hell. Out."

"It'll be a pleasure to." Looking rather self-satisfied, she shrugged passed Jared and Max. As she was passing me, she made an extremely stupid move: she abruptly reached out and clawed my face with her nails like some sort of wildcat.

Without hesitation I dived on her, or at least I meant to. Instead, the strangest thing happened. I fell *into* her. My body invaded hers, fused with hers, melded with hers. It was an odd feeling. It was like stepping into an all-in-one suit, stretching my limbs into place; a suit that I could see out of. Then the other senses came to me; hearing, smelling, touching, tasting. And then the feeling changed again, as though the suit was being burned into my skin so that it became part of me, but the pain was only slight and brief.

And just like that, I felt utterly invincible. I knew that I wasn't, but I felt it. Power was coursing through me, making me feel drunk on it. It was like a caged, pacing, agitated tiger: it wanted to be released, and I knew that if I unleashed it, I'd have a hard job controlling it.

"What the hell happened?" My voice didn't sound like my own, nor did it sound like Joy's; it was kind of a mixture of the two. I looked down at my body and gasped: it was neither me nor Joy; there was a likeness of us both. I realised then that I hadn't possessed her body. By merging with her, I had made us one being — one stronger being.

"Sam," drawled Jared in a soothing voice. "It's all right."

I looked at him incredulously. "Are you kidding me! I'm far from all right." I could hear Joy's voice in my head: it wasn't a shock that she was cursing me. Oddly, I could pick up everything about her, as though I now had total access to her thoughts and feelings and memories. What I learned surprised me: she loved Jared, and she believed he loved me. Had she always been daft?

"Holy shit," muttered Max. "It looks like you've developed a new gift or something."

Then it all fell into place. "Antonio. I'll kill him."

Max looked pale even for a vampire. "I think you might be a Merger."

"Oh really, whatever made you think that?" said Jared sarcastically before turning back to me. "Sam, I can sense how you're feeling but I swear you're going to be fine, just concentrate. You can undo this. I know it must be weird and unfamiliar, baby, but you can control it just like you control anyone else's gift."

I nodded, sucking in a long breath. His presence was like an anchor, and I so needed one of those right now. I concentrated on my water tank metaphor. I imagined water filling me so completely that there was no room for Joy any longer. I realised that I seemed to be involuntarily draining the energy from her half; taking it into me, soaking it up.

Then suddenly I was myself again and she was stumbling away; it was an odd sensation, like peeling away a bulky layer of clothing that was attached to your flesh like Velcro. It left a weird sensation behind on my skin like little bugs crawling over me. Thankfully it quickly faded, as did the feeling of being omnipotent.

Immediately Jared was there, his hand massaging my nape. "You okay?" His concern was beating at me; I could feel it as distinctly as if it was my own. It seemed that drinking his blood had made that weird link stronger. Great.

"I'm fine," I said. "But I still intend to kill Antonio."

He smiled a half-smile. "You'll have your chance soon. There's a meeting for all the commanders. Bran, Connelly and Kaiser will be there too. Apparently Bennington very briefly hinted at the idea of invading The Hollow and they came to tell tales on him."

"That's one of the weirdest things I've ever seen in my life." Max shuddered. Then he looked at Jared, his eyes seemed to be searching for something. "You knew it wasn't her." He still seemed confused. His gaze flicked between us both and then he sighed as if he had resigned himself to something. "What happened today at the arena won't happen again," he assured me with a semi-smile. Then he strode out, roughly dragging a dazed Joy with him.

Jared pulled me against him, still massaging my nape.

"You all right?" I asked him.

"You're asking me if I'm all right when you're the one who's just discovered you're a Merger as well as a Feeder?"

I shrugged. "You're feeling really, really unsettled about something, I can sense it."

"Of course I am. I've just watched you merge with another person."

But it wasn't just that, I *knew* it wasn't. I wondered if maybe he was just shocked after hearing Joy make it clear she cared about him. It probably wouldn't be a great idea to tell him she actually loved him. Nor was it a good idea to tell him that I cared about him as well.

Evan was just as freaked as Max had been when I revealed, on the way to the meeting, I was now a Merger. I almost stumbled in surprise as he stopped statue-still as we entered the conference room, staring hard at something with his mouth hanging open. Following his gaze, I saw a red-headed woman who was sitting beside Bran – I remembered her as his Consort – looking rather bored. By the awed look on Evan's face, I had a good idea who she could be.

"Is that her? The girl from the vision?" I asked discretely.

He only nodded. His words came out in a whisper. "She's real. She's here."

Jared put a hand on my back, urging me forward. "Who?" When neither Evan nor I responded, he frowned at Evan who quickly turned to look at him. I gathered that they were having a telepathic conversation and I wondered how much Evan would tell him.

Seeing that people were looking at us curiously, I made my way to one of the few empty seats. Evan and Jared placed themselves either side of me. Evan was then directly opposite Bran's consort, who was staring at Evan like he was a snack. Well it was a start.

"Why Samantha, how are you?" asked Connelly after having greeted Jared and Evan and talked to them like they were gods. It almost made me laugh.

"Fine and dandy, thanks."

I don't know how you're not drained, you should've took some energy from me, said Jared.

The person who went away drained was Joy. Besides, I don't fancy teleporting to the arena and the bottom of the pool every five minutes like last time. Feeling particularly put out by my new gift, I added, *When Antonio and Luther come in, let them know about my gift having manifested itself, but don't tell them what it is.* He smiled at my eagerness to have them kept in suspense.

"I was telling Jared last night that he may set off a trend by having a Sventé as a consort," Connelly said to Evan.

Jared smiled. "Actually, consort isn't the correct word. She's a commander."

"Within the legion?"

Still smiling, Jared nodded.

Kaiser scoffed, "A Sventé, a *female* Sventé, working as a commander within the legion? Absurd."

Yes I should be used to this by now, but apparently I wasn't. Before he could twist the cap off his NST bottle, I – in a movement so swift he hadn't seen it coming – sucked energy into my hands and manifested my whip, which I then cracked toward him and used to snatch his bottle. Brining the bottle to me with the whip, I picked it up and read the label as I let the whip fade away. "Nah, I don't like that flavour." With that, I placed the bottle back on the table and released a gust of air from one hand, sending it zooming back to Kaiser. The commanders chuckled.

"A Feeder," gasped Bran.

"A Sventé Feeder," said Kaiser. I winked at him and leaned back in my seat. "But that is only a Pagori gift."

"And that is only one of many things that make Sam unique," announced a new, deep, rhythmic voice as he, Luther, and Sebastian strolled into the room. Antonio.

As usual, Nero came to greet me with a lick to my arm and then he squeezed himself between mine and Evan's chair, eager to be stroked. When both Antonio and Luther looked sharply at me with intrigue written all over their faces, I knew Jared had told them telepathically about the surfacing of my new gift. I could see that they were itching to know more. I merely smiled.

After Antonio made all the introductions, he began, "Bran, Rupert," – he called Connelly by his first name, the same as Jared did – "and Kaiser have arrived to inform me about certain things that Bennington of Great Britain was heard to have said last night at Rupert's gathering. All of it supports Luther's vision: Bennington intends to attack The Hollow and is trying to recruit as many vampires as possible.

"Bran, Rupert, and Kaiser have agreed to support the defence of The Hollow by adding their own legions to ours, which has increased our numbers greatly. In fact, their legions are being teleported to the Guest House and other accommodations as we speak. This sense of urgency I have is in light of what we didn't otherwise know before: Bennington intends to attack at midnight tomorrow."

There were gasps, mutterings and curses. I was pretty much mute with the dread running through me. That gave us no additional time to train: we would literally have to put ourselves in place tomorrow evening and lie in wait. Jared's hand gripped mine under the table. I could sense his rage and his unease. Bennington might himself be nothing but a little fart, but his army of specially gifted vampires were a big concern. And God only knew how many allies he'd manage to secure.

"It would seem that he decided to bring his time-table forward, probably because he suspected that my Advisor may have had a vision and so he hoped to catch us off-guard. We may not have had as much time to prepare as we would have liked, but had it not been for Luther's earlier vision, we might never have been as psychologically prepared as what we are now. I would advise all commanders to spend this evening familiarising yourselves and your squads as much as possible with the surrounding rainforest.

"I have additional security measures in place, including a stronger shield over The Hollow so that *no one* may teleport there until I have removed it. Even now, the other vampires and humans are being hidden underground." Antonio cast a look at the three High Masters. "If you wish for your consorts to also be hidden, that can easily be arranged."

"I think I can help," the redhead blurted out. Bran castigated her with a look but Antonio waved away the break in etiquette.

"We have become used to outspoken females," said Antonio with a smile. "How is it you believe you can help, Miss...?"

"It's Alora. Well, you said you'd be using the rainforests. I can communicate with and charm animals. Ordinarily they wouldn't aid us in any way: they see us as the ultimate predator. However they'll sense that Bennington's lot are a threat to their surrounding environment, they won't like that. Even having them as spies would be useful."

I saw how Evan had stiffened and I knew he fully intended to suggest she was locked away for safekeeping. I subtly kicked him under the table. "I agree that she might be able to help." She smiled at me gratefully for that. Last night she'd looked at me like I was no better than a dung beetle just because I was a Sventé. I felt Evan's eyes drilling into me and condemning me. "Haven't you learned anything from me being here?"

He sighed and looked away, mumbling something about God needing to save him from women with iron wills.

"Jared, Lou, Will," began Antonio, "I consider you three to be the specialists on formations. Where do you suggest we place each squad?"

Jared spoke immediately, his voice filled with determination, "I'm covering the front line."

"We agree that it would be an advantage for Jared and Sam's squad to be one of the squads covering the outer perimeter," said Lou. "From what we have heard and seen, although the squad is reasonably new, the recruits are as prepared as any can be."

"They kicked the ass of my squad," grumbled Evan.

Antonio nodded. "The fact that they will have both Jared and Sam leading them makes them an excellent choice for that position."

"Wait," said Jared. "I'm not sure Sam should—"

My voice was like a whip. "I really would ask yourself if you like your eyes because if you finish that sentence there's a good chance I'll gouge them out."

He raised his hands in a placatory gesture. "It's nothing personal, Sam, I just—"

"When are you going to grow up and accept that we have to work together?"

"Sam—"

"This 'I don't need help' crap is getting old now. Hurts your pride that you have a female Sventé backing you up, does it? Tough. That squad is mine just as much as it is yours."

"I didn't say it wasn't. There are plenty of other places you could cover."

"I believe I already stated, Jared, that I wished for you and Sam to lead the squad together during the attack," said Antonio. "It wasn't a request. Now, let us move on."

While Will and Lou put forward suggestions for the placing of the squads during the attack and what tactics each should use, I sat there seething. I didn't care that the irritation and lividness was pouring off me, or that everyone in the room could sense it. That sod had just tried to cut me out again. I felt utterly betrayed.

He hadn't ever really seen me as an equal at all, had he? Not as a colleague and probably not even as a person. He definitely didn't respect me if he thought he could shag me one minute then turn on me the next. I'd understand if I didn't take my job seriously or something, but it was the opposite. I loved my job and I had tried so hard with those recruits. I'd invested time and sweat in their training and it had paid off. And now Jared was happy to cut me out again.

I was surprised by how much it stung. This was a person I had come to care about and, as painful as it was to face, Joy had been totally spot-on: I was just 'another piece of ass' to him.

Sam, will you just—

I didn't want to hear it. I slammed up my mental shields. Victor had made sure I had strong ones to ensure I could resist any vampiric attempts at brainwashing. If Jared was going to shut me out then I'd shut him out as well. He remained uncharacteristically quiet through the entire meeting, which I thought was pretty wise because keeping a low profile in front of me was the only way I was going to calm down.

After much debating, it was eventually decided that The Hollow's legion would cover the north of the island, Bran's legion would cover the east, Connelly's would cover the west, and Kaiser's would cover the south. It was also agreed that Alora would join Evan's legion for the attack; I suspected that this was the only way he'd be able to function, having her there where he could see she was safe.

The second Antonio announced that the meeting was over, I was on my feet. Apparently Jared's common sense had left him because he tried to speak to me again. I pointed at him hard. "You stay out of my face."

"Why can't you just—"

"Sam," called Antonio as he approached, "might Luther, Sebastian and I have a word?" He gestured for me to follow them, and Jared, the cheeky twat, actually went to follow. "Alone," Antonio added. Jared spat a profanity at the ceiling and stormed off, muttering to himself.

It wasn't until we were inside one of Antonio's many parlours, settled on a bulky sofa that he spoke again. "I can only apologise for Jared's behaviour. I had thought that he would have accepted the situation and swallowed his pride by now."

"I don't want to talk about him," I said as I stroked Nero attentively, hoping to calm myself. "Let's just get down to business, shall we. You want to know what my new gift is, right?"

"The wait has been agonising," admitted Luther with a smile.

"I doubt your suffering was much worse than the shock I had when it surfaced." Seeing their looks of expectation, I decided to teasingly spoon-feed them info. Simple pleasures and all that. I smiled. "It's really good."

"How good?"

"It turns out that this gift doesn't run in Svanté lines either." I heard them all gasp slightly. "Should I be shocked by that, or did you expect it to not be a Svanté gift considering that my other one isn't?"

"We had no way of knowing," replied Antonio.

"It runs in Pagori lines, just like Feeders. Oi, you don't think I'm really a Pagori, do you?"

"You're definitely a Svanté, as you well know," said Antonio impatiently.

Sebastian appealed to me with a look. "Is the suspense really necessary?"

"It's pretty rare."

"Oh Sam do stop this and satisfy three old men's raging curiosity."

"It turns out I'm now a Merger as well as a Feeder."

All three men gasped again before smiling approvingly.

Luther puffed. "I hadn't seen that coming."

"Oh this is even better than what my guesses were," said Antonio. "I've only ever met one Merger before. It is a substantial gift. He described the sensation of Merging with someone as slightly painful and uncomfortable, but also very empowering."

I nodded. "You feel full of power, like you could do just about anything."

"That is why it can also be a very dangerous gift to have."

I nodded again. "It was so odd. I could tap into every single bit of energy that was inside Joy—"

"Joy?" asked Antonio, a brow arched. I continued on, regardless.

"—but I knew there was no way I'd be able to use her gift because she was resisting the whole experience. But I could have drained her." Full points to me for resisting.

"As I said, it is a dangerous gift to have. People can become drugged on the energy and power. But, then again, being a Feeder can be just as dangerous and yet you have more than mastered that. Still, be careful with it, Sam. Be wary of using it during the attack. You are still new to it and that would be the wrong time to experiment with it."

"What would be the point of having these gifts if I ain't going to use them?" I'd be using them for something else very soon too, and I was as eager as hell for it. Jared would have no room to moan because he'd brought this on himself.

(Jared)

Shit! Shit! Shit!

There was no denying that I had well and truly fucked up. Just when I'd had Sam starting to relax around me and open up to me, I went and said something that pretty much guaranteed that she would hate me. I knew what leading the squad meant to her. I knew that she was capable of leading them during an attack. In fact, she was one of the most capable commanders I'd ever met. I knew how much the squad would benefit from having her there during the attack. I knew how much I'd benefit from having her there. I knew that she could take care of herself and didn't need mine or anyone else's protection.

So why didn't I want her covering the front line with me?

Because just the thought of her being in that level of danger made me feel ill inside, no matter how capable she was.

And why did the idea of her in danger make me feel ill inside?

For the same reason that the idea of her in danger scared the crap out of me: I loved the crazy bitch.

I'd realised it the second I teleported into the office and saw her with Max. Or, I should say, I saw *Joy* with Max. It explained so much: why I hadn't been able to shake her off, why I'd wanted her so badly and so completely, why I sensed her and her emotions. For the first time in a long time, I had let a woman passed my mental barriers – and I hadn't even realised I'd done it. I had no idea when it had happened or if it had been a gradual thing that had only crept up on me tonight. I just knew that it was real and that if anything at all ever happened to her I'd never be able to get through it.

I also knew that I couldn't tell her.

Sam had once told me that she didn't want to love anyone ever again, that she didn't want anything complicated. Telling her I loved her would be a sure-fire way to make her keep as far away from me as possible. I was going to have a hard enough time getting her to calm down for me after what went on in the meeting, so mentioning the word 'love' was out of the question.

Sick of twiddling my thumbs and procrastinating, I teleported from my apartment to the office: time to face the music. I frowned at the empty room. Next I tried her apartment. No Sam there either.

Was she staying away from the obvious places because she didn't want to see me? She had to know that all I had to do was tap into that link we had and use it to find her. Unless she wasn't aware of it...?

Sighing, I reached for her through the link and immediately teleported myself to her. Suddenly I was at the arena, which was empty apart from Sam. She was pacing at the northern side and smiled evilly at me when she saw me.

"Took your bloody time," she snapped.

Then I watched as she sucked the surrounding energy into her palms and shaped it into her silvery-blue energy whip. Oh shit. She'd known about the link, she'd known I could use it to find her, and she'd been counting on me doing it.

CHAPTER FIFTEEN

(Jared)

"Sam," I drawled in a calming tone, "let's talk, I don't want to duel with you." She cracked the whip at me. I jerked back a few steps and it missed me by inches. "Look, I know you're mad at me but—"

"I'm not mad, I'm pissed." She cracked the whip at me again. This time it caught the hand I'd held up in a white-flag gesture, and it stung like fuck.

"Jesus, Sam, will you just listen."

"What's the point? There's honestly nothing you could say that would change the fact that I want to whip your arse around this arena until you beg me to stop. Not that I will stop."

Again she lashed the whip, and again it caught me; this time on my ear. Even in spite of the pain, I couldn't help noticing how sexy she looked right then with her eyes smouldering and that whip threading through her fingers. "Baby, just listen to me—"

"Oh no, you don't get to call me that. I'm not your baby." As if to punctuate that, she cracked the whip again and it slashed my chest, tearing my t-shirt and also the flesh underneath. It burned even as it healed itself. What burned more were her words.

"Like hell you're not." I released a stream of electric sparks through my fingers, zapping the ground near her feet. I could tell by the maddened expression on her face that she knew I'd purposely missed.

"Fight me!" Abruptly she cracked the whip hard; it sliced along my cheek, lips, and jaw. It hurt like a bitch! Without giving me time to recover, she cracked it again. A sharp, burning pain ran along my thigh.

"I told you, I don't want to duel with you! Now will you just calm the hell down so we can talk?!"

"About what, Heir Boy? About how I'm okay to shag and feed from but I'm not good enough to lead alongside you? About how you're cutting me out again? About how you're a sexist, lying, backstabbing bastard?" The whip slashed through my t-shirt again so there was now an X running through it.

"It wasn't that I was trying to cut you out."

"You've been trying to cut me out from day one!"

This time the whip cut through the flesh of my shin. Jesus, this woman was merciless!

"You know what's funny? Last night at the gathering when everyone was looking down on me 'cause I'm a Sventé, I wondered if you'd go back to being like that after you'd shagged me. Hmm. Seems like that was more of a premonition really."

"Dammit, Sam, I don't look down on you." The whip caught my earlobe so hard I jumped. "Goddammit!"

"I can't believe I ever thought you might just respect me. Not that I thought you respected me as much as the others do, but I thought you might just be getting there. But no, you're still the sexist twat I met at the pool."

"If you'd just lower that whip for a minute and let me speak I can expl—" The whip clipped my earlobe again where it hurt the most; which was obviously why she'd done it. Although my blood had only seeped to the surface slightly with each tear of my flesh before repairing itself, the scent was still potent in the air. I could see that it was getting to her by the way her nostrils were flaring and how she was repeatedly swallowing hard. I was thinking of how I might be able to use it to my advantage but her next words cut off all thoughts.

"Max was right about you, I should've listened to the bloke. I should've stayed well away from you. I should've shagged *him*!"

And there went my patience and my rationality. With my Pagori speed, I was on her before she'd even finished lashing the whip, slamming her into the wall. "I don't want you on the front line because I don't want you being hurt, you insane bitch!" Then I closed my mouth over hers, forcefully thrusting my tongue into her mouth to stroke her own. It was a punishing, possessive, hungry kiss.

That same blast of fire that always came with kissing her rushed through me just as it rushed through her, but I could sense she was still ready to fight me off. I palmed her breast and then, with my thumb, zapped her nipple with a brief electric discharge. She jerked and moaned, so I did it again.

"How could you think I look down on you?" I demanded, but I kissed her again before she could speak. "Whether you believe it or not, I admire you, I respect you and I care about you." I held back the 'L' word. Maybe there would come a time to tell her, but it wasn't now. I sensed the shock she was feeling quickly give way to scepticism. Cutting off whatever she was about to say, I cupped her and zapped her clit. "It's true. And I can't stand the idea of anything happening to you." While zapping her clit again with one hand, I zapped a nipple with the other. She half-moaned half-whimpered and gripped my t-shirt as if to anchor herself. "Like that, baby?"

Her eyes flipped open and her glare was fierce. "I said don't call me that."

I cupped her harder and zapped her clit again. "I'll call you that as often as I damn well want."

"You're a bastard!"

I freed my painfully hard cock from my jeans. "Yeah? Well this bastard's about to fuck you, baby." With Pagori speed I slipped my hands under her thighs, hoisted her up, tore open her pants and plunged inside her; seating myself to the hilt in one harsh stroke. We both groaned. "Jesus, Sam," I breathed against her lips as her muscles clamped around my cock. She was so hot and tight and wet, and she was all mine whether she liked it or not.

(Sam)

Why did it have to feel so good to have him inside me? The way he filled me and stretched me made me feel completely and utterly taken. I wanted so much to hate him. I wanted so much to be able to snort at his claim to care about me and air-blast him away. If it hadn't been for that link, I'd have been convinced that he'd been talking tripe, but I'd sensed his honesty and also his fear that I might be hurt. I had to admit to myself, though, that even if I hadn't sensed those things, I probably wouldn't have been able to fight this need to have him, especially when this might actually be our last night together.

"Can you feel how much I love being deep inside you?" His voice was thick with lust and a need to move that, for whatever dumb reason, he was resisting. I nodded. "I can sense how much you love it too."

It was at times like this that that stupid link really cheesed me off; him knowing things like this gave him power over me. To add to that, it made me feel exposed and vulnerable, like I was an open book to be read at his leisure. What was frustrating me even more now, however, was that he wasn't moving. I tightened my legs around his hips and squeezed my inner muscles around his dick, hoping to incite him.

"You want me to fuck you, baby?"

"You dare ask me to beg again and I'll rip your bollocks off."

"I don't want you to beg. I want you to admit that it's only me you want, no one else. What, you thought saying you wished you'd fucked Max wasn't going to make me pissed?"

Oh and he *was* pissed. In fact, I'd never seen Jared this agitated before. In all fairness, though, if he'd said something like that to me about another woman, I'd have set him on fire and done a celebratory dance around his ashes.

"Admit it, it's not him you want buried inside you like this, is it?"

"No."

Rewardingly he withdrew and then drove himself deep. I groaned and locked my arms around his neck. "And it's not any other guy you want like this either, is it?"

"No."

Again he withdrew and then surged into me, wringing another groan from me. "Who is it you do want? Tell me."

"You."

"That's a very good thing, baby, because if another guy even tries to touch you, I'll fucking kill him." Palming my arse to hold me still, he began pounding into me like he was possessed. And that was exactly how I wanted him. God, it was absolutely amazing. Each thrust was harsh and ruthless. It was as if each time he drove into me, he was driving home his words. "I've needed to fuck you since the second I laid eyes on you, Sam. Even then, even that very first day, I couldn't shake that goddamn feeling that you were mine."

I opened my mouth to say something, but all that came out was a moan. I realised then that I had no idea what to say. Part of me wanted to deny that I was his or anyone else's, yet another part of me wanted to growl at him that he was mine too and that he'd better remember that.

I wasn't sure what he saw in my expression but suddenly he raised a brow and growled, "Are you going to tell me you're not mine?" He knotted a hand in my hair. "Are you?"

Begrudgingly I said, "No, but you're still a bloody bastard."

He gave me a lopsided smile and then there was an odd sensation in my stomach and suddenly I was lying on my back on golden silk sheets. Jared was stood at the edge of his bed, tugging off what was left of my pants and thong. He then rid himself of his own clothes but I didn't get much time to ogle because abruptly he closed his mouth over my clit and suckled. Jesus! At the same time, he ripped my top and bra wide open and started zapping my nipples again, subjecting me to a sensory overload. He really was a bastard.

I hated the way I was writhing, and twisting, and whimpering, but I couldn't help it. I wanted to tell him to stop, but if anyone knew how to tease it was Jared, and he was such a master at it that he robbed me of the ability to speak. He continued until I was not only speechless but mindless. Then my entire body clenched and jerked, and it felt like I'd imploded as my release hit.

When I opened my eyes again, it was to find him gazing at me wearing the cockiest, self-satisfied expression. I just wanted to wipe it right off his face. Oh and I was going to. I crooked my finger at him and instantly he crawled over me and meshed his lips with mine. His kiss was hungry and, again, possessive.

If he hadn't been off-guard, I doubt I'd have been able to do it, but I actually managed to flip him onto his back. He looked up at me as I straddled him; surprised but pleasantly surprised. I didn't impale myself on him as he was obviously expecting. No, because I had a point to prove: that I could make him as mindless as he could make me.

I shrugged off my ruined top and bra and then crawled backwards until my head was level with his cock, which was, I have to say, a very impressive one. I licked the entire length of it from base to tip and then swirled my tongue around the head. Jared shuddered and groaned. Knowing this was going to shock the hell out of him, I couldn't help smiling. I inhaled the energy around me just as I had that time in our office while we duelled and wrecked it. But instead of releasing a concentrated air blast, I threw my head back and exhaled a timid flame of fire, heating up my mouth. Jared's brows shot up and I smiled, but before he could speak I'd closed my mouth over his dick.

(Jared)

As Sam took my cock into her scorching hot mouth I almost came right then. I'd never felt anything like it before. "Christ, baby, that feels so fucking good." It would've felt amazing having her deep-throat me purely because it was Sam, but this...Jesus she was going to kill me.

She sucked me deeper each time, gliding her hot tongue along the underside and occasionally grazing with her teeth. I was completely hypnotised by the sight of my cock disappearing into her luscious, talented mouth. She was sucking so hard that her cheeks hollowed. "Christ, Sam." And now she was playing with my balls at the same time. God I loved this woman: this very crazy, borderline-homicidal – on second thought, scrap the borderline – woman.

I drove my hand into her hair and began lifting my hips, surging up to meet her burning hot mouth. I was practically fucking it but she just smiled around my cock. Knowing I wasn't going to last much longer, I pulled her head away. "I need to be inside you now."

"Wait," she said as I tried to tug her toward me. "One more thing first." I watched as she curled her soft hand around the base of my cock and lowered her mouth onto the head. She sucked hard and then there was a sharp sting.

Shit, the crazy bitch had bitten my cock. I was a vamp so sure I liked to be bit, but my dick: hell no. But then her Sventé saliva got to work in my system as she continued to suck and, Holy Mary Mother of God, I thought my entire cock would explode. "Oh *fuck* yeah." I didn't think it was possible for her to suck harder, but then she did. Only seconds later a loud, guttural groan left my throat as I erupted into her mouth.

Wearing that wicked smile on her beautiful face she was like a sinful angel. "Come here." Slowly she slinked her way over me. "You're amazing, do you know that?" I grabbed her by her nape and pulled her face to mine, taking her lips in a searing, greedy kiss. I clutched and moulded those breasts that were, hands down, the most incredible pair I'd ever seen. You couldn't look at them without wanting to bury your face between them, so that was exactly what I did. Then, unable to resist the taut buds, I closed my mouth over one, suckling and nibbling.

God I loved those husky moans she made. Already my cock was hard again just listening to them. I flicked her other nipple repeatedly with my tongue then plucked at it with my teeth. "You like that, don't you?" She moaned in response. Unable to wait any longer to be inside her again, I grabbed her by the hips and poised her above my dick. "Ride me, Sam." Even if my life had depended on it, I couldn't have moved my eyes from the vision of her lowering herself onto my cock. One inch. Two inches. Then she stopped.

"Let go." The second I dropped my hands from her hips, she slammed down onto me, impaling herself to the core.

"Son of a bitch." When another wicked smile split the tricky bitch's lips, my cock seemed to harden even more, if that was possible. Slowly she elevated herself until only the head remained inside her, and then she slammed down on me again. "Jesus, Sam." She did it again, and then it seemed as though her restraint had snapped and control became nothing more than a distant memory. She rode me hard and fast, slamming down on me over and over. Nothing had ever felt better.

Needing to touch her, I squeezed her breasts, and tweaked and pinched her nipples. It wasn't enough. I needed her lips again. Fisting a hand into her hair, I dragged her down and ravished her mouth as she continued to ride me so hard I thought my cock would snap. So close to the edge now, I gripped her hips and began lifting to meet each of her downward thrusts. Seizing her gaze, I growled, "Come for me, baby. I want to hear you scream my name for me again." I sank my teeth into her neck, groaning at the taste of her.

Her body tightened and jerked, and her muscles contracted around my cock as she screamed my name. I slammed her down onto me one final time and then held her there as I exploded inside her, growling, "Mine". With my body then totally replete, I sank into the mattress as she flopped down over me, flaccid against my chest. I curled my arms around her, panting and shuddering with the aftershocks. This here and now was the ultimate definition of sated.

After a couple of minutes of comfortable silence she spoke. "I'm working the front line with you and the squad whether you like it or not."

Playing with her incredibly soft hair, I sighed. "Is it really that terrible that I want you safe?"

"If I asked you to cover a safer position, would you?"

Dammit the woman knew what cards to play.

"I wouldn't ask you to because I know that hiding in the back isn't who you are. And if you honestly think I'd leave our squad to cover the front without me then you're an extremely dense individual."

The protectiveness in her voice made me smile. I released a groan of surrender. "If you let anything happen to you, I'll strap you to this bed for a month."

"Tell me how I lose in this situation."

Laughing, I lifted her chin with my finger and mashed my lips with hers. "Come on then, let's go gather up our squad. We need to inform them about the upcoming attack and go over the plan for tomorrow evening. Then we eat."

Needless to say, none of the guys took it well, but they were pleased to know that they were covering the front line. In the past, both Sam and I had – separately of course – taken the guys through the rainforest many times, so they were familiar enough with it by now. Still, we took them again.

What they were not familiar with was Sam and I putting up a united front and I could see how awkward they felt, as if not knowing who to focus their attention on. And didn't that just make me feel like shit. I'd done that; I'd actually let my pride get in the way of the guys' training.

Thinking about the way I'd acted, it was a wonder that Sam even entertained my existence, let alone slept with me. I refused to let myself hope that there must therefore be feelings involved on her part. I'd told Sam I cared about her, but she hadn't said the same. Nor had she expressed the same protectiveness over me that she had over the squad. It hurt more than I cared to admit. But, then again, she'd said it was only me she wanted, right? She didn't dispute that she was mine. Even if it was all physical for her, it was enough for now. It had to be, because there was no goddamn way I could give her up.

CHAPTER SIXTEEN

(Sam)

God bless the excellence of vampire night vision. The forest floor was generally dark even in daylight due to the canopy overhead, so right now it was pitch black. The humidity was bad as well; if it wasn't for the natural glamour that came with vampirism my hair would be frizzy and wild. Currently I was crouched beside the buttress roots of a canopy tree, letting my eyes scan through the scattered, interlaced hanging lianas, vines, and climbers. I knew I'd hear anything before I saw it, but still I had all my senses on high alert.

The animal sounds that I usually loved about the rainforest were gone tonight. There was a tense hush; like each and every creature was holding its breath, waiting for the war to start. I knew that Alora had already whispered news of the upcoming attack to some of the animals, so it would seem that word had gotten around fast.

Taking advantage of our intimate knowledge of this area, Jared and I had placed the squad members on different levels of the forest. It wasn't the same for all rainforests, but here it could be broken up into five vertical layers. At the top you had the overstory, which was the crowns of scattered trees. Up there were David and Butch, as they had better agility than the others. Next you had the canopy, which was the ceiling of closely spaced trees. There, Stuart and Denny were perched because they had the next best agility.

Then there was the understory, which was the layer of trees that were spaced further apart than those above; there we had Salem and Max, as they were the best climbers. Then there was the shrub layer, which was made of even more widely spaced trees – all of which were much shorter. Covering that were Harvey and Reuben, merely because Chico and Damien didn't like trees – or, more specifically, they didn't like the insects that crawled along them — so I had to put them on the forest floor.

Jared was supervising the overstory, canopy and the understory. I was covering the shrub layer and forest floor, but both of us were keeping in contact using his telepathy.

It was comforting to know that he was just a, well, thought away. I knew that no matter what he was doing or what was happening, if I called for him, he'd come straight away. That was why I had no intention of calling for him if I needed help. Another person would weigh the situation wisely and if the situation was that I'd need to wait, I'd be left waiting. During an attack like this, that was how it needed to be.

Still, the idea that he would come for me like that gave me a warm feeling. Just as it had when he'd told me he saw me as his. Just as it had when he'd been inside me that last time before we fell asleep; every thrust had been leisurely, deliberate, and sensual. He'd held my gaze with his the entire time, and nothing in my life had ever felt more intimate. It had scared me as much as it had electrified me.

I couldn't work out whether, when he said he thought of me as his, he meant he actually *wanted* me to be. He'd said he couldn't shake the feeling off, but he'd said it in such an aggravated voice that I didn't know whether to take that as him meaning that he *wanted* to shake it off and it annoyed him that he couldn't, or that he wasn't going to try. There was a big difference between someone saying they felt like you were theirs and them wanting to claim you as theirs. Once a vampire claimed someone for their own, they bound themselves to them with a Binding Ceremony (a vampy wedding), and they never took anyone else after that. I couldn't envision Jared making that kind of commitment with anyone.

God, if anything at all happened to him…

Even the thought of that was a lot to bear. I already knew exactly what it would feel like to lose him because I'd felt it with Bryce. But I suspected that it would hurt more with Jared. What I knew for a downright fact was that if I lost him tonight to Bennington's crew, I'd kill every last one of them. Where the hell were they? It had to be around midnight now.

You okay? Jared. I guessed he must have sensed my mental restlessness.

Just wishing we could get this over with. Patience isn't a quality of mine.

Oh, but you do have plenty of qualities to compensate for that. There was no mistaking what kind of qualities he was talking about.
How you can be thinking about sex right now is anyone's guess.
Thinking about you makes me think about sex.
I had to smile at that. *Then don't think about me.*
I already tried that, failed miserably.
Try harder.
After about ten seconds he came back with, *No, it's still not working.*
Please don't tell me you have a hard-on, I joked. But there was no response. Nothing. It made the hush around the rainforest feel even worse. *Jared?* No answer. *Jared, don't ignore me you've got me nervous now.*

A few seconds later he responded: *They're here. That was Evan contacting me. A few of the animals told Alora that a load of vamps have just been teleported to the outer edge of the north.*

That meant they were no less than a hundred feet away. Stretching out my senses, I searched our surroundings. *I can hear them. Alert the squad.* I waited while, telepathically, he relayed to the recruits what he had told me. *We've been over this formation a thousand times so they better remember it or I'll jam bamboo up their arses.*

As the vampires neared, the tension in the rainforest seemed to increase. There were eight in total. Most had red tints to their irises whereas two had amber. Their nervousness and apprehension was apparent in the air. I watched as, wearing clothes as dark as ours, they moved separately and stealthily through the trees. No covering each other's backs or working as a team? This couldn't be Bennington's *real* army of firecrackers then; these were obviously the expendables sent in to test the waters.

Things were going exactly as Jared predicted then.

As he'd suggested earlier, we let the group of expendables pass by. Letting Bennington believe he'd found himself a safe passage was the way to draw him out. An effective method to getting to people who were difficult to reach was to make them come to you. We knew Evan's and Lou's squads could take care of the expendables.

Minutes went by, but there were no more vamps. I wondered if any had teleported to the other areas yet. We doubted that Bennington would attack from all sides – he was too much of a Bulldozer. He liked to just barrel right into the thick of things. But his allies were a different matter.

HERE BE SEXIST VAMPIRES

Evan's just been in touch; the expendables are nothing but ashes now, Jared told me.

Good.

It was a few minutes later before there was more movement. This time, it was a group of ten and they were all Pagoris. I held my breath as I waited for the squad to act as Jared and I had instructed. Suddenly, the ten stopped dead and swerved their heads slightly – and I knew that Max had stolen each of their senses.

Quick as anything, Chico appeared from behind a protruding tree trunk and shot the ten with thorns. As Reuben had amplified Chico's gift beforehand, the thorns had placed the vamps into a long but temporary coma. Of course we could kill them, but we didn't want the scent of blood in the air or a lot of noise going on. Besides, Antonio had expressed a wish to have some live captives.

Before the ten vampires' bodies could flop to the ground, Max, Salem, Reuben, Harvey, Stuart, and Denny were there, silently hurling them up on to the tree branches to be hidden. A silent sigh of relief left me. It was over in seconds. So far so good.

More minutes of nothing passed, and I started to wonder if something had tipped Bennington off. Then I heard a large number approaching.

Twenty heading this way, announced Jared. I knew that each time he announced something to me he was also informing the squad. *We let them pass us and then pick them off from behind using the formation we went over at dusk.*

This cluster of Pagori vamps was more covert than the others. They each moved fluidly and silently, covering each other and reaching out with their senses. As such, they got a terrible shock when Max stole them. Before they could blindly use their gifts and hint at what was happening, Chico was there again exhaling his thorns while Salem dealt some psychic punches. Denny reached out from the canopy, shooting green, sticky ooze out of his hands to trap some of the vamps and bounce them up to him. Again the squad hid them in the trees, and again I gave a silent sigh when all went smoothly.

It was only about forty seconds or so before more came. Thirty this time. Because they were all slightly spaced out, Max couldn't encompass all of them to steal their senses. Shit. *Do you think if we let them pass, Evan could take care of the first ten or fifteen and then we'll pick off the rest from behind?*

That was exactly what I was thinking. If they pass, they can't retreat. Five seconds or so later Jared informed me, *Evan's squad will be taking on the first half.*

Just as covert as the last lot, these Pagoris noiselessly made their way along the forest floor. One came dangerously close to where I was hid, and then halted. The amount of energy I had absorbed was begging to be released, and I was expecting that I would need to do exactly that to defend myself. But then the tall, stocky Pagori continued onwards. Relief coursed through me. If we could get rid of this group without drawing attention we would have gotten rid of fifty eight in total, and that was bound to make Bennington feel confident and secure and get him moving.

I hadn't wanted to use David so early — he was only young and I knew this was his first battle. Not that I thought he wasn't up to the challenge. I just wanted him to have a chance to get a grip on his nerves. However, it was imperative that we completely assassinated this lot discreetly, and so I needed David's gift.

Jared, tell Harvey to telekinetically bring David down here after Max has done his thing: we're going to need him. Then he can take him back up.

Roger that, baby.

The very second the last Pagori intruder had passed, Max did his thing. Then Chico, Salem, David, and Denny were there as quick as anything. Chico and Salem put their targets into a coma while Denny wrapped his in ooze. David, as Reuben had amplified his gift, put an end to the life of his own targets. It was done and dusted in the space of three seconds. Thankfully there was no chance of us running out of trees, and so were we able to successfully hide the fifteen vampires.

Evan's attack was just as successful, Jared informed me. After a pause there was a: *Goddammit.*

What is it?

On the plus side, Bennington and his little army are on their way over.

The downside?

Some of them are using the trees.

Crap. How big is his army? Please say no more than one hundred!

HERE BE SEXIST VAMPIRES

There are forty vampires surrounding him, but there's an additional eighty encircling them. Time to unite the squads, baby. No more letting people pass. None of them are to get near The Hollow. On my signal, we attack.

I might have griped about him talking to me like he was my superior if I wasn't so tremendously focused on the approach of the vampires. One hundred and twenty?! That meant that he'd brought, in total, one hundred and sixty eight: a number that exceeded Antonio's legion. Worse still, he had his allies lurking somewhere.

Suddenly an arrow of fear shot through me. Not for myself, but for Jared and the squad. I'd come to care about each and every one of them.

I loved how protective Chico was of them all. I loved how Butch could look so calm even as he was plotting someone's death. I loved how Damien could make any damn thing funny just by his mannerisms. I adored Denny's innocent face and smile. I enjoyed watching Salem constantly bounce around like a boxer in the ring as if he actually believed he was there. I loved that proud expression Stuart wore every single time he'd travelled around as molecules. I could listen to Reuben's distorted French accent all day long and never get bored of it. I liked the way, even when he was being a wanker, Max could always make me laugh. I even liked Harvey's cockiness. I loved David's vulnerability that lay beneath his maturity.

And as for Jared…well I loved that sexist twat just because.

As Bennington's vamps got close, I peered up at Max, who was watching me from his place on the understory layer and waiting for my signal to act. One thing I'd always been especially clear on was that they should never give the enemy the chance to make the first move – not when you were dealing with vampires as you never knew just what gift they had. Finally, when the first row of vamps – some Pagoris, some Kejas – was directly in front of me, I nodded to Max.

Quicker than lightning, Max paralysed the senses of the twenty he was able to encompass. While Harvey, David, Denny, and Jared attacked them, Damien was astral projecting to the far right, distracting a chunk of the other vamps. While they were distracted, Chico, Salem and I dealt with them. Then there was a battle-cry from one of Bennington's vamps, and then everything went bloody mental.

Vampires were zooming around thanks to Harvey's telekinesis or my air blasts. Others were being hit with deadly electric discharges, compliments of Jared. Some were wrapped in ooze or itching like crazy after having met Denny. Many others were in comas thanks to Salem and Chico. Then there were those wondering aimlessly due to Max. Others were dying by psionic boom courtesy of David who, as I predicted, was an immediate target of Bennington's army but being protected by Butch's shield. Then there were others twirling constantly as Damien and Stuart continually distracted them.

And of course there were vampires who were being hit by energy balls, energy beams, energy bolts or an energy whip. Plenty found themselves alight, but only for as long as it took for someone else to kill them – then I put the flames out as I didn't want the rainforest catching fire.

The rest of our legion also came forward, and those other gifts together with ours created the party of a lifetime. But Bennington's army were in good shape also. There was that bloke who kept shooting acid at me; if it hadn't been for my energy shield, I'd be dead by now. There was one who was turning some of the vamps to stone with his breath and who almost got Jared; he then instantly died from an energy beam to the heart. There was the one who kept reducing himself to sand every time anyone aimed anything at him. Stuart and Denny chased him around and eventually got a grip of him.

The most distracting was the Keja who had the ability to mentally project; in other words, he could manifest your thoughts, which could be your fears or memories, and that meant my squad and Evan's kept seeing things that weren't there. Reuben eventually got close enough to touch him and then reduced the power of his gift – one of Evan's squad then conjured a stake and killed him. There was also the vamp who had the power of suggestion and was trying to rule the minds of those around him. He very nearly got Chico to shoot himself with his own thorns, but Salem threw his psychic punch in time.

When it looked as though Bennington's numbers were decreasing swiftly, I started to think that maybe it was too good to be true. *Jared, ask Evan if Alora has heard anything from the animals about any more attacks on the other sides of the rainforest.*

Seconds later he replied with: *He's not answering. He's not dead, but I think he might be unconscious. I'm going to track him through our link.*

Feeling terribly distraught and irate at the thought that something might have happened to Evan, I increased the force of my air blasts until even the trees looked likely to topple over. Then I saw something that riled me even more: Bennington was turning back.

Oh he did *not* think he could cause this and then scarper off, did he?

Wrapping my energy shield around me I dashed at vampire speed after Bennington and what was left of his army; there appeared to be about eighteen to twenty. Ripples of power and various weapons bounced off my shield as other vamps targeted me, but I didn't stop.

It was when I got close that I heard the screech. I turned to see Alora being dragged along by two Pagoris. That was when I noticed other vamps also being dragged along. It hit me then: Bennington was collecting himself some more powerful vamps. Right now, however, I only had eyes for Alora; Evan would never forgive me if anything happened to her, and I didn't want him to know that feeling of losing someone you cared about.

I shot both the Pagoris that had been restraining her with energy balls, and she dropped to the floor like a sack of spuds when they disintegrated into ashes. "You all right?"

She nodded and gripped my hand as I pulled her upright. "Thank you so much. They knocked Evan unconscious. Is he okay? Where is he?"

I was just about to wrap my energy shield around us both when suddenly she was sucked away from me as if by a vacuum, but instead she was in the arms of a Keja. Before I could act, I found myself in a large frosted cube. No matter how many beams, or bolts, or balls I hit it with, it remained strong. "Bastard," I hissed at Bennington as he approached and studied me curiously.

"I had to have you, Samantha. There was no way I was going to leave without taking you with me. You had to have known that." His smile was self-satisfied and slimy.

"If you honestly think you'll leave here alive, you're dafter than Victor was."

"Oh things may not be going so great over here, but then I had expected Antonio's legion to be the strongest. My allies are having a lot of success attacking the other sides, thankfully. The Hollow will be mine."

"Let me ask you a question, Bennington. If your little helpers are winning the battle on the other sides, what makes you think they'll hand The Hollow over to you?" His smile faded. "The Hollow's not exactly an apartment building, is it? I can't see someone handing such a grand place over to you like that. It strikes me that whoever penetrates the walls will be the one who takes it. Looks like that won't be you, eh."

"Then perhaps I shall use my new Feeder to aid my cause."

"I'd sooner see to my own death before I'd help you."

"Don't worry, baby. It won't come to that." Jared's voice sent a bolt of warmth through me.

Bennington chuckled as his army gathered around him and the cube. "You really are very fond of your consort, Jared. Victor was much the same. I must assume, then, that she is quite the performer in the bedroom. Perhaps I should take a leaf out of your and Victor's book and take her as my consort as well as having her in my army."

I snickered as I appraised him. "Sorry, your Monopoly Man look does nothing for me."

"She's not my consort," said Jared. His voice was dripping with rage.

"Oh? Then what?" Bennington seemed confused.

"She's *mine*." He left no doubt as to what he meant by that. He must have felt my shock because he nodded slightly at me to assure me of his honesty. Bennington's confident smile faltered.

When a vampire chose someone for their own, it was considered an extremely serious thing: they each belonged to the other and had the right to stage a full-scale war over them. It had happened plenty of times. Taking the Heir's chosen was as good as signing your own death warrant; Bennington would be automatically putting a bounty on his head. If Jared didn't kill him, some random vampire could, and would, just to collect on whatever reward came with his death.

Bennington chuckled nervously. "I have to say I'm surprised you have allowed anyone to claim you, Samantha. I saw you as too much of a free spirit for that."

"Stop stalling, Bennington," ordered Jared. "Give her back to me." He didn't follow that up with an 'or', and that made his words sound all the more threatening. His tone made it clear that there was no room for bartering, or negotiating, or making any deals. Bennington was to hand me over: The End.

I heard a slight crack and frowned. Then there was another. I swerved to see a large crack forming in the wall of the cube. On the other side of the cube was Reuben with his palms slapped up against it, trying to weaken it. He nodded at me and shrugged as if to say the rest was up to me now.

I sucked the energy around me into my palms and then I placed my hands on the wall of the cube, just as Reuben had done. Then I released a scorching heat near the crack. As I'd hoped, the crack widened and split until more cracks were branching off it. I kept emitting the heat, conscious of Bennington and Jared talking but not hearing their words. Then the cube began to tremor and quake as the split ran through the floor of it. I absorbed more energy into my palms and then slammed a massive energy bolt into the base of the cube. The entire thing cracked and fragmented.

Everyone turned to look at me and then, taking advantage, my squad appeared and attacked using their formations. Jared created and projected an extremely high voltage bolt of lightning and aimed it at a distracted Bennington. The sad little man shook and convulsed and made the most ear-piercing noise as the electricity ran through his body, stealing his life. I almost danced at the sight of his ashes.

Instantly Jared was there, holding me tight to him. At the same time, those who were left of Bennington's army suddenly looked unsure and apprehensive. While some surrendered completely, others fought harder as if they'd sooner die than be caught – we happily indulged them in that. Within seconds it was over and all was quiet around us. There were still sounds of battle in the distance, but at least Bennington was dead.

Jared scrunched his hands in my hair and rested his forehead to mine. "I could kill you for getting caught."

"I didn't do it on bloody purpose."

He kissed me hard. "I'm still strapping you to the bed."

"Coach! Look!"

I turned to see Denny pointing through a gap in the trees. At least three hundred more vampires had just teleported to the island. Twat. The Monopoly bloke had had more allies than we'd expected. Or were they allies? It seemed more likely that they had acted as though they were working in league with Bennington when in fact that had planned to let him fight most of the fight and then jump in at the last minute to steal the victory.

Suddenly there was a lot of cursing, and shouting, and movement, and the squad retreated to join the others and prepare for the new invaders. But when Jared tried to drag me along behind them, I resisted and shook my head. "We can't fight off that many, you know that." He was going to electrocute me for this but I couldn't see any other choice. "Don't resist it."

"What?"

That was when I merged into him. Just like last time, there was that sensation of fusing and melding with this other body as though I was encasing myself in an all-in-one suit. Each of my five senses came to me, one by one. And then there was that burning pain as though I was melting into the suit, into Jared, and our cells knitted together. Again, I felt totally and utterly omnipotent. But unlike with Joy, there was another feeling: that I was complete, which made no sense but it was there.

I examined first my hands and then the rest of me; my hands were slightly larger and calloused, I was burlier and taller. I was exactly as I'd been in the vision that I'd had via Luther. Just like in that vision, I felt more alive than ever; my entire body buzzed with power and energy. Jared's energy was fifty times the strength of Joy's.

There were two potential problems. One, I wasn't sure I could channel such a large concentration of power that mine and Jared's combined made. Two, I didn't seem to care that I might not be able to channel it. I was filled with this sense that nothing could happen to me. All I could think of was releasing this caged power against the attackers.

Sam, no! The voice reverberated around my head. *You need to unmerge with me right now. I told you not to do this — you can get drugged on the power!*

Although his words didn't quite penetrate, Jared's voice still somehow snagged my attention.

That's it, baby, just think for a minute. Think. I know the power feels good to you but it's too much, it could take over you! It could kill you!

That couldn't be right. I was invincible. Wasn't I?

That might be how it feels, but it's not real. Baby, please, listen to me: you have to unmerge with me right now.

He was right, I finally fully realised; I could be hurt, the power really could overwhelm me. But I couldn't unmerge with him like he wanted. Not when I knew the attackers were coming. I could even hear them. *I have to do this, Jared.*

Fuck, no!

With my Sventé agility and Jared's Pagori strength and speed all mixed together, leaping from tree to tree in my ascent was practically effortless. Finally I reached the overstory layer where I perched myself steadily on the top of a large, sturdy tree.

Sam, baby, please don't do this?!

I need to do this, you know I do. We *do. Now stop resisting or this won't work. Please?!*

From where I stood I had a clear view of the approaching vampires. I could also see flashes of energy and light in the distance where the others were battling. I raised my arms straight above my head, shoulder width apart, with my hands balled into tight fists. I then closed my eyes as I tapped into the eager power inside me that seemed to have a life of its own.

It was like it was impatiently clawing at my insides, bumping against my organs and making me feel as though I was going to burst. For a moment I wondered if Jared was right, if it was too strong for me to channel. But then he spoke, and although I wasn't sure what he said, his voice grounded and anchored me.

Praying that the combination of my ability to tap into the natural elements and Jared's gift of electrokinesis was enough, I opened my fists. My entire body seemed to spasm as the energy streamed out of me and manifested itself into a massive grey cloud; a cloud that increased in size with each second. I watched as it continued to grow and darken until it was like a smoky blanket hanging over the island. A harsh wind picked up and then there was a loud clap of thunder.

Then came the lightning. I directed the bolt at the High Master vampire, Winston Jones, who had been fast approaching until the storm began. Instantly he was ashes. Seeing that his vampy friends were ready to make a run for it, I sent a massive gush of wind at them, sweeping each one of them up, and then shaped the wind into a gigantic tornado.

The tornado touched nothing but what I instructed it to as, sweating and shaking, I directed it around the island, sweeping up each and every enemy that I could see. It was easy to tell them apart from the friendly vamps, because they were the only ones running away. Any that somehow managed to escape the tornado got struck by a lightning bolt.

Once I had them all, I lifted the lid on the last bit of power I had contained inside me, and created a large ball of fire that engulfed the tornado and every vampire within it.

And then I collapsed, greeting an unconscious state with gratefulness.

(Jared)

She obviously wanted me to kill her. That was the only explanation I could think of as to why she'd place herself in that much danger. I'd felt how it had been for her when she Merged with me and our energies clashed; it was as though she'd been standing at the edge of a precipice, fighting against a wind that could possibly throw her over the edge.

I'd sensed each time the power almost overwhelmed her enough to throw her over that edge into oblivion. And I hadn't been able to do a goddamn thing about it. I'd tried over and over to undo what she'd done, but as the Merging gift was hers, I'd had no choice but to be nothing more than a voice in her mind, grounding her.

As soon as she'd collapsed with exhaustion, her own body had peeled away from mine, leaving my skin itching like crazy for a minute. Having teleported her crazy ass out of the tree, I laid her on the forest floor and squatted beside her. "Sam, baby, wake up," I coaxed, running my hand through her hair. "Come on, wake up." Becoming aware of a presence behind me, I turned to find Antonio, Luther and Sebastian being teleported by one of the guards.

"How is she?" Antonio immediately asked.

"Totally wiped out. She'd known from what happened with Joy that she could drain me if she wasn't careful, but she'd ended up draining herself."

"Thank God it wasn't to the point of death," said Luther.

"A coma?" enquired Chico as the entire squad suddenly appeared from the trees with Alora. Most of the guys were worse for wear, but they were alive.

I heard some of them cursing at the sight of a very still Sam. "She's just unconscious," I assured them. "But she's sapped."

"So she'll be okay?" David was swallowing hard in panic.

I nodded. The only thing I could think of that might rouse her from this state was blood. I slid my hand under her upper back and raised her slightly, allowing her head to fall back a little. Then I bit hard into my wrist and swiftly put it to her mouth. Although the skin quickly healed itself I still managed to get a few drops onto her tongue. "Come on, Sam." Nothing – no movement, no sounds, not even the flicker of an eyelid. "Sam, I swear to God, if you don't wake up I'll spank your ass."

Bastard, I heard in my head.

Instantly a smile curved my mouth. "She's all right, she's waking up."

Denny raised a brow, still tense and anxious. "How can you tell?"

"She's just telepathically called me a bastard." There were laughs at that, but the air was still filled with worry. Then she inhaled a long breath through her nose, and everyone seemed to sigh and sag in relief. Aquamarine eyes found mine and she smiled a little. I pulled her onto my lap as I sat down. "Hey baby."

"I told you not to call me that."

"Was there a reason why you felt it necessary to turn into Storm out of the X-Men?"

"Oh shut your noise." She looked up at Antonio then. "Many casualties?"

His smile was sad. "Although there wasn't as many as I would have expected, given how outnumbered we were, we unfortunately lost an entire squad from the legion. However, it seemed that Rupert's legion suffered the worst. I think things would have been much worse if you hadn't...turned into Storm, as Jared so aptly put it."

"It was so cool," said Harvey with a wide smile. I shot him a scowl.

She turned to the squad and smiled, her eyes flicking to each one of them. "I don't mind saying I'm proud of you lot." They each grinned. "But if you let it get to your heads and rods reappear up your backsides, it'll be Storm time again, all right?"

They each chuckled but nodded.

"If you think we'd risk your wrath you're crazy," said Damien.

Jared? It was Evan, anxious.

"Evan's awake," I told her. "I stashed him out of sight further into the rainforest when I found him unconscious."

Alora dashed forward. "Can you take me to him? Please?"

I nodded then stood upright, Sam still in my arms. "See all you guys later."

"Put me down." She kicked her legs until I planted her on her feet, an arm around her waist, waiting while she steadied herself before grabbing Alora's hand. In under a second we were stood before Evan, who stopped his anxious pacing and quickly locked his arms around Alora. To my surprise, she eagerly returned the embrace.

I looked at Sam. "That was fast work for Evan." She only smiled. Then her smile wobbled a little and she suddenly seemed nervous. "What is it?"

She cleared her throat, but when she opened her mouth she didn't say anything, as if she wasn't sure she should say whatever it was. I encouraged her with a look.

"When I Merged with you…it meant I could access – I wasn't snooping, it's just part of the Merging – your thoughts, and memories, and…feelings."

I knew where this was going. I'd suspected that the process would allow her to do that.

After a second, she murmured in disbelief, "You love me. Or at least you think you do."

"I *know* I do." I wrapped my arms around her. "And you love me." Her eyes widened; clearly she hadn't known that I'd had the same access to her mind as she had to mine. "If you sensed I love you then you must've also sensed that I meant it when I said I was claiming you as mine. And no, I'm not asking, and the reason I'm not asking is because the answer 'no' is unacceptable. I want the Binding Ceremony – everything."

A wicked, crooked smile formed on her face. "If I *do* say no…will you strap me to the bed for longer than a month?"

My smile mirrored hers. "You'll leave me no choice but to have to. And then, of course, I'll have to spank your ass, bite your nipples, and tease your clit with my tongue until you change your mind."

"Then the answer is definitely a resounding no."

"Note that I'll also be giving it to you up the—"

"Bro, we can hear you over here," whined Evan. "Those are visuals I could live without."

I sighed while Sam giggled. "Come on, time to go to my apartment and get started on that spanking."

The second we arrived at my apartment, she smirked. "You'll have to catch me first."

And then the insane bitch turned back into Houdini.

SUZANNE WRIGHT

ACKNOWLEDGMENTS

I have to say a sincere thank you to my unfailingly supportive husband and my amazing (albeit slightly demonic) children – three very special people who love me in spite of the fact that I hear voices in my head and lack a fully functioning mind-to-mouth filter.

I also wish to deeply thank Ruby José for the fabulous cover she did for both 'Here Be Sexist Vampires' and its sequel, 'The Bite That Binds'. Ruby, you are so unbelievably talented and I truly appreciate what you've done. I'm literally floored by how you were able to create exactly what's in my head like that.

A big thank you to Anna Campbell from 'a.g. Proof and Edit' for her proofreading skills. When I'm working, I write what I see, and I'm scribbling or typing so fast to keep up with what's playing in my head that I make the dumbest mistakes ever. So thank you, Anna, for catching them for me.

And a huge thanks to all my readers. Not just for buying the book, but for taking the time to read this story that I worked so hard on and lost so much hair over. I said when I first released this book a year ago that if it received a positive response, I'd love to make a series of it. Your support has made it possible for that to happen, and I thank you so much for that!

If for any reason you would like to contact me, whether it's about the book or you're considering self-publishing and have any questions, please feel free to e-mail me at: suzanne_e_wright@live.co.uk.

Website: www.suzannewright.co.uk
Blog: www.suzannewrightsblog.blogspot.co.uk
Twitter: @suz_wright

ABOUT THE AUTHOR

Suzanne Wright lives in England with her husband, two children and her bulldog. When she's not spending time with her family, she's writing, reading, or doing her version of housework - sweeping the house with a look.

TITLES BY SUZANNE WRIGHT:

The Deep in Your Veins Series

Here Be Sexist Vampires
The Bite That Binds
Taste of Torment
Consumed
Fractured

The Dark in You Series

Burn
Blaze
Ashes
Embers
Shadows

SUZANNE WRIGHT

The Phoenix Pack Series

Feral Sins
Wicked Cravings
Carnal Secrets
Dark Instincts
Savage Urges
Fierce Obsessions
Wild Hunger
Untamed Delights

❦

The Mercury Pack Series

Spiral of Need
Force of Temptation
Lure of Oblivion
Echoes of Fire
Shards of Frost

❦

Standalones

From Rags
Shiver

Printed in Great Britain
by Amazon